W9-BSW-051

RANDOM
HOUSE
LARGE
PRINT

metropolis

Also by Philip Kerr
Available from
Random House Large Print

Greeks Bearing Gifts
Prussian Blue

philip kerr

RANDOM HOUSE
LARGE PRINT

This is a work of fiction. Names, characters, places, and incidents either are the product of the author's imagination or are used fictitiously, and any resemblance to actual persons, living or dead, businesses, companies, events, or locales is entirely coincidental.

Published in the United States of America by Random House Large Print in association with G. P. Putnam's Sons, an imprint of Penguin Random House LLC, New York.

Cover design: Pete Garceau
Cover images: (background) ullstein bild/Contributor/GettyImages; (male figure) Mark Owen/Arcangel

Grateful acknowledgment is made to Erich Lessing/Art Resource, New York, for permission to reproduce photographs of the triptych **Metropolis** (1928) by Otto Dix (Kunstmuseum Stuttgart).

The Library of Congress has established a Cataloging-in-Publication record for this title.

ISBN: 978-1-9848-8287-5

www.penguinrandomhouse.com/large-print-format-books

FIRST LARGE PRINT EDITION

Printed in the United States of America

10 9 8 7 6 5 4 3 2 1

This Large Print edition published in accord with the standards of the N.A.V.H.

For Jane

Now and forever

one: women

two: decline

three: sexuality

metropolis

prologue

LIKE ANYONE WHO'S read the Bible, I was familiar with the idea of Babylon as a city that was a byword for iniquity and the abominations of the earth, whatever they might be. And like anyone who lived in Berlin during the Weimar Republic, I was also familiar with the comparison frequently made between the two cities. At the Lutheran St. Nicholas' Church in Berlin where I used to go with my parents as a small boy, our brick-faced, shouty pastor, Dr. Rotpfad, seemed so familiar with Babylon and its topography that I believed he must once have lived there. Which only provoked my fascination with the name and prompted me to look it up in the **Conversations-Lexicon,** which occupied a whole shelf in the family bookcase. But the encyclopedia wasn't very enlightening on the abominations. And while it's true there were plenty of whores and scarlet women and an ample supply of sin to be found in Berlin, I'm not sure it was worse than in any other great metropolis such as London, New York, or Shanghai.

Bernhard Weiss told me the comparison was and always had been nonsense, that it was like comparing apples with oranges. He didn't believe in evil and reminded me that there were no laws against it anywhere, not even in England, where there were laws against almost everything. In May 1928, the famous Ishtar Gate, the northern entrance to Babylon, had yet to be reconstructed in Berlin's Pergamon Museum, so the Prussian capital's notoriety as the wickedest place in the world had yet to be underlined in red by the city's moral guardians, meaning there was still some room for doubt. Perhaps we were just more honest about our own depravities and more tolerant of other people's vices. And I should know; in 1928, vice in all its endless permutations was my departmental responsibility at the Police Praesidium on Berlin's Alexanderplatz. Criminalistically speaking—which was a new word for us cops, thanks to Weiss—I knew almost as much about the subject of vice as Gilles de Rais. But in truth, with so many dead in the Great War and the flu that came immediately after, which, like some Old Testament plague, killed millions more, it hardly seemed important to worry about what people put up their noses or what they did when they got undressed in their dark Biedermeier bedrooms. And not just in their bedrooms. On summer nights, the Tiergarten sometimes looked like a stud farm, there were so many whores copulating on the grass with their clients. I suppose it's hardly surprising that after a war in which so many Germans were obliged to kill for their country, they now preferred to fuck.

Given everything that went before and everything that followed, it's difficult to speak accurately or fairly about Berlin. In many ways it was never a pleasant place and sometimes a senseless, ugly one. Too cold in winter, too hot in summer, too dirty, too smoky, too smelly, too loud, and, of course, afflicted horribly with far too many people, like Babel, which is the other name for Babylon. All the city's public buildings were constructed to the glory of a German empire that hardly ever existed and, like the city's worst slums and tenements, made nearly everyone who encountered them feel inhuman and insignificant. Not that anyone ever cared much about Berlin's people (certainly its rulers didn't) since they were not very agreeable, or friendly, or well mannered; quite often they were stupid, heavy, dull, and relentlessly vulgar; always they were cruel and brutal. Violent murders were commonplace; mostly these were committed by drunken men who came home from the beer house and strangled their wives because they were so befuddled by beer and schnapps they didn't know what they were doing. But sometimes, it was something much worse: a Fritz Haarmann or a Karl Denke, one of those peculiar, godless Germans who seemed to enjoy killing for its own sake. Even this no longer seemed so surprising; in Weimar Germany there was perhaps an indifference to sudden death and human suffering that was also an inevitable legacy of the Great War. Our two million dead was as many as Britain and France combined. There are fields in Flanders that contain the bones of so many of our young men that they are more German than Unter den Linden. And even today, ten years after the war, the streets are always full of the maimed and the lame, many of them still in uniform, begging for a few coins outside railway stations and banks. It's a rare day when Berlin's public spaces don't resemble a painting by Pieter Brueghel.

And yet, for all that, Berlin was also a wonderful, inspiring place. Despite the many previously listed reasons to dislike the city, it was a large, bright mirror to the world and hence, for anyone interested in living in that world, a marvelous reflection of human life in all its fascinating glory. I wouldn't have lived anywhere else but Berlin if you'd paid me, especially now that Germany was over the worst. After the Great War, the flu, and the inflation, things were getting better, albeit slowly; things were still hard for a lot of people, in the east of the city most of all. But it was difficult to see Berlin ever going the same way as Babylon, which, according to the **Conversations-Lexicon,** was destroyed by the Chaldeans, its walls, temples, and palaces razed and the rubble thrown into the sea. Something like that was never going to happen to us. Whatever followed now, we were probably safe from a biblical destruction. It wasn't in anyone's interest—not the French, nor the British, and certainly not the Russians—to see Berlin and, by extension, Germany, become the subject of divine apocalyptic vengeance.

part one
women

Everywhere the mystery of the corpse.

—Max Beckmann, **Self-Portrait in Words**

FIVE DAYS AFTER the federal general election, Bernhard Weiss, Berlin's chief of the Criminal Police, summoned me to a meeting in his sixth-floor office at the Alex. Wreathed in the smoke from one of his favorite Black Wisdom cigars and seated at the conference table alongside Ernst Gennat, one of his best homicide detectives, he invited me to sit down. Weiss was forty-eight years old and a Berliner, small, slim, and dapper, academic even, with round glasses and a neat, well-trimmed mustache. He was also a lawyer and a Jew, which made him unpopular with many of our colleagues, and he'd overcome a great deal of prejudice to get where he was: in peacetime, Jews had been forbidden to become officers in the Prussian Army; but when war broke out, Weiss applied to join the Royal Bavarian Army, where he quickly rose to the rank of captain and won an Iron Cross. After the war, at the request of the Ministry of the Interior, he'd reformed the Berlin police and made it one of the most modern forces in Europe. Still, it had to be said, he made an unlikely-looking policeman; he always reminded me a little of Toulouse-Lautrec.

There was a file open in front of him and from the look of it, the subject was me.

"You've been doing a good job in Vice," he said in his plummy, almost thespian voice. "Although I fear you're fighting a losing battle against prostitution in this city. All these war widows and Russian refugees make a living as best they can. I keep telling our leaders that if we did more to support equal pay for women we could solve the problem of prostitution in Berlin overnight.

"But that's not why you're here. I expect you've heard: Heinrich Lindner has left the force to become an air traffic controller at Tempelhof, which leaves a spare seat in the murder wagon."

"Yes, sir."

"Do you know why he left?"

I did know, but hardly wanting to say, I found myself pulling a face.

"You can say. I shan't be in the least offended."

"I'd heard it said he didn't like taking orders from a Jew, sir."

"That's correct, Gunther. He didn't like taking orders from a Jew." Weiss drew on his cigar. "What about you? Do you have any problems taking orders from a Jew?"

"No, sir."

"Or in taking orders from anyone else, for that matter."

"No, sir. I have no problem with authority."

"I'm delighted to hear it. Because we're thinking of offering you a permanent seat in the wagon. Lindner's seat."

"Me, sir?"

"You sound surprised."

"Only that it's the splash around the Alex that Inspector Reichenbach was going to get the seat."

"Not unless you turn it down. And even then I have my doubts about that man. Of course, people will say I don't dare offer the seat to another Jew. But that's not it at all. In our opinion you've the makings of a fine detective, Gunther. You are diligent and you know when to keep your mouth shut; that's good in a detective. Very good. Kurt Reichenbach is a good detective, too, but he's rather free with his fists. When he was still in uniform, some of his brother police officers nicknamed him Siegfried, on account of the fact that he was much too fond of wielding his sword. Of hitting some of our customers with the handle or the flat of the blade. I don't mind what an officer does in the name of self-defense. But I won't have a police officer cracking heads open for the pleasure of it. No matter whose head it is."

"And he hasn't stopped for the lack of a sword," said Gennat. "More recently there was a rumor he beat up an SA man he'd arrested in Lichtenrade, a Nazi who'd stabbed a communist. Nothing was proven. He might be popular around the Alex—even some of the anti-Semites seem to like him—but he's got a temper."

"Precisely. I'm not saying he's a bad policeman. Just that we think we prefer you to him." Weiss looked down at the page in my file. "I see you made your Abitur. But no university."

"The war. I volunteered."

"Of course."

"So then. You want the seat? It's yours if you do."

"Yes, sir. Very much."

"You've been attached to the Murder Commission before, of course. So you've already worked a murder, haven't you? Last year. In Schöneberg, wasn't it? As you know, I like all my detectives to have had the experience of working a homicide alongside a top man like Gennat here."

"Which makes me wonder why you think I'm worth the permanent seat," I said. "That case—the Frieda Ahrendt case—has gone cold."

"Most cases go cold for a while," said Gennat. "And it's not just cases that go cold, it's detectives, too. Especially in this city. Never forget that. It's just the nature of the job. New thinking is the key to solving cold cases. As a matter of fact, I've got some other cases you can check out if you ever get such a thing as a quiet moment. Cold cases are what can make a detective's reputation."

"Frieda Ahrendt," said Weiss. "Remind me of that one."

"A dog found some body parts wrapped in brown paper and buried in the Grünewald," I said. "And it was Hans Schnieckert and the boys in Division J who first identified her. On account of the fact that the killer was thoughtful enough to leave us her hands. The dead girl's fingerprints revealed she had a record for petty theft. You would think that might have opened a lot of doors. But we've found no family, no job, not even a last-known address. And because a newspaper was foolish enough to put up a substantial reward for information, we wasted a lot of time interviewing members of the public who were more interested in making a thousand reichsmarks than in helping the police. At least four women told us their husbands were the culprit. One of them even suggested her husband was originally going to cook the body parts. Thus the newspaper epithet: the Grünewald Pork Butcher."

"That's one way to get rid of your old man," said Gennat. "Put him up for a murder. Cheaper than getting a divorce."

After Bernhard Weiss, Ernst Gennat was the most senior detective in the Alex; he was also the largest, nicknamed the Big Buddha; it was a tight fit in the station wagon with Gennat on board. Weiss himself had designed the murder wagon. It was equipped with a radio, a small fold-down desk with a typewriter, a medical kit, lots of photographic equipment, and almost everything needed to investigate a homicide except a prayer book and a crystal ball. Gennat had a mordant Berlin wit, the result, he said, of having been born and brought up in the staff quarters at Berlin's Plötzensee Prison, where his father had been the assistant governor. It was even rumored that on execution days Gennat had breakfasted with the headsman. Early in my days at the Alex, I'd decided to study the man and make him my model.

The telephone rang and Weiss answered it.

"You're SPD, right, Gunther?" Gennat asked.

"That's right."

"Because we don't need any politics in the wagon. Communists, Nazism, I get enough of that at home. And you're single, right?"

I nodded.

"Good. Because this job ruins a marriage. You might look at me and think, not unreasonably, that I'm very popular with the ladies. But only until I get a case that keeps me here at the Alex day and night. I'll need to find a nice lady copper if ever I'm going to get married. So where do you live?"

"I rent a room in a boardinghouse on Nollendorfplatz."

"This job means a bit more money and a promotion and maybe a better room. In that order. And you'll be on probation for a month or two. Does this house you live in have a telephone?"

"Yes."

"Use drugs?"

"No."

"Ever try them?"

"Bit of cocaine once. To see what all the fuss was about. Not for me. Besides, I couldn't afford it."

"No harm in that, I suppose," said Gennat. "There's still a lot of pain relief this country needs after the war."

"A lot of people aren't taking it for pain relief," I said. "Which sometimes leaves them with a very different kind of crisis."

"There are some people who think the Berlin police are in crisis," said Gennat. "Who think the whole city is in crisis. What do you think, lad?"

"The larger the city, the more crises there are likely to be. I think we're always going to be facing a crisis of one kind or another. Might as well get used to that. It's indecision that's more likely to cause us crises. Governments that can't get anything done. With no clear majority, I'm not sure this new one will be any different. Right now our biggest problem looks like democracy itself. What use is it when it can't deliver a viable government? It's the paradox of our times and sometimes I worry that we will get tired of it before it can sort itself out."

He nodded, seeming to agree with me, and moved on to another issue.

"Some politicians don't think much of our clear-up rate. What do you say to that, lad?"

"They should come and meet some of our clients. Maybe if the dead were a bit more talkative they'd have a fair point."

"It's our job to hear them all the same," said Gennat. He shifted his enormous bulk for a moment and then stood up. It was like watching a zeppelin get airborne. The floor creaked as he walked to the corner turret window. "If you listen closely enough you can still hear them whisper. Like these Winnetou murders. I figure his victims are talking to us, but we just haven't understood what language they're speaking." He pointed out the window at the metropolis. "But someone does. Someone down there, perhaps coming out of Hermann Tietz. Maybe Winnetou himself."

Weiss finished his telephone call and Gennat came back to the meeting table, where he lit his own pungent cigar. By now there was quite a cloudscape drifting across the table. It reminded me of gas drifting across no-man's-land.

I was too nervous to light a cigarette myself.

Too nervous and too respectful of my seniors; I was still in awe of them and amazed that they wanted me to be part of their team.

"That was the ViPoPra," said Weiss.

The ViPoPra was the police president of Berlin, Karl Zörgiebel.

"It seems that the Wolfmium light-bulb factory in Stralau just blew up. First reports say there are many dead. Perhaps as many as thirty. He'll keep us posted.

"I would remind you that we are agreed not to use the name Winnetou when we're referring to our scalping murderer. I think it does those poor dead girls a grave disservice to use these sensationalized names. Let's stick to the file name, shall we, Ernst? Silesian Station. Better for security that way."

"Sorry, sir. Won't happen again."

"So welcome to the Murder Commission, Gunther. The rest of your life just changed forever. You'll never look at people in the same way again. From now on, whenever you stand next to a man at a bus stop or on a train, you'll be sizing him up as a potential killer. And you'd be right to do so. Statistics show that most murders in Berlin are committed by ordinary, law-abiding citizens. In short, people like you and me. Isn't that right, Ernst?"

"Yes, sir. It's rare I ever meet a murderer who looks like one."

"You'll see things every bit as bad as the things you saw in the trenches," he added. "Except that some of the victims will be women and children. But we have to be hard. And you'll find we tend to make jokes most people wouldn't find funny."

"Yes, sir."

"What do you know about these Silesian Station killings, Gunther?"

"Three local prostitutes murdered in as many weeks. Always at night. The first one near Silesian Station. All of them hit over the head with a ball-peen hammer and then scalped with a very sharp knife. As if by the eponymous Red Indian from Karl May's famous novels."

"Which you've read, I trust."

"Show me a German who hasn't and I'll show you a man who can't read."

"Enjoy them?"

"Well, it's been a few years—but yes."

"Good. I couldn't like a man who didn't like a good western by Karl May. What else do you know? About the murders, I mean."

"Not much." I shook my head. "Chances are the killer didn't know the victims, which makes him hard to catch. It may be the instinct of the moment that drives his actions."

"Yes, yes," said Weiss, as if he'd heard all this before.

"The killings do seem to be having an effect on the number of girls on the streets," I said. "There are fewer prostitutes about than there used to be. The ones I've spoken to tell me they're scared to work."

"Anything else?"

"Well—"

Weiss shot me a quizzical look. "Spit it out, man. Whatever it is. I expect all my detectives to speak frankly."

"Just that the working girls have another name for these women. Because they were scalped. When the last woman was murdered I started hearing her described as another Pixavon Queen." I paused. "Like the shampoo, sir."

"Yes, I have heard of Pixavon shampoo. As the ads would have it, a shampoo used by 'good wives and mothers.' A bit of street corner irony. Anything else?"

"Nothing really. Only what's in the newspapers. My landlady, Frau Weitendorf, has been following the case quite closely. As you might expect, given how lurid the facts are. She loves a good murder. We're all obliged to listen to her while she brings us our breakfast. Hardly the most appetizing of subjects, but there it is."

"I'm interested: What does she have to say about it?"

I paused, picturing Frau Weitendorf in her usual vocal flow, full of an almost righteous indignation and hardly seeming to care if any of her lodgers were paying attention. Large, with ill-fitting dentures, and two bulldogs that stayed close to her heels, she was one of those women who liked to talk, with or without an audience. The long-sleeved quilted peignoir she wore at breakfast made her look like a grubby Chinese emperor, an effect that was enhanced by her double chins.

Besides Weitendorf, there were four of us in the house: an Englishman called Robert Rankin who claimed to be a writer; a Bavarian Jew by the name of Fischer who said he was a traveling salesman, but was probably a crook of some kind; and a young woman named Rosa Braun who played the saxophone in a dance band but was almost certainly a half-silk. Including Frau Weitendorf, we were an unlikely quintet, but perhaps a perfect cross section of modern Berlin.

"As for Frau Weitendorf, she would say something like this: For these girls who get their throats cut, it's an occupational hazard. When you think about it, they were asking for it, really. And isn't life cheap enough without risking it unnecessarily? It wasn't always like that. This used to be a respectable city, before the war. Human life stopped having much value after 1914. That was bad enough, but then inflation came along in 1923 and made our money worthless. Life doesn't matter so very much when you've lost everything. Besides, anyone can see this city has grown too big. Four million people living cheek by jowl. It isn't natural. Living like animals, some of them. Especially east of Alexanderplatz. So why should we be surprised if they behave like animals? There are no standards of decency. And with so many Poles and Jews and Russians living here since the Bolshevik revolution, is it any wonder these young women go and get themselves killed? Mark my words, it will turn out to be one of them who killed these women. A Jew. Or a Russian. Or a Jewish Russian. You ask me, the tsar and the Bolsheviks chased these people out of Russia for a reason. But the real reason these girls get killed is this: The men who returned from the trenches came back with a real taste for killing people that needs to be satisfied. Like vampires who need blood to survive, these men need to kill someone, **anyone.** Show me a man who was a solider in the trenches who says he hasn't wanted to kill someone since he came home and I'll show you a liar. It's like the jazz music that those Negroes play in the nightclubs. Gets their blood up, if you ask me."

"She sounds positively awful," said Weiss. "I'm surprised you stay in for breakfast."

"It's included in the room price, sir."

"I see. Now tell me what this awful bitch says about why the killer scalps these women."

"Because he hates women. She reckons that

during the war it was the women who stabbed the men in the back by taking their jobs for half the money, so when the men came back, all they found were jobs paying joke wages or, more likely, no jobs at all because the women were still doing them. That's why he kills them and why he scalps them, too. Pure hate."

"And what do you think? About why this maniac scalps his victims."

"I think I'd want to know more of the facts before I speculate, sir."

"Humor me. But I can tell you this much: None of the scalps have been recovered. Therefore we have to conclude he keeps them. He doesn't seem to favor any particular hair color. We might easily conclude he kills in order to claim the scalp. Which begs the question: Why? What's in it for him? Why would a man scalp a prostitute?"

"Could be a weird sexual pervert who wants to be a woman," I said. "There are lots of transvestites in Berlin. Maybe we've got a man who wants the hair to make a wig." I shook my head. "I know, it sounds ridiculous."

"No more ridiculous than Fritz Haarmann cooking and eating the internal organs of his victims," said Gennat. "Or Erich Kreuzberg masturbating onto the graves of the women he'd murdered. That's how we caught him."

"When you put it like that, no, I suppose it isn't."

"We have our own theories why this man scalps his victims," said Weiss. "Or at least Dr. Hirschfeld does. He's been advising us on this case. But I'd still welcome your ideas. Anything. No matter how outlandish."

"Then it comes back to simple misogyny, sir. Or simple sadism. A wish to degrade and humiliate as well as to destroy. Humiliation is easy enough to inflict on a murder victim in Berlin. I've always believed it's unspeakable that this city continues the practice of allowing the general public to come and inspect the corpses of murder victims at the city morgue. For anyone who wishes to ensure his victims are humiliated and degraded, you need look no further than there. It's time the practice was stopped."

"I agree," said Weiss. "And I've told the Prussian minister of the interior as much on more than one occasion. But just as it seems something is going to be done about it, we find ourselves with a new PMI."

"Who is it this time?" asked Gennat.

"Albert Grzesinski," said Weiss. "Our own former police president."

"Well, that's a step in the right direction," said Gennat.

"Carl Severing was a good man," said Weiss, "but he had too much on his plate, what with having to deal with those bastards in the army—the ones already training in secret for another war. But let's not get too carried away with Grzesinski. Since he's also a Jew, it's fair to say that his appointment isn't likely to meet with universal enthusiasm. Grzesinski is his stepfather's name. His real name is Lehmann."

"How come I didn't know that?" asked Gennat.

"I don't know, Ernst, since they tell me you're a detective. No, I'd be very surprised if Grzesinski lasts long. Besides, he has a secret his enemies are bound to exploit before long. He doesn't live with his wife, but with his mistress. An American actress. You shrug, Bernie, but it's only the Berlin public who are allowed to be immoral. Our elected representatives are not permitted to be truly representative; indeed, they are forbidden to have any vices of their own. Especially when they're Jews. Look at me. I'm virtually a saint. These cigars are my only vice."

"If you say so, sir."

Weiss smiled. "That's right, Bernie. Never accept anyone's word for their own recognizance. Not unless they've already been found guilty." He wrote a note on a piece of paper and pressed it on the blotter. "Take this to the cashier's office. They'll give you a new paybook and a new warrant disc."

"When do I start, sir?"

Weiss pulled at his watch chain until a gold hunter lay on the palm of his hand.

"You already have. According to your file, you have a few days' leave coming up, is that right?"

"Yes, sir. Starting next Tuesday."

"Well, until then you're the Commission's weekend duty officer. Take the afternoon off and acquaint yourself with the Silesian Station files. That should help you stay awake. Because if anyone gets murdered in Berlin between now and Tuesday, you'll be the first on the scene. So let's hope for your sake it's a quiet weekend."

I CASHED A check at the Darmstädter and National Bank to tide me over the weekend and then walked over to the enormous statue of Hercules; muscular and grumpy, he carried a useful-looking club over his right shoulder and except for the fact he was naked, he reminded me a lot of a beat copper who'd just restored order to some east-end drinking den. Despite what Bernhard Weiss had said, a bull required more than just a warrant disc and a strong word to close a bar at midnight; when Germans have been boozing all day and half the night, you need a friendly persuader to help you bang a beer counter and command their attention.

Not that the children leaning over the edge of the fountain paid Hercules much attention; they were more interested in the coins that had been tossed into the water over the years and in calculating the huge fortune that lay there. I hurried past the place and headed toward a tall house on the corner of Maassenstrasse with more scrollwork than a five-tier wedding cake and a top-heavy balcony facade that put you in mind of Frau Weitendorf herself.

I had two rooms on the fourth floor: a very narrow bedroom and a study with a ceramic stove that resembled a pistachio-colored cathedral and a marble-topped washstand that always made me feel like a priest when I stood in front of it to shave and wash myself. The study was also furnished with a small desk and chair, and a squarish leather armchair that creaked and farted more than a Baltic sea captain. Everything in my rooms was old and solid and probably indestructible—the sort of furniture the Wilhelmine manufacturers had intended to last at least as long as our empire, however long that might have been. My favorite piece was a large framed mezzotint of Georg Wilhelm Friedrich Hegel; Hegel had thin hair, hammocks under his eyes, and what seemed to be a very bad case of wind. I liked it because whenever I had a hangover I looked at it and congratulated myself that however bad I felt I couldn't feel as bad as Hegel must have felt when he'd sat for the man laughingly known as the artist. Frau Weitendorf had told me she was related to Hegel on her mother's side and that might have been true except that she also informed me Hegel was a famous composer, after which it became clear she meant Georg Friedrich Händel, which made her story seem a little less likely. To maximize her rental income her own room was on the upper-floor hallway, where she slept behind a tall screen on a malodorous day-bed she shared with her two French bulldogs. Practicalities and the need for money outweighed status. She might have been the mistress of her own house, but she certainly never saw any of her lodgers as slavishly subordinate to her will, which was quite Hegelian of her, I suppose.

The other lodgers kept themselves to themselves except at mealtimes, which was when I got to know Robert Rankin, the good-looking, cadaverous Englishman who had the rooms underneath mine. Like me he'd served on the Western Front, but with the Royal Welch Fusiliers, and after several conversations we realized we'd faced each other across a stretch of no-man's-land during the Battle of Loos, in 1915. He spoke near-perfect German, probably on account of the fact that his real name was von Ranke, which he'd been obliged to change during the war for obvious reasons. He'd written a novel about his experiences called **Pack Up Your Troubles,** but this had proved unpopular in England and he was hoping to sell it to a German publisher just as soon as he had translated it. Like most veterans, myself included, Rankin's scars were mostly invisible: he had weakened lungs from a shell blast at the Somme, but more unusually he'd been electrocuted by a field telephone that had been hit by lightning and this had left him with a pathological fear of using any telephone. Frau Weitendorf liked him because his manners were impeccable and because he paid her extra for cleaning his room, but she still called him "the spy" when he wasn't around. Frau Weitendorf was a Nazi and thought all foreigners were not to be trusted.

I arrived back at the house with the briefcase full of police files and crept quickly up the stairs to my room, hoping to avoid anyone who might be at home. I could hear Frau Weitendorf in the kitchen talking to Rosa. Most recently Rosa was playing her tenor sax at the upmarket Haller-Revue on Friedrichstrasse, which was the classiest of all the titty shows in Berlin, with a casino and VIP sections, and a very good restaurant. But there were lots of reasons to dislike the place—not least the number of people crowded into it, many of them foreigners—and the last time I'd been there I'd promised myself and my wallet that I'd never go again. I was certain that when she finished playing her sax Rosa wasn't above earning extra cash on the side. Once or twice I had returned very late from the Alex to find Rosa sneaking a client upstairs. It was none of my business and I certainly wouldn't have told "the Golem"—which was what all the lodgers called Frau Weitendorf, on account of the fact that she wore a large stiff yellow wig that resembled a large loaf of bread and was exactly like the monster's in the horror movie of the same name.

The fact was, I had a soft spot for Rosa and hardly felt qualified to judge her for trying to earn a bit more. I could have been mistaken, but eavesdropping on the stairs one day I gained half an idea that Frau Weitendorf might have been trying to set Rosa up with one of her friends from the Nollendorfplatz Theater, where, as she never tired of telling us, she'd once been an actress—which meant that the Golem was probably doing a bit of pimping on the side.

In fact, after the inflation of 1923, nearly everyone, including a lot of cops, needed a little back-pocket business to help make ends meet, and my landlady and Rosa were no different from everyone else. Most people were trying to make enough to get by, but it was never enough to get ahead. I knew plenty of cops who sold drugs—cocaine wasn't actually illegal—illicit alcohol, homemade sausage, foreign currency, rare books, dirty postcards, or watches lifted from the bodies of the dead and the dead drunk they found in the streets. For a while I supplemented my own wages by selling the odd story to Rudolf Olden, a friend at the **Berliner Tageblatt.** Olden was a lawyer as well as a journalist and, more important, a liberal who believed in free speech; but I stopped when Ernst Gennat saw me talking to him in a bar and threatened to put two and two together. Not that I'd ever have given Olden any sensitive information; mostly it was just tips about Nazis and communists in Department 1A, the political police, which was supposed to be staffed by cops who were free of any party allegiances. For example, I gave Olden some notes I took of a speech Commissioner Arthur Nebe gave at a meeting of the Prussian Police Officers' Association, the Schrader-Verband. And while Olden didn't mention Nebe by name, everyone at the Alex knew who was being quoted in the paper.

> An unnamed and supposedly independent commissioner in the Berlin political police made a speech last night to a private meeting of the Schrader-Verband at the Eden Hotel during which the following remarks were made by him: "This is no longer a healthy nation. We've stopped striving for something higher. We seem quite happy to wallow in the mire, to sink to new depths. Frankly, this is a republic that makes me think of South America, or Africa, not a country at the heart of Europe. And Berlin makes me almost ashamed to be German. It's hard to believe that just fourteen years ago we

were a force for moral good and one of the most powerful countries in the world. People feared us; now they hold us up to scorn and ridicule. Foreigners flock here with their dollars and pounds to take advantage not just of our weakened reichsmark, but also of our women and our liberal laws regarding sex. Berlin especially has become the new Sodom and Gomorrah. All right-thinking Germans should feel the same way as I and yet this government of Jews and apologists for Bolshevism does nothing but sit on its gold-ringed fingers and feed the people lies about how wonderful things really are. These are terrible people. They really are. They lie all the time. But there is, thank God, one man who promises to tell the truth and to clean up this city, to wash the filth off Berlin's streets, the scum you see every night: the drug dealers, prostitutes, pimps, transvestites, queers, Jews, and communists. That man is Adolf Hitler. There's something sick about this city and only a strongman like Hitler, with his Nazi Party, has the cure. I'm not a Nazi myself, just a conservative nationalist who can see what's happening to this country, who can see the sinister hand of the communists behind the erosion of our nation's values. They aim to undermine the moral heart of our society in the hope that there will be another revolution like the one that's destroyed Russia. They're behind it all. You know I'm right. Every cop in Berlin knows I'm right. Every cop in Berlin knows that the current government intends to do nothing about any of this. If I weren't right, then maybe I could point to some judicial sentences that might make you think the law is respected in Berlin. But I can't because our judiciary is full of Jews. Answer me this. What kind of deterrent is it when only a fifth of all death sentences are ever carried out? You mark my words, gentlemen, a storm is coming—a real storm, and all these degenerates are going to get washed away. That's what I said: **degenerates.** I don't know what else to call it when you have abortion on demand, mothers selling their daughters, pregnant women selling the mouse, and young boys performing unspeakable acts on men in back alleys. I went to the morgue the other day and saw an artist drawing the corpse of a woman who'd been murdered by her husband. Yes, that's what passes as art these days. If you ask me, this killer the press has dubbed Winnetou is just another citizen who's had enough of all the prostitution that's ruining this city. It's high time the Prussian police recognized that crimes like Winnetou's are perhaps the inevitable result of a supine, spineless government that threatens the very fabric of German society.

Gennat must have guessed it was probably me who'd fingered Arthur Nebe for the **Tageblatt** and while he didn't say anything at the time, later on he reminded me that it wasn't just cops from Department 1A who were supposed to leave their politics at home, it was Praesidium detectives, too. Especially detectives who disliked Arthur Nebe as much as he and I did. A higher standard was expected of people like us, said Gennat; there was, he said, enough division in the Prussian police without adding to it ourselves. I figured he was right and after that I stopped calling Olden.

Alone in my room I rolled and lit a cigarette, moistened the end with a little rum, and opened the window to clear the smoke. Then I unloaded my briefcase and settled down to read the Silesian Station files. Even for me they made uncomfortable reading, especially the black-and-white pictures taken by Hans Gross, the Alex police photographer.

There was something about his work on crime scenes that really got under your skin. They say every picture tells a story, but Hans Gross was the kind of photographer whose work made him the Scheherazade of modern criminalistics. This was only partly down to the fact he favored a big Folmer & Schwing Banquet camera on a rolling platform and a mobile version of the same carbon arc lamps they used at Tempelhof airport, both of which took up at least half the space in the murder wagon. More important than the camera equipment, it seemed to me, Hans had a feel for a crime scene that was nothing short of cinematic; Fritz Lang couldn't have framed his pictures better, and, sometimes, Gross's Murder Commission photographs were so sharp it seemed that the poor victim might not be dead at all, might in fact be faking it. It wasn't just the framing and sharp focus that made the photographs effective, it was the way all the background details helped to bring them alive. Detectives often saw things in his photographs they'd failed to spot at the actual crime scene. Which was why detectives at the Alex had nicknamed him Cecil B. DeMorgue.

The picture in the first case file, that of Mathilde Luz, found murdered in Andreasplatz, was so clear you could see every line of Red Front graffiti on the dilapidated brick wall her body lay next to. A pair of thick-framed glasses lay to the right of her head as if she'd just taken them off for a second; you could even see the label in one of the Hellstern shoes she'd been wearing and which had come off during death. But for the fact that a strip of her scalp was missing, Mathilde Luz looked as if she'd just lain down for a moment to take a nap.

I read the notes and various statements and then tried to imagine the conversation I might have had with her if she herself had been able to tell me what had happened. This was a new technique Weiss was encouraging us to try, as a result of a paper he'd read by a criminalist called Robert Heindl. "Let the victim talk to you," was what Heindl had said. "Try to imagine what she might tell you if you were able to spend some time with her." So I did.

MATHILDE LUZ WAS a good-looking girl all right and still wearing the clothes she'd been murdered in: the hat, the coat, and the dress all from C&A, but no less becoming for that. There are some girls who manage to wear cheap fashion and make it look good and Mathilde Luz was one of those. The police report noted her perfume was 4711, worn in the kind of quantity that made you think it served to disguise rather than allure. The report also stated she was dark, with large brown eyes and lips the same red as her nail varnish. Her face was powdered dead white; at least I thought it was powder. It might have been that way just because she was dead.

"I made incandescent mantles at the German Incandescent Light Company for two years," I heard her saying. "Liked it, too. I had some good friends there. The wages weren't much, but with my husband Franz's wage—he works at the Julius Pintsch factory, making gas meters for a living—we had just about enough to keep a roof over our heads. It wasn't much of a roof, it's fair to say. We lived on Koppenstrasse in a one-room apartment, if you can call it that—slum more like. It's a poor area, as you probably know. There were two butter riots there in 1915. Can you imagine Berlin without any butter? Unthinkable. I remember them well. I guess at the time I must have been about fourteen."

"Which made you twenty-seven at the time of your unfortunate death."

"That's right. Anyway, the landlord, Lansky, was a Jew like us, but he was never the kind to put his own tribe ahead of profit; if we hadn't paid the rent on time the bailiff would have had us out double-quick. He always told us how lucky we were to have the place at all, but then he never had to live there himself. I know for a fact he lives in a nice apartment off Tauentzienstrasse. A real **gonif,** you know? Anyway, I got laid off just after Christmas last year. I looked for another, of course, but half the women in Berlin are looking for jobs now, so I knew that wasn't ever going to happen. If I hadn't been laid off, I wouldn't ever have had to go on the sledge. With the rent due, it was Franz's idea and I went along with it because it was better than taking a beating."

"The shoes you were wearing. Style Salome, by Hellstern. Expensive."

"Girl needs to look her best."

"Where did you get them?"

"A friend stole them to order from Wertheim."

"And the glasses?"

"Some men like the secretarial type. Especially around that pitch north of Silesian Station. Makes them feel like you're the girl next door, which gives them confidence."

"It's a stone's throw from the Julius Pintsch factory, isn't it?"

"That's right. Sometimes my darling husband worked a late shift and came and found me just to take what I'd earned so he could go and buy himself a beer or two. Franz was thoughtful that way. He told me he was looking out for me, like a proper Alphonse, but I knew different.

"Of course it was dangerous. I knew that, too. We all did. Everyone remembers Carl Grossmann. He killed God only knows how many women in the very same part of Berlin. When was that?"

"Between 1919 and 1921."

"They say he ate his victims."

"No, that was Haarmann. Grossmann merely chopped his victims up after he'd killed them. Usually in his apartment on Lange Strasse. But you're right. It's not far from where you were killed."

"Bastards. If you ask me, all men are bastards."

"You're probably right."

"You, too, probably. Bulls are just as bad as all the others. Worse. You're all taking stocking money or shoveling snow, pretending you hold the law in respect. But sometimes you're worse than anyone. Who was that cop bastard at the Alex who was killing women a few years ago? The one they let off with a smack on the wrist?"

"Bruno Gerth."

"Did you know him?"

"Yes. But I wouldn't exactly say they let him off."

"No? He kept his head, didn't he?"

"True, but he's in a mental asylum now. And likely to stay there for the rest of his natural life. As a matter of fact I went to visit him a couple of months ago."

"That must have been very nice for you both. They say he put it on for the trial judge. The loony act. He knew how to work the system and the court bought it."

"That may be right. I don't know. I didn't attend the trial myself. But let's get back to what happened to you, Mathilde. Tell me about the evening you were murdered. And I'm sorry for what happened."

"I spent the early evening in the Hackebär. That was common. Lots of **chontes** like me would drink a couple of glasses of courage before we went out looking for a client."

"There were traces of cocaine in your system, too."

"Sure, why not? Puts a bit of spring in your step. Helps you when you're coming onto a likely-looking Fritz. It even helps you enjoy it, you know. When they actually fuck you. And it's not like the stuff is hard to get or particularly expensive. The sausage vendor in front of the Silesian Station is usually good for a toot."

"We asked him. But he denied it."

"You probably asked him at the wrong time. When all he had was salt and pepper."

"Then what happened?"

"A couple of us girls went to the Rose Theater and maybe the Zur Möwe."

"The dance hall. On Frankfurter."

"Right. It's a bit old-fashioned, but there are usually plenty of men looking for it. Mostly men like Franz, it has to be said. Someone saw me leave with a man, but I can't tell you anything at all about him for obvious reasons. Things start to get a little bit fuzzy. Somewhere on Andreasplatz there's a fountain with a statue of a Fritz holding a hammer."

"A witness says he saw a man washing his hands in that fountain about ten or fifteen minutes after we think you must have been murdered."

"It figures. Anyway, I reckon that's what killed me. A hammer like that one. I felt a heavy blow on the back of my neck."

"That's what killed you, Mathilde. Your murderer broke your neck with one blow."

"After that. Nothing. The big blank. Over to you, copper."

"And then he scalped you."

"Shame. I always had nice hair. You ask Franz. He used to brush it for me when he was feeling sweet. I found it very relaxing after a night on my back. Like someone really cared for me as a person, and not just a bit of mouse."

"He told us that. But it struck my bosses as a bit strange. Not many men would brush their wives' hair. It's like he was perhaps abnormally interested in a woman's hair."

"Nothing abnormal about it. He could see I was tired and wanted to do something for me. Something nice. Something that would help me to relax."

"Let's talk about Franz. We interviewed him several times. Mostly on account of the fact that you and he were reported to have had several violent arguments."

"It was Koppenstrasse, right? Not a suite at the Adlon Hotel. Everyone argues in a dump like that. Show me a couple who lives there who doesn't have violent arguments."

"He has several convictions for assault. And he owns plenty of sharp knives. Knives sharp enough to have scalped someone easily."

"He did a lot of woodworking. Made toys to

sell for the Christmas markets. To bring in a bit of extra money. Wasn't bad at it, either. But the night I was killed he had an alibi. He was working the night shift at Julius Pintsch."

"It's my job to break alibis. So he was close enough to sneak out of the factory for ten minutes, kill you, and then go back to work."

"Kill his golden goose? I don't think so. I was good at being a whore, copper. Franz may be a bastard, but he isn't entirely stupid. And lots of his fellow workers—including the factory foreman—say they never had him out of their sight."

"The police also found several novels by Karl May in your apartment. Including **Winnetou.** In fact, that was what persuaded the press to start calling your killer Winnetou."

For some reason, I couldn't bring myself to think of the murderer as the Silesian Station killer. I knew Gennat felt the same way and so long as Weiss wasn't around he always called him Winnetou; everyone did, and I was no exception.

"I'm not much of a reader myself. But from what Franz told me, half the men in Germany have read those damn books."

"You're probably right."

"Look, Franz was a lot of things, my friend. But somewhere deep inside that barrel chest of his was a heart that loved me. That's what kept us together. We quarreled, yes, but usually because he'd had a skinful. What Fritz doesn't drink himself into a state on a Friday night and then knock his wife around for the hell of it? You wouldn't know much about that in a nice little room like this. Carpet on the floor. Curtains on the windows. Windows that you can see through. I gave Fritz a couple of smacks with a chair leg on occasion when he was properly out of line. One time I even thought I'd killed him. But he has a head like a walnut and he came around after an hour or so, full of apologies for having kicked off. Didn't even bear me a grudge. In fact, I'm pretty sure he didn't even remember me hitting him. We made it up nicely that time."

"Sounds very romantic."

"Sure, why not? That's romance, Berlin style. Let me tell you something, copper; it's only when a man is lying insensible at your feet and you realize you could beat his head to a pulp with a chair leg if you wanted to that you really know if you love him or not."

"Like I said before, I'm sorry for what happened to you. And I'll do my very best to catch the man who did it. You have my word."

"That's very sweet of you, Herr Gunther. But to be honest, it really doesn't matter to me now one way or the other."

"Is there anything else you can tell me?"

"No."

"According to the lab report you were pregnant. Did you know?"

"No. I—we always wanted a baby. Not that we could have afforded one." She wiped away a tear and was very quiet for a moment; and then she was very quiet forever.

I WASN'T USUALLY back home in Nollendorfplatz for supper, but it being a Friday and having missed lunch, I was glad I was, because this was the night Frau Weitendorf usually went to the theater and left a lung hash that only had to be heated up on the stove. There was always enough for about ten people and, having been quite particular to lung hash since I was a schoolboy, I was pleased to join my fellow lodgers around the dinner table. Rosa did the honors with the hash and some boiled potatoes, while Fischer, the Bavarian salesman, cut the black bread, and Rankin poured malted coffee into large mugs. I laid the table with the second-best china. They were curious as to why I was there at all, of course, but didn't ask me why directly; not that I would have told them I'd been promoted to the Murder Commission. The last thing I wanted to talk about when I was at home was crime. But most of the talk was about the explosion at the Wolfmium factory and all the workers who'd been killed, and Fischer told us that this was one of the reasons he was going to march through Berlin with the communists the next day, which he would never have mentioned if Frau Weitendorf had been at home. If there was one subject likely to make our landlady fly into uncontrollable rage it was Bolshevism. It wasn't just the fact that she was a Nazi that made her so vehemently anti-communist; it was the several bullet holes in the front of the house made by the Spartacist militia during Berlin's Bolshevik revolution of 1919. Frau Weitendorf took each one of them personally.

"Which part?" I asked. "Of Berlin."

"We're starting in Charlottenburg."

"Not many communists there, I'd have thought."

"And heading east, along Bismarckstrasse."

"I didn't know you were a communist, Herr Fischer," said Rosa.

"I'm not. But I feel I have to do something after the terrible tragedy at Wolfmium. You might say I want to show a bit of worker solidarity. But it's no surprise to me that this kind of thing happens. Employers in this country don't care anything about their workers and the conditions they have to endure. Some of the things I see when I'm on the road and visiting customers, you wouldn't believe. Underground illegal factories, slum sweatshops; places you wouldn't believe could exist in a city like Berlin."

"Good for you, Herr Fischer," said Rankin. "I agree with you about worker conditions. Here and in England, they're awful. But you're not saying that what happened at Wolfmium was the result of the employer's negligence, are you? I mean there's no evidence of that, surely. It was an accident. I imagine some of the materials they use in the manufacture of electric light bulbs are inherently dangerous."

"I'll make you a bet now," insisted Fischer. "That someone's to blame. Someone who ignored fire safety codes just to make a bigger profit."

Rankin lit a cigarette with a handsome gold lighter, stared into the flame for a moment as if it might provide a clue to the origins of the explosion, and then said, "What do you think, Herr Gunther? Are the police investigating what happened?"

"Not my department," I said. "It's the fire brigade that has charge of this kind of investigation." I smiled patiently and helped myself from Rankin's cigarette case. As I leaned toward his lighter I caught a strong smell of alcohol. I puffed on the nail for a minute and then rolled it thoughtfully between my fingers. "But I will say this: A nail is always the most effective way to start a most effective fire. Chances are that's all it was. A careless cigarette end. To that extent we're all potential arsonists."

Fischer looked scornful. "The Berlin police,"

he said. "They're part of the same conspiracy. These days the only crime is getting caught."

Rankin smiled politely. He might have been a bit drunk, but he was still equal to the task of changing the subject on my behalf for the sake of politeness.

"I was reading in the newspaper," he said to no one in particular. "Benito Mussolini has ended women's rights in Italy on the same day that my own country has lowered the age of women voters from thirty to twenty-one. More or less the same day, anyway. For once I'm almost proud to be an Englishman."

We finished supper not saying anything of much consequence, which suited me very well. After we'd cleared up, I returned to my room and was preparing to read the case file of Winnetou's second murder when I heard the telephone downstairs. A minute or two later Rosa came up and spoke to me. She'd changed her clothes and was now clad in the male evening attire she was required to wear to play in the Haller-Revue's band. The white tie and tails made her look oddly sexy; as a Vice detective, I was used to seeing transvestites—the Eldorado on Lutherstrasse was notorious for transvestites and a frequent source of information about what was happening in Berlin's underground scene—but I wasn't at all sure I was the kind of man who felt comfortable in the company of a woman dressed as a man. Not while there were still so many women who dressed like women.

"That was the Police Praesidium at Alexanderplatz on the telephone," she said. "Someone called Hans Gross said he'll pick you up outside our front door in half an hour."

I thanked her, glanced at my watch, and quietly enjoyed the scent of her Coty perfume in my room. It made a nice change from rum, cigarettes, Lux, Nivea, fried potatoes, and cheap hair oil, not to mention a lot of old books and unwashed laundry.

"Think you'll be working late?" she asked.

"I won't know for sure until that police car turns up. But yes, maybe. That's the nature of the job, I'm afraid."

At the same time, I was thinking that it was still a little early for a murder. Berliners usually wait until they've loosened up with a few drinks and a couple of songs before battering someone to death. Only a few weeks before I'd seen a prisoner in the main reception hall at the Alex singing "From the Age of Youth" at the top of his voice. He was drunk, of course, but he'd also just beaten his elder sister to a pulp with a golf club.

"She comes, she comes no more! She comes, she comes no more!"

Which, sadly, was all very true, of course.

Chances were it was just an accident we were to attend, what some of the uniformed boys called a Max Mustermann; a body some citizen had found in circumstances that raised the question of foul play.

"Why don't you come by the club tonight?" she said. "I'll be there until well after midnight. Hella Kürty is on the bill."

I shook my head blankly.

"Singer. She was in that movie **Who Throws the First Stone.**"

"Didn't see it."

"I could leave you a ticket at the box office if you like."

"I can't promise I'll be there," I said. "But sure. If I can. Thanks."

"It's probably not your thing, I know," she said, a little sadly. "The show is very empty and pretentious, it's true. But these days, tell me what isn't? If you ask me, the inflation didn't just affect our money, but everything else, too. Sex, drinking, drugs, nightlife, art, you name it. It's like everything is rampantly out of control, you know? Especially in Berlin. The inflated money was just the beginning. The city's become one great big department store of debauchery. Sometimes when I walk along the Kurfürstendamm and see all the boys powdered and rouged like tarts and behaving outrageously I fear for the future. I really do."

"How do you mean?" I asked.

"All of this fake sexual freedom and eroticism, it puts me in mind of the last days of ancient Rome. And I keep thinking that ordinary Germans just wish it would all go away so that they could get back to living calm, orderly lives."

"You're probably right. But I worry what we'll replace it with. Something worse perhaps. And that maybe we'll regret its passing. I don't know. Better the devil you know."

When she'd gone I realized, too late, that Rosa had looked a bit lonely and that I should have talked to her more and even made it a little clearer that I liked her, but at that particular moment I had something else on my mind. Ernst Gennat would probably have said that a living girl—even one dressed like a man—is always more interesting than a dead one, especially a girl as pretty as Rosa, but I was keen to prove that Bernhard Weiss had been right about me, that I wasn't another cynical Berlin bull, that I believed in the job and that I was the right man for Lindner's seat. So I sat down in the armchair and lit another rum-moistened roll-up. There was just time to read the facts of the second Winnetou case before the Alex murder wagon showed up.

THE MUTILATED BODY of Helen Strauch was found in the old cemetery of St. Jacobi's Church, just south of Hermannplatz, in Neukölln. The wide shots of the cemetery showed a not-unattractive mourning chapel resembling a small Greek temple, a Doric colonnade, several lime and chestnut trees, and a shapeless figure at the feet of a statue of St. Jacob as if prostrate in prayer. Close-ups of the head and the body showed Helen Strauch was lying facedown on some blackened flagstones that had been previously chalk-marked for the children's hopping game called heaven and earth. According to the police pathologist, death had been more or less instantaneous; she'd been struck a mortal blow on the back of the neck—which is the weakest and most vulnerable part of the human body—leaving behind a bruise the size and color of a red cabbage, and then scalped from the center of her forehead to the occipital bone at the back of her skull. Like Mathilde Luz, there was no evidence that the killer had sex with his victim; there was even a ten-mark note still in her garter. The time of death was not long after midnight on the twentieth of May.

Helen had lived on Hermannstrasse, which ran along the eastern perimeter of the cemetery. According to the police report you could see the murder scene from her bedroom window; at least you could when the window was clean. The area, generally known as the Bullenviertel, was one

I'd policed as a uniformed bull, the kind of area where a cop learned his trade fast—a gray and desolate place where people worked long hours for not much money, the air stank of roasted malt, barefoot children ran wild at all times of the day and night, every second cellar shop was a bar selling cheap and often illegal booze, and the Salvation Army was in almost permanent residence. I'd often had to shoo prostitutes out of the cemetery at St. Jacobi's; they were inclined to use the colonnade to service their clients. But safe in my rooms in Nollendorfplatz and wearing a clean shirt collar and tie, I already felt like a stranger to the slums.

Helen Strauch was a prostitute who'd previously worked at the Bergschloss Brewery, which was only a short distance from where she was found dead. When she'd been laid off last summer, it seemed she'd had little choice but to become a full-time prostitute. This already looked like a typical Berlin story. On the night of her death she'd spent the evening drinking absinthe cocktails in the brewery bar on Hasenheide before going on the street. No one remembered her with a client or seeing her talking to any particular man. One girl did think she remembered Helen talking to someone in a car, with her foot up on the running board, but she didn't remember the type of the car or the number plate, nor indeed the man, if it was a man. Opposite the brewery on Hasenheide was a hospital where Helen had gone for an appointment the previous day—a pregnancy test, which proved negative.

The body had been found by Walther Wenders, a drayman from Babel's Brewery in Kreuzberg; beer in that part of Berlin is more than just a drink, it's a way of life. Wenders lived on Berlinerstrasse and his walk to work took him west, past the little cemetery where he'd stopped for a quick pee, which was when his eye caught something unusual. At first he thought it was just an old coat someone had thrown away. It looked like a good coat and his wife certainly had need of one, but as soon as he saw the blood on the ground he realized exactly what he was looking at. It was obvious that there was nothing to be done for the girl, so he walked quickly west to the hospital on Hasenheide and raised the alarm there. The regular detective attached to the Murder Commission on that occasion had been Kurt Reichenbach who, having carefully searched the area on his hands and knees, found a man's gold cuff link engraved with a Freemason's symbol—the set square and compass. For a while it had looked like an important clue since Helen's poor head had been resting on the chalked number nine, which has a special meaning in freemasonry; or so Reichenbach had argued.

Born in Thuringia in 1904, Helen Strauch had lived nearly all her life in Neukölln; her mother had left her drunken woodcutter father and come to Berlin to become a piecework seamstress in a garment factory before she had drowned herself in the Landwehr Canal aged just thirty-five, when Helen was only fifteen. The reason: early onset of arthritis that had stopped her from making her living. Helen then had an on-and-off relationship with a man called Paul Nowak who was employed at the gasworks on Fichtestrasse and who lived in a room on Friedelstrasse. But Paul Nowak was also a part-time prostitute and he had a fistful of alibis for the night of the murder, having spent the evening at several queer bars in Bülowstrasse—the Hollandais at number 69, the Continental at number 2, the Nationalhof at number 37, the Bülow Casino at number 41, and the Hohenzollern lounge at number 101—before bringing a gentleman home to his room on Friedelstrasse. All the barmen remembered seeing him that night, and even his client, a Dutch businessman called Rudi Klaver, who happened to be a Freemason himself, had provided him with an alibi, which says a great deal about how open homosexual men were in Berlin. "Berlin means boys" was a widely held thought throughout the Weimar Republic. But the fact was that ever since Frederick the Great had forbidden women to his Praetorian Guard in the 1750s, obliging the guards to seek the company of boys for their sexual pleasure, Berlin had been identified with soldierly inversion and uranic sexuality. Paragraph 175 of the Federal Criminal Code still forbade all homosexual activity but there were so many male prostitutes in Berlin—at the Alex it was generally held there were at least twenty-five thousand of them—that the law was more or less unenforceable.

Nowak had a criminal record for car theft and from the police photograph, he was no one's idea of a rent boy; he was a large, powerful bearded youth who hunted wild boar in the Grünewald on his weekends and often skinned the beasts himself. He had knives, sharp knives, but then so did most Berlin men. I kept a folding knife in my jacket pocket myself; made by Henckels of Solingen, it was as sharp as a razor and could have scalped a bowling ball. Nowak wasn't a violent man, however; if anything, Helen Strauch had been the abusive partner in their relationship. She was a boot whore, which is to say, she was a dominatrix who got paid to beat up her clients. Now and then she took a cane to Nowak, who, friends said, frequently took a whipping without complaint. Gennat liked Nowak for the murder and he liked his sharp knives, too, but with all those alibis in the back pocket of the boy's greasy leather shorts—Nowak was only eighteen years old—he couldn't make it stick. But most of all, on the night Mathilde Luz had been killed, Nowak had been in a cell at the police station on Bismarckstrasse following an allegation that he'd robbed another client with whom he'd had sex—an allegation that was subsequently withdrawn.

Meanwhile, Reichenbach had pursued the Freemason link all the way to the manufacturer in Rosenthaler Strasse, but after interviewing the masters of all three Berlin Grand Lodges, the trail finally went cold—though not before the Nazi Party unilaterally decided in the pages of **Der Angriff** that the link with freemasonry was all too real and only proved what it had always argued: that freemasonry was an insidious cult that threatened to undermine Germany and should be outlawed. Since it was generally known there were many Freemasons employed as policemen at the Alex, the Nazi theory provided the Party with yet another means of criticizing the Berlin police.

We were an easy target, of course, not least because Berlin now had almost nothing in common with the rest of the country. Increasingly the capital city was like a large ship that had slipped its mooring and was slowly drifting farther and farther away from the coast of Germany; it seemed unlikely we were going to return to its more conservative ways, even if we'd wanted to. It's not just people who outgrow their parents and origins; it's metropolises, too. I'd read that a lot of Franzis hated Paris for much the same reasons: Parisians always made them feel like poor relations. Maybe it's the same with any great metropolis; for all I know the people of Mexico hate the citizens of Mexico City for the very same reasons that Berliners are despised by the citizens of Munich. And vice versa, of course; I've never been particularly fond of Bavarians.

Helen Strauch's case was life in the metropolis writ horribly, swinishly large, squalid and depressing, like lifting a wet stone in a very dark forest to see what was crawling underneath, and when I finished reading the file I felt obliged to wash my hands and face; but my evening was just beginning and there were many more unpleasant things about to come crawling my way.

I KNEW WE were probably in the right place when, approaching the Fischerstrasse bridge at the end of Friedrichsgracht, I recognized the uniformed policeman seated on a mooring bollard; his name was Miczek and he was a good copper who could usually be relied on. The shine on his boots would have told you that much: Miczek was a real spit-and-polish copper and as tough as his steel toe caps. Seeing the murder wagon, he stood up, buttoned his tunic collar, replaced the fire bucket of a leather helmet on his head, tossed his cigarette into the black water behind him, and approached with a two-finger salute. It was the wagon that drew the respect, not me, even though I was now nominally in charge of the homicide.

"Where's our Max Mustermann?" asked Hans Gross, climbing out from behind the wagon's enormous steering wheel. Along with the two uniformed policemen who'd accompanied him from the Alex, I followed. Our stenographer, Frau Künstler, stayed put behind her typewriter; she had no appetite for seeing a dead body, and I couldn't say I blamed her. Especially not a body that had been in the river. The haze of cigarette smoke in front of her bespectacled face was probably there to make sure she didn't see or smell anything unpleasant.

"Still in the water," said Miczek. "We've hooked him but didn't want to pull him out in case we lost any evidence."

Bodies were frequently found floating in the Spree and just as often remained unidentified. When a corpse was being manhandled onto the quayside it was easy for a wallet or a purse to fall out of a pocket and sink to the bottom of the river. After that it was surprisingly difficult to put a name to a human face, especially if the fish had already lunched there.

"Good work," said Gross.

Miczek pointed down at three bargemen who were playing skat on top of an upturned fish basket. All had caps, pipes, and enough facial hair to stuff a small sofa.

"Come to see our catch, have you?" said one, and reaching behind him, he pulled on a length of line that brought closer to the oily surface of the water the upper part of a man's body.

Meanwhile, Hans Gross had already unfolded his portable Voigtländer and was taking pictures.

"Who found him?" I asked.

"Me," said the man holding the line. "Spotted him just after lunch."

Half an hour later we had landed him on the quayside and a small crowd of bystanders started to gather. The man didn't look as if he'd been in the water for very long. He was about fifty, with a small mustache that resembled a smudge on his upper lip. He was wearing a double-breasted, pinstriped suit, and a pair of shoes that already told me he wasn't a bargee. On his lapel was an Iron Cross. And in his chest, right up to the hilt, was the knife that had killed him.

"Anyone recognize this fellow?" I asked.

No one said a thing. I touched the handle of the knife and found it was lodged so firmly in the dead man's chest it must have gone all the way through into his backbone. As he lay there, his mouth slowly sagged open and, much to everyone's horror, a small crayfish came wandering out, almost nonchalantly. Restraining my own disgust, I searched the man's pockets, which were empty save for one thing: a plain wooden ball a little smaller than a tennis ball. I looked at it without much comprehension. I was thinking I might have encountered a real mystery of the kind that are supposed to fascinate good detectives when I heard a voice and realized that the discovery of the wooden ball had prompted a response from someone in the growing crowd.

"I reckon that's Bruno Kleiber," said a woman. She was wearing a cotton smock and a man's old army cap, and she carried a broom. Her legs were so heavily covered with varicose veins they looked as if several small sea creatures had burrowed underneath her skin. And from the angle of her head on her shoulders I supposed there was something wrong with her spine. She spoke in a Berlin accent that was as thick as her forearms.

"Let her through," I told the constable, and the woman stepped forward.

"You are?"

The woman snatched off her army cap to reveal a head that was so deeply scored with an old bullet wound it almost resembled a center parting and looked like the very definition of a lucky escape. "Dora Hauptmann, sir. I sweep the quays clean. For the Cölln Canal Company. Everywhere on this island, sir, south of Schlossplatz."

"And you think you recognize the dead man?"

"Wasn't sure of it until I saw that ball in his pocket. But now I am. No mistaking that wooden ball and that Iron Cross. His name is Bruno Kleiber and that wooden ball was his living for ten years, I reckon." She took out a handkerchief, dabbed at the corner of each rheumy eye, and then pointed west along Friedrichsgracht. "I can show you where he worked, if you like."

"Thanks. I'd appreciate it."

We started along the quayside.

"Three-shell game was it?" I asked. "Kleiber's racket?"

"Nah. Ball's too big. He used to run a street roulette wheel underneath the Gertrauden Bridge. Every morning, at exactly nine thirty a.m., he'd open up his table and start the ball rolling. That's when everyone who works at the Cölln Fish Market finishes for the day. They go and get a few beers in, or maybe a whore who doesn't mind the smell of fish so much, and sometimes they'll stop to make a bet at Kleiber's table. Little Monte Carlo they call it. An illegal game, of course, but it didn't do any harm and the game wasn't crooked, neither. Kleiber didn't need to be crooked. Ran a straight game, everyone knew that. That Iron Cross he wore was supposed to be a guarantee of his integrity and it was. He made just enough money to make it worthwhile for himself but not so much that folk around here ever resented him. He always paid up when he lost, which is how he stayed in business for so long."

"Well, someone resented him," I said as we walked along.

"I doubt that. He was a decent sort, was Kleiber. Always had a joke for you. Or a penny for some snot-nosed kid. You ask me, someone wanted to get their hands on his float. The cash he kept in his back pocket to pay up on a winning number."

"Sounds like you knew him reasonably well."

"Well enough to regret his passing. He used to give me a few coins every day to sweep up all the cigarette ends that people left on the ground under the table. He was scrupulous that way. As if his pitch really had been the red carpet at Monte."

"And today?"

"I'm late today. I was on my way down to the bridge when I saw you lot fishing him out of the water."

"By the way, not that it's any of my business, but that scar on your head. How did you get it?"

She fingered the scar without any sign of discomfort. "This? I was lucky. That's how I got it. I was a nurse on the Eastern Front in 1916 with a Catholic confessional sisterhood. Got hit by a piece of shrapnel from a Russian shell. Same piece of shrapnel that killed my sister, who was also a nurse. I was lucky once, and I might just get lucky again."

"Sorry. It's just that you don't see many female war veterans on the streets."

"That's because most of us who were injured died. Women were less important than men."

"Must be something a man said."

Under the Gertrauden Bridge, chained to a mooring ring, we found what looked like a folded-up billboard of the kind a sandwich man might have carried. It was about four feet in length, painted green and quite heavy. I took out my knife, twisted the point in the padlock, and a minute later we were unfolding a trestle table about eight feet long that was squared off in numbers and combinations of numbers; in the middle was a sunken round dish with ten crude round slots numbered from zero to nine. The operation was fairly obvious. The croupier would spin the wooden ball around the dish, wait for the ball to drop onto a slot, and then reckon up the game's losers and winners.

"Kleiber was quick at making calculations and he never got it wrong. Had a mind like a slide rule."

"That float," I said. "How much cash did he carry, do you think?"

"Maybe a hundred marks. Enough to make it worth someone's while to rob the poor bastard."

"Anyone spring to mind?"

"No one from Cölln. Folk around here are tough but honest, in the main. Some mad bastard from somewhere else, probably. Whole country has gone mad, if you ask me. Fact is, there used to be a madhouse nearby, but they closed it. Seems to me as if we need our madhouses more than ever."

"You got that right. But with all that money you'd have thought he had a human watchdog."

"He did. Ex-boxer. Corduroy suit. Matching cap. Tall fellow with an ear like someone's kidney on toast. What was his name? Kube. Kolbe?"

"I wonder if he barked or not." I fetched a roll-up from a tin and lit it quickly. "And if not, why not? Where did Kleiber live?"

"No idea, lad. But every day, after the game, regular as clockwork, he'd go to the Nussbaum Inn on Fischerstrasse and have his lunch there. They might know. In fact, I'm sure of it."

We walked back to the crime scene and I waved Miczek over; I wanted him to hear me as I dictated to Frau Künstler through the rear window of the murder wagon. Without looking up, she typed on a sleek black Torpedo that was the same color as the lacquer on her fingernails. That was the first time I realized our stenographer was a much younger woman than I'd supposed;

younger and more unconventional perhaps. On the back of her head she wore a little black beret, while on the shoulder of her black dress was a brooch shaped like a large black grasshopper. What with her white face and heavy black eye makeup, she resembled Theda Bara. Meanwhile, Hans Gross was taking pictures under the arc lamps, using the Folmer & Schwing now. While I was there a call came through on the radio from the Alex; it was Gennat. I told him what I knew, and when he'd gone off the air, I told Miczek and one of the other uniformed coppers to accompany me to the Nussbaum Inn.

"Do you know the place?" I asked Miczek.

"Everyone on the island knows the Nussbaum. Oldest bar in Berlin. And five minutes' walk from here. But they don't much like coppers in there. Especially on payday."

"Good. That suits me just fine."

"It might be a good idea to call for some backup."

"We won't need it."

When we got to the Nussbaum, I told the two cops to wait outside front and back while I went in to ask questions.

"Are you sure about this, lad? There are some tough Fritzes in there. And likely most of them are drunk."

"If anyone comes out in a hurry, I want you

to stop them leaving. Just so I can get a look at them. You never know. My guess is that Kleiber's murderer waited until his man had finished lunch and then followed him out, so maybe his killer is still on the grounds."

"All right, lad. I see what you're driving at. But be careful. No sense in you getting yourself murdered today."

The Nussbaum had been at 21 Fischerstrasse since 1505 or 1705 depending on who told you the story. It was every American tourist's idea of what an old Berlin bar should look like; it had a tall saddlebag dormer roof that was a little wonky and the kind of windows that made you think the place belonged properly in a fairy tale involving a witch with a very long nose. There was a ramshackle garden out front that was mostly one lime tree, and a green picket fence next to which stood a line of ragged children who were probably waiting for their parents to finish drinking away their wages in the bar. From ten feet away you could smell the beer and hear the raucous laughter of men and women who'd already had far too much to drink. And as I walked through the front door I tried to banish my nerves to the deepest pocket of my trousers.

At the bar I picked up a glass and tapped it loudly with a knife. "Could I have your attention, please?"

Gradually the noise died down.

"I'm a detective from the Alex—"

Several people booed and catcalled. The usual friendly Berlin welcome.

"And I'm investigating the murder of a man who came in here every day. His name was Bruno Kleiber and he ran an illegal roulette wheel under Gertrauden Bridge. Someone robbed him this afternoon. Stabbed him to death and pushed his body into the Spree. I'd like to speak to anyone who saw him today or who can shed some light on what happened to him."

"He was a Jew," someone called out. "So who gives a damn? Maybe someone just did to him what he used to do to other people."

"Yes, rob them," said someone else, laughing.

"I don't believe that. According to what I've heard he ran a straight game."

"He was in here today," said the man nearest to me. "Same as always. Had his lunch and a beer and then left."

"What time was that?"

"Came in about twelve. Left about two. Must have happened after that."

"Did you see him talk to anyone?"

"He kept himself to himself," said another man. "Never bothered anyone."

The publican came around the counter with a small billy club in his hand. "Dead, you say?

That's too bad. Bruno Kleiber was a good customer and a good man and I'll bar any one of you bastards who says different. Got that?"

The noise died down again.

"I'm at the Alex if anyone remembers anything, and you can telephone me in confidence. The name's Gunther. Bernhard Gunther."

It wasn't my most subtle performance, but then it wasn't meant to be. My intention had been to behave exactly like a loud yapping dog, and hopefully to drive some sheep into my pen.

Outside the Nussbaum were the sheep; well, one anyway. Miczek and the other policeman had arrested the man who was now my number one suspect; straightaway I recognized him from Dora Hauptmann's description. Both cops had drawn their batons and looked ready to deal with a man resisting arrest, even one who looked as tough as this fellow.

"He came out just as soon as you started your spiel," said Miczek. "In a hurry, too. Like maybe he didn't want to help the Berlin police."

"You Kube?" I asked.

"Nope."

"Kolbe, then?"

The big man shrugged. "Who wants to know?"

He stank of beer and was sufficiently unsteady on his feet to persuade me that he'd been drinking all afternoon.

"I've heard you were paid to watch Bruno Kleiber's back."

"Who told you that?"

"Doesn't matter. Just answer the question."

"You've got the wrong Fritz, copper. I played the Jew's numbers just like lots of people around here, but I was never his dog."

"You've got something against Jews?"

"Hasn't everyone?"

"It didn't sound like it in there," I said. "Besides, who would be dumb enough to admit he didn't like Jews when there's a dead one lying on the quayside just five minutes' walk from here?"

"I don't like Jews. What of it?"

"Gives you a motive to kill him, I'd have thought. That and a hundred-mark float that was in the dead man's back pocket. Which is reason enough for me to search you."

"Try it and see what happens, copper."

"Search him."

Kolbe raised his huge fist, which was as far as it got before Miczek tapped him on the back of the head with his police baton; not hard, but just hard enough to drop him onto the cobbles, leaving him dazed for several minutes, in no position to resist us. We went through his pockets and just about the first thing we found was a solid-gold signet ring; on this was a Star of David.

"For a man who doesn't like Jews you have some interesting jewelry," I said.

Miczek had a good-quality leather wallet open on his palm and anyone could have seen it wasn't Kolbe's; for one thing there was a wedding picture of Kleiber and his wife; for another, the wallet held two hundred-mark notes. We even found an empty leather sheath for the murder weapon in Kolbe's pocket. It was probably the easiest murder arrest I ever made, but I was soon to discover that not all Berlin's murderers were as dumb as Herbert Kolbe.

WE WENT BACK to the Alex to put Kolbe in the lockup. As usual the main front door was so heavy I had to push it open with both hands—Gross was carrying the camera, and the two men in uniform each held one of Kolbe's muscular arms. The door closed behind us with an enormous hollow boom like the sound of a howitzer at the last judgment. Inside the entrance hall everything was as busy as the front line during wartime: drunks being processed for a night in the cells, typewriters clattering away, telephones ringing, coppers shouting, keys jangling, women crying, police dogs barking, and always the front door closing loudly on the peculiar metropolitan hell that was the Berlin Police Praesidium. Leaving the boys in green to process our prisoner I grabbed a quick coffee and a smoke in the canteen and then went up to the Commission offices to file my report. But on the stairs, I met none other than Kurt Reichenbach. There was an awkward silence between us for a moment, and then Reichenbach lifted his hat politely.

"I've just heard that you got the seat in the murder wagon," he said affably. "Congratulations, my dear fellow. It's a good break for you. And very well deserved."

"Thanks. That's good of you, Kurt."

"Not at all. Word is you'll go far, Gunther. You'll be a commissar in no time. Me, I've got a big mouth so it's probably just as well I didn't get the seat. Truth be told, two Jews in the one car is one Jew too many. But you know when to keep your lip buttoned, lad. That's the secret to advancement around here. Knowing when to keep your trap shut. And when to forget about politics. Besides, there are too many damn lawyers in the force already. The ranks of the commissars are stiff with them. You're precisely the kind of new blood this place needs."

Reichenbach was small and bearded, with an easy smile. He wore a fine black leather coat in nearly all weathers and carried a thick walking stick. Since there was nothing wrong with either of his legs it was assumed, rightly, that he carried the stick in lieu of a truncheon.

He was well dressed for a detective. There was a feather in the band of his gray bowler hat and a handsome gold pin in the knot of his green woolen tie. Even when it was empty, the amber cigar holder he favored rarely left his mouth, but on this occasion it was filled with a sweet-smelling Dominican Aurora. I was sure about the brand because even as he was speaking he was generously tucking one into the breast pocket of my jacket.

"Anyway, there's something for you. A good cigar to celebrate your promotion and show there's no hard feelings from me. I get these sent from a special shop in Amsterdam."

"Thanks, Kurt. They must be expensive."

"Sure they're expensive. But there's no wisdom in smoking cheap cigars, is there?"

I was almost sure this was a reference to Bernhard Weiss, but if it was he didn't make a big thing of it and I didn't pick him up on it.

"My wife, who's a nurse, disapproves of all kinds of smoking, but where would Kripo be without tobacco? That's what I say. It's hard enough being a detective as it is without giving up something that stimulates the old gray machine." He tapped his head and grinned. "I suppose if I ever stopped to think about it, I might give it up. But until then I shall keep puffing away. In spite of my wife."

I ran the cigar under my nose, savoring it gratefully and quietly wondering where he got the money for such luxuries. I was quite sure I'd seen his leather coat in the window at Peek &

Cloppenburg costing over a thousand reichsmarks. I'd heard it said he had a loan-sharking business on the side; then again, that might just have been plain anti-Semitism; he certainly never offered me a loan. Still, it's true that being a detective with the Prussian police wasn't particularly well paid.

"By the way, Gunther, there's a favor you might do me if you're so inclined."

"Sure. If I can."

"I have a friend who's a filmmaker. Her name is Thea von Harbou and she's a scriptwriter who's married to Fritz Lang, the film director." He paused. "I take it you've heard of Fritz Lang."

"I've heard of Fritz Lang."

"Thea writes his film scripts. She's researching a new movie about a sex murderer and would dearly like to speak to someone who's employed by the famous Berlin Murder Commission."

"Look, I've only just started. I'm not sure what I can tell her that you couldn't tell her. It's not like you haven't worked for the Commission."

"True, but I'm not a **permanent** member. And not actively on a murder case right now. Which is an important distinction. To her, anyway. Also, she has ambitions of being able to speak to the Big Buddha, and the plain fact of the matter is that there's bad blood between Gennat and me, as is now obvious to everyone. Gennat would certainly have refused if I'd asked him about Thea von Harbou. He thinks I'm a thug. Well, maybe I am. I try to carry out my duties as best I can, but sometimes I am a little overzealous; particularly where Nazis are concerned. Either way, I can't help Thea in this particular respect and I was hoping you might speak with her. Look, all she really cares about is that the person she meets is a **permanent** member of Berlin's famous Commission. I imagine so she can tell her husband as much. He's a very demanding fellow, by all accounts."

"Sure, I'll do it. If Gennat gives his permission."

"I'm sure he will. If **you** ask him. Gennat loves cinema. Almost as much as he loves attractive women. And now that you're his blue-eyed boy he won't deny you much. Especially if what I hear is true; that you've already felt your first collar."

"Yes. But there was nothing to it. We virtually caught the Fritz red-handed."

"I'm sure you're just being modest. Which is very commendable. Weiss loves a bit of modesty in his detectives. He hates anyone to outshine his beloved department. He only tolerates the fame of the Big Buddha because Ernst Gennat doesn't give a damn for reputation. You can see that by the way he dresses. He's not a threat to anyone. Those suits of his look like they were cut with a cheese knife."

"On the whole modesty suits me better; I don't sound good when I'm bossing people around."

"Well, congratulations anyway. Even an easy collar can come away in your hand, Gunther. Remember that. And make sure you don't neglect the paperwork. Weiss is above all a lawyer and lawyers love to read reports."

"I was just heading upstairs to finish my report."

"Good man. So then, here's Thea's business card—" He sniffed it before handing it over. "Hmm. Scented. Anyway, you can telephone her yourself. She's quite attractive. A bit too old for you, probably. But an interesting woman nonetheless."

"You've met her then?"

"Oh yes."

"Here?"

"No. Although she'd dearly love to get a look around the Commission offices as well. At the time, I didn't dare bring her here in case it scuppered my chances of getting Lindner's seat. No, I took her to the Police Museum, the Hanno showhouse, and then Hirschfeld's Institute for Sexual Science at In Den Zelten, just to give my stories some extra color, so to speak. The institute is mostly photographs of perverts and Japanese dildos. But she seemed to find it all quite interesting. Especially the dildos. At the very least you'll probably get a nice dinner out of her. She took me to Horcher's."

I pocketed the woman's business card and nodded. "I said I'd do it," I said again. "And I will. I like a free dinner as much as the next man."

"Good, good." Reichenbach tipped his hat and started down the stairs, swinging his stick and puffing his cigar back into life. "I can't understand it myself. A movie about a man killing whores in Berlin? I mean, who cares about that?" He laughed. "Nobody in this place, that's for sure. You might just as well shoot a movie inside the Reichstag. Sometimes I think I should have been a movie producer, not a cop. I understand the public, you see. I know what scares them. And it certainly isn't someone crushing a few grasshoppers. Most Germans think those girls have got it coming."

I WANTED TO contradict Reichenbach, to shout into the vertiginous stairwell that I cared. In fact, I cared very much and not just because I was now attached to the Murder Commission. I was thinking of Rosa Braun, wondering how I might feel if she turned up in the Spree with her neck broken; nobody deserved a death like that, not even if she was taking a risk selling it for money. But it wasn't just Rosa I cared about.

In my time with Vice I'd got to know a great many girls who were on the sledge and quite a few of them struck me as honest, good people. I even knew one or two who had made their Abitur. None were the worthless grasshoppers Reichenbach had spoken of. For many single women in Berlin, life was a slippery slope, which of course was one reason prostitution was called the sledge in the first place. And the whole city seemed morally degraded when a girl turned up in an alley with her neck broken and her scalp missing. But it hardly seemed worth disagreeing with Reichenbach now that he was halfway out of the building. Besides, keeping my mouth shut about a lot of things was probably best for the present. He was my superior after all. And it wasn't as if he was wrong; most of the cops at the Alex didn't care that much about the fate of a few prostitutes.

Nor was there much wrong with his advice to me, even if it was obvious. Bernhard Weiss didn't appreciate it when Kripo detectives started to get their names in the newspapers and he did like things in his department to be well documented. Watertight paperwork was the best guarantee of our own investigative integrity: his words, not mine. You could hardly blame the boss for that; he was often suing the Nazis for libel, and he never went into court without a set of meticulous police records, which was why he always won, of course. He must have sued them successfully at least ten times, and they hated him for it. He ought to have had a bodyguard, but he scorned any police protection for himself on the grounds that the Nazis would only criticize him for that, too. Weiss did carry a gun, however; after the assassination of his friend the socialist journalist Kurt Eisner in 1919, every Jew in public life carried a pistol. In 1928, a pistol was the best kind of life insurance you could buy. Which was probably why I had two.

Weiss and Gennat came and found me not long after I'd sat down at my new desk to type out my report. The offices overlooked Dircksenstrasse and commanded a good view of the railway station and the western half of the city beyond. Berlin looked bigger at night: bigger and quieter and even more indifferent than it did by day, as if it were someone else's bad dream. Looking at all that neon light was like staring up at the universe and wondering why you felt so insignificant. Not that there was any great mystery about that; really there was just light and darkness and some life in between, and you made of it what you could.

"Here he is," said Gennat. "Berlin's very own Philo Vance."

My feet hurt but I stood up anyway. Weiss and Gennat were wearing their coats and it looked as if they were about to go home; it was almost eleven o'clock after all. They made an odd pair, like Laurel and Hardy: Weiss small and precise, Gennat large and shapeless. Weiss had the superior mind, but Gennat the better jokes. He glanced at the report on the carriage of my typewriter and rubbed his jowls noisily with the flat of his hand. It sounded like someone sweeping a path with a heavy brush. The Big Buddha badly needed another shave.

"You can forget that for now," Gennat said, pointing at the typewriter. "Do the report later."

That sounded good; in my mind's eye I was already turning up at the Haller-Revue and imagining what it might be like to undress a woman who was dressed like a man. It had been a long day.

"Good work, Gunther."

I told them what I'd told Reichenbach—that we'd caught the killer almost red-handed. "He was boozing away the spoils of the robbery in the very place where he'd met with his victim." I laughed. "He was supposed to be the dead man's bodyguard. But he'd got himself into debt. The dumbhead even had the dead man's gold ring and wallet in his pocket."

"That's the thing about bodyguards," said Weiss. "I've seen it happen again and again. They always end up despising the person they're supposed to be protecting. Easy enough, I suppose. You guard a man, you get to know his foibles and weaknesses. And before he knows it, he's trusted his life to someone with a gun who badly wants to put a hole in him."

"It's just as well most of our clients are stupid," said Gennat. "I don't know how we'd catch half of them if they all had their Abiturs."

"A murderer is still a murderer," said Weiss, polishing his glasses. "However you catch him. And catching him is what counts, not the mystery, nor the detection, nor the intellectual showdown between you and the killer. Just the arrest. Anything else is a sideshow. Remember that, Gunther."

Gennat was pouring us each a glass of schnapps from a half liter he kept in his coat pocket. He raised his glass and waited for Weiss and me to do the same. In his fat pink fingers the glass looked like a crystal thimble.

"What are we drinking to?" I asked, thinking that it might be my own early good fortune.

"We're not drinking to anything, lad," said Gennat. "We've got another body to go and look at."

"Now?"

"That's right. Now. Tonight. This minute. And by all accounts we're all going to need a bit of liquid backbone. Victim looks pretty tasty apparently."

"Another girl's been scalped," added Weiss, and rather to my surprise he necked his drink in one.

I swallowed the schnapps, grabbed my hat and coat, and followed them out the door.

IN THE MURDER wagon, outside the Praesidium's main entrance, Weiss asked if I had read all the Silesian Station files.

"Not yet, sir. I've read the files on Mathilde Luz and Helen Strauch. I was just about to read the third case—the attempted murder—when the call came through about the floater in the Spree."

"We're waiting on Hans, are we, Eva?" Gennat was looking at Frau Künstler, who was busy lighting a cigarette.

"He said he wouldn't be long. That he had to fetch some new plates for the camera."

"I expect the dead girl will wait," said Weiss. "They usually do. It's me who's in a hurry to get home, not her. Poor thing."

"Yes, sir."

"Ernst, bring Gunther up to speed with the most recent attack," said Weiss. "Do you mind listening to this kind of talk, Eva?"

"No. I don't mind. I type up the victim reports, don't I? What, do you think I just forget all that stuff? Sometimes I think this city has more dead bodies than a battlefield. I try and forget but not for long and not long enough. To really forget you need a hobby and I don't have time for one on account of the fact that I'm always in this damn car."

"Sorry, and I'm sorry to ask you to work late again," said Weiss.

"That's all right. Fortunately for you I need the extra money. Besides, I don't sleep so well since I started working for you people."

"I'm not surprised," said Gennat.

"Oh, it's nothing to do with the murders and the details of what happened to the victims. That I can deal with. Just about. It's the man downstairs in the building where I live. He's a singer in a choral group called the Comedian Harmonists. And when he's drunk, which seems to be at all hours of the day and night, he sings."

"I've heard of them," said Gennat. "They're famous."

"Yes, well, not for much longer," said Eva Künstler. "One night you're going to get a telephone call to attend an address in Potsdamer Chaussee, and you'll find a singer with his throat cut and me standing over him with a razor in my hand."

"That's a good address," said Gennat. "We've never had a murder there. It will make a nice change to go somewhere like that one day. And I'll certainly make a point of forgetting that we ever had this conversation. Now, I can't say fairer than that."

"Ernst remembers every detail of every murder

he's investigated," said Weiss. "Isn't that right, Ernst?"

"I don't know. Maybe. If you say so."

"That's one reason why he's such a good detective. The Big Buddha never forgets. So then. Fill Bernie in on girl number three. Fritz Pabst."

"Fritz? She's got a man's name?"

"Believe me," said Weiss, "the similarities are just beginning."

"Fritz Pabst, also known as Louise Pabst, was a transvestite prostitute," said Gennat, "and a good one, too, which is to say that even in broad daylight it was difficult to tell that she was really a man. The pictures of Fritz dressed as Louise are salutary for anyone who thinks he's an experienced man of the world. Right down to his Goschenhofer underwear."

"Wish I could afford nice stuff like that," murmured Frau Künstler.

"Pabst kept a photo album and was planning to become a singer at the Pan Lounge. By day he worked at Wertheim's department store, in haberdashery, and by night he frequented the Pan and the Eldorado lounge, not very far from where he was attacked and left for dead. That's right: left for dead. Because girl number three there survived the attack.

"Pabst insists he hadn't picked anyone up and that his attacker came out of a dark doorway and just hit him. As with the previous victims, a blow from a hammer broke his neck. We think that when the killer tried to scalp him, Fritz's wig came off in his hand and the killer ran for it. The victim stayed alive, however, and gave us a clue, which, so far, we've managed to keep out of the newspapers. He doesn't remember anything about the killer except for the fact that in the immediate seconds before he was attacked, he heard someone whistling a tune we've now identified as being from **The Sorcerer's Apprentice,** by a French composer called Paul Dukas. He wasn't sure about the name but he hummed it to me and I whistled it to a musician from the Philharmonie in Bernburger Strasse, who identified it. The only witness—the woman who found him—doesn't remember a man whistling but she does remember seeing a man washing his hands in a horse trough near Fritz's unconscious body. A man wearing a soft wide-brimmed hat with lots of longish fair hair on one side, Bohemian style. Like an actor, she said. Fritz Pabst is recovering in hospital but so far he has been unable to remember anything else. And frankly he isn't likely to; it's touch-and-go if he'll ever walk again, poor devil. And certainly not in high heels."

Hans Gross arrived and, opening the rear door of the murder wagon, proceeded to place a box of camera plates in the back alongside his tripods and arc lamps before climbing in with Frau Künstler. He squeezed the woman's knee and stole a puff of her cigarette; to my surprise she objected to neither.

"Sorry to keep you waiting. Sir, I'm going to need some more things from Anschütz. We're running a bit short."

"Investigating murder is an expensive business," said Weiss. "Especially in Berlin. I'll sort it out, Hans. Leave it to me."

The driver—a cop in uniform—started the big engine and we drove off, followed by a squad car.

"Where are we going?" asked Gross.

"Wormser Strasse," said Weiss.

"That's much farther west than the previous victims."

"Can I continue?" said Gennat.

"We're all ears," said Weiss.

"Now, at the time I couldn't figure out exactly why the killer should have felt the need to wash his hands in the trough if he hadn't scalped his victim. There was no blood to speak of. But walking around the area in daylight I discovered that there were wet-paint signs on the Patent Office on Alte Jakobstrasse, and it occurred to me that perhaps the killer wasn't washing blood off his hands, but green paint. So we unscrewed the doors, scrutinized them for fingerprints, and found a partial handprint, which of course may or may not belong to the killer. Sadly, it doesn't match anyone we have on record, and for the moment, we've drawn a blank on that one, too."

"Now, that was a clever bit of thinking," said Weiss. "I'm sure I wouldn't have thought of that. The Big Buddha is very like his ancient namesake, Gunther. Not only is he perfectly self-awakened, he is also endowed with the higher knowledge of many worlds. Learn the nine virtues of detective work from him. Learn them and make them your own."

"Fritz Pabst had no boyfriend," continued Gennat, ignoring the compliment, "no girlfriend, and nothing in the middle, if you know what I mean. So we can't go blaming it on any poor bastard who loved him. But. And this is interesting. We did find a British pound note next to Fritz's discarded wig. As if it might have fallen out of the killer's pocket."

"How much is that worth?" I asked.

"About twenty reichsmarks."

"Which is about twice the going rate for a street whore," I said. "So maybe the killer offered it to Fritz Pabst, or Louise. In lieu of German money. Not that it really mattered."

"How do you mean?" asked Gennat.

"If the murderer was going to kill Fritz Pabst anyway, what difference would it make how much it was, or if it was even legal tender? By the time Fritz was holding it up to the light to see what it was, it was probably too late."

"So you think Fritz could be lying about having picked someone up."

"Not necessarily. If someone has hit you with a hammer with intent to kill, you probably forget more than just the latest rate of exchange. You forget everything, I shouldn't wonder. I know I would. Either way it means the killer could be an Englishman. Or someone who wants it to look like an Englishman." I shrugged. "Or perhaps it was someone else completely unrelated to the case who dropped it."

"We found traces of green paint on the note," said Weiss. "The same paint that was used on the Patent Office wet-paint signs. We contacted the Bank of England for some information on the banknote, but all they can tell us is that it was one of a batch sent to a bank in Wales. Which doesn't get us much further forward."

"I don't know," I said. "It might let an awful lot of Germans breathe more easily at night if the killer should turn out to be British."

"Why do you say that?" asked Weiss.

"I suppose I worry that, as a people, we've become very cruel since the war. The fact is, we're still coming to terms with what happened. With our immediate history."

"You make it sound as if history is something

that could be over," said Weiss. "But I'm afraid the lesson of history is that it's never really over. Not today and certainly not tomorrow."

"That may be so, but it cannot be denied that people get an appetite for blood and human suffering. Like the ancient Romans. And I think any German who was proud of his country would prefer Winnetou to come from somewhere other than Germany."

"Good point," admitted Gennat.

"Perhaps our man is a sex tourist," I said. "Berlin is full of Englishmen and Americans getting the best rate of exchange in our nightclubs and with our women. They screwed us at Versailles and now they screw us here at home."

"You're beginning to sound like a Nazi," said Weiss.

"I never wear brown," I said. "Brown is definitely not my color."

"It wasn't the English and the Americans who screwed us at Versailles," said Weiss. "It wasn't even the French. It was the German high command. It's them who've sold us all that stab-in-the-back horseshit. If only to get themselves off the hook."

"Yes, sir."

"I'd like you to meet Dr. Hirschfeld sometime, Gunther," said Weiss. "He's convinced that the killer isn't a man who hates women, but a man who loves women so much he wants to be one."

"He's got a funny way of showing that love, sir," I said. "It seems to me that any man who really wants to be a woman only has to do what Fritz Pabst did—buy himself a nice dress and a good wig, call himself Louise, and head for the Eldorado. There are plenty of men in there who want to be women. Not to mention quite a few women who want to be men."

"That's not quite the same thing as actually becoming a real woman," said Weiss. "According to Hirschfeld."

"True," I said. "And I'll certainly be hanging on to that fact for dear life when I next talk to a strange girl. Real women are born that way. Even the ugly ones. Anything else is just hiding the family silver and moving the ornaments to the back of the shelf. But who knows? Maybe he's just dumb enough to cut off his own private parts. And when we arrest him we'll find there's just one thing missing."

"No one's that stupid," said Gennat. "You'd bleed to death."

"I thought you said most of our clients were stupid."

"Most. But what you're describing is plain crazy," said Gennat.

"Nobody's that crazy," said Hans Gross. "Not even in Berlin."

"Could be this fellow comes the closest," I said.

"If he slices off his manhood in pursuit of becoming a woman, he'll certainly save us the trouble of cutting off his head."

Weiss laughed. "You know, I'm beginning to think that glass of schnapps was too much for Gunther. This is the most I've heard him say since we gave him the seat. Some of it even makes sense."

I wound down the window and took a deep breath of the damp night air. It wasn't the schnapps I found intoxicating, it was the tobacco smoke; I could see that if I was ever going to make it as a homicide detective I was going to have to work on my smoking habit. Beside these people in the murder wagon, I was a rank amateur. And I was beginning to appreciate why both Ernst Gennat and Hans Gross had a voice like a farrier's rasp. Frau Künstler's voice was more like black coffee, like her manicure.

"Sorry, sir."

"No, I like my detectives to talk because, surprising as it might seem, I need food for thought, no matter how strange and exotic that food might be. You can say anything in this car. Anything, to me or the Big Buddha, just as long as it doesn't offend Frau Künstler."

"Don't worry about me," she said, taking the cover off her Torpedo. "I'm from Wedding and I can take care of myself."

"But if you do talk, do try and make it entertaining. We hate boring people. And drop the sir when you're in the wagon. I like things in here to be informal."

THE MURDER WAGON'S window was still down because I was feeling a little nauseous and the rain and cool air felt good on my face. Southeast of Alexanderplatz, we stopped at a traffic light on Friedrichstrasse, immediately outside the James-Klein Revue, which, at number 104A, was right next door to the Haller-Revue. Both establishments were brightly lit and looked full of life, full of people—full of people with plenty of money who were drunk or on drugs. It seemed unlikely that any of them were thinking about the Wolfmium factory explosion and the dead workers, now at a count of fifty. At the very least it was probably a better Friday night out than our expedition in the murder wagon. You could hear their screams of laughter as well as a cacophonous mixture of jazz blaring out from both clubs, which only added to the feeling of corruption and intemperance in the air. An SA brownshirt was positioned between the two clubs with a collection box, as if any of the clubs' patrons might be inclined to forget that the Nazis wanted to close down all of Berlin's showgirl nightclubs. The Jimmy Klein doorman, a very tall Russian named Sasha carrying an umbrella as big as the dome on the Reichstag, approached the car with an oily, gap-toothed smile and leaned down toward my open window.

"Gentlemen," he said, "please, why not join us inside? I can promise you won't be disappointed. We have completely nude dancers in here. Seventy-five naked models—more than any other club in Berlin—whose daring and audacity is nothing short of priceless. The James-Klein Revue is proud to present an evening without morals in twenty-four scenes of startling eroticism."

"Just an evening?" murmured Weiss. "Or a whole decade?"

It was about now that Sasha recognized me. We were old acquaintances from my time in Vice. Now and then he'd been a useful informer.

"Oh, sorry, Herr Gunther," he said. "I didn't realize it was you. You going into the undertaking business, then?" He was talking about the murder wagon and its occupants and it had to be admitted that we did resemble a group of mourners. "You want some free tickets? Paul Morgan's the **conferenciér** tonight. He's got the best dirty jokes in Berlin, if you ask me."

But I was hardly listening. My eyes were on the Haller-Revue next door, trying to make out the sound of a saxophone and wondering how much of the music I could hear was being played by Rosa Braun. Clearly I wasn't going to make it into the Haller that night to see her. If Weiss and Gennat hadn't been with me, I might have dashed inside and informed the box office that the ticket she'd left for me was no longer required, and that she wasn't to expect me. As it was, the traffic light changed and we drove off in search of our cadaver, a carful of ghouls with no discernible interest in the living or in scenes of eroticism, startling or otherwise. Nobody said anything now. There's something about the imminent prospect of viewing a violent death that stops most normal conversation.

The car slowed at Wittenbergplatz, then turned south onto Wormser Strasse where there was a large courtyard surrounded by well-maintained offices and apartments. Guided by a uniformed officer, we drove into the yard and followed a flashlight to a distant corner. At the top of a steep basement stairwell, we found the lead detective. He was from the Police Praesidium on Sophie-Charlotte-Platz, north of the Ku'damm. His name was Johann Körner, and he was Erich Ludendorff under a false name with slightly less wax on the dead badger he called a mustache—a real old-school Prussian cop with a **pickelhaube** up his ass. Which is to say he disliked modern, lawyerly cops with new ideas like Bernhard Weiss almost as much as he disliked clever Jews like Bernhard Weiss. They'd crossed swords before but you wouldn't have known it from the easy way Weiss spoke to him.

"Commissar Körner, good to see you. It's my understanding that you have a dead girl here who's been scalped."

"It's the work of Winnetou, all right. I've no doubt about that, sir. Hammer blow to the back of the neck and scalped. She's lying at the foot of this stairwell. Been dead since the early hours of this morning, I'd say."

"This is your case, of course, until you decide differently. But as you know we've already investigated two or three similar cases, which gives us a certain insight into the killer's modus operandi. So we can remain here in a largely advisory capacity; or we can work together with you; or we can take over the case—as you prefer. Really, it's entirely up to you."

Körner glanced at his wristwatch as if considering that it was past his own bedtime, brushed his mustache, and then lifted himself up on his toes.

"Why don't I just tell you what my men and I have been able to find out and then leave you to it, sir? I'm sure you and your people know much more about this sort of thing than I ever will."

I wasn't sure if "your people" meant everyone in the murder wagon or something more insidious, but if Weiss felt insulted, he certainly didn't show it. As always he was a master of polite restraint and professional courtesy. He could have been speaking to a lawyer in court instead of to an anti-Semitic **Pifke** like Johann Körner.

"That's very generous of you, Johann. Thank you. So tell us what you think you know."

"Eva Angerstein, age twenty-seven. Payday prostitute. Worked as a stenographer by day for Siemens-Halske in Siemensstadt. And lived in a room at the far end of the Ku'damm on Heilbronner Strasse, number twenty-four. We found her office clothes in a large cloth handbag we presume must be hers."

A payday prostitute was a girl who only went on the sledge toward the end of the month, before payday, when money was tight. Common enough in a city like Berlin, where there were always unexpected expenses.

"The building caretaker found her when he went down these stairs to check the boiler. Rancid fellow named Pietsch. He said there was a problem with half-silks bringing their clients down here from Wittenbergplatz. Up against the wall at the bottom of these stairs looks as good a place for a quick jump as any, I suppose. That's what we figure must have happened. They went down there together, he hammered her on the neck, and then scalped the poor bitch."

"Any witnesses?"

"None."

"Have you spoken to any of the working girls on Wittenbergplatz?"

"No. There was a receipt in her handbag from the Kakadu club, on Joachimstaler Strasse, from last night, so that's where we figure she may have met her killer. We haven't been there either."

One of Körner's men handed him a pocketbook, which he handed to Weiss, who handed it to Gennat, who wiped his hands and then handed it to me. I opened it, dropped my flashlight inside, and noted that it had been bought from Hulbe, a quality leather goods shop on the Ku'damm. I was about to search through the contents when I became aware that the bag was covered in coal dust; it was more or less empty, too, apart from her identification papers.

"The cloth bag containing her clothes we found in the stairwell next to her body; the handbag we found in the coal bunker up on ground level. One of my men discovered it more or less by chance, just a short while ago."

"I wonder why it was in there. Any ideas?"

"The bag was open, he said. Like someone had been through it, looking for something, and then tossed it."

"Apart from the girl's papers, the bag's empty," I said. "No money, no purse, no wallet, no valuables. Nothing."

"Not our man's normal behavior," said Weiss. "Not normal at all. Our previous victims were still in possession of some money."

"There's nothing normal about this bastard."

"True. I meant, he doesn't normally rob his victims."

I could tell that Weiss was thinking the same thing I was: that one of Körner's men had stolen the money from Eva Angerstein's handbag and divided it with his commissar. This wasn't exactly unknown among Berlin cops. Neither of us said a thing.

"Who knows what's in the mind of a twisted maniac like Winnetou?" said Körner. "It's always been my experience that a man like that exhibits all kinds of criminal behavior. Thieving, arson, rape, you name it. If you told me he was also planning to commit treason I wouldn't be surprised. It's not like murderers are scrupulous about breaking the law. In my humble opinion, sir."

"Bag's from Hulbe," I said to Weiss. "A good bag from a good shop. You wouldn't expect a girl who could afford a bag like this to take a client and bang him up against a wall in an apartment courtyard. You'd think she would have used a room. Somewhere she could wash." I continued searching the bag even as I spoke.

"You make it sound like she was something better than a whore," said Körner. "Look, it's just a handbag, right? I don't know that it tells you anything. Perhaps her Fritz was in a hurry. Didn't want all the fancy silk trimmings and lingerie that some of these girls offer. Just a quick bit of mouse and then a bit of cash for a taxi home."

"I expect you're right, Johann," said Weiss.

"This is interesting," I said. "There's a secret pocket in this bag. The zip is at the bottom of the pocket instead of the top and underneath a fold of leather so it would be easy enough to miss, I suppose. Certainly anyone in a hurry might not realize it was there. There's something in it, too." My hand came out of the handbag holding a couple of gold rings and a new ten-mark banknote.

"Let me see that," said Körner irritably.

I handed over the rings but not the note.

"I think you'd better not touch Herr Thaer," I said. "This one looks brand-new. Like it was issued yesterday. We might even be able to trace this, sir."

"Good work, Gunther."

Ten-reichsmark notes were green and featured an agriculturalist called Albrecht Thaer, whose only real fame was that he was on the money. I'd never heard of him. The heroes of the Weimar Republic always seemed underwhelming, which is perhaps the hallmark of true democracy; under the Kaiser, German money had looked altogether more patriotic and inspiring.

I slipped the banknote into a paper bag and

carried it back to the murder wagon before returning to the top of the stairwell. I left Weiss speaking to Körner and then descended the stairs to where Ernst Gennat was now giving the corpse the benefit of his many years' experience in homicide. His flashlight was all over the ground around the body like an anteater's nose. Her head was covered with blood and she looked like she'd fallen downstairs and cracked her skull. Her clothes were good quality and her stockings were made of silk; her discarded gray cloche hat was from Manheimer on Oberwallstrasse and resembled a steel helmet that hadn't worked.

"Rigor's set in," said Gennat. "I figure she's been dead about twenty-two or twenty-three hours. Like killing a seal pup."

"How's that?"

"She comes down here in front of him, he batters her with his hammer, one powerful blow, breaks her neck, and before she's even hit the ground he's got his blade out and is preparing to take her pelt. Start to finish maybe as little as sixty seconds."

"Christ, that's fast."

"That's because he takes no pleasure in it. This much is obvious. If he did there would be more evidence of him going into a frenzy. Sometimes when a killer actually gets up the courage to kill, it opens the floodgates and he inflicts multiple stab wounds. But this girl's skirt hasn't even been lifted and as far as I can see there's not a mark on her body. So this is not about sex, Gunther. It's not even about killing. It's all about that trophy. The hair. Her scalp." Gennat paused. "Find something in her handbag, did you?"

I told him about the banknote.

"A ten's what he'd have given her to go with him somewhere," he said. "Down here. Just enough to silence any misgivings she might have. And more than enough to blow him."

"That's what I figured. Only maybe he worried about that banknote. And came back to see if he could retrieve it. Which is why he ransacked her handbag." I lowered my voice. "And here was me thinking that it was one of Körner's men who did that."

"It doesn't mean that Körner's boys didn't pinch some stuff from her bag. The police from Sophie-Charlotte-Platz have always had a reputation for unofficial taxation, if you know what I mean. You notice they were careful to leave her ID so as not to have the trouble of the legwork needed to put a name to her face. Look, it's a nice theory you have there, Gunther. About the banknote. Now see if you can prove it. Perhaps you can find something else out there that could have come from her handbag. A lipstick or a powder compact. A purse or a set of keys. Then, when you've done that, go to the Kakadu and see if anyone remembers her. Not forgetting some of the other girls on Wittenbergplatz. Maybe they'll have seen her with someone. Hopefully someone with the word **murderer** chalked on his back."

"Right you are, sir." I started back up the steps, with the beam from my flashlight straight ahead of me. Something white reflected light back at me; I leaned over to take a closer look. It was an ivory cigar holder.

"I doubt that could have come from her handbag, don't you?"

Gennat leaned toward the cigar holder and picked it up on the end of his Pelikan. He cursed loudly.

"You know what this means, don't you?" he said.

"That the killer smokes cigars?"

"It means we have found an important clue at three of the murder scenes. A cuff link. A pound note. And now this."

"You believe the killer is playing games with us?"

"I'm beginning to think so. Christ only knows how much police time Reichenbach was obliged to waste on the idea that the killer might be a Freemason."

"Of course, they might all be genuine, those clues. He really could smoke cigars, wear Freemason cuff links, and have a pocket full of foreign currency."

"Sure, why not? If it helps you to believe that a little mouse will pay you a nice shiny penny if you leave a tooth on your bedside table, then go right ahead. But I think Winnetou's playing us for fools. It's always been my experience that clues are like wine; they need a bit of time to grow in stature. Clues only look like clues in stories. But I'm smelling a rat because my nostrils are more sensitive to rats than yours. The question is why? Why tease us like this? It looks very premeditated."

"He wants to waste our time. Doubles back like a fox to throw us off the scent. Surely that's got to be a good thing for him."

"Looks that way. To my mind that banknote looks like the real clue here. Now go and back it up."

I STALKED AROUND the courtyard with my flashlight, staring at the ground like a heron. From time to time I glanced up at the surrounding windows, some of which were occupied by interested onlookers. Nothing like a murder to bring Berliners out of their pigeonholes. A few of them shouted to me but I couldn't hear what was said and even if I had, I wouldn't have answered.

Close to the stairwell was a solitary tree that had seen better days. At the base of the tree was a hole; I pushed my arm in up to the elbow and quickly found a leather wallet that matched the dead girl's Hulbe handbag. There was no money in it but there was a bus ticket and a photograph of Eva Angerstein. She was pictured standing on Potsdamer Platz in front of the famous traffic-light clock. Behind her you could see the equally famous Haus Vaterland on Köthener Strasse, which would have been exactly the kind of place a half-silk like Eva would have plied her trade. She was wearing a little navy cloche and a loose blue dress, which she had raised with one hand just enough to show off her red garter: a provocative pose for laughs, it looked like. It was the first time I'd got a proper look at her face. She was pretty, with a Cupid's-bow mouth, dark hair, and a nice smile. Someone's daughter, I thought; someone's sister, perhaps; and now someone's victim.

I had another feel around inside the tree and came up with a lipstick. I put the lipstick in a paper bag and the photograph in my pocket. Then I brought the evidence back to the murder wagon, told Bernhard Weiss where I was going, and said I might get back before they left, and if not, I'd catch them in the morning. Then I set off for the Kakadu, a five-minute walk away, in the hope that someone there would remember her.

But nobody did.

Over every dining table was a caged cockatoo

that was supposed to squawk for the bill when you tapped the glass with a knife, and probably I'd have been better off asking the birds for information for all the help I got. But on my way out I got lucky when I asked the hatcheck girl if she recognized the girl in the photograph. She said she did, and even mentioned another girl she'd been with for part of the previous evening. Her name was Daisy and she was an American and the hatcheck girl thought I'd probably find her in the small lounge, which I'd forgotten existed.

The lounge was full of cozy corners with lots of little fireplaces and sofas and chaises longues and couples getting to know each other, some of them quite intimately; fortunately for me, Daisy wasn't one of these. She was easily distinguishable from the other women in the Kakadu: American women always looked better-dressed than German women. She was sitting on her own, drinking champagne, and, seeing me out of the corner of her eye, she glanced at her watch impatiently as I approached. She was slender, small-breasted, and good-looking, probably in her twenties, and quite sure of herself, the way girls are when they have plenty of money. The wristwatch told me that much; it was all jade and diamonds and she probably couldn't have cared less what time it was.

"Daisy?"

"I'm waiting for someone, Fritz," she said. "And he'll be here any minute, so don't bother sitting down."

"It's no bother. At least not for me. And my name's not Fritz." I sat down and showed her my new beer token. "It's police. Maybe police trouble for you, maybe not. That's what we need to find out."

"What do you want?"

"Some information. First of all, your full name."

"Torrens. Daisy Torrens. What's this about?"

"You seem nervous, Daisy."

"Like I said, I'm waiting for someone."

"Then I'll make it quick." I took Eva's photograph out of my pocket. "Ever seen this girl before?"

"No." Daisy might have been looking at someone's tram ticket for all the attention she paid to the picture.

"I think you should look at it again. Because I've a witness who says you were speaking to her last night. And it wouldn't do for an American girl to mislead a German policeman. It will look bad for international relations when I'm forced to arrest you on suspicion of withholding evidence."

"All right, I spoke to her. So what?"

"What about?"

"Look, I really don't remember. We just spoke

for a few minutes. About nothing at all really. Girl talk. Men. This place. How the cockatoos shit on the tables in the other room. I don't know."

"We could always do this at Alexanderplatz if you prefer. But I can't promise that someone won't shit on the tables there, I'm afraid."

"What's the big deal? I speak to all kinds of people in here. Everyone does. There's no law against it."

"The big deal is that Eva Angerstein was murdered after she left here last night. And there is a law against that. For all I know you were the last person to see her alive."

"Oh, I see. That's terrible. I'm sorry." She didn't sound in the least bit sorry. She thought for a moment, bit her pouty lip, and then looked squarely at me. "Look, if I tell you what I know, which really isn't much, will you go away and leave me alone? My gentleman friend won't like it if he sees me talking to the police."

"Sure. Why not. But I'll need to see an identity card. Just to know you're on the level."

She grabbed her purse and handed me her identity card. Hers was a good address, and easily remembered: villa G, street 6, number 9, in the fashionable suburb of Eichkamp. The kind of address where diamond-and-jade wristwatches were easily afforded. I handed the card back.

"So. Talk to me."

"Eva used to buy me cocaine," said Daisy Torrens. "There's a dealer on Wittenbergplatz. Outside the station. Sells sausages as well as dope. But he doubles his price when he sees me coming. Because I'm an American, he figures I'm good for it. And I don't much like the smell of sausages. That's one of the reasons I come here; the vegetarian restaurant. It's the best in Berlin."

"You're supposed to have a prescription to buy cocaine," I said. "And only from a pharmacist."

"Yes, I know, but at this time of night where are you going to get one of those?"

"So Eva was your go-between. You'd done this before?"

"Sure. Lots of times. We met in here a while ago. I wouldn't say we were friends. But I'd give her ten percent for the trouble. She used to do that for lots of people. They don't like anyone selling drugs in here. Anyway, Eva was always reliable. Until last night. I gave her fifty marks to get me some coke and she never came back." Daisy glanced at her watch again. It was worth a second look. "I guess now I know why."

"Did you know Eva was a prostitute?"

"She never said as much, but I had a pretty shrewd idea she was at it. A lot of girls in here are."

"But not you."

"No." Her tone stiffened and her chin raised

a little as if she was thinking of telling me to go to hell, and she might have done if I hadn't been a policeman. "I'm an actress, as a matter of fact. And now if you don't mind, I'd like you to leave me alone."

"One more question and then I will. Did you see her talk to any men last night? Any men at all."

"Honestly? No. The lighting in here is a little subdued as you can see and I wasn't wearing my glasses, so even if I had seen her talking to someone I wouldn't have recognized them."

"You're shortsighted?"

"Yes."

"May I see those glasses?"

"Sure." She opened her handbag and took out a spectacle case, which she handed me. I took out a pair of glasses and held them up, inspecting the lenses. "Satisfied?" she asked.

I handed them back. "Thank you." I stood and walked away without another word but at the edge of the small lounge I hung back behind a pillar in the hope I might see the gentleman friend on whom she was waiting. Daisy didn't see me. I was sure about that; she wasn't wearing her glasses. But I did see the man she'd been waiting for, whom she now kissed very fondly. Dressed in a dinner jacket, he was probably twice her age and certainly twice her size: dark, fleshy, balding, with eyebrows like hedgerows and a nose the size of a car horn. In short, he was every German bigot's idea of what a rich Jew was supposed to look like and, what's more, I recognized him and only to see him was to feel as if I had stepped onto the roller coaster at Luna Park. His name was Albert Grzesinski, once Berlin's chief of police and now the new Weimar government's minister of the interior.

I WAS DOG-TIRED by the time I reached Wittenbergplatz. My feet hurt even more than before and my brain felt like a half lemon in a bartender's fist. There's something about all that neon light at night that seems to bleach out a man's spirit. I was much too tired to be as polite as I'd been in the Kakadu and I was already regretting I hadn't been a little harder on Daisy Torrens. The indifference she'd demonstrated at the news of Eva Angerstein's murder had shocked me a little; in those days I was still capable of being shocked at human behavior, in spite of having worked in Vice for two years.

Wittenbergplatz was known for two things: the Hermann Tietz department store, formerly known as Jandorf's, where I did most of my own clothes shopping, and the art nouveau U-Bahn station; with its neoclassical facade and grand entrance hall, it looked more like a church than a railway station. That was Berlin for you. Make something look better, nicer, a little more grand than what it was. The same way that the UFA Cinema on Nollendorfplatz looked more like the ancient Temple of Dagon before Samson turned up and rearranged the architecture.

Inside the entrance hall of the Wittenbergplatz station was the usual gauntlet of whores through which men coming up from the trains were obliged to pass, and indeed there was a man balancing a boiler tray of sausages on his chest, and a couple of beggars—injured war veterans trying to make a few pennies. It was a fairly typical metropolitan scene right down to the fat lawyer type coming into the entryway who looked at the whores and the beggars and then harrumphed loudly.

"Disgraceful," he said to the two beggars. Why he should have singled them out for criticism I don't know. "You should be ashamed of yourselves. The way you degrade that uniform. And those medals."

Which was my cue to walk over and drop a handful of coins into each man's cap and that was more than enough to send the fat man scuttling down to catch his train to somewhere as respectable as his opinions.

I bought twenty Salem Aleikum, presented myself in front of the sausage seller, and asked for a bag of salt, which, without the sausage, only meant one thing; when I was certain it was in his hand, I showed him my beer token. Selling cocaine without a prescription didn't count as much of a crime but it was probably enough for me to have taken him in, and might even have been enough for him to have lost his street vendor's license.

"You can put the bag of salt away," I said. "I'm not interested in that. I'm more interested in talking about one of your regular customers. Half-silk. Name of Eva Angerstein."

"They've got names? You surprise me."

"This one has a photograph."

I handed him the picture and he took it between a greasy thumb and forefinger, found some glasses in the breast pocket of his jacket, looked at the photo, ate a bit of a sausage he obviously wasn't going to sell that night, and then nodded.

"Nice-looking girl."

"Isn't she just."

"All right, I know her," he admitted. "Buys from me two or three nights a week. Too much to use herself. Takes it to one of the clubs, I reckon, and probably sells it in the ladies' toilets. I take that into account when I give her the price."

"When did you last see her?"

"Last night. About this time. Why? What's she done?"

"She's been murdered."

"Pity. Lot of that about these days. As a matter

of fact it's got so bad that some of these girls are afraid to work. You wouldn't think it, but there's only half as many girls on the streets these days. Afraid of getting scalped by Winnetou. Well, who wouldn't be? Was she scalped?"

"I couldn't say."

"You just did. So Eva bought some salt and then went to talk to those girls over there. At least I think it was them. Hard to tell them apart from this distance. Then after a few minutes this fellow comes into the station and eventually she leaves with him. Out the front door."

"Could you describe him?"

"Now you're asking. These girls talk to more men than I sell sausages. It'd be like you asking me to describe a würst I just sold."

"Try."

"Well dressed. Gentleman, looked like. Wore his hat on the side of his head. Sort of rakishly. Big raincoat. I was only half paying attention." He shrugged. "That's about it. You'd best ask the grasshoppers. They don't miss anything. In less than ten seconds they can size you up and tell how much you've got in your pockets and if you're in the mood for some mouse or not."

HE WAS RIGHT.

I turned toward the girls, but they'd already taken a good look at me talking to the sausage seller, concluded I was police, and scattered to the four winds. I walked back to my informant.

"See what I mean?" He laughed. "They had you fingered as a bull the minute you handed me that photograph, son. Hard enough to make a living without you scaring away the fish."

I nodded and turned away wearily. My bed in Nollendorfplatz felt very close by and I badly wanted to be there. On my own.

"One more thing," said the sausage seller. "I don't think it was him who killed her. The Fritz with the hat, I mean."

"Why do you say so?"

"Because it's my opinion he didn't look or sound like he was going to kill anyone."

"How do you mean?"

"Well, he was whistling, wasn't he? Fellow who's going to scalp a girl and kill her doesn't whistle before he does it. Does he? No. I wouldn't say so. A man whistling is a carefree sort of sound, I'd say. Hardly the type to go on the warpath."

"You're probably right. But just as a matter of interest, do you remember the tune he was whistling?"

"No. Not a chance, I'm afraid. I'm tone deaf. Here. Have a sausage. On the house. I'm not going to sell these and I'm knocking off soon. They'll only go to waste."

—

BACK OUTSIDE THE courtyard in Wormser Strasse, eating my sausage in the darkness, I barked my shins on some short wooden crutches and a vagrant's trolley, the type a legless or partially paralyzed man might have used in lieu of a proper wheelchair to get around the city. It reminded me of some medieval painting of amusing German beggars wearing cardboard crowns and foxtails on their backs. We always had a cruel sense of humor in Germany. The trolley was homemade and crude, but many men had little choice but to use one. Modern orthopedic wheelchairs of the kind produced by Germany's agency for the disabled were expensive and, immediately after the war, there had been many instances of men being robbed of them. Maybe that's why it struck me as strange that one of these "cripple-carts," as they were commonly known, should have been abandoned in this way. Where was the man who'd been using it? And it says a lot about my own attitude to Germany's disabled that I should have forgotten about this cart almost as soon as I'd encountered it earlier in the evening. Ten years after the armistice, Berlin's disabled veterans were still so ubiquitous that nobody—myself included—gave them a second thought; they were like stray cats or dogs—always around. The few coins I had dispensed at the station on Wittenbergplatz had been the first I'd parted with in more than a year.

I hurried inside the courtyard in search of further head-swelling praise for what I had recently discovered.

Commissar Körner had gone home, leaving behind just a few uniformed cops from Sophie-Charlotte-Platz to help police the crime scene. People were still leaning out their high windows to see what was happening; it was that or listen to the radio, or maybe go to bed. I knew which one I was keenest on. My bed couldn't have felt more enticing if it had contained a bottle of good rum and a clean pair of pajamas. Hans Gross had finished taking his photographs. Frau Künstler had pulled the cover on top of the typewriter and was lighting another cigarette. Weiss was checking his pocket watch; his own car and police driver had arrived to take him home and he looked as if he was getting ready to leave; at least he was until I took him and Gennat aside to tell them what I'd discovered on Wittenbergplatz and, more intriguingly, in the Kakadu.

"Before she was murdered, the victim met up with a woman she sometimes bought drugs for," I explained. "An American girl, name of Daisy Torrens."

Weiss frowned. "Now, why does that name ring a distant bell?"

"Perhaps because she was awaiting the arrival of a man you yourself know, sir. That man's name is Albert Grzesinski."

"The new minister?" said Gennat.

"Unless he has a twin brother."

"Are you sure?" asked Weiss. But he didn't sound as if it was me he doubted so much as his own ears.

"Positive."

"He was really with that woman in public?"

"Not just with her, but all over her."

"Jesus."

"Who is Daisy Torrens?" asked Gennat. "I've never heard of her."

"An actress," said Weiss. "She had the leading role in a recent UFA movie called **We'll Meet Again in the Homeland.** I thought you were interested in cinema."

"That was a dreadful film," said Gennat.

"I don't doubt it. Anyway, Grzesinski's been having an affair with Miss Torrens but, until recently, he was much too discreet ever to be seen with her in public. He's married, after all. But they share a house in Eichkamp."

"She gave me the address," I said.

"So far, the press have been ignoring the affair, but if the Nazis were to find out about it they could easily finish off his career in the pages of **Der Angriff.** There's nothing they like more than a Jew with his hand in an American girl's pants. Especially one who's involved with drugs." Weiss removed his pince-nez, polished the lenses gently, squeezed them back onto the bridge of his nose, and then shot me a look. "You're sure about that part."

"She told me herself," I said.

"What kind of woman would you say she was?"

"A rich bitch. Glamorous and heartless."

"That's what I heard," said Weiss. For a moment he seemed overcome with a mild fit of coughing, which he stifled with the back of his hand.

"If this gets out," said Gennat, "the new government will be over before it's even started. The last thing we need now unless you're a goddamn Nazi is another election. There's only so much democracy that one country can take before it starts to get tired of the idea."

"Then we'd best keep this to ourselves," said Weiss.

"Agreed," said Gennat.

I nodded my assent as if that were important; the idea that I might have some influence over the fate of the government seemed absurd to me.

"I'll speak to Grzesinski and suggest that he and his American friend might like to behave a little more discreetly in future," added Weiss. "For his sake and the country's. Anyway, this is all beside the point. You obtained another description of the murderer, Gunther. Which fits the one we already had from the woman who found Fritz

Pabst. Good work, my boy. First thing in the morning I want you to visit the Reichsbank on Jägerstrasse and get them to start checking up on that ten-mark banknote you found. If you have any problems with this, telephone me at home and I'll speak to Heinrich Köhler himself. He owes me a favor."

Köhler was the German finance minister.

"But right now, you should go home. You, too, Ernst. We've done all we can tonight, short of staging a candlelit vigil for the dead girl." He glanced up as someone in one of the higher windows whistled down to us. "If we stay out here any longer they'll be wanting a few bars of 'Berliner Luft.' "

"ACCORDING TO THE serial number, the banknote I found in Eva Angerstein's handbag was issued just a week ago," I said. "I've traced it to a branch of Commerzbank, in Moabit. The manager believes it was part of a batch of notes from the German central bank that was divided up and paid out to one or two local businesses in time to be distributed in workers' wage packets last Friday. By far the largest of these payments was made to the Charité hospital, which means the killer could be a medical man. And that would certainly be consistent with the killer's fondness for—and skill with—a sharp knife. It's my belief that we should probably speak to the hospital director and arrange to have all male employees of the Charité interviewed by police officers from the Alex as soon as possible. We have a description of the man, we even have a possible handprint, and we can certainly check alibis. This note might be just enough to narrow down our inquiry quite significantly."

Weiss listened carefully and then nodded. It was Monday afternoon and we were in his office at the Alex. I sensed I only had half his attention, which was perhaps hardly surprising. It had been a difficult weekend for the Berlin police and for him in particular—the large bruise on his face told me that much. At the communist march in West Berlin, the police had charged after the Reds had broken through their lines, shots had been fired, and a communist workman had been killed. And if all that wasn't enough, Weiss had been assaulted on Frankfurter Allee by Otto Dillenburger while he himself was watching a different communist demonstration. An openly right-wing police colonel in command of the eastern police region, Dillenburger had previously alleged that Weiss was secretly colluding with the communists, and he was now suspended from duty pending an inquiry by the Praesidium. But already he'd lodged an appeal with the PPPO—the Prussian Police Officers'

Association—and it was widely held that the colonel would be quickly reinstated. The PPPO was almost as right wing as Dillenburger himself.

You didn't have to be a detective to work out why Weiss was suspected of being a communist; not in Germany. Everyone who was sympathetic to the Nazis believed that a Jew was just a communist with a big nose and a gold watch. I felt desperately sorry for this man whom I and many others much admired, but I didn't mention the incident with Dillenburger; Weiss wasn't the type to dwell on his own misfortunes or to seek sympathy.

"Approximately how many people would you say work at the Charité hospital, Bernie?"

"I don't know. Perhaps a thousand."

"And how many men do you think work here, at the Alex?"

"About half that number."

Weiss smiled. "True. I fear there are many reforms still needed to make this the force it might yet become. A great many policemen are just hanging on for a severance payment or a police maintenance claim with which to start up a business. Between you and me, I've heard of some patrolmen leaving the force with several thousand marks in their pockets."

I whistled quietly. "So that's why the uniformed boys wear those riding breeches. You need big pockets with that kind of money on offer."

"Ironic, isn't it?" said Weiss. "For all its antipathy to socialism and to trade unionism and workers' rights, I know of no organization in the whole of Germany with more powerful unions than the Berlin police."

He relit his cigar and stared up at the three-arm brass gasolier, as if things were clearer near the ceiling.

"Bernie, what you recommend is certainly what should be done, without question; and I've no doubt that in the future, all investigations will be conducted on the basis of cross-referenced witness statements. But I'm afraid that what you're suggesting is quite impossible. For one thing, we don't have the time, but even if we did, I'm not sure I should follow your recommendation. You see, there's the politics of it to consider. Yes, the politics, although I hate mentioning a word like that in this building. Let me explain. I'm not one of those who believe that Berlin society is improved by the presence of fewer girls on the street, but there are many—Commissar Körner, for example—who believe exactly that. And the plain fact of the matter is that if we're going to catch this psychopath it will have to be with the immediate resources of the Murder Commission and a few like-minded Kripo officers, rather than the whole police department. So as far as the Charité is concerned, feel free to speak to the hospital director; maybe he can identify a few doctors who present themselves as morally insane. I've certainly met a few of those in my time. But I fear that if you do conduct any more interviews, it will have to be a mostly solo effort. I'm sorry, Bernie, but that's just how it is and how it has to be. Understand?"

"I understand."

"Was there anything else?"

"Yes. There's a writer who'd like a little help with a script she's writing about a police detective investigating a series of murders. Background research, I suppose. I'd like your permission to bring her into the Commission's offices on one of my days off this week. Her name is Thea von Harbou."

"Married to Fritz Lang, the film director. Yes, I've heard of her. Permission granted. With one proviso."

"And that is?"

"Thea von Harbou comes from a family of minor Bavarian nobility. The same cannot be said of Fritz Lang. Lang is a Jew who identifies as a Roman Catholic but that means nothing to the likes of Hitler and his local ape, Josef Goebbels. Once a Jew always a Jew. So bring her here to the Alex by all means, and give her all the assistance you think appropriate, but please make sure you deal with her and with her husband discreetly, as if your name was Albert Grzesinski and hers was Daisy Torrens."

IT WAS LIKE visiting Berlin Zoo but without the entry charge, which probably was why there was a longer line to be admitted to the place. Berlin's showhouse for the dead—otherwise known as the police morgue—was just that: a popular spectacle and perhaps the last place in Europe where the murdered corpses of your fellow citizens could be viewed in all their anonymous rumination, no matter how horrific that might be. People queued along Hannoversche Strasse as far as Oranienburger Tor to get in to see the "exhibits." Grouped in glass cases around the central hall, they most resembled the inhabitants of the zoo's famous aquarium. Certainly many of these corpses looked as torpid as any ancient moray eel or crusty blue lobster. Children under sixteen were forbidden entry but it certainly didn't stop them from trying to sneak past attendants who were employed not by the police, nor by the Charité hospital across the street, but by the city's animal hospital next door. As a schoolboy, I myself had tried to get into the Hanno showhouse; and once, to my everlasting disgust, I had succeeded.

There was, of course, a sound forensic reason for this exhibition; it was argued that information about a deceased person was often very hard to obtain from a metropolitan citizenry that was enormously diverse except for a shared dislike of Prussians and the Berlin police, and the display of corpses, while no doubt titillating, sometimes produced valuable information. None of this counted for much with me. You just had to eavesdrop on what was said to know that the people who went to see the stiffs and be horrified were the same ones who would have bought a sausage and gone to watch a man broken on the wheel. Sometimes there is nothing quite so dreadful as your fellow man, dead or alive.

None of the bodies already exhibited in the central hall were familiar to me, but I wasn't in search of a name or evidence so much as to confirm something I'd heard Arthur Nebe talking about in his speech to the Prussian Police Officers' Association: that the Hanno showhouse was very popular with Berlin's artists in search of something to draw. I assumed, wrongly as it transpired, that these artists were merely following in the tradition of Leonardo da Vinci and perhaps Goya, looking for human subjects that wouldn't or couldn't move while you were drawing them.

As it happened I only saw one artist at the Hanno showhouse that Tuesday afternoon. To my surprise, he wasn't drawing anatomical studies but actual wounds—throats that were cut or torsos that had been comprehensively disemboweled—and he seemed not at all interested in drawing dead men, only dead women, preferably in a state of undress. He was about forty, thickset with dark hair and, for some obscure reason, dressed as an American cowboy. A pipe was in his mouth and he was almost oblivious of everyone around him—everyone who was alive, that is. Several times I looked over his shoulder at his sketchbook just to check my own appraisal of his work before I eventually introduced myself with the Kripo warrant disc. I'm no art critic but the word I'd have used to sum up his style was **depraved.** I suppose if he'd been dressed like an Apache Indian I might even have arrested him.

"Can we talk?"

"S'up? Am I in trouble?" he asked, and almost immediately I knew he was a Berliner. "Because I'm quite sure there's no law against what I'm doing. Nor any rule in here that I'm breaking. I already asked the people in charge of this place and they said I was free to draw anything I liked but not to take photographs."

Despite his eccentric appearance—he was even wearing spurs—the Fritz was a Berliner, all right: asserting your rights in the face of Prussian officialdom was as typical as the accent.

"Well, then, you know more than I do, Herr—"

"Grosz. George Ehrenfried Grosz."

"No, you're not in any trouble, sir. At least none that I know of. I'd just like to talk to you, if I may."

"All right. But what shall we talk about?"

"This, of course. What you're drawing. Your preferred subject. Murder. In particular, murdered women. Look, there's a bar nearby, on Luisenstrasse—Lauer's."

"I know the place."

"Let me buy you a drink."

"Is this official? Perhaps I should invite my lawyer."

"What's the matter? Don't you like our fine capital's police?"

He laughed. "Clearly, you haven't heard of me, Sergeant Gunther. The law and my work don't seem to get on very well right now. And not for the first time, either. Currently I'm being prosecuted for blasphemy."

"Not my department, I'm afraid. The only picture on my wall at home is a mezzotint of Hegel and you would think it had been originally drawn by his bitterest enemy. If he had his throat cut and his arse hanging out of his trousers he couldn't look any worse."

"History teaches us that no one ever learned anything from Hegel. Least of all about art or even history. But yours is a compelling image. I shall borrow it."

In Lauer's I bought us each a beer—two foaming glasses of Schultheiss-Patzenhofer, which was the best beer in the city—and we sat down at a quiet table. Not that it mattered much to George Grosz; he didn't seem to mind that people looked at him as if he were a lunatic; maybe that was supposed to be artistic in itself, like walking your pet lobster through the streets on a blue silk ribbon. While we talked and sipped our beers he was also drawing me with pen and ink, and doing it with great skill and speed.

"So what's with the Tom Mix outfit?"

"Did you ask me here to talk about my clothes or about my art?"

"Maybe both."

"You know, I might be tempted to dress up as a police officer if I could buy myself a uniform."

"You wouldn't like the boots. Or the hat. Or for that matter the pay. And it probably **is** a crime to dress up as police in this town. On the whole, cops in Berlin don't have much of a sense of humor about such things. Or about anything else, now I come to think about it."

"You would think they would, considering those boots and that leather hat. There is one thing that cannot be denied, however: the truncheon always seems to hit at the left. Never at the right."

I smiled weakly. "Haven't heard that one before."

"Witness Saturday's demonstration in which a communist worker was shot."

"Are you a communist?"

"Would it surprise you to learn that I'm not?"

"Frankly, yes."

"I once met Lenin, that's why I'm not a communist. He was a most unimpressive figure."

"So might I ask, why would a man who's met Lenin dress up as a cowboy?"

"You might call it a romantic enthusiasm. I guess I've always loved America more than I love Russia. When I was a boy I read a lot of James Fenimore Cooper and Karl May."

"Me too."

"I'd have been surprised if you told me any different."

"It's said that as well as his fascination for the Old West, Karl May had a peculiar enthusiasm for using pseudonyms."

"True."

"So is George Grosz your real name? Or is it something else?"

Grosz fished in his jacket, took out his card, and handed it to me silently. I glanced over the details, held the card up to the light—this wasn't just for show, there were plenty of forgeries around—and handed it back.

"But as it happens you're right," he said. "I also enjoy using pseudonyms. Anything like that seems not only possible when you're an artist, but excusable, too. Even necessary. The reason a man becomes an artist these days is to make his own rules."

"And here was me thinking a man only becomes an artist because he wants to paint and draw."

"Then I guess that's why you became a policeman."

"What's your favorite book by May?"

"It's a toss-up between **Old Surehand** and **Winnetou the Red Gentleman.**"

"I assume you must have heard about the killer the Berlin newspapers have dubbed Winnetou."

"The one who scalps his victims? Yes. Ah, now I begin to understand your interest in me, sergeant. You think that because I sometimes draw murdered women I might actually have killed someone in real life. Like Caravaggio. Or Richard Dadd."

"It certainly crossed my mind."

"Tell me, did you see any active service?"

"Four fun years in one place after another. But always the same nasty trench. You?"

"Jesus, four years? I did six months and it damn near killed me. They had me training recruits and guarding prisoners of war, on account of how I was partly an invalid."

"You look all right now."

"Yes, I know. I'm ashamed to tell you they

kicked me out twice. First because of sinusitis, and the second time because I had a breakdown. They were going to execute me as a deserter, but then the war ended. But before it did I saw more than enough for it to affect my work. Perhaps now and forever more. So my themes as an artist are despair, disillusionment, hate, fear, corruption, hypocrisy, and death. I draw drunkards, men puking their guts out, prostitutes, military men with blood on their hands, women pissing in your beer, suicides, men who are horribly crippled, and women who've been murdered by men playing skat. But chiefly my subject is this: hell's metropolis, Berlin itself. With all its wild excess and decadence, the city seems to me to constitute the very essence of true humanity."

"Can't argue with that."

"But I expect you think I should paint nice landscapes and pictures of pretty smiling girls and kittens. Well, I simply can't. Not anymore. After the trenches there are no pretty girls, no nice landscapes, and not many kittens. Every time I see a landscape I try to imagine what it would look like if there was an enormous shell hole in the middle of it, a trench in the foreground, and a skeleton hanging on the barbed wire. Every time I see a pretty smiling girl I try to imagine what she'd look like if she'd been cut in half by a Vickers machine gun. If I was ever to paint a kitten I'd probably paint two men without noses tearing it apart over the dinner table."

"Is there much of a market for that kind of thing?"

"I don't do it for the money. We paint that way because we have to paint that way. Yes, that's right, I'm not the only one. There are plenty of artists who think and paint the same way as I do. Max Beckmann. Otto Dix—yes, you should really see what Dix draws and paints if you think there's something wrong with me. Some of his work is much more visceral than anything I might paint. But for the record I don't think either of them is a murderer. In fact, I'm sure of it."

For a moment he made me feel glad that I was just a stupid policeman—clearly it was what he thought. Still, I was determined to prove him mistaken on that score. Just because I thought I could. But I was probably wrong about that, too, and later on I felt as if I'd been swimming against the wave machine in the indoor pool at Wellenbad.

"Frankly, I don't give a damn what you choose to draw and paint, Herr Grosz. That's entirely your affair. This is Berlin, not Moscow. People can still do more or less what they like here. Like you, I, too, sometimes think that after the war nothing can ever be the same again. But I suppose the major difference between you and me is that I haven't yet given up on beauty. On optimism. On hope. On a bit of law and order. On a little bit of morality. On Holy Germany, for want of a better phrase."

Grosz laughed, but his teeth clenched his pipestem tightly. I swam on, still against the tide.

"Oddly enough I still see the best in women, too. My wife, for example. Until she died I thought she was the most wonderful person I'd ever met. I haven't changed that opinion. I guess that makes me an incurable romantic. Something incurable, anyway."

Grosz smiled thinly, while his Pelikan raced across the page. From time to time his shrewd eyes flicked up at me, appraising, measuring, estimating. No one had ever drawn me before and it made me feel strange, as if I were being stripped bare, to my very essence, like one of the corpses in the Hanno showhouse.

"When a man talks about a wonderful woman," he said, "usually that just means he likes her because she tries very hard to be very like a man. Have you looked at women in this town, lately? Christ, most of them even look like men. These days it's only the men who look like real women. And I could give a damn about what's best in women."

"Well, you've certainly answered one question. Why you like drawing dead women so much. It's because you don't much like women. But I do like the drawing you've done of me. Very much. I wonder if you might give it to me."

Grosz tugged the page out of his sketchbook, added the date, his signature, and the location, and swept it across the table as if it had been the check.

"It's yours. A gift from me to the Berlin police."

"I shall pin it on my wall. Next to Hegel." I looked at it again and nodded. "But you've made me look too young. Too smiley. Like a schoolboy who's just got his Abitur."

"That's how I see you, sergeant. Young and naïve. It's certainly how you see yourself. Which surprises me given all you must have been through in four years at the front."

"Coming from you, sir, I count that as a great compliment. Makes me feel like that English queer who only gets old in his portrait and loses his soul."

"I think you must mean Dorian Gray."

"Yes, him. Except that I've still got mine. Yes, in future I shall look at this picture and think I've been lucky. I've come through the worst of it with my soul still intact. And that's got to be worth something."

THE FOLLOWING DAY, a Wednesday, was another day off and I'd planned to walk up to Tietz and buy some things for my new office at the Alex to celebrate my promotion to the Commission: a city map for the wall, a decent-size ashtray, a table lighter, a desk set, and a bottle of good Korn and some glasses for the drawer, just in case anyone came visiting; and then to spend a quiet morning in my room reading some police files. But over breakfast that morning—coffee, Tilsit cheese, and fresh rolls from the Jewish baker's shop on Schwerinstrasse—I learned that Frau Weitendorf, her hair even more rigidly Golem-like than normal, which made me think it must be a wig, had other ideas as to how I might spend at least the first part of my morning. Sticking a cigarette into her fat ruddy face and lighting it with a match struck on the pewter novelty monkey's backside, which often made her smile (although not on this occasion), she came tortuously to the point:

"I suppose you haven't seen Herr Rankin," she said as she turned down the volume on the Firma Telefunken radio that stood on the sideboard beside a vase of yellow flowers and underneath an Achenbach print of a seascape.

"Not today."

"When was the last time you saw him, Herr Gunther?"

"I don't know. Last Friday evening, perhaps? When we all sat down to eat your delicious lung hash."

"That was the last time anyone at this table saw him," she added ominously.

I looked around at the two others, who were down for breakfast.

"Is that true?"

Rosa nodded and left the table.

Herr Fischer nodded as well, but felt obliged to add his three pennies' worth of information, none of which was in the least bit relevant.

"Yes. It was Friday evening. I remember that because the next day I marched with the communists on Bismarckstrasse, and your lot opened fire as they held up our brass band to allow motor traffic over the intersection at Krumme Strasse. Which was quite uncalled for. But entirely typical of what we've come to expect from the Berlin police."

My lot were the police, of course. I shrugged. "Traffic takes precedence over Marx and Engels."

"I meant the shooting."

"Oh that. Look, all this is beside the point. I thought we were talking about Herr Rankin, not public order."

"He's gone missing," said Frau Weitendorf. "I'm certain of it."

"Are you sure? Perhaps he just went away for a few days. I'm beginning to wish I had."

"His suitcase is still here."

"You've been in his room?"

"He pays me to clean it. And to change his

sheets once a week. When I went in yesterday it was plain he hadn't been there in days. There were several empty bottles lying on the floor and some blood in his shaving basin."

"You're sure about that?"

"Go and take a look for yourself."

We all went upstairs and she unlocked Rankin's door from a bunch of keys on a pink silk ribbon and ushered me inside.

"I don't think we all need to be in here," I said to Fischer in particular. "No matter what might have happened, I think we still have to respect Rankin's privacy."

While I spoke I was eyeing several of the drawings on the wall, which were of naked men in various states of arousal and left nothing to the imagination.

"Typical copper," said Fischer. "Always telling people what to do. Just like the Nazis he and his kind serve so enthusiastically. Look, we all live here. And Robert Rankin's a friend of mine. A good friend. It's not like he hasn't invited me in here before. And I think I'm entitled to know if something's happened to him."

I had become tired of Fischer's constant baiting and the assumption that because I was a cop I was also a Nazi lackey.

"I think you're entitled to know nothing," I said, pushing him back out the doorway. "Although it does seem to me that nothing is usually what a Bolshevik heel hound such as yourself knows best of all."

"Listen, I'm a citizen. You should be more polite. Or I'll feel obliged to report you to your superiors."

"Go right ahead. Meanwhile, I think I'm all through being polite with you, Herr Fischer, so please don't be in any doubt about that."

I closed the door on him, leaving me alone with Frau Weitendorf, whose smile told me she'd quite enjoyed the way I'd spoken to Herr Fischer.

"Lefty bastard," she muttered.

"Mostly I don't have anything against communists," I said. "But I'm beginning to make an exception in that man's case."

Rankin's rooms were much like my own, though bigger and better appointed, with the same sort of furniture except there were more pictures and a large Royal typewriter on the desk. The lip of the basin was spattered with blood and full of pinkish water. Among the shards of broken phonograph records on the floor were several empties that had once been filled with good Scotch; the ashtray beside the typewriter was full of English butts; and a handsome leather suitcase was still on top of the wardrobe. There were at least ten copies of his book, **Pack Up Your Troubles,** on the shelves, almost as if he'd tried to improve its sales by buying it himself. I went into the bedroom and inspected the narrow single bed. The pillow smelled strongly of Coty perfume, perhaps suggesting that Rosa Braun had a better acquaintance with Robert Rankin than I might have supposed.

I picked up one of the records and inspected the label; the vocalist was Bessie Smith.

"Why does a man smash his records like this? It's not normal."

"That all depends on whether you like Bessie Smith," I said. "Me, I can take her or leave her."

"I don't mind telling you, Herr Gunther, I'm worried something's happened to Herr Rankin." She stubbed her cigarette out in Rankin's ashtray and folded her arms under her substantial bosom.

"I can't say I'm inclined to agree with you. Not yet. Not on the basis of what I've seen in here. He drinks a lot. More than he should, perhaps. He smashed a few records. People do things like that when they're drunk. And he cut himself shaving. If it wasn't for the absence of a stick of alum on the shaving stand I'd see no real reason to worry."

Apart, I might have added, from the smell of Coty perfume on the missing man's pillowcase.

I sat down at Rankin's desk. There was a diary and, beside the big black Royal, a pile of typed pages I assumed were part of the book he'd been translating into German. I thought these might give me a clue as to what might have happened to him. "Why don't you leave it with me for a few minutes? I'll poke my muzzle through his desk drawers. See what I can find out."

"I don't know," she said. "I should stay here and keep an eye on things. For Herr Rankin's sake."

"True. You can't trust anyone very much these days. And the cops not at all."

"I didn't mean to suggest you would steal anything, Herr Gunther."

"That's because you don't know as many cops as I do." I thought of Commissar Körner and the way he or his men had helped themselves to what was in Eva Angerstein's handbag. "Okay, take a seat. Here, have a smoke while you're waiting."

I fished out my packet of Salem Aleikum, lit one for each of us, and then tugged open the top drawer. The little Browning .25 caught my eye right away; I sniffed it carefully; it had been recently cleaned. Everything else looked harmless enough, even the dirty postcards featuring boys from the Cosy Corner, which was a queer bar not very far away. What with the cards and the drawings on the wall, I was beginning to wonder if the Coty perfume on his pillow hadn't been worn by Rankin himself; of course that was just wishful thinking and I knew better. For one thing, there wasn't a bottle of the stuff anywhere in his drawers, and for another, it wasn't every queer who didn't like women. Besides, Rankin was a very handsome man, with a bit of money, which made him almost irresistible to every woman in Berlin, including Rosa. I'd seen the way she looked at him, and the way he'd looked at her, and given his obvious predilection for boys and her habit of dressing as a man, they seemed to have a lot in common.

I looked in the diary and learned nothing, except that he often went for lunch at Höhn's Oyster Saloon, and that he was a frequent visitor to the opera, which seemed like a questionable use of anyone's time.

"According to his diary he's going to the Comic Opera on Friday night," I said. "So if he is dead he's still got time to get his money back."

"Don't joke about such things, Herr Gunther."

"No. Perhaps you're right." I lifted the pile of typewritten paper and started to read. I must admit that I got slightly more than I had bargained for.

In April I rejoined the First Battalion of the Royal Welch Fusiliers on the Somme. We were billeted in Morlancourt, a very pretty village, and our trenches—formerly French, and hence more rat-infested than was normal—were at Fricourt, in close proximity to the Germans who were much inclined to throw all sorts of new bombs and grenades at us; the worst of these experimental weapons was one that we began to call the kitchen sink—a two-gallon drum full of explosive and every bit of scrap metal and frangible rubbish they could find to use in it as shrapnel. Once, we found an unexploded kitchen sink and discovered that as well as the usual nuts and bolts it also contained the complete skeleton of a chicken. If that sounds funny it wasn't. Fragments of bone were every bit as dangerous as screws and rusted rifle parts, perhaps more so. I even saw a man who'd been struck in the head by a piece of his own officer's jawbone after a mortar fell on the trench; it took him days to die of his injuries.

A few weeks later I was posted to the Second Battalion and was discovered to be unfit for trench service by the MO; this was something of a surprise to me since, apart from a cough, which turned out to be bronchitis, I felt reasonably all right. So I went back to Frise and took command of the headquarter company, where things were much more relaxed, or so I thought. Almost immediately something happened that persuaded me I would have been better off back in the trenches with the rats, facing down the Germans. I was obliged one day to borrow a horse and ride to the nearest field hospital with a case of trench foot that was to cost me all my toenails. I was lucky; for many men the only treatment was surgical debridement, and sometimes amputation. As soon as I had been treated, Brigade told me to take command of a firing squad, following the court-martial of a Welsh corporal who was charged with cowardice.

His case was already well known to me as it was to almost everyone in the Royal Welch; the day before throwing away his rifle in the presence of the enemy, the corporal had walked into no-man's-land close to the German wire to retrieve his wounded sergeant, whom everyone had thought was dead but had now revived and was calling for help. In broad daylight the corporal had climbed over the parapet and, armed with only a white handkerchief that he waved in front of him like a flag of truce, walked slowly across no-man's-land to where the wounded sergeant lay. At first the Germans fired shots around his feet to halt his advance, but he was not deterred and gradually their guns fell silent as they recognized the man's enormous courage. Having reached the injured sergeant the corporal dressed the man's wounds, gave him some rum, and then hoisted him up onto his back, carrying him all the way to his trench. Everyone who witnessed it said it was the bravest thing they'd ever seen and how it was a miracle that he hadn't been shot for his trouble; even the Germans cheered him. The corporal might have been recommended for a medal but for the fact that there were no officers present to witness the action.

All would probably have been well if the sergeant had survived, but the next day he died of his wounds, and someone at Brigade was stupid enough to make sure the corporal found out about it, minutes before the Germans mounted an attack, which was when the incident with the rifle occurred. Instead of helping to defend the trench, the corporal threw away his rifle in disgust and walked back toward Brigade HQ, where he was eventually arrested.

With a better advocate he might have survived; an army order stipulated that in the case of men on trial for their life, a sentence of death might be mitigated if conduct in the field had been exemplary. By any standard the corporal's heroic actions in saving the sergeant the previous day ought to have been more than enough to have saved his life. But asked by his court-martial exactly why he had thrown away his rifle, he had replied that if he'd held on to it any longer he might have shot the idiot of a lieutenant who was leading the company or indeed any of the general staff he might have run into. Not that there was any chance of that, he added, since in his opinion the general staff were even bigger cowards than he was. Any threat of injury to an officer was enough to have aggravated the corporal's cowardice charge, and he was found guilty and ordered to be shot at dawn by a firing squad made up of his own company, who drew straws for the duty.

Of course I might have refused this duty, but to do so would have resulted in my disobeying a direct order and being court-martialed myself; besides, someone else would only have taken command of the firing squad with the same inevitable outcome. As it was, and still limping, I was able to visit the corporal the night before his execution and leave him a small bottle of rum and some cigarettes. I don't suppose he slept any more than I did.

At dawn the following morning we marched the corporal around to the church graveyard where death sentences were carried out and there, in the presence of the French military governor, we tied him to a small obelisk erected to the victims of the Franco-Prussian war—which struck me as ironic. The morning was as beautiful a morning as I'd ever seen in that benighted country; the graveyard was full of evening primrose flowers and reminded me of a perfect May morning at Oxford. I offered him a blindfold, but he shook his head stubbornly and stared bravely at his comrades, nodding encouragement at them as if trying to give them the strength to carry out their appointed task. His final words were the battalion calling cry:

"Stick it, the Welch." A braver man I never saw, which also struck me as ironic since we were shooting him for an act of gross cowardice. The lads botched it, however, and missed the cardboard target pinned over his heart, which left it to me as the officer commanding to finish the poor bastard off.

The French call this shot delivered to the head the **coup de grâce,** but there is nothing graceful about it. And the worst part of it was that the corporal's blue eyes were wide open throughout his final ordeal. I say his final ordeal, but it was, of course, an ordeal for me, too. He looked at me as I unbuttoned the holster of my Webley and I swear he smiled. That was bad enough, but then he whispered after the health of my foot; for the rest of my life I shall remember his expression and even today, ten years afterward, I can remember these events as if they were yesterday; many's the time I have awoken from a most vivid nightmare in which I am back in Frise with that Webley in my hand. The nightmare alone is enough to cause me to suffer the most severe depression for days afterward and there have been many times when I have wished it had been me who had been shot in the head, and not the poor corporal.

Even as I write this now I can see his skull implode like a burst football; I choose my words carefully. The corporal had played football for Wrexham United before the war and helped to win the Welsh Cup three times. Meanwhile, the sight and scent of evening primrose is always enough to reduce me to a gibbering wreck.

It was there that Rankin had stopped typing his book although according to the original text he was only halfway through the chapter and but for my lack of English I might have read that, too. I put aside the manuscript, took a puff on my Salem, and thought for a moment. It felt strange reading the account of a man who'd once been my enemy even if he was half German, but if anything it made me realize how much more we had in common than what had divided us. It felt a little as if we were brothers-in-arms. And like Frau Weitendorf, I realized that I, too, was now feeling a little worried about Rankin.

"Well? What do you think?"

I'd almost forgotten that I was not alone in the Englishman's rooms.

"Those flowers on the sideboard in the dining room," I said. "The yellow ones. What are they called?"

"Evening primrose," said Frau Weitendorf. "I pick them from the Heinrich-von-Kleist-Park. At this time of year there are thousands of them. Lovely, aren't they? Why?"

"When did you put them there?"

"Saturday afternoon. Is it important?"

"I think in future it might be a good idea to choose something else. It seems those particular flowers awaken terrible memories in our Englishman's mind. Suicidal memories, perhaps."

"How is that possible?"

"I don't know. But it certainly fits with my own experiences. The smallest thing can trigger all sorts of unpleasant thoughts of the war." I finished my cigarette and stubbed it out. "I'll make some inquiries at the Alex and have someone check the hospitals. Just in case."

I might also have mentioned the Hanno showhouse but for the fact that I'd just been there and I was more or less sure I hadn't seen a corpse who resembled Robert Rankin.

THE ALEX TELEPHONED, asking me to cut short my leave and come in the following day, which left me only enough time to have dinner with Thea von Harbou. She suggested we meet at the Hotel Adlon.

THEA WAS TALL, handsome rather than beautiful, full figured, and about forty. Looking at her, it was hard to believe she'd written the screenplay of a movie about robots and an industrialized future. I might more easily have believed she was an opera singer; she certainly had the chest for it. She was wearing a light tweed two-piece suit, a man's shirt and tie, white stockings, and a pair of silver earrings. Her shortish blond hair was parted to one side, her mouth was maybe a bit too wide, and her nose a bit too long, but she was as elegant as Occam's razor and just as sharp. She had come armed with some expensive stationery from Liebmann and a variety of accessories that made me think she might have been to India: a gold enameled cigarette case that resembled a Mughal's favorite rug; a variety of silver and ivory bangles; and a green clutch bag with an embroidered Hindu god that was home to a lorgnette and several large banknotes. This was just as well; the Hotel Adlon's restaurant was the most expensive in Berlin. I knew that because I saw the ransom demands that were amusingly called prices on the menu, and because Fritz Thyssen was at the next table. Naturally Thea von Harbou was a friend of his; I expect she knew everyone who was worth knowing and Thyssen was worth a lot more than that. He was wearing an extremely fine double-breasted gray suit that made my own gray suit look more like the hide on a dead rhinoceros.

"So when did you become a policeman?" she asked.

"Immediately after the war."

"And it's taken until now to get into the Murder Commission?"

"I wasn't in any hurry. How about you? How did you get into the picture business?"

"The usual way. A man. Two men, if I'm honest. My husband. And the husband before him. I suppose I always wanted to be a writer more than I wanted to be a wife. Still do, if the truth be known."

Hers was the kind of voice that licks your ear slowly, inside and out, as if it contained the sweetest honey: dark and sexy and very assured, with just a hint of whisper on the edge of it, like the lace on a pillowcase. I liked her voice and I liked her, too. It's hard not to like a woman who buys you a good dinner at the Adlon.

"How does your husband feel about that? The present one, I mean."

"We have an understanding. He sees other women—a lot of women; actresses, mostly—and I try to be understanding. There's a club he enjoys going to. The Heaven and Hell, on Kurfürstendamm. He's probably there with some little **minette** right now."

"I'm sorry."

"Don't be. In many ways Fritz is a very selfish, narcissistic man. But he's also enormously talented. And I admire him a lot. So most of the time we're a pretty good team."

"I know. I saw your last picture. **Metropolis.**"

"What did you think?"

"What didn't I think? I thought it was very thought provoking. I especially enjoyed the part when the workers rise up against their masters. I'm only surprised they haven't done it already. That's what I think."

"Then we think the same way."

"Although not so as you'd notice from the people you know." I glanced sideways at Thyssen.

"Thyssen? He's not so bad. He puts money into a lot of our pictures. Even the losers. And that's good enough for me."

"So how did **Metropolis** do?"

"It's had a mixed reception. Even from my darling husband. When he hears bad things about **Metropolis** he blames me; but when he hears good things about the movie, he prefers to take full credit. But that's directors for you. It's not just our movie cameras that need a tripod, it's his ego, too. Writers are a lesser species. Lesser and cheaper. Especially when they're women. Anyway we're through making pictures about the future. Nobody in Germany gives a damn about the future. At least for the present. If they did, they wouldn't keep voting for the communists and the Nazis. We'd have a proper government that could get things done. So right now we're focusing on something very different, something with more popular appeal. In particular, the subject of mass murderers like Fritz Haarmann and this other man who's been killing and scalping Berlin prostitutes: Winnetou. Fritz is fascinated with sex murders. These murders, in particular. You might even say he's obsessed."

"Why's that, do you think?"

"Sometimes I wonder, you know?"

"And what answers do you come up with?"

"It might be the fact that the victims are prostitutes. Fritz has always had a thing about Berlin's **demi-monde.** But it might also be the scalping. Yes, I think it must be that. It's so very extreme. If Fritz wasn't a film director and interested in all sorts of other extreme stories I might even be worried about him."

"I don't think he's the only one, Thea. Sex murder seems to be an obsession he shares with a lot of Berlin artists." I mentioned my meeting with George Grosz and what he'd told me about Otto Dix and Max Beckmann.

"I guess that doesn't surprise me. Fritz says Berlin has become the sex-murder capital of the Western world. And maybe it has, I don't know. Certainly you'd think so from what's in the newspapers. So we've decided we want to make a picture right here in Berlin about a sex killer like Winnetou. And a detective like Ernst Gennat."

"He'll be delighted."

"What sort of man is he, anyway?"

"Gennat? Buddha with a large cigar and a voice like a black bear with a heavy cold. Berlin's best detective and probably Germany's, too, but don't say it to his face. Fat, a bit clownish to look at, grumpy and easily underestimated."

"Is he married?"

"No."

"Girlfriend?"

"You'd have to teach him how that kind of thing works these days. And I doubt he's got the time or the inclination."

She nodded and sipped some of the excellent Mosel she'd ordered with dinner. Then she smiled. Her smile was bright and full of warmth and meant, I realized too late, for the man seated behind me.

"That's what Kurt Reichenbach said."

"I'm not sure I can improve on anything he's already told you."

"Perhaps. But Fritz says our investors are very keen on us having a source who actually works for the Murder Commission. It's the sort of thing that impresses such people. Fritz says that having you to advise me will help persuade them our film is as true to life—as realistic—as possible. And that you'll be able to help explain why the killer does what he does. How he gets away with it, for a while at any rate. And eventually how he's caught."

"You make that part sound like a foregone conclusion."

"Isn't it?"

"Not at all. You'd be surprised how many killers get away with it. If murderers were all that easy to catch I'd be directing traffic on Potsdamer Platz. Or looking for missing cats and dogs."

"That's a comforting thought."

"There's a lot of thumb twiddling and navel-gazing in the detective business, Thea. And a good measure of luck. Not to mention incompetence and stupidity."

I might have added dishonesty, too, but for the fact that I'd already gained the impression that she and Fritz Lang wanted to make a detective the hero of their movie.

"Would it surprise you to learn that most detectives are dependent on professional criminals to help them solve crimes? Criminals who for one reason or another become informers. Fact is, most cops would be lost without them. Even in the Murder Commission we often have to rely on Berlin's lowlife to get a handle on what's what. Sometimes the best detective is just the guy with the most reliable informer. Or someone who's better at squeezing a lemon, if you know what I mean. You want to know the reason that most murderers get away with it?"

"Do tell."

"Because they're people who look just like you and me. Well, me, anyway. There are not so many women killing prostitutes. Even in Berlin.

You want realism? Then make your murderer nice. The guy next door. That's my advice. The type of clean-shirt and bow-tie sort of guy who is kind to children and animals. A respectable fellow who takes a regular bath and wouldn't hurt a fly. At least that's what all the neighbors will say when he's arrested afterward. No hideous scars, no hunchback, no staring eyes, no long fingernails, no sinister rictus smile. So you can forget about Conrad Veidt or Max Schreck. Make your character insignificant. A little guy. Someone hardly like a villain at all. Someone whose life has run out of meaning. It might lack drama but that's realistic."

Thea was silent for a few minutes. "So tell me about Winnetou."

"I'll tell you what I'm allowed to tell you. Another time, I'll invite you back to the Commission offices, maybe introduce you to Gennat himself, show you the murder wagon, but tomorrow I have to work."

"Do you mind me taking notes? Only, my secretary will type them up and Fritz will read them, too."

"That's okay."

Thea lit a cigarette, spread her notebook expectantly on the table, and started writing down everything I told her as if I were dictating holy writ. Which was probably why, when I'd finished talking, I told her that a lot of people at the Alex—which is to say, a lot of men—didn't think the Winnetou killings were important.

"What I mean is this, Thea. Dead prostitutes in this city are ten for a penny. And while I'm very keen to catch this bastard, as are Weiss and Gennat, there are plenty of others at the Alex who really don't give a damn. And not just at the Alex but across the whole city: there are Berliners who believe that many of these girls got what was coming to them. Who think that Winnetou is doing the Lord's work, and cleaning out the Augean stables. They're probably the same misguided people who think Germany needs a strongman to lead her out of our current situation. Someone like Hitler. Or the army perhaps. Hindenburg. Or maybe the Pied Piper of Hamelin, I don't know."

"So what are you saying? That I shouldn't write this movie?"

"No, I'm not saying that at all. I'm saying why take the risk of choosing a murderer who preys on people who are already perceived by some to be part of the problem? Why not choose another sort of killer? Another kind of victim. For maximum sympathy. The kind of victim no one could argue with."

"Like who?"

"I don't know. I'm a cop, not a writer. But if you were to choose a killer who preys on children, perhaps, then there's no one who could ever suggest that they deserved it, that they were courting disaster. Everyone likes children. Even Gennat."

"A child murderer." Thea's eyes widened. "That **is** something new. But it might be too much. Could people stand a film like that?"

"Make them stand it." I lifted my glass, leaned back in my chair, and watched Thyssen screw a cigarette into a gold holder; vulgarly I wondered how much he was worth and what kind of house he was going home to. I expect he was looking at me and doing the same.

"But there's another reason why I'm saying this. If you're writing about a child murderer, then your screen killer will look very different from Winnetou. This helps put a bit of distance between Bernhard Weiss and your husband."

"And that's important? Why? Because they're both Jews, I suppose."

"Because they're both Jews. The Nazis love to see conspiracies where none exist. So let's give them as little ammunition as possible. And by the way, this is Weiss's thinking, not mine. I'm just a detective."

She gave me a ride home in her car. When I got inside the house on Nollendorfplatz, I found Rankin had turned up safe and sound. He'd been on a bender with some old friends who were over from England and had stayed in the house they'd rented over in Schmargendorf.

"I'm sorry but it simply didn't occur to me that any of you would worry," he said.

"That's all right," I said. "We'll know the next time that you're probably all right. Won't we, Frau Weitendorf?"

"Well, I think you've been very selfish," she said. "Fraulein Braun and I thought something dreadful must have happened to you, Herr Rankin. All those broken records on the floor of your room. And the empty bottles of whiskey. What were we supposed to think? Even Herr Gunther was concerned about you."

"It's true, I drink too much sometimes. And when I do I get very strong opinions about music. I should never have bought those records. You might say they were a sort of failed experiment in taste. The fact is, I much prefer Wagner and Schubert."

"That is no excuse," said Frau Weitendorf, and waddled off irritably.

"I think she'd almost have preferred it if you were dead," I said.

"I think you're right. But she'll come around. They always do. I'll give her a bit extra for cleaning the room and she'll be fine." Rankin grinned at me sheepishly. "Women, eh? Can't live with them, can't live without them."

I thought about my pleasant evening with Thea von Harbou and reflected that possibly her husband felt exactly the same way as Rankin.

My own opinion of women wasn't in the least bit equivocal: Living without my own wife was much less preferable than living with her. In fact, there were times when it was nothing short of intolerable. If women were good for one thing it was this: that they take the sharp edge off feeling forever like a man.

part two
decline

Deep below the earth's surface lay the workers' city.

—**Metropolis,** directed by Fritz Lang from a screenplay by Thea von Harbou

Berlin's summer finally arrived in earnest and the city bloomed with light and shrugged off its greasy loden overcoat. Lovers sat on five-penny benches in the Tiergarten not far from Apollo, who stared at his stringless stone lyre and wondered impotently what to play for them. On Sundays, workers in their thousands took an S-Bahn train to the white sandy beaches of Wannsee. One day I went myself and you couldn't see the beach for the people, so that it was hard to make out where the sand ended and the water began; they paddled their dirty feet in the warm shallow water before returning home to the gray eastern slums, their faces pink from the sun, their sweating bellies full of sausage and sauerkraut and beer. Pleasure steamers headed noisily down the Spree to Grünau and Heidesee, and the statue of Victoria at the top of Berlin's victory column blazed in the bright sunlight like a fiery angel as if it had come to announce some new apocalypse.

At the Alex, we paid lip service to summer by calling in the painters and plasterers, by hosing down the basement cells and leaving the upper-floor windows ajar all day, allowing the air to blow away some of the gloom and the stink of tobacco smoke and perspiration. But it never lasted very long. A cage is still a cage however wide open you leave the doors, and it always stinks of the animals who've been kept there: murderers, thieves, gartersnappers, queers, grasshoppers, control girls, drug addicts, alcoholics, wife beaters, and gangsters. But mostly just cops. No one smells worse than us.

There's something about a big Police Praesidium on a broiling summer's night; it's easy to think that crime kicks off its tight shoes and takes a holiday like the rest of Berlin, but that would be a mistake. It's never the cold that brings out the worst in people, it's the heat. If you can call them people: the sick, venal, lowlife that lies oozing at the bottom of the strata we are wont to call Berlin society. Sometimes I had the strong idea that George Grosz was right and I was wrong; that he was only recording what was already there: the indifferent fat bankers, the crippled veterans, the mutilated beggars, and the dead prostitutes—that this was how we really were, ugly and obscene, hypocritical and callous.

But there's always something new in this job that surprises you. Something that throws you off guard, such as the kind of murder you never expected to see because naïvely you thought you'd seen everything. That's what happened in the long hot summer of 1928.

It was on a day when public interest in Winnetou was at its highest that everything changed abruptly and, almost overnight, a very different sort of killer took his place in the febrile imagination of the metropolis. One moment the Kripo's Murder Commission was investigating Eva Angerstein's killing, and the next it seemed as if she and Winnetou's other unfortunate victims had never existed. For a while I tried to keep a discreet handle on the case but it was to no avail. The orders came from the very top.

One day Bernhard Weiss found himself summoned to a meeting at the Ministry of Justice on the Wilhelmstrasse, where he was told, in no uncertain terms, that the Murder Commission was to lay off the Winnetou murders and devote all its energies to catching the man the press had dubbed "Dr. Gnadenschuss," which was how he had represented himself in the letter he'd sent to all the city's newspapers. In it, he had claimed responsibility for these latest murders while also mocking the Berlin police and, in particular, the Murder Commission. And since those present at the meeting included the minister of justice, Hermann Schmidt; the minister of the interior, Albert Grzesinski; and the ViPoPra, Karl Zörgiebel, Weiss had little choice but to bite his lip and comply with his orders. It was as if someone had overheard my conversation at dinner with Thea von Harbou. The word from the Wilhelmstrasse was that almost nobody in government gave a damn about a few dead grasshoppers—not when there was a killer at large deemed to be of much greater political importance. Our government and politicians had deemed what Dr. Gnadenschuss was doing to be a disgrace to the Republic, and catching him was now to be the Murder Commission's top priority. Meanwhile, Police Colonel Magnus Heimannsberg, who was also briefed in the same meeting, had his uniformed boys in Schupo advise Berlin's prostitutes to stay off the streets or to sell it at their own risk.

As it happened, Magnus Heimannsberg knew a lot more about risk than he did about prostitutes, at least the female ones. According to Gennat, he lived with a handsome police major called Walther Encke, in an apartment on Apostel-Paulus-Strasse, in Berlin Schöneberg. Which probably also explained why he was not one of the Republic's great police reformers. But he was very popular with the common patrolmen by virtue of the fact he'd started his career at the bottom of the ladder and also was totally apolitical, which is to say he was a staunch republican, like me. Neither a communist nor a Nazi, he was interested only in the welfare of the men whom he commanded and he suffered a lot of fools gladly in a way that Weiss would never have countenanced. There was no love lost between these two senior officers but they both agreed on the importance of avoiding any further national scandal, and of avenging the published insult to the Berlin police by capturing this Dr. Gnadenschuss as soon as possible.

WHAT OTHER NATIONS called the **coup de grâce,** we Germans called the **Gnadenschuss:** a single shot to the head that puts a badly injured man out of his misery. Except that the men to whom this dubious mercy was accorded on the streets of Berlin in broad daylight in 1928 had been severely injured more than a decade before. All these new murder victims were disabled war veterans, half-men on cripple-carts who for years had been begging for coins in front of the city's S-Bahn stations. The victims were men who couldn't run away. The first three were shot through the head at point-blank range with a .25-caliber pistol in less than a week; the small-caliber shot was barely heard above the noise of the trains in the station overhead. And in the case of two of the victims, it took several hours before anyone noticed they were dead, such was the commonplace status of these disabled veterans and the almost silent method by which they had been dispatched.

We case-reviewed these three killings in Gennat's office: Weiss, Heller, Gennat, Otto Trettin, and me, with Frau Künstler typing up the transcript of what was said. Trettin had just returned after a length of time at a local sanatorium, which meant we were at last back to full strength.

"Take Otto through the facts as we know them, Bernie," said Weiss. "He can read the files later."

"The first victim was Werner Schlichter," I said. "Age thirty-six, with no family that we know of. Formerly a sergeant with the 180th Infantry. Took a bullet in the spine in 1916 at the Battle of the Somme, which left him paralyzed from the waist down. A Berliner, he'd been a gardener at the Botanical Garden in Dahlem before the war. More recently he lived in the Salvation Army hostel on Müllerstrasse. His body was found near the railway station at Wedding, just south of Nettelbeckplatz, on June 6. He'd been shot once through the forehead in broad daylight at close range with a .25-caliber automatic. There was no used brass found at the scene, which means the killer felt confident enough to pick it up and take it away with him. The body was found by a schoolteacher from the Lessing Gymnasium on Pankstrasse—a Herr Kesten. A veteran himself, he'd spoken to Schlichter on previous occasions, when he put a few coins in the man's cap. Except that on this occasion, the cap was on the dead man's head, covering the bullet wound, instead of lying on his thigh, where it could more usefully collect coins. Again, it's assumed that it was the killer who put the man's cap on his head. Still on Schlichter's army tunic were the Honor Cross with Swords and a German Imperial Wound Badge, black grade, and in his pockets were several marks. The Salvation Army commander at the hostel is a man called Harfensteller, also an army veteran, who said that Schlichter kept to himself and had no particular friends or enemies that he could think of. Before going on the streets to beg he had worked at the Oskar-Helene Home here in Berlin but apparently he didn't care for the regime there and left."

"Nobody saw anything?" asked Trettin.

"Not a thing," I said, and handed Trettin the photograph taken by Hans Gross. From the picture it was easy to see why the murder had gone unnoticed for several hours; Schlichter was seated on his **klutz** cart and looked to all the world as if he was asleep; the entry wound resembled nothing more than a small carbuncle on his forehead.

"Why didn't he like the Oskar-Helene?" asked Trettin.

"I'll come back to that in a minute."

Otto Trettin was a good detective but, like Kurt Reichenbach, he was at times a little bit heavy-handed; he'd once been attacked by two thugs from a criminal ring called Apache Blood and had put both men in hospital, with one losing an eye. He was not a man to tangle with. He'd also been rapped over the knuckles by Gennat for fiddling his expenses. He was said to be working with another detective on a book about famous Berlin murder cases. A moneymaker, perhaps; all of us were interested in making a little extra money, of course. Even Bernhard Weiss had recently published a book, **Police and Politics.** Somewhat dull, it didn't have much appeal to the general public and it was bruited that one or two Berlin coppers hadn't liked what he had to say about them in print. Gennat was also rumored to be working on a book. Sometimes I thought I was the only detective in the Commission who wasn't planning a separate career as a writer.

"Thirty-six hours later," I said, "we found the second victim: Oskar Heyde, age forty. The body was underneath the Friedrichstrasse station bridge. He'd been shot twice through the head at close range. Originally a businessman from

Silesia, he joined the Fiftieth Reserve Division as an infantry lieutenant and was badly injured at the Third Battle of Ypres in September 1917, when he was blown up by a British mine, which cost him both legs and the sight in his left eye. For which he was awarded the Iron Cross. After the war he went to live with his brother Gustav in Potsdam, but the brother lost everything in the inflation and killed himself. Heyde then went to the Oskar-Helene Home, but he didn't care for the regime either, and left soon afterward, since when he was on the street. Again, the body was undisturbed for several hours before anyone noticed anything suspicious."

"So what is it with the Oskar-Helene?" asked Trettin.

I looked at Weiss. "Boss? Perhaps you'd like to take that question."

Weiss removed his pince-nez, relit his cigar, and leaned back in his chair. "Gunther and I visited the home, which is in Berlin-Zehlendorf, the day before yesterday," he said. "It was most informative. And utterly depressing. Quite the most depressing experience I've had in a long time. It's my opinion that those who run it represent everything that's wrong with modern Germany. The place is under the control of two doctors, Konrad Biesalski and Hans Wurtz, who have very definite, not to say inflexible, ideas on rehabilitation and social integration. They believe hard work is the only true cure for an injured man's maladies; that a man who remains work-shy and dependent on society demonstrates 'a crippled soul' and is constitutionally deficient to the extent of being degenerate. Frankly, they leave nothing for a man's pride, even half a man, with half a face, as was the case with several of the men we encountered.

"I don't doubt that their intentions are good. But it seems to me that not every man who was badly injured is capable of work. If you submit to their regime and become a morally healthy, curable cripple, then you agree to be retrained and to become a useful member of society, or at least society as it is perceived by these two doctors. If you don't, you find yourself classed as a feebleminded, morally unhealthy, incurable invalid; more important, you put yourself beyond any financial compensation for war-related suffering."

"Jesus," muttered Trettin.

"Effectively, they're both eugenicists, which is to say that the logical conclusion of their theories is nothing short of euthanasia, according to which, men who won't work are not only a burden on society, but are psychopathic, unpatriotic, and unworthy of life. They are war neurotics deserving only of extermination." Weiss replaced his pince-nez on his nose. "Now, tell him about the third victim, Bernie, if you would."

"Boss. Age forty-two, Werner Jugo lived with

his wife in a basement in Meyerheimstrasse. Before the war he was a bus driver with the Berlin Transport Company. Joined the Twenty-Seventh Field Artillery Division in 1914. In 1918, he was hit by mortar fire at the Battle of Amiens."

"The blackest day of the German Army," muttered Weiss, quoting Ludendorff.

"Lost an arm and both legs. After the war, he spent several years at Spandau Hospital. Then served a year in Fühlsbuttel Penitentiary in Hamburg for an assault on a prostitute."

"It's an occupational hazard," said Trettin. "That is, if you're a gartersnapper."

"We don't know why he attacked her. He then spent a year in St. Joseph's Sanatorium."

I paused for a second, acutely aware that this was the same place from which Otto Trettin had just returned. St. Joseph's was a monastery near the lake in Weissensee where Berliners were treated for cocaine addiction.

"It's all right," he said. His face was a thick-lipped rictus with a broken nose and large, cold dark eyes, a bit like a totem pole with piles. "I don't mind talking about it. I had a little habit that got out of hand, that's all. Well, you know how the hours are on a job like this. Up and down. Sometimes I needed a lift just to function. Anyway, all that's behind me now. Thanks to the boss here."

"We're glad to see you back in harness, Otto,"

said Weiss. "That's what matters. And especially now."

Gennat grunted and got up to adjust the clock on the wall of his office, which he did several times a day; it was an old railway clock and more decorative than useful. Every time I looked at it, it was wrong and there was a general suspicion that Gennat liked it that way, that it gave him an excuse to interrupt a meeting he wanted to end, and the fact was, he didn't like Otto Trettin very much. He didn't trust anyone who'd been addicted to drugs. While Gennat corrected and then rewound the clock, I carried on with my exposition of the case.

"He may have been a beggar, but Werner Jugo was strongly suspected of having been a coke dealer. We found several grams of the stuff on his body. His wife, Magda, is an attendant in the ladies' lavatory at the Excelsior, and it's possible she also sells drugs. But given the two previous cases, we are of the opinion that the murder was not drug related. Like the two previous victims, Jugo was shot through the forehead at close range. The body was found under the station on Schönhauser Allee, still on his cripple-cart. This was just twenty-four hours after victim two was found dead. Again, no one saw or heard anything, with the noise of the train concealing the gunshot.

"The day after Jugo's murder, four Berlin

newspapers—the **Morgenpost,** the **Vossische Zeitung,** the **Lokal-Anzeiger,** and the **Tageblatt**—received an identical typewritten letter that claimed to have been written by the murderer. The letter to the **Morgenpost** was accompanied by an army cap on which was written Oskar Heyde's name. It also contained his army number, which we have since checked with the Bendlerblock, and the Reichswehr have confirmed that the number is genuine."

"Which would seem to make the letter genuine also," said Weiss. "Incidentally, Gottfried Hanke, Kripo's in-house typewriter and graphology expert, believes the letters were typed on an Orga Privat Bingwerke machine. Not only that, but he says the machine displays a defect in the horizontal alignment: the capital letter **G** prints to the right. I've asked Hanke to check out office-supply companies in Berlin to see if they have a record of sales of that particular machine. The postmark on the envelope was Friedrichshain, but I doubt there's any significance in that. I live in Friedrichshain. Anyway, read the letter, Bernie."

> "Dear Editor, This is the killer of the three disabled war veterans. But you can call me Dr. Gnadenschuss. To prove I killed these men: I used a .25-caliber pistol and shot them through the forehead at close range. Close

enough to burn the skin. I didn't leave any spent rounds on the ground near the bodies. I shot the first man once, the second, twice, and the third three times. But the next man I shall shoot just once; and I will also take one of his medals, if he's wearing any. Also in one previous case, I took a souvenir—a soldier's forage cap—which I have enclosed in my letter to the **Morgenpost.** No exclusives here; sorry, gentlemen. His name was Heyde. The reason I have killed these three men should be obvious to anyone who calls himself a patriotic German. The men I shot were dead already and I was merely putting them out of their very obvious misery; while they existed they were not only a disgrace to the uniform, they also reminded everyone of the shame of Germany's defeat. You've heard of the stab-in-the-back theory; well, these men represent a stab in the front. For everyone who sees them crawling around the sidewalks like rats and lice, they represent an affront to the human eye and to the very idea of civic decency. In short, I have only done what needs to be done if Germany is to begin to rebuild itself, to put the past behind it. The fact is, a new Germany cannot emerge from the ashes of the old while ragged, degenerate, crippled reminders of its ignominious past continue to haunt our streets like so many ghosts and ghouls. They are a burden on the state. A future in which the German Army assumes its rightful place in the nation's destiny cannot begin until these obscene blots on the national landscape are wiped out. We all know that I am only stating what has been apparent for a long time. Besides, everyone knows that many of these malingering beggar veterans are fakes and frauds; I myself saw one get up and walk away from his cripple-cart as if his middle name had been Lazarus.

"No need to thank me, so hold the applause. Anyway, you have been warned. I will kill more war cripples than the cops can count, so you can expect more blood on the streets of Berlin before very long. Not that the police can do anything. The cops, and more especially Berlin's famous Murder Commission, know that they stand little or no chance of stopping me from carrying out these random attacks. Even if they were not the bunch of incompetent idiots that they are—did they ever catch Winnetou? No, of course not—they couldn't stop me now. Real detective work is not what it once was in this city. Most of Kripo couldn't catch a cold. You had better print this letter if you know what's good for you. Heil Hitler. Yours, Dr. Gnadenschuss."

"Any comments, gentlemen?" asked Weiss. "It's been two years since we had the Murder

Commission," said Trettin. "He's not very up-to-date with current police practice."

"Perhaps that's just as well," said Weiss.

"I've a comment," said Gennat. "And it relates to the very peculiar sort of anti-Semitism that's demonstrated in this letter."

"There is no anti-Semitism in that letter," observed Weiss.

"That's what's peculiar about it. This must be the first time anyone made a criticism of Kripo and the Murder Commission that didn't make mention of the fact that there's a Jew in charge of this department. Specifically, you. Especially when they've signed off with a Heil Hitler."

"Yes, that's true," admitted Weiss. "I never thought of that."

"In every other respect he sounds exactly like a Nazi," added Gennat.

"Or someone who wants to sound like a Nazi," I said. "But I agree with Ernst. It's curious that a Nazi of all people should miss out on a good opportunity to libel you, sir. They're not normally so careless about such things."

"Especially that bastard Goebbels," agreed Trettin. "Hey, wouldn't it be great if a Nazi really had killed these men? Hitler loves to pose as the veterans' friend. Something like this would truly embarrass him."

Weiss said nothing but I could tell he was thinking the same thing.

"You know, boss," added Trettin, "listening to that letter reminded me of how you described those two doctors at the Oskar-Helene Home in Zehlendorf. You said they were eugenicists. Only more so. That they believe in the extermination of those who serve no useful purpose in society."

"Sadly, this kind of perverted science is a commonly held view today," said Weiss. "Especially in Germany. And among some quite respectable people, too. Until his death a few years ago, Karl Binding was a leading exponent of 'mercy' killing, as he called it. And psychiatrist Alfred Hoche has been advocating euthanasia for the disabled and mentally ill for many years."

"Nevertheless," said Trettin, "maybe there's some useful purpose in seeing if Doctors Biesalski and Wurtz are somehow involved in these killings."

"You mean, in seeing if they're murderers?"

"I'm not sure I would go that far. No, in seeing if perhaps they counseled others at the home to carry out the murders."

Weiss frowned. "I think it's highly unlikely. I didn't like them. I didn't like them at all. But I don't think there's any German doctor who would put a gun to a man's head and pull the trigger in the name of so-called racial hygiene, or ask someone else to do so. Things are morally bad in Germany, yes, but they're not that bad. But by all means pursue it as a possible lead if you think it's worth it, Otto. It's not as if we have a lot of other theories to work with right now. Only do it discreetly. I don't want them complaining to the Ministry."

Gennat came back to the meeting table and clasped his pink hands in front of his belly, like an innocent choirboy. He didn't sit down. Looking as if he wished to make a point, he addressed the table with the air of an angry chairman berating a board of directors.

"If you ask me, it's teenagers who are behind these killings," he said. Gennat seemed a little more red-faced and pop-eyed than usual, and his voice could have blunted the edge of a saber. "That's right. Our delightful, all-important, patriotic German youth who don't know anything and want to know even less. Lazy little bastards. Most of them regard cops as figures of comedy." He stared up at the ceiling with a look of sarcastic innocence and tried to speak like an adolescent. " 'What, me, Officer? I really don't know what you're talking about, Officer. No sir, I can't remember where I was last night. And I wouldn't dream of doing what you suggest. As a matter of fact, I've just come from church, where I was praying for my grandmother.'

"They make me puke." Gennat caught the smile on the face of Bernhard Weiss and pointed his cigar holder the boss's way. "And why not them? You know what I'm talking about, boss.

A gang of juveniles looking for amusement. And what could be more amusing than murder for the hell of it, especially when you're just killing off a few old men who've outlived their usefulness? That's just Darwinism, according to some lawyers I've spoken to."

"You're exaggerating a bit, Ernst," said Weiss. "Young people are really not as bad as that, are they?"

"No, they're far worse than that. You don't believe me, then go down to the Juvenile Court and take a good look for yourself, Bernhard. They have no souls, half of them. But why should that be a surprise to anyone? Many of them have grown up without any kind of discipline in their lives because their fathers were killed in the trenches."

"What about the letter? Are you seriously saying a juvenile could have written that?"

"Excuse me, chief, but why not?"

With a magnanimous gesture of his hand, Weiss encouraged Gennat to continue.

"They can write. They've been educated. Some of these teenage swine are a lot cleverer than you think, chief. Paul Krantz, for example. Remember him? He was attending a good school, a gymnasium, and would have got his Abitur but for the small matter of a murder trial."

Paul Krantz was a juvenile whose case had

recently come before the Berlin courts; he'd been accused of murdering two of his teenage friends, youngsters from a nice, middle-class home in Berlin-Steglitz, along with another boy who was his rival for the affections of a local girl. The murders had been a source of enormous fascination in the Berlin newspapers.

"But Paul Krantz was acquitted of murder," protested Weiss.

"All the worse. But everyone in Berlin knows he did it. Three murders and all he gets is a rap over the knuckles; three weeks in the cement for the illegal possession of a .25-caliber pistol. That's what I call clever. You think I'm exaggerating? Well, I'm not. I seem to recall the trial judge in his case referring to **dangerous tendencies** that are present in the German youth of today. Frankly a lot of German teenagers are communists or Nazis and don't even know it yet. Maybe Dr. Gnadenschuss is just one of those: young **Pifke**s the Nazis are working hard to recruit because none of them possesses so much as a vestigial conscience. The ideal Nazi.

"And by the way, you notice I made mention of Paul Krantz owning a .25-caliber pistol. That's because lots of kids in juvenile gangs have them. Forget about knives and saps; a lot of these wild boys own small automatics. It's a status symbol. Like an earring, a good pair of leather shorts, or an old tuxedo. They're a lawless breed bent only on their own lawless pleasure."

"So what are you suggesting?" asked Weiss, fiddling with his immaculate shirt cuffs. He seemed like a study in patience—the very opposite of his more passionate deputy.

"Let's have Schupo round them all up for questioning early one morning. See what we can shake out of their **lederhosen** pockets. If nothing else it will look to the minister like we're doing something. Who knows? Maybe we'll get lucky. It's about time we did. We find one kid in possession of a typewriter that has a misaligned **G** and we're laughing all the way to the falling ax."

"But where are they? These gangs of teenagers?"

"They're easy enough to find. They hang out in encampments in park sites, abandoned warehouses, and old beach huts on the outskirts of Berlin, mostly to the west. Did you know that some of these gangs even call themselves after names in Karl May's novels?"

"How do you know all this, Ernst?" asked Weiss.

"Because there's a fourteen-year-old runaway in a cell over in Charlottenburg who stabbed another gang member in a knife fight. A vicious little queer who thought he was playing bare-arsed Boy Scouts. He just happens to be my brother-in-law's cousin. My sister telephoned to see if I could help him and I told her she could forget it. Help was something he needed a year ago in the shape of a thick ear; now he needs a good lawyer. Besides, I'm a detective, not a damn psychiatrist."

"We had noticed," said Heller.

"So what do you say, boss? Shall we round them up for questioning?"

"I don't like the idea of mass arrests," said Weiss. "It smacks of the Freikorps and the right wing. But if you think it's worth a shot, then let's do it. I'll speak to Magnus Heimannsberg and see when we can arrange it."

"The sooner, the better," said Gennat. "The last thing we need is another letter, let alone another murder."

"Yes, indeed," agreed Weiss. "It's awkward the way this letter puts Kripo on the spot. It makes it harder for us to deflect criticism from both conservatives and communists. I think perhaps I shall have to write a newspaper article for the **Tageblatt** myself. Dr. Gnadenschuss isn't the only one who can command some newspaper space. I'll speak to Theo Wolff."

Gennat looked as if he were about to say something but Weiss silenced him with a raised index finger.

"I know you'll say I should pick a newspaper that isn't run by Jews, but the **Berliner Tageblatt** has a circulation of a quarter of a million. And the others are bound to pick it up. It's high time we persuaded our citizens that they should become the eyes and ears of their own police force. Maybe we can persuade the people to catch Dr. Gnadenschuss for us."

"'Good luck with that' is actually what I was going to say."

"You don't think such a thing is possible?"

Gennat looked momentarily exasperated. "Newspapers are in the business of creating mass hysteria," he said. "They don't give a damn if we catch this bastard. All they care about is stoking fear and spreading panic and selling even more newspapers. You write an article in the paper about Dr. Gnadenschuss, then you're showing the world that we're taking this lunatic seriously."

"What's wrong with that?" asked Weiss.

"It's as good as telling every spinner and nutcase in this city that he'll be taken seriously, too. It was before your time, chief, but the last time the newspapers published a murderer's letter to the editor was the Ackermann case in 1921. There was a press conference then, too, after which we had two hundred people who walked into this police station, each of them claiming to be the murderer. All of whom had to be checked out, of course. It was as if all the metronomes in Berlin suddenly started to swing in time with one another. Not to mention the three copycat murders that followed. In my opinion, public enthusiasm to catch a murderer can hinder progress as much as it can promote it."

"I hear what you say, Ernst. But we can't have it both ways. Public apathy or public hysteria—we have to choose the lesser of two evils here. Yes, I feel we have to do something. At the very least, the honor of the department demands that I answer this man's taunts. And, of course, disabled veterans need to be warned to take precautions, to stay off the streets if they can. Not to mention the fact that we need to mobilize their help as well."

"They're beggars," objected Gennat. "Most of them don't have much choice but to beg on the streets, let alone enough money to buy a newspaper."

"Nevertheless, we're going to need their help," said Weiss.

For the rest of us seated around the table in Ernst Gennat's office, seeing these two men argue was like watching Dempsey versus Firpo, but on the whole it was easier for me to agree with Gennat than with Bernhard Weiss: Gennat was the older dog who knew all the tricks of the trade. Weiss commanded attention, but Gennat commanded respect. Not that I would have commented either way; it certainly wasn't for me to offer my opinion on the arguments of my superiors. Still, I thought it was greatly to Weiss's credit that he tolerated—even encouraged—his deputy's dissenting view, like Wilhelm I and Bismarck perhaps, except that Gennat didn't threaten to resign if he didn't get his way.

But in truth, most of my mind was still back at the Oskar-Helene Home in Zehlendorf. Some of the things I'd seen in that creamy-white building on the edge of leafy Dahlem had left me feeling profoundly depressed and wondering how it was I'd been lucky enough to come through the whole war with a face, two eyes, and four limbs. Almost ten years had passed since the 1918 armistice, but what had happened in the trenches was still powerfully inside my head, as if it had been yesterday. Where did it come from, this sudden recrudescence of horror, this revival of mental anguish and pain that I thought had been long forgotten? For the life of me I couldn't explain it, but seeing all those badly maimed men had brought things flooding back so powerfully I'd barely slept since our visit. Now, whenever I went to bed, I encountered the prologue to a nightmare that was indelibly printed on the inside of my eyelids—grotesquely vivid images of myself back in the trenches, the complete mud-encrusted disaster. In particular there were three silent films that kept coming back to haunt me: my best friend's brains in my hair after a stray bullet from a Lewis gun shattered his skull; a man screaming his last breath into my face, followed by most of his blood and guts; a field surgeon amputating wounded limbs with a guillotine, to save the time a surgical saw would have demanded.

And because of this, ever since our visit to the home, like some shaky neurotic trying to stave off madness, I'd been drinking more than was good or usual for me—with Rankin; with Gennat; with Trettin; but mostly on my own. Whiskey, schnapps, and rum, it was all the same to me. Drinking so that I was always on the edge of being drunk, sucking lots of mint PEZ to try to hide the booze on my breath, and saying very little in case I spoke one adventitious word that would give the game away. But there was no hiding that kind of thing from a man like Ernst Gennat, who knew a bit about drinking himself. After the meeting in his office he took me aside.

"Tell me, Gunther, did you always drink a lot?"

"I don't drink a lot. Just often. And lately, more often than I should, perhaps."

"Why's that, do you think? Is the job getting to you already? It's the most interesting job in the world, but the pressure it creates can break a man."

"It's not the job. At least not directly. The fact is, I've been drinking much more since I visited that damned home for the disabled in Zehlendorf. It awoke all sorts of bad thoughts—things from the war I thought were asleep forever. Being at the home just reminded me of how many had gone. Comrades. Friends. Men I cared about. I still see their faces, you know. Hundreds of them. I heard a car backfire last night and I damned near shit myself. You'll laugh but I saw a ditch today in the Tiergarten and wanted to climb in and get my head down. A ditch looks like somewhere nice and safe. Getting into a glassful of schnapps looks a bit cleaner, that's all."

Gennat nodded and put an avuncular hand on my shoulder. It felt as heavy as a military kit bag. "I don't trust a man who doesn't drink," he said. "It means he doesn't trust himself and I've no use for a man who doesn't trust himself. You can't rely on a man like that. Not in this business. But there's a drink and then there's drinking. One's a cop's good friend and the other's a cop's worst enemy. You know that, of course, otherwise you wouldn't have tried to cover it up with those mints you keep sucking on, not to mention that terrible cologne. And because you know that, you also know it'd be best if you were to try and put the cork back in the bottle, lad. Get over it. Sooner than later. You'll have to try to live with those trench demons of yours without the help of the holy spirit. Because neither I nor the chief has any use for a man who smells like a bar towel at eleven o'clock in the morning."

But as things turned out he was wrong about that.

"WEISS IS QUITE right, you know," said Trettin when, toward the end of the day, he and I were ensconced in the Zum. "If we're ever going to catch Dr. Gnadenschuss we are going to need the help of the city's vagrants and beggars. It stands to reason that one of them must have seen something. But I'm afraid Gennat is also right. Those people don't buy newspapers. And plenty of them don't even speak German, let alone read it. As I see it, there's no point in interviewing them one at a time. That would take too long. So we should go to the barrel and talk to them in number."

"The barrel?"

"That's right."

"What do you mean?"

"You'll see." He looked at his watch. "I think we'll be just in time."

We finished our drinks and then Trettin drove us northwest to Weissensee and parked on Fröbelstrasse, next to the gasworks. A long line of the city's poor, some of them barefoot, were waiting to get inside the building opposite while a couple of SA men did their best to recruit new members for the Nazi Party.

"The Palme," I said. "Of course."

With five thousand beds, the Palme was Berlin's oldest and largest night shelter for the city's homeless. Support was limited to the bare necessities: accommodation in one of the dormitories for no longer than five consecutive nights, disinfection of clothing, access to personal-hygiene facilities, a plate of soup and a piece of bread mornings and evenings. Berliners sometimes called it the pauper's Adlon. It was almost as inaccessible: more than two kilometers northeast of the Alex, it was far enough away from any respectable people that no one could have complained.

"You know, it doesn't matter where you go," I said, "it seems there's a Nazi there ahead of you."

"A brown shirt is at least a clean shirt. But if ever those bastards get into power they'll arrest everyone in this place. Mark my words. They're recruiting homeless men today, but they'll be arresting them tomorrow. On the grounds of being a public nuisance or something like that."

"They can't arrest them all," I said. "Besides, they'd only have to accommodate them somewhere else."

"You think that will stop them? I don't."

"Poor bastards."

"Why? Because they're homeless? Listen, for a lot of them that's the life they've chosen. And the rest are just crazy."

"I don't believe that."

"It's true."

"You're hard enough to ice skate on, Otto, do you know that?"

WHY IT WAS called the Palme, Trettin didn't know for sure.

"It might have been because there used to be a palm tree in the entrance hall," he said. "At least there was back in 1886, when the Palme got started."

"A palm tree? In Berlin? Someone's idea of a joke, perhaps."

He pulled a face. "I agree, that does sound unlikely." He fetched a little tin from his vest pocket and handed it to me.

"What's this?"

"Mentholated camphor. I keep some in my pocket in case I have to attend a police autopsy. Wipe some on your nostrils. It will help with the smell when we're in there."

We left the car and, pushing our way through the line of unwashed bodies, went inside. Trettin had been right about the mentholated camphor. The place smelled like a trench on a hot day. Toothless, gnarled gray faces surrounded us; it was like stepping onto the page of some mildewed engraving of grim metropolitan life.

Trettin led the way to the closed-in admissions

counter, showed the warder his beer token, and asked to see the director.

Five minutes later we were in a large office overlooking the courtyard of the main building. On one wall was a portrait of the Berlin planning commissioner who'd helped found the Palme, and on another a picture of St. Benedict Joseph Labre. The director, Dr. Manfred Ostwald, was a stout man with white hair and very dark eyes; with his stiff collar and morning coat he reminded me of a badger in a children's story. On his desk were several copies of a magazine called **The Tramp;** he said it was published by the International Brotherhood of Vagabonds, which sounded like a joke but wasn't. He listened to our request and then invited us to use a newly installed public address system that, he explained, was connected to a loudspeaker in every one of the Palme's forty dormitories.

"If I might add a word of advice, gentlemen," he said. "Write down what you want to say first. That way you won't repeat yourself and you'll avoid any hesitation while you work out what to say."

"Good idea," said Trettin, and then handed me his copy.

"You want me to read it?"

"You've had more to drink than I have."

"What's that got to do with anything?"

"You're relaxed. I get nervous when I read my wife a story in the newspaper."

"Yes, well, I've seen your wife and that doesn't surprise me. She'd frighten a hyena with a law degree."

Trettin chuckled. "That she would."

After reading our appeal for information under my breath several times, I read it out loud into the microphone, and while we waited to see if anyone would come forward, Dr. Ostwald pressed a glass of schnapps on us, which was brutal of him, but we weren't about to complain. There's nothing like a glass in your fingers to make a line of inquiry seem as if it's going well. Fifteen minutes passed and then Ostwald's secretary knocked on the door to tell him that we had someone who wanted to give us some information. But she also added a name that made her boss hesitate.

"Well, show him in," said Trettin. "That's why we're here, isn't it?"

By now Dr. Ostwald's hesitation was accompanied by a grimace. "Wait, I know this fellow of old," he said. "Stefan Rühle is one of our regulars and a little bit of a troublemaker. Quite apart from the fact that he will want money, he has some eccentric, not to say lunatic, ideas. And by the way, **don't** give him any money, at least not right away, or there'll be another ten just like him in this office. You spend six minutes talking to this man and if you're still in your right mind, then you can tell me I was wrong. Otherwise I'll simply say I told you so."

"We can spare him six minutes," I said. "Even those Nazis outside probably gave him more than that."

"All right. Just remember not to swallow all of what he says. Not unless you want your stomach pumped." Dr. Ostwald waved at his secretary. "Show him in, Hanna, dear."

She went outside and returned trying not to smell the air surrounding the man behind her. He was a shifty, pop-eyed individual, with a cap that looked like it was moss growing on his head, and a jacket that was more grease than wool. Seeing us, he grinned and swung his arms excitedly.

"You the police?"

"That's right."

"If you're the police, where are your warrant discs? I'll need to see some identification before I say anything. I'm not stupid, you know."

I showed him my beer token. "So. Have you got some information for us, Herr Rühle?"

"Stefan. Nobody calls me Herr Rühle. Not these days. Not unless I'm in trouble. I'm not in any trouble, am I?"

"No trouble at all," I said. "Now then. How about it? Have you any information about this man who's been killing disabled war veterans?"

"If I tell you what I know, how can I be sure that you're not going to kill me?"

"Why would we want to kill you?" asked Trettin.

"You'll know why when I give you the information you're looking for. Besides, you're police. That means you have the right to hurt people like me."

Trettin smiled patiently. "We promise not to kill you, Stefan. Don't we, Bernie?"

"Cross my heart and hope to die."

"Sounds like a copper's promise. Which is to say not a promise at all. Maybe if I had a drink. That might help me believe you're sincere."

I looked at Ostwald, who shook his head.

"If you tell us something interesting then we'll take you out for a beer," said Trettin. "As many beers as you like if we get a name."

"Don't like beer. Schnapps. I like schnapps. Same as you fellows. I can smell it on your breath."

"All right. We'll buy you a schnapps. Until then, why not have a cigarette?" Trettin opened his case and let Rühle help himself to several. He put them in his pocket for later.

"Thanks. Well, then, to business, as you say. The man who is killing these war veterans is a copper, like you. I know that because I saw him shoot a man."

It was my turn to smile patiently. "Why do you say that?"

"Because it's true. I recognized him. It was a

policeman who killed those men. I saw him do it. And if you ask me, it was an act of mercy."

"Was he wearing a uniform?"

"No."

"Then how did you know he was a policeman?"

"How? I mean, I knew. All right? I'd seen him before. Somewhere. I don't remember where, exactly. But I'm sure that at the time he identified himself as a policeman. This was the same man who shot one of those **schnorrers**."

Rühle spoke in an abrupt, runaway manner, with almost no eye contact, which immediately made me think he was a little unhinged. Most of the time he was staring at the carpet as if there was something in the pattern he found fascinating.

"Yes, but why would a policeman do such a thing?" asked Trettin.

"Oh, simple. Because he probably believes that these men are vagabonds. That they're part of an infectious epidemic that's afflicting this city. Because they are indecent and beneath contempt. That's why he's doing it, for sure. Because beggars force their poverty upon people in the most repulsive way for their own selfish purposes. People will only feel that things are improving in Germany when someone launches a successful action against beggars of all descriptions. That's why he's doing it. I should have thought that was obvious. He's doing it for reasons of urban hygiene. And frankly I agree with him. It's a necessary defensive measure against uneconomic behavior."

"What my colleague was saying," I said, "is that he doesn't believe that a policeman is capable of cold-blooded murder like this."

"Well, that doesn't surprise me. Everyone believes that policemen are a necessary evil. But they are **evil.** They—you—do the devil's work. When a policeman shoots someone because he's committed a crime it's the most cold-blooded murder there is because it's his job, see? He gets paid to do it. There's no emotion or feeling involved. A policeman does that work because we need evil men to do evil work to keep us safe from other evil men. Or so he imagines. But really he does it because the devil told him to. And when he goes home at night he can sleep because he can tell himself that he was only obeying the devil's orders."

"The devil." Trettin sighed and shook his head. It was clear he'd already given up hope of getting any sensible information from Stefan Rühle.

"What did this policeman look like?" I asked.

"He looked like a demon, that's what he looked like. I'm not sure which one. But his face was covered in hair. His eyes were red. And he wore the very finest clothes available to man. As if money was no object. His shoes were like snow. The scepter he carried was the symbol of his power on earth. And his smile was as white as a wolf's. I don't doubt he would have torn out my throat with his teeth if I'd stayed to speak with him. If you have a police artist I will be glad to help him draw the man's portrait."

"I don't think that will be necessary," I said, looking at my watch. The man had had his six minutes. And when finally we managed to get rid of him, Dr. Ostwald looked at me with a twinkle in his eye.

"I told you so."

THE ROUNDUP AND temporary detention of Berlin's wild boys went ahead as planned but revealed very little that was of interest to us in the Murder Commission. Petty crime and general delinquency. Ernst Gennat shrugged off the disappointment. Just because the sweep hadn't found anything didn't mean it wasn't the right thing to do; that was the way he looked at it. Meanwhile, the **Berliner Tageblatt** published the article by Bernhard Weiss and, as predicted, the department was quickly overwhelmed with men—and one lesbian transvestite—who claimed to be Dr. Gnadenschuss. And it was perhaps fortunate for us that almost immediately afterward a fourth war veteran turned up dead and we were able to shoo them all out the door with a warning about wasting police time.

Age thirty-seven, Walther Frölich had been born in Dresden and served with the Third Army's Ninth Landwehr Division as a corporal, winning a second-class Iron Cross. Shot through the spine at Verdun in October 1918 and paralyzed from the waist down; his body was found under the Oberbaum Bridge, near Schlesisches Tor, which was a stone's throw from the Wolfmium factory, its blackened ruins still overlooking the Spree like a modern gate of hell. He'd been shot just once through the head.

IF BERNHARD WEISS still didn't realize that his newspaper article was a mistake, it wasn't very long before he had to.

At Uncle Pelle's Circus in Wedding, there was a famous freak show. Some of its members were actually war veterans, including a man without arms and legs who was billed on the posters as "the human centipede." A couple of days after Weiss's article appeared in the **Berliner Tageblatt,** he received a telephone call at the Alex from this man alleging that Surehand Hank, the celebrated circus marksman, had confessed to being Dr. Gnadenschuss and was now threatening to shoot Weiss. Since Surehand Hank was a known Nazi who often gave shooting lessons to SA members and had been linked to a violently right-wing anti-Semitic organization previously involved in several political assassinations, it was a persuasive-enough profile. Quite how the human centipede made the telephone call was anyone's guess, but Weiss felt obliged to go and check it out himself when his informant insisted that they meet in person. Since the human centipede could hardly come to him, Weiss asked me to drive him to the circus.

The chief's own private car had been chosen for safety: a blue Audi Type K that was easily distinguishable from most other Berlin motorcars by virtue of the fact that it was a left-hand drive. I liked driving it although changing gear with my right hand took some getting used to. The car provided a better view of oncoming traffic and seemed a lot safer than the majority of right-hand-drive cars, an impression enhanced by the fact that beside the driver's seat was a door pocket containing a broom-handle Mauser. That was a good gun, but if I had as many enemies as Bernhard Weiss I think I'd have kept a sawn-off in the car.

Turning out of the Alex courtyard I steered the Audi north and west toward Wedding, and it wasn't long before I realized that the chief was paying attention to every one of the decisions I was making behind the wheel. His eyes were all over my gear changes.

"Does the human centipede have a name?" I asked, missing a gear change.

"Kurzidim, Albert Kurzidim. He says that he's suspected Togotzes from the beginning, but that my article persuaded him he had to call. That's Surehand Hank's real name. Hans Togotzes."

"Haven't been to the circus since I was a boy," I said, missing another gear.

"Are you up to this?" he asked, as we drove up Oranienburger Strasse and then Chausseestrasse.

"Up to what, sir?"

"This. What you're doing now. Driving."

"What are you getting at, sir?"

"What I mean is, are you fit to be behind the wheel of this car?"

"Is there something wrong with my driving, sir?"

"Then let me put it another way: Have you had a drink today?"

"Not since last night," I lied.

"I believe you," he said in a way that made me think he didn't believe me at all. "Gennat mentioned he thought you were drinking too much since we visited that damned disabled home. And I just wanted to say, I understand you, Bernie. Perhaps in a way that Ernst doesn't. In fact I'm sure of it. Ernst didn't see any army service during the war. Not like us. I was the officer in charge of a medical company before becoming a captain in a cavalry unit, and I saw things I never want to see again. As I'm sure you did. And I don't mind telling you that I've had a few drinks myself since we went to the Oskar-Helene. I may even have had a bit of a problem myself a few years ago. There's no shame in this, Bernie. There's even a name for it, these days. Shell shock, or neurasthenia. Did you know there are as many as eighty thousand German veterans still being treated in hospitals for this condition? Men who are every bit as seriously injured as some of those we encountered the other day; but mentally."

Seeing the sign for Uncle Pelle's I turned off the main road and headed along a narrow gravel track between two small cemeteries. The track was lined with poplar trees beyond which could be seen the distinctive candy stripes of the circus big top.

"So take some time off if you need it. As much time as you need. I'd rather have you back in Kripo as a recovering drinker than not at all. Drunk or sober, you're one of the best men I've got."

"Thank you, sir. But I'll be fine."

IT WAS ALL a setup, of course. I might have drunk my breakfast out of a bottle, but there was nothing wrong with my eyesight. Even at thirty meters I could tell that the man emerging from the side of the track with one hand in the air had an MP-18 in the other. The MP-18's thirty-two-round left-side drum-magazine, which resembled the wing mirror on a car, was all too distinctive, not to mention deadly. And as he raised it to fire at us, I swerved to the right, braked hard, pulled Weiss down onto the floor of the Audi, and then reached for the Mauser.

"Stay there," I yelled, and, opening the driver's door, rolled out of the car even as I heard several rounds hit the bodywork, startling the crows but startling me even more. But these were wild shots, since thirty meters was on the far side of what was comfortably in the Bergmann's range; it was a better weapon for clearing a trench at close quarters.

I ran around the back of the Audi, climbed into the cemetery on my left, and, using the wall as cover, ran in the direction of the shooter. Even as I ran I slipped the safety off the Mauser and thumbed back the hammer so that it was ready to use. There was another burst of gunfire and I guessed the gunman must have thought I'd run away and that he now had all the time in the world to finish his attack on the deputy police president; I smelled his cigarette, heard his footsteps on the gravel, and then the unmistakable sound of another magazine being loaded into the machine gun. I was now behind our assailant and so I climbed over the wall again, which is one advantage of a rum breakfast and exactly why they used to give us a tot in the trenches before we went over the top.

The assassin was standing with his back to me about ten meters away, working the bolt action on the machine gun and getting ready to fire again. He was tall, with a workman's cap, a sleeveless pullover, and boots that laced up to the knee. Over his shoulder was a small kit bag containing the used magazine and possibly another weapon. There was little or no time for a fair warning, especially as I had half an idea that there was another man lurking in the undergrowth of the other cemetery, but I tried all the same.

"Police. Put your gun down."

The man threw away his cigarette and turned, and I saw that he was no more than twenty, with a hard, empty face and bright blue eyes that were still full of murderous intent—that much was clear; he was going to shoot if he could. I think he smiled because he had so much more gun in his hands than me. The hot summer sun flashed intermittently through the leaves above our heads, dappling the ground beneath our feet so that it was like standing on a lake, which only added unreality to the reality that confronted us both now. On a perfect summer's day, in a place of almost preternatural quiet, one of us was going to die. He started firing the MP-18 even before he'd aimed it my way, as if he was hoping that might stop me from pulling the trigger on the Mauser, but of course it didn't.

I shot him in the chest and he fell back, still shooting for a second, before he hit the ground like a starfish. I walked toward him carefully, ready to fire again, saw that he was still alive, kicked the MP-18 out of his hand, and then retrieved a Nazi Party badge from his pullover. The heels of his big hobnailed boots shifted as if he was trying to stand, but it was hopeless. He was drowning in his own blood and that was all there was to it; in ten or fifteen minutes he'd have expired, and nothing I nor anyone else could have done would prevent that. But this was of lesser importance beside the continuing danger of our situation: I was already looking around for a second and even a third assassin, as this was how an ambush worked, and since there was little time or inclination on my part for anything other than mercy of the kind practiced by Dr. Gnadenschuss, I put the barrel of the Mauser against the dying man's head, pulled the trigger, and ran back to the car.

Bernhard Weiss was still on the floor of the Audi where I'd left him. He had a Walther in his hand and almost shot me as I jumped into the driver's seat. The engine was still running and without further explanation I ground the gear into reverse and accelerated backward down the track before a grenade could be tossed at the car or someone else started shooting. Holding his hat on his head, Weiss stared straight ahead at the body of the man who'd just tried to assassinate him.

"I like your car," I said, trying to improve his spirits.

"For Christ's sake, Bernie, forget about the car; he was going to kill me."

"He would have killed us both. Had to. No witnesses. We were lucky."

"I guess there is no connection with Surehand Hank or the human centipede. Never was. The whole thing was a hoax, cooked up to lure me into a trap."

"I have to tell you I had my doubts. When something's too good to be true it usually is."

"Goddamn, why didn't I see that? What kind of a detective am I if I couldn't spot that?"

"I reckon that's what comes of posting articles in the newspapers. One of your readers decided to offer a critique of your writing."

"That's one way of looking at it."

"It beats a letter to the editor."

At the end of the track I spun the Audi around on the gravel and then steered the car south and east, away from the scene as quickly as possible. Weiss turned around in the passenger seat and pointed through the rear window.

"What about **him**?"

"Who?"

"The gunman, of course. Maybe he's still alive."

I didn't answer.

"Is he still alive?"

"I sincerely hope not."

"What do you mean?"

"He's dead, chief. I made sure of that. But right now that's hardly our concern. He might have some partners. These cowards usually do. That's how they killed Rathenau. And Erzberger. In armed groups of two. I don't figure you'll be safe until we're back at the Alex." I stamped on the accelerator, hoping the speed would reduce Weiss to silence. It didn't.

"We can't just leave him there."

"Can't we? That's what he'd have done to us."

"But we're not like that."

"No?"

"We're police, which means we should stop and telephone this in."

"If you take my advice you'll say nothing about this to anyone except your car mechanic. You chose a left-hand-drive car for the sake of your safety; now you have to listen to me and do what I say for exactly the same reason."

"That's not possible."

"Isn't it?"

"I'm the head of Kripo, Bernie. The deputy

police president. And a lawyer. An officer of the court. I can't leave the scene of a crime even if I am the intended victim. It wouldn't be right. And it certainly wouldn't be legal."

"There's only you and me know about this, chief. Why not keep it that way?"

"What are you talking about, Bernie? You know very well we can't do that."

"Look, chief, do you want to be in the evening newspapers? Do you really want your wife and daughter to know that someone tried to murder you today? Is that what you want? Because the minute we report this, that's what will happen. You'll never leave home again without Lotte worrying for the rest of the day that something dreadful has happened to you."

Weiss was silent for a moment.

"You're right about that much, anyway," he said eventually. "Ever since Otto Dillenburger assaulted me, my daughter Hilda's been begging me to resign from the force. My wife hasn't said anything about it but I know she agrees."

"And another thing: leaving that body there for his friends to find is a clear message to these nationalist bastards. After all, they don't know that it was me who shot him and not you. Maybe now they'll think twice about trying to kill you again. Maybe they'll think you're tougher and more ruthless than you look. There's all that and the fact that you don't know what the Nazis will make of it in their newspapers if you report exactly what happened. Who knows? Maybe they'll find that poor boy back there had a mother and a sister, and that he sang in a church choir and was kind to little animals, and that he didn't stand a chance against us. That he only meant to scare you. Maybe someone like Goebbels will call him a martyr and write a poem about what a great Fritz he was and how a dirty Jew helped shoot him down like a dog."

"You don't know that he was a Nazi."

"Don't I?"

I handed Weiss the party badge I'd pulled off the dead man's pullover.

"And just in case you thought I'm only thinking of you, chief, here's another thing. You make this thing public and it's not only you that's on a Nazi death list. It's me, too. Maybe you're used to it by now, being a Jew and all. But I've got enough to worry about seeing snakes in my boots, with the booze. The last thing I want is to have to look over my shoulder as well."

Weiss was silent until we reached the safety of the Alex. I parked the car in the central courtyard, turned off the engine, and lit us each a cigarette.

"And if none of those arguments convince you, then consider this, if you would, sir. You're a decent man and you have my respect and my admiration; but you're also a Jew in Germany, which means that whether you like it or not your people are at war with the Fatherland. Have been since 1893, when anti-Semites won sixteen seats in the Reichstag, including Prussia. In case you've forgotten, that election made the hatred of Jews in this country socially respectable. You may not like it, sir, but you should remember that when you're at war the most important thing is to win at all costs. And by any means. You won't win doing things by the book, sir. You'll only win by being more ruthless than they are, by doing things the Prussian way. By killing them before they kill you."

Weiss took a puff of his cigarette and then looked at the end thoughtfully. "I can't tell you I like what you say, but you're probably right."

"I wish I wasn't, but I am. So. We don't tell anyone. Not the ViPoPra, not your secretary, and not even Ernst Gennat. Although I happen to think he might agree with me."

"He might at that. Although not on much else. He wants you out of the Murder Commission. He thinks I should send you back to Vice. At least until you've stopped drinking. He thinks you're about to crack."

"That's not an unreasonable assumption."

"Are you about to crack?"

"This is Berlin. Who'd notice? But no, I'm not about to crack, chief. I'm hard-boiled, at least ten minutes. I may have had a drink in my coffee this morning, but you didn't see me going to pieces. The way I feel now you could write the works of Goethe on my shell with a fountain pen without putting a hole in me."

"You saved my life. I won't forget that. If it hadn't been for you, I'd be dead and my wife, Lotte, would be a widow. **A sheynem dank,** Bernie Gunther."

I delved into my jacket pocket and produced a hip flask full of good Austrian rum. I unscrewed the cap and took a large bite off the top that was part nerves and part bravado; I didn't care what Weiss thought about me now. Having just saved his neck I figured I could afford to stick mine out a bit.

"Then here's to your wife," I said. "You get to go home and see her and your family. That's all that matters. You get to go home. That's all that matters for anyone who's a cop in this city."

I handed him the flask and watched him take a drink with hands that looked as unsteady as my turbulent heartbeat. It had been a while since I'd killed anyone. I wondered if I would have shot the assassin a second time if I hadn't already enjoyed a few drinks. When you think about it, sometimes that's all it takes to kill anyone.

—

IT WASN'T A detective's instinct that led me back to the scene of Eva Angerstein's murder off Wormser Strasse so much as my dismay at the ferocious indifference of the authorities to her death and the deaths of the other girls. That as well as a perverse and insubordinate desire to disobey the Ministry's orders in the name of true justice; somehow it's easier to understand what justice amounts to when you've had a drink. Besides, it wasn't like we had a lot of clues to work with in the case of Dr. Gnadenschuss. That's the trouble with random murders and why they're so hard to solve; where there is no connection between murderer and victim, you might as well try to mate a German mastiff and a dachshund.

As it happened not everyone was indifferent to Eva Angerstein's death; at least that was the conclusion I drew from the large bouquet of flowers—twenty-seven white lilies—that someone had left at the foot of the stairs where her body had been found. There was a damp handwritten card on the flowers with a name that was hard to read but the identity of the florist was clear enough: Harry Lehmann's on Friedrichstrasse. Twenty-seven flowers from an expensive florist that was at least four or five kilometers east of Wormser Strasse meant that the buyer was someone close to the dead girl, someone who'd made a special journey to the scene of her murder. I wondered about the number until I remembered Eva Angerstein had been twenty-seven years old, which seemed to indicate the buyer was **very** close to the dead girl. We'd tried and failed to trace Eva's next of kin. Not that I was surprised at this outcome; most girls who went on the sledge lost contact with their families, for obvious reasons. So I was keen to speak to the person who'd bought these flowers and decided to look in at Harry Lehmann's on my way back to the Alex. Twenty-seven white lilies was the kind of order that would be easy to remember.

I went back up the stairs and was met by a man wearing a blue pinstriped suit with lapels like halberds, a bowler hat, and leather gloves. He was carrying a thick cane, his fair hair was longish, and the lines on his red forehead were so deep they looked as if they'd been carved there by a glacier. It was obvious he'd seen me looking at the flowers.

"Can I help you with something?" he asked.

"Not unless these are your flowers," I said, facing him now. He was about fifty and a Berliner; his accent was as thick as Stettin soot.

"Who wants to know?"

I showed him my beer token and his eyes narrowed.

"You don't smell much like a cop."

"I'll take that as a compliment, shall I?"

"What I mean is, I could put a match to your breath and torch this whole damn neighborhood. That's what I mean. Most cops I've met at this time of the morning are still digesting their first coffee."

"Who are you? The local insurance man?"

He nodded over my shoulder down the stairs. "You're investigating Eva's death?"

"That's right."

"From the Murder Commission?"

I nodded. "Try it sometime. We see a lot of dead bodies in various stages of disrepair. And we like a drink to edit some of that shit out. It helps keep us sane, if not always sober."

"I can imagine."

"I hope not, for your sake, Herr—?"

"Angerstein."

"Eva's father?"

He nodded.

"I'm Sergeant Gunther, Bernhard Gunther, and I'm sorry for your loss."

He nodded again, barely hanging on to his composure. "They cremated her before I even knew she was dead."

"We tried our best to trace the next of kin."

"Not that you'd have found me. I've been away." He glanced around pugnaciously as if trying to decide if he should punch the wall or me. "According to the locals they haven't seen many cops down here since the night Eva was killed. So what brings you back?" His voice was more animal than human, all bared teeth and smoked tonsils.

"I'm looking for something."

"Mind telling me what?"

"I'll know it when I see it. Something I didn't see before, perhaps. Until then, I don't mind telling you at all. The job's like that, Herr Angerstein. Like playing the tray game, you know? You keep on looking at it, then maybe later on, you'll remember an object that you missed the first time."

"Eva wasn't a whore, you know. At least not full-time. She had a good job. I just want you to know that." He took out his wallet, found a fifty-mark note, and tucked it into my breast pocket like a handkerchief. "Find her killer, son, clear her name, and there's more where that came from. A lot more if you let me deal with him myself."

I removed the crushed note and handed it back to him. "It's rum I have on my breath, Herr Angerstein, not greed. So thanks, but I can't take this. If I did, then you'd start to think I owed you something. You might feel sore about your fifty if I don't catch the killer."

"Not catching him. Is that a possibility?"

"It's always a possibility when the killer doesn't leave a name and address."

"Catch the bastard who killed her and I'll give you something else. Something better perhaps."

"There's nothing I want from you."

"Sure there is. You're a copper, aren't you? You catch him and you clear her name and I'll give you the name of the man who burned down the Wolfmium factory. That's fifty murders solved in one fell swoop. Maybe more—the final death toll isn't in yet. I'll give you his name and I'll give you his address and I'll even give you a reason why." He returned the fifty to his wallet. "Think about it. That's the kind of collar that could make your career, son. Always supposing you're interested in that kind of thing. The way you smell today, I'm not so sure about that."

"What makes you think it was murder?"

"Let's just say that I move in the kind of circle that occasionally overlaps yours. Or perhaps I should say, the kind of ring."

The rings were professional criminal gangs, mostly in the north of Berlin, of which there were a great many, all with names, strict codes of conduct, and sometimes distinctive tattoos. Organized crime, German style. There wasn't much professional crime in Berlin they didn't have a finger in. They were powerful, too, with an influence that extended all the way into the Reichstag. I'd once seen the funeral of a ring leader, a gangster called Long Ludwig, and you'd have been forgiven for believing the Kaiser himself had died.

"Which one?"

"Now, that would be telling and I've told you enough for now. But I'll tell you a lot more if you get a result, Gunther. If you find this bastard."

"Fair enough."

"What's fair got to do with anything? If there was any fairness in this world my little girl would still be alive." He lit a cigarette and smiled a crocodile sort of smile. "**Fair,** he says. Listen, son, this country—and this city in particular—are full of shit. And the shit keeps on piling up around our ears. Communists, Nazis, Junkers, Prussians, military men, pimps, drug addicts, perverts. You mark my words, Gunther, one day there's going to be nowhere clean left for anyone to stand on and we'll all be in the shit."

And with that he walked off.

I'd walked the length and breadth of the courtyard when a man arrived with a barrel organ and started to play "The Happy Wanderer," except it sounded about as happy as a wander across a field in Flanders. But some women came out of a door and started to dance with each other as if they were in a ballroom. The ballroom of Berlin, that's what it was. With men in short supply, older women who wanted to dance were obliged to dance with each other. I had another look inside the coal bunker and inside the bole of the tree where I'd found Eva's purse, but there was nothing.

Some kids were playing with a cripple-cart, which reminded me that it was probably the same one I'd seen abandoned on Wormser Strasse the night Eva Angerstein had been killed. Then, it had meant nothing; now, since Dr. Gnadenschuss, it perhaps meant something. Why had the cart been abandoned in the first place? How would the disabled man who'd once used it have got around Berlin without it? A cart like that represented not just a means of transport but also a way of making a living. Just seeing it again begged all kinds of questions.

I walked over to the kids, showed them my beer token, and confiscated the cripple-cart before shooing them off; I could more kindly have bought it from them, I suppose, for the price of a couple of ice creams, but I was feeling a little short. Turning down Angerstein's fifty hadn't been easy for a man like me.

I took the cripple-cart and examined it. There seemed to be nothing remarkable about it; it was made of wood, with a worn leather seat and four wheels taken off an old pram. It was only very gradually that I began to see things a little differently. The platform, which was meant for a legless man, was actually an artfully designed box on wheels, about forty centimeters deep, so that its occupant might have sat back on his haunches and presented his knees to the world as if they'd been the stumps of severed legs. The more I looked at the cart, the more I began to understand that the person using it hadn't been a cripple at all but a swindler, a yokel catcher, a **zhulik,** a man posing as a disabled veteran for gain. There was a name painted on the inside, **Prussian Emil,** which sounded like an underworld name, the kind Angerstein might have used himself. I decided to speak to the disabled veterans I'd seen begging outside the station on Wittenbergplatz.

IT WAS TOO early for the whores, but the sausage salesman was in the station entrance and he waved me over.

"Hey, copper, I was hoping I'd see you again. I remembered something that might be useful to you. That girl who was scalped. The one who used to buy snow from me. Eva something. Couple of times she had a Fritz with her. Not a client, though."

"How do you know he wasn't?"

"He was queer, that's how I know. Eva said his name was Rudi something. Geise, I think. That's it, Rudi Geise. He came on his own a couple of times with a boy who looked like a girl with a prick and bought some dope himself. Said he worked at UFA Babelsberg and that some of the movie stars liked a bit of a lift when they were filming. Which was why he usually bought a lot of stuff from me. And carried quite a bit of money in his pocket. I asked him if it was safe carrying so much coal and he showed me a knife inside his coat. Not just any knife: a big fixed blade about twenty centimeters long, with a cross guard. Like he was planning to skin a bear or something. Said it was for show. But I don't think it was the kind of show they have at the Wintergarten, know what I mean?"

"Yes, indeed. Thanks for the tip."

"What's with the wheels?"

"I was looking for the two legless wonders I saw here the last time."

"Cops moved them on. For their own safety. Because of this killer who's been preying on them."

"Any idea where they went?"

"You could try outside the aquarium. That's a popular pitch. Safer there, too. At least that's what the Schupo men said."

"How'd they work that out?"

"No trains there. Not much noise to cover the sound of a gunshot. Just the occasional bark of a sea lion."

STILL CARRYING THE cripple-cart I walked north up Ansbacher Strasse and onto Kurfürstenstrasse, at the western end of which was the recently built zoo and aquarium. The two disabled veterans I was looking for were on either side of the main entrance, each positioned under the relief of one of the ancient animals that embellished the exterior. Farther down the street was a life-size iguanodon. There was something about it that reminded me of the Reichsadler, the red-legged German imperial eagle; maybe it was the dinosaur's beak-like snout, but it might have been the fact that both the iguanodon and Germany's empire were extinct.

As well as being a dual amputee, the first man I spoke to was blind and a bit deaf, which made asking questions a more or less pointless endeavor; it seemed unlikely that he would have seen or heard anything of much interest to me. But the other man—a veteran staff sergeant with one leg and a pair of polished wooden crutches who was sitting underneath the stegosaurus relief—looked like a better bet. He was wearing a field cap with the canvas camouflage strip—safer than the previous red, and the transitional gray tunic that was typical of men from the early part of the war. On his remaining foot, he wore an ankle boot with puttees—a lot more comfortable than jackboots; the ribbon on his tunic was for the Prussian second-class Iron Cross, worn, correctly, in the second buttonhole, which was usually the quickest way of telling if a man was faking it. He had a thick white mustache that resembled a couple of sleeping polar bears, the kind of bright blue eyes that belonged in a German jeweler's shop window, and two well-tanned ears that were almost as large as the Metzger biscuit tin now functioning as his begging bowl. I dropped several coins into the tin and then squatted down beside him. I lit a couple of Salem cigarettes and handed him one.

"I hope you're not here to feel sorry for me," he said.

"I'm not even going to try, sarge."

"Or tell me I'm a disgrace to the uniform."

"You're not. Any fool can see that. You get around the city much?"

"Like a Canada goose. What do you think?"

"No, I can believe it."

"You believe that, you believe anything, which is unusual in a cop. Listen, me and Joachim, my friend over there, we've already been moved once today. We're not about to get up again."

"I am a cop. But I don't intend trying to move you on. Besides, I don't imagine you're so easy to move when you don't want to move."

"So I guess you want to talk about Dr. Gnadenschuss."

I pointed to his companion. "What about him?"

"He doesn't talk so well. Not since he got a

bullet through his windpipe. But I don't mind talking. I don't mind talking at all."

"You're not afraid of Gnadenschuss?"

"Were you in the trenches yourself, young man?"

"Yes."

"Then you already know the answer to that question. Besides. I'm not going to die today. I can't."

"You seem very sure about that."

"They say that on the day you die you see your name written on the Spree. And since I already looked this morning, I'm not at all worried. I'd say I'm certain to outlive this government, wouldn't you?"

He had a little tin mug on a piece of string that was tied to one of his crutches, into which I poured a generous measure of rum, before offering him a toast.

"I'll drink to that."

He took the drink and I sipped from my flask.

"Anyone wave a .25-caliber automatic in your direction, lately?"

"No."

"Anyone else you know report anything like that?"

"No."

"What about abuse? Respectable-citizen outrage. Get any of that?"

"Plenty. Just the other day I got bawled out by some right-wing prick who thought I was a disgrace to the uniform. And once or twice from some kids. Queers from up west." He smiled. "These days, I come prepared for almost anything." From his puttee he drew a trench dagger, which had been meant to replace an off-duty soldier's bayonet. "I used to say to myself, 'How low can you get?' Then, in Berlin, I found out. What's that you've got there, anyway? Looks like some Fritz's **klutz** wagon."

"That's exactly what it is. I found it abandoned on Wormser Strasse just a short way south of Wittenbergplatz. There's a name inside it. Prussian Emil. I was wondering if you knew who he was, and maybe why he might have left it behind."

"The who is easy. Prussian Emil is a drug dealer, a burglar's **achtung**—his lookout—and a very occasional beggar, for the sake of appearances. He carries a bugle and gives the brass a blow if the owner or the police should unexpectedly show up while the burglary is still in progress. He was in the army and was nearly shot for desertion, but he's not crippled, which is one reason genuine beggars like me haven't managed to put a stop to him; the other is that he's a member of a ring. Only don't ask me which one. He usually gives genuine **schnorrer**s like me a few marks to help keep us sweet. But supposing we were to inform on him to the local police or take the law into our own hands—assuming we could get near him—then we'd soon find the ring had something to say about it. The why is pure speculation. If he abandoned that **klutz** wagon, the chances are he was obliged to leg it for some reason. Come to think of it, it's a while since I saw him around."

"Does he work with one man in particular? Or just anyone who pays?"

"Anyone who pays, I think."

"Can you give me a description?"

"I'll say one thing for him, at least, he looks like the real thing. Standard 1910 uniform with Swedish cuffs. Brown corduroy trousers. If you asked him he'd swear he was with the 248th Regiment from Württemberg. That's deliberate and clever because he knows that if he was wearing a Prussian military uniform, there's always a chance he might run into trouble in this town. Also a Charlotte Cross ribbon and a silver military merit medal. Dark glasses, which make him look like he's blind. Of course, that's when he's working. When he's not working, he's thin, painfully thin. Cadaverous, even. And completely hairless. Oh, and he has a port-wine stain on his neck, like a careless waiter spilt something down his shirt collar."

"You know where I could find him? Or just look for him?"

"No. Besides, for a drink, a cigarette, and a few coins, I think you did pretty well out of me, copper."

"Would it make any difference if I put some paper in your box?"

"Probably not. Look, there's a club called Sing Sing, like the American prison. They say they've even got an electric chair, just for laughs. You could look for him there, if you dare. It's the kind of place you need a steel undershirt. Just don't say I mentioned it."

I nodded and started to walk away. "There's a password to get in," he added. "That has to be worth a couple of marks."

I put a couple of notes in his hand and he saluted me and told me the password.

"It was nice talking to you," I said. "If you think of anything else, my name is Bernhard Gunther and I'm at the Alex."

"Sergeant Johann Tetzel."

ERNST ENGELBRECHT HAD left the Berlin police but he was frequently to be found behind his regular table at the Zum, in the arches of the S-Bahn station near the Alex. It was an atmospheric place. The owner, Lothar Kuckenburg, was an ex-cop and he'd decorated the walls with photographs of Schupo men and police athletic clubs. In pride of place, next to the till, was a picture of Lothar shaking hands with a previous Schupo commander, Hugo Kaupisch. Until he'd left, Engelbrecht had been an expert on local crime syndicates, and figuring he still was, I'd sought him out to ask what he knew about Angerstein. He might have disliked Jews and, of course, one Jew in particular, but he and I got on well enough and he never seemed to mind me picking his brains; indeed he always seemed to welcome it.

"Bernhard Gunther," he said.

"Buy you a beer?"

"Sure. I'll take a beer. And maybe an explanation."

"About what?"

"The Schrader-Verband. What were you doing there?"

"I pay my dues."

"Yes. But there's the Schrader-Verband and then there's a drinks party with the right wing of the Schrader-Verband. They're very different things. One's a union and the other's a new way of looking at things."

"Maybe I wanted to hear Arthur Nebe talk before I made up my mind about that."

"And?"

"I'll take a drink with more or less anyone. Listen to anyone, anywhere. Work with anyone if it gets the job done. But when it comes to politics, I'm a natural independent."

"Fair enough. But very soon that will be a luxury you can't afford."

"I'm a cop. There are lots of luxuries I can't afford. But that doesn't include principles."

"You know there are financial advantages for a cop in Berlin to be allied with the Nazis. A cop like you for instance. Expenses. Walking-around money."

"Cops get paid to take risks not money."

"Oh sure, but this isn't a bribe. This is just a top up. I could speak to someone and work something out for you. A little dash of raspberry sauce in your beer, you might say."

"I never did like the taste of that. I like my beer just the way it comes out of the tap. Talking of which."

I went to the bar and brought back some beers.

"So what can I do for you, Bernie?"

"Tell me about the rings. And Herr Angerstein."

"Any particular reason you mention him?"

"No reason other than he's a gangster. Last I heard it's men like him who are our client base."

"There are at least eighty-five underworld clubs in Berlin," he told me. "Strictly speaking, Angerstein—his given name, by the way, is Erich, in case you're wondering—isn't a member of any of them, for the simple reason that he's part of a syndicate that supervises a large number of these clubs. The Middle German Ring. They impose rules on the clubs, control their activities, and exact a financial tribute that is supposed to provide legal assistance for club members. I haven't met him myself; he's very private. But from what I've heard, he's to be feared, the kind of man other criminals would obey without question. That makes him very dangerous. Every year he hosts a banquet for the clubs at the Eden Hotel and over a thousand men and women attend. Even a few cops are invited. The Middle German maintains good relations with all the top police councilors and quite a few politicians. Which makes him a man of some influence. If you're planning to have any dealings with him, son, be careful. That man has very sharp teeth."

"Thanks. I'll bear it in mind."

"Almost as sharp as Arthur Nebe's."

"Why should that worry me?"

"Just don't get too independent, Bernie. When a cop gets too independent he's got no friends. And when he's got no friends, his luck runs out."

"AND WHERE THE hell have **you** been, Gunther?"

Ernst Gennat was wearing a new suit, but his temper was badly frayed. His eyes were bloodshot and restless, his face was red, and there was a whole shingle beach of sweat on his brow. As usual his pink fists were raised in front of his substantial belly, as if he was ready to fight someone off: me perhaps. His rasping, bass tenor voice was sounding just the one note, a sour one, as if he'd been gargling with vinegar.

"I've been looking for you, Gunther. According to your diary you should be here. And you weren't. You know the way we work. If you're out on a case you're supposed to write it up on the chart outside my office. So that I can keep track of you bastards. At least that's the theory."

"Sorry, boss. I was scratching an itch. I wanted to take another look at the place where Eva Angerstein's body was found."

"Drinking in a bar more like. And didn't you hear the chief's order? We're to lay off the Winnetou cases until we've caught Dr. Gnadenschuss. Besides, Winnetou hasn't killed in a while."

"You noticed that, too? As a matter of fact, he hasn't killed since Dr. Gnadenschuss started work. Maybe that should tell us something."

"It tells me you're not listening to the orders. Now, listen—no, don't interrupt, this is important—I want you to equip yourself with a criminalistics kit and then get over to the Mosse building in Friedrichstadt. Apparently the **Tageblatt** has received another letter from Dr. Gnadenschuss, and this time a medal, too. There's a fingerprint on the letter and I want you to go and take a look at it before the world and his dog have contaminated any possible evidence. Ask for the editor in chief, Theodor Wolff. He's expecting you. And for Christ's sake suck some mints before you speak to him. Your breath smells like a brewery."

"None of the other papers have received it?"

"Not as far as I'm aware."

"Can I take a car from the pool?"

"No. Take the tram. It's quicker at this time of day. And probably safer for a soak like you. Then, as soon as you're back here, I want you to interview some of these spinners who've walked in off the streets to claim responsibility for the Gnadenschuss murders. We've got at least five of them locked up in the cells right now." He shrugged. "One day someone in this department is going to listen to me when I advise against doing something."

I caught a number 8 from Alexanderplatz going west to Potsdam Station, where I got off and walked northeast. The Mosse publishing group owned a stable of magazines and newspapers, of which the **Berliner Tageblatt,** with a daily circulation of a quarter of a million, was easily the most important. Even if you didn't buy it, nearly everyone in Berlin, including me, managed to read the **Tageblatt;** it was essential reading for anyone of a vaguely liberal disposition and only the fact that the paper's owner—Hans Lachmann-Mosse—and editor—Theo Wolff—were both Jews probably prevented Germany's conservative right wing from reading it, too.

The building where the Mosse group was headquartered was more like a fortress, complete with rusticated walls, enormous iron-bound oak gates, and stone balustrades, which probably explained why it had been taken over and fortified by the right-wing Freikorps during the Spartacist uprising of 1919. It was even said that several left-wingers had been executed in the courtyard where now there were dozens of bicycles awaiting the men who would deliver the papers to all corners of the city. Stacked nearby were several giant rolls of newsprint. Just to see the place was to conclude that a free press in Germany was something that needed to be defended at all costs.

I showed my warrant disc to the burly doormen at the castle gates and an elevator carried me to the upper floor where the **Tageblatt** was put together. In the enormous reception area, a messenger boy took my name and then went to find someone while I sat down on a bench along the back wall and amused myself by watching brass capsules drop out of a pneumatic tube into a net next to the main door. It made being a journalist look a lot easier than being a detective. Eventually the boy returned and led me down a long hall in which a whole crowd of trolls, gnomes, and goblins might have paid court to some urban mountain-king.

Theo Wolff was almost as powerful, I suppose. As well as founding a political party—the

DDP—Wolff had once refused the post of German ambassador to Paris, preferring to remain in journalism, which said a lot for his belief in the importance of newspapers in Germany. He was about sixty, small and pugnacious, and he viewed my arrival in his office with no more enthusiasm than if I'd belonged to the anti-Semitic Hugenberg publishing group. I may have worked for Bernhard Weiss, but the Berlin police wasn't exactly known for its liberal views.

Also around his editorial table were a number of men whose names were more familiar than their faces: Rudolf Olden, Ernst Feder, Fred Hildebrandt, Kurt Tucholsky, and, most famously, Alfred Kerr.

I shook hands with Wolff, nodded at the others as he made the introductions, and then pointed at the letter, which lay flat on the table in front of him, next to the envelope it had arrived in, the medal it had also contained, and a typewriter that someone had probably already copied it on.

"Is that it?"

"Yes."

"How many people have handled this, sir?" I asked.

"Three, I should think. The postboy. My secretary. And me. As soon as I saw what it was I called the Alex."

I put on the surgeon's rubber gloves I'd brought

from the Alex and pulled a pair of tweezers from my pocket. I drew the letter carefully across the table, sat down, and checked that it had been typed on a machine with the capital letter **G** printed to the right. Then I read it to myself.

Dear Editor,

I am the killer of Walther Frölich over by Oberbaum Bridge. I shot him just once through the forehead with a Browning .25-caliber automatic pistol. To prove this, here is the medal I removed from the dead man's tunic and a lock of bloodstained hair I cut from the back of his skull. This gives you an excellent indication of how much time I had to carry out this murder and how little I was concerned that I might be apprehended by the police. They can check the blood type on the hair, and the brooch-back Iron Cross first class, and they will know that I am telling the truth. I am the same man who killed the other three parasites, who also called themselves disabled veterans. And I am enjoying myself.

You could easily help put a stop to this, of course. You need only publish an editorial calling on the government to remove these rats and lice from our streets. If they heed your words and do this—might I suggest that these vermin all be arrested and taken somewhere outside the city and disposed of hygienically; or accommodated in special camps or hospitals, perhaps? This would render our capital city's streets fit for patriotic Germans to walk in. At the present moment it's impossible to take any pride in a country where there are so many living reminders of our national shame begging for coins on every street corner.

One day Germany will thank me for prompting it to clean up our cities. When I am done with Berlin's cripples I will perhaps move on to some others I have on my little list; yes, I have a little list—pestilential nuisances we wouldn't really miss. Gypsies perhaps. Street urchins. Whores. Freemasons. Communists. Or queers—they certainly wouldn't be missed. I shall certainly enjoy killing them, too.

Meanwhile, the police are not going to catch me, but please understand that this is not arrogance on my part; it isn't that I am too clever for them, but that they are too stupid. The Murder Commission run by the Jew Bernhard Weiss has a great deal in common with my victims in that it is crippled and has already outlived its usefulness; indeed, you might think that Bernhard Weiss had a hole in his own head the way he goes about running that department. The self-serving article he wrote for your newspaper was as badly written as it was ill-advised.

Mark my words: All that his so-called journalism will succeed in doing is giving the police a lot more work as they attempt to deal with those misguided Berliners who wish to take false credit for my work. Take my advice and don't give him any more space in your paper.

But to prove to you how useless Kripo is I am providing you with a very nice thumbprint—mine!—so that the fingerprint people at the Alex can spend a great deal of time trying to match this with something they already have on file. This will be in vain, of course, for the simple reason that I am not a criminal but a patriot. Long live Germany.

Heil Hitler.

Yours,
Dr. Gnadenschuss

"Where's the lock of hair?"

"Still in the original envelope," said Wolff. "Untouched by anyone around this table. The letter was posted in Humboldthain."

"Are you going to print this?" I asked.

"We're a newspaper. Not a church magazine. And that's front-page news."

"I'll take that as a yes, shall I, sir?"

"I can see that you don't think we should print it. But this is Germany. Not Soviet Russia. Unlike the Bolsheviks we don't practice press censorship in this country. It's what makes our readers know they can trust the **Tageblatt.** News is news. The minute we start deciding on what news we choose not to print, then people might as well subscribe to **Pravda.**"

"That's a nice speech, sir. And on the whole I agree with it. All I'm asking is that you delay printing the letter until we've had a chance to read and digest it. To give us time to check this fingerprint. In case that or something else here gives us a lead."

"How long would you suggest?"

"Seventy-two hours."

"Twenty-four."

"Forty-eight."

"Thirty-six."

"Agreed."

"Anything else?"

"Yes. If you don't mind, maybe you could leave out the make of the gun and the fact that it was an automatic. It's important for us to know just a little more than your readers. That's fair, isn't it?"

"Agreed," said Wolff. "What about that fingerprint? Think it's genuine?"

"Oh, it's a genuine fingerprint, all right. The question is, who does it belong to? Emil Jannings, Gösta Ekman, or Werner Krauss; Hindenburg perhaps. But I'll stake my life on the fact that it doesn't belong to the good doctor. I've got a feeling this fellow likes wasting police time the way the Nazis like beating drums and waving flags."

I picked the letter up with the tweezers and carefully slid it into a thin manila file: I repeated the procedure with the enclosing envelope and the medal before glancing around the smoke-filled room and asking myself a question. I knew what I thought about the letter, but I was curious what they thought.

"I'm not often in such illustrious company," I said. "I wonder if any one of you distinguished gentlemen might care to speculate on why someone would do something as heinous as killing four disabled men? What's his motive?"

"Seriously?" said a voice.

"Of course."

"Now?"

"Now, this minute, yes. If you can do it sooner I'd appreciate it. Look, thousands of people already pay attention to your daily opinions. So why not give me the scoop on your thinking. On what you're going to write in the paper. I'm a reader. But I'm also a listener."

"He sounds quite intelligent," said someone.

"He means the killer," said someone else. "Not you, sergeant."

I smiled at the general laughter that followed this remark. "I'm not very handsome, either.

Next time I'll comb my hair, brush my teeth, wear a clean shirt, and bring a nice sharp pencil."

"You're rather assuming Dr. Gnadenschuss doesn't actually believe the reasons he provides in his letter," said Wolff.

"I'm a cop, there's a lot I don't believe. I think that letter is just him ringing a few bells at the funfair. That's right. The ones he thinks people like us want to hear. Frankly, I'm not convinced by any of that monkey talk."

"Surely you're just saying that to undermine our resolve to publish it," said Wolff.

"No, not even if I thought I could. But I've heard this kind of political testament before. It's the sort of crap that people write when they're pulling a stretch in Landsberg Prison."

"He signs off with **Heil Hitler.** That's all we need to know, isn't it? Surely it's obvious the murderer's a Nazi."

"Exactly," said another man.

"That's certainly what he'd like you to believe," I said. "Only, I do wonder why he sent his letter only to a Jewish-owned newspaper. So far as we know, none of the other papers has received it. And let's face it, gentlemen, it's not like he's preaching to the choir here. I imagine none of you believes in ridding this city of disabled beggars at the barrel of a gun."

"No, of course not."

"So I'd say he sent this letter to you because you printed the article by Bernhard Weiss and because you'll believe this latest letter **was** written by a Nazi. And because it suits your agenda to print a murdering Nazi letter, doesn't it? But you should ask yourself this: Do you think the **Völkischer Beobachter** or **Der Angriff** would publish this letter? Or any of the newspapers in the Hugenberg publishing empire?"

"That's a fair question," said Wolff.

"And what's the answer?"

"I suspect they would not publish it."

"You're not a Nazi yourself, are you, sergeant?" asked Wolff.

"I guess you didn't understand my joke about Landsberg Prison."

"It's only that you seem a little anxious for us to believe it might not be a Nazi who wrote the letter."

"Anxious, no, sir. I want the truth, that's all. The first letter contained no references to Bernhard Weiss's Jewishness. Which for a Nazi shows a degree of restraint that's hardly typical."

"He's got a point."

"This new letter mentioned his Jewishness only once. And not in any really poisonous words, which would be more usual."

"What are you saying, sergeant?" asked Wolff.

"I'm not sure, sir. Right now all I have are

questions and not enough facts. That kind of journalism might be good enough for **Der Angriff,** but not for the newspapers I like to read."

"I'm just the theater critic," said a bald, horse-faced man with a Charlie Chaplin mustache. This was Alfred Kerr, perhaps the most famous writer working for the **Tageblatt.** "But in answer to your question about what I'd like to write about this fellow, Shakespeare teaches us that a man like this is probably someone who's been disappointed in life. Who's fallen short of his own expectations. Who desperately wants significance and power. Above all I should say this is a man who knows how to hate. Motiveless malignancy, as Samuel Taylor Coleridge put it when talking about Iago in **Othello.** Yes, there's your problem, sergeant. Quite possibly this man **has** no real motive. It may be that he is someone who simply enjoys wickedness for its own sake. I'm afraid you may be dealing not just with the mystery of whodunit but with the mystery of life itself."

I scratched my head and nodded. "Thank you, sir. I'm certainly glad I asked."

ON MY WAY back to the Alex I stopped in at the Berlin Fire Department to see the chief fire commissioner, Walter Gempp. He was a genial, helpful man of about fifty whose modernization of the fire department and public allegiance to the left-leaning German Democratic Party made him a natural ally of men like Grzesinski and Weiss. Gempp was accompanied by Emil Puhle, the senior fire chief at Linienstrasse and, effectively, Gempp's second-in-command.

"I asked you to come and see me because I heard from Waldemar Klotz that you'd been asking him questions about the Wolfmium factory fire."

Klotz was the fire chief of Company 7, in Moabit. After what Angerstein had told me about the Wolfmium factory fire, I'd telephoned him to ask if there was any evidence of arson.

"That's right, sir." Reluctant to mention that my information about the fire had come from a Berlin gangster, I decided to make less of my interest than there was, especially as I hadn't yet shared these suspicions with Gennat or Weiss.

"Might I ask why?"

"You might say it was a routine inquiry. With at minimum fifty workers dead, I just wanted to check that there was nothing in it for the Murder Commission. Which there would be if there was any evidence of arson."

"Yes, of course. Well, we've found nothing that raises any cause for suspicion. Nothing at all. Our investigating officers are convinced that the fire started in a faulty electrical switchboard. Once the fire got hold, there was every chance of it becoming a disaster. Osmium, which is used in the production of light bulbs, has an oxide—osmium tetroxide—that is extremely flammable. It also produces a highly toxic gas, which is what killed all those people. Indeed, several of my own officers are still recovering in hospital after sustaining respiratory tract injuries. Thirty years after the Schering company fire in Wedding, this city still does not have enough breathing respirators, despite the fact one of my predecessors, Fire Chief Erich Giersberg, died as result of that fire.

"I will say this, Gunther, as someone who is often publicly associated with the DDP, I care very much about the safety conditions for workers in this country. And the workers at Wolfmium were no exception, in spite of their being mostly Russians and Volga Germans. So anything you yourself discover that gives me cause for believing there was any criminal negligence would be of great interest to me."

"I understand, sir."

"For example: I have a relation who's a broker at the Berlin Bourse. And he tells me that in recent months Wolfmium had lost a large contract to Osram, one of their major competitors. And that, before the fire, the price of shares in Wolfmium had halved. I mention that because the Hamburger Fire Insurance Company has just settled the factory owners' claim in the amount of more than a million reichsmarks. Which more than compensates for any losses the owners might have sustained on the stock market. Obviously it's not the sort of thing I'm able to investigate myself, but someone in the police might very well conclude this alone could constitute grounds for further investigation. Wouldn't you agree?"

"Yes, sir. I would."

I WASTED THE rest of the day interviewing a few of the men who'd been inspired by Bernhard Weiss's article in the **Tageblatt** to claim that they were Dr. Gnadenschuss. It was hard to believe Ernst Gennat had been wrong regarding the wisdom of Weiss in writing a newspaper article about the Gnadenschuss murders. I doubt that the Holy Inquisition would have accepted the confessions that came in, and my instinct was to call the lunatic asylum at Wuhlgarten and have these men taken away in straitjackets so that they might be subjected to the old tried and tested cure, which was a half hour under a fire hose. The only one of these time wasters who struck me as sane was the youngest and probably the strangest.

Just fifteen, Sigmar Gröning was a pupil at the Leibniz Gymnasium on Wrangelstrasse, which was about a ten-minute walk from where Frölich's crippled body had been found. He was one of a group of schoolboys who'd discovered the body. Gröning had white-gold hair, pitiless gray eyes, a high forehead, a rather self-satisfied, sneering mouth, and a prominent chin. He was wearing a tailored black jacket, black knickerbockers, long lace-up black boots, a stiff white collar and tie, and a naval-style black cap with a small shiny peak that probably resembled his soul. Bloodless, coldhearted, straight-backed—he was likely everyone's idea of a fallen angel.

Unlike the others I'd questioned, he at least had done his homework and knew all the details of what had been printed in the first letter to the newspapers. In fact, he knew almost as much about the Gnadenschuss killings as I did. But it was immediately obvious to me that he hadn't killed anyone; just as obvious was the fact that he would have liked to kill someone, probably anyone would do. I'd looked enough murderers in the eye to recognize what was lurking inside this young man's skull. After half an hour in the company of this ruthless little monster, I wondered where the country might be going if this was a sample of its youth. I tried to envisage Gröning in ten years' time and concluded that in all probability I was talking to a future lawyer, assuming I didn't throw the book at him for wasting police time.

His father was the manager at the Luisen Theater on Reichenberger Strasse and his middle-class family lived in a comfortable apartment on Belle-Alliance-Platz. Nice people, probably. I wondered what they might say if I telephoned and told them that their son was being questioned at the Alex.

"Do you own a typewriter, Sigmar?"

"I think my father has one. Why do you ask?"

"Do your parents know you're here?" I asked. "Confessing to five murders?"

It was four murders, of course, but he didn't contradict me.

"It's nothing to do with them," he insisted. "And I came here of my own accord. I'm the man you're looking for."

I shrugged. "Why not keep going? Until your confession we were nowhere near catching you. Why quit now when you're making such a good job of running rings around the police?"

Gröning shrugged. "I'm bored with it. And I think I've made my point."

"That you have. That you have. You know, I hate to break it to you, sonny, but they'll probably execute you for this."

"That's a matter of small importance to me."

"To you, maybe. But I would think your mother might be upset to see you sent to the guillotine at Plötzensee."

"Might wake her up a bit. She's horribly complacent. I'm actually looking forward to her having to see my death."

"Only because you've never seen what the falling ax can do. I have. It's not a pretty sight. One time I saw the condemned man—a real skinny-looking Fritz, like you—pull his head back in the lunette, just a couple of centimeters, but enough for the blade to lodge in the skull instead of slicing cleanly through the neck. It was a terrible situation. Took us almost fifteen minutes to get the blade out of his cranium. And all the time this Fritz was still alive, screaming like a pig—it was a real mess. I almost threw up, myself."

"You don't scare me."

"That's what they all say, sonny. But believe me, when they first catch sight of the man in the top hat, they soon change their minds."

I lit a cigarette and leaned back in my chair. "Your father. Let's talk about him, shall we?"

"Must we? I hate him."

"Oh sure. That goes without saying. All fifteen-year-old boys hate their fathers. I know I did. But I would think that his is an interesting job. He must see a lot of plays. In his theater. You, too, for that matter."

"Could I have one of those, please?" he said, nodding at my cigarettes. He placed a hand on the table between us; it was a violinist's hand, slender, delicate, with badly bitten fingernails.

"You're too young to be smoking."

Gröning bit his lip, perhaps irritated he wasn't being treated with the respect he had expected.

"Well, does he? See a lot of plays?"

"Dumb question."

"I guess it was. All right. Let's get to it, Siggy. Why did you kill them? That's more to the point. Wouldn't you agree? I mean, I have to write something on my report to the public prosecutor. It doesn't look good in court if I just write down any old reason. **I killed them because I could and stopped because I got bored.** Nobody will believe you. That is the point of you coming in here and confessing, isn't it? You do want us to believe you, don't you, Sigmar?"

"Yes."

"So why did you do it? Why did you shoot those five men?"

"Like I said in my letter. They're Germany's shame, not to mention a burden on society."

"You don't actually believe that crap, do you?"

"Of course I believe it. Just as I believe that this country has a destiny."

"And you really think Hitler has the answers?"

"I think only he can deliver Germany from its present humiliation, yes."

"Fair enough. You know, I expect this will

make you famous, Sigmar. I can't think of any other fifteen-year-old boys who've killed five people. You'll probably end up a Nazi hero. They seem to admire this kind of decisive action."

"The deed is everything, the glory nothing."

I smiled, recognizing a quote from Goethe's **Faust,** and suddenly I thought I understood exactly what he was doing. I got up and wandered around the room before coming back to him and blowing some smoke in his face. What I really wanted to do was hit him very hard with my fist. To knock some of the arrogance out of him before it was too late—for him and for Germany.

"You know what I think? That you're playing a part. Like an actor playing Faust in your daddy's theater. You've taken on this very difficult and challenging role—the part of a murderer—and you want to play it out, to see how far you can get with it before an expensive lawyer pulls your chestnuts off the brazier and tells the court that your confession is all a pack of lies. You fancy yourself to be a great actor—the next Emil Jannings. Get your name in the paper, and everyone will be impressed that you've pulled this off. That you've convinced those dumb cops you did it. Now, those are real notices that any actor would be proud of."

The boy reddened.

"That's it, isn't it? Look, did someone at school put you up to this nonsense, Sigmar? Or is there someone in the theater you want to impress? A girl perhaps. An actress."

"I don't know what you're talking about."

"Sure you do, sonny. Maybe you think you can beat the rap, like Paul Krantz did. That in spite of your confession people will look at your sweet chorister's face and think it impossible you could have done such a thing. Or maybe you think the worst that can happen is that you'll be charged with wasting police time. Although a good lawyer could probably make that go away, too. 'My client is just a boy, Your Honor. It was all a stupid prank that got out of hand. He's at a good gymnasium and is a promising student. It would be a shame to spoil his chances of his Abitur and going to university by imposing a custodial sentence.'

"So you know what we do with snot-nosed kids like you who waste our valuable time? We let the police dogs have them for a few minutes. That way we can let the dogs take the blame when you get injured. Nobody's about to prosecute an Alsatian for police brutality."

"You wouldn't dare."

"Let's find out, shall we?"

I stood up and took hold of his ear, twisting it hard for good measure. I was tired and pissed off and keen to go home. And much as I would have liked to have left him alone with a police dog, it was time to put a quick end to the whole charade.

"All right, sonny, out you go."

I hauled him onto his feet and dragged him to the door of the interview room, picking up speed as we passed through the main hall. One or two uniformed cops laughed as they realized what was happening; none of us liked time wasters, especially when they were just out of short trousers. Once through the big door, I let go of the **Pifke**'s ear and then kicked his skinny behind, hard.

"And don't come back. Not without a sick note from your mother."

I watched him sprawled on the pavement for a moment and smiled, recalling my own gymnasium days.

"I always thought I should have been a schoolteacher."

"I'D LIKE YOU both to listen to my theory," I told Weiss and Gennat. My office was the size of a goldfish bowl and, walled mostly with glass, just as public. A phone was ringing in the next office, and the hot twilight and the noise of traffic were coming in through the open window.

"A theory," said Gennat. "You need a long gray beard to make one of those sound persuasive in this temple of cynicism, Gunther. Like Feuerbach. Or Marx."

"I can stop shaving if it helps."

"I doubt it. A cop with a theory is like a lawyer going into court with an empty briefcase; he doesn't have a shred of evidence. And that's what matters in this place."

"Not a theory, then. A new interpretation of some facts."

"Still sounds like a theory."

"Just hear me out. Then you can have as much fun as you like picking it apart."

"Let the boy talk, Ernst," said Weiss. "He's been right before."

"I don't wind up my pocket watch and it's still right, twice a day."

I pointed to the cripple-cart I'd brought with me, which now lay on the floor like a child's toy.

"I found this **klutz** wagon at the entrance to a courtyard on Wormser Strasse. On the same night Eva Angerstein was killed."

"I told you to drop that damn case," said Gennat.

"It was previously used by a yokel catcher and burglar's lookout called Prussian Emil. From what I've heard he's not even disabled. He positions himself outside a house that's being turned over by his partner and then blows a bugle if the owner comes back or a cop shows up. I've been wondering why the cart was left abandoned at the scene of Eva Angerstein's murder. So I checked with Commissar Körner. There was a burglary in an apartment on the corner of Bayreuther Strasse on that same night. Just a short way along from the Wormser Strasse courtyard."

"Interesting," said Weiss.

"So what are you saying?" asked Gennat.

"I'm saying that Prussian Emil may have seen the man who killed Eva Angerstein. Maybe even recognized him. And legged it before Winnetou could murder him, too. Since when he's been trying to do exactly that."

"So you're saying that Winnetou is also Dr. Gnadenschuss," said Gennat. "Jesus Christ. Is that your damn theory?"

"That's right. Look, it can't have escaped your attention that Winnetou hasn't struck since Dr. Gnadenschuss started killing disabled war veterans."

"It's nice and neat. I'll give you that. Two murderers for the price of one. They should put you in charge of the shop floor at Teitz."

"It might just be that he's killing them in the hope of eliminating someone who could identify him as Eva Angerstein's killer. Since when, maybe he's developed a taste for it. Maybe he prefers what he's doing now. After all, there was never anything sexual about the Winnetou killings."

"Killing and scalping a girl seems like a very different crime from shooting a **klutz** in the head," said Gennat.

"True. But you said yourself that it was murder

for the sake of it. He enjoys killing and nothing else. That and tormenting the police, of course."

"Maybe Prussian Emil abandoned his **klutz** wagon when the police showed up to investigate Eva Angerstein's murder," objected Gennat. "That seems just as likely, to me. Where does that leave your theory?"

"In tatters," I conceded. "But why suppose yours is the only explanation, when there's at least a possible chain of causation between Winnetou and Gnadenschuss? That's the kind of chain of causation that helps us."

"Or wastes valuable police time."

"You're both right," said Weiss. "And you're both wrong. But that's the true character of police work. Right now we have to work on the assumption that you're both right. I can't think of any other way of advancing this investigation, Ernst. We'll let Gunther run with his theory for a while and see how far it carries us. Any ideas on that, Bernie?"

"There's a club on Chausseestrasse, near Oranienburger Tor. A place called Sing Sing. Prussian Emil has been known to drink there with other members of his ring. I thought I'd go there and see what I can find out."

"Bar work." Gennat laughed. "I might have known. Just up your street, I'd have thought."

"That used to be the Café Roland," said Weiss. "I've never been there myself but I've heard about it. The headwaiter is a loan shark called Gustav. Wasn't a Schupo man found dead near there, a year ago?"

"On Tieckstrasse," said Gennat. "But it was an accident. Live wire underneath the pavement electrocuted him when he walked through a deep puddle after some heavy rain."

"I have a question that potentially undermines your theory, Bernie," said Weiss. "If Dr. Gnadenschuss saw Prussian Emil run away from the scene of Eva Angerstein's murder, then surely he'd know that Emil was a yokel catcher. A fraud. And that there was no point in shooting other disabled veterans on **klutz** wagons. So why bother with them at all?"

"Prussian Emil isn't the only yokel catcher in Berlin. Everyone knows that a good percentage of these men are faking it to make a living. In his first letter, Dr. Gnadenschuss actually mentions he'd seen one get up and walk away from his cripple-cart **as if his middle name had been Lazarus.** Well, suppose it was Prussian Emil that he saw get up and walk away. Suppose he concentrates only on men who are using **klutz** wagons. Suppose he figures that maybe he'll shoot the right man eventually."

"Why suppose when you can say **pretend**?" said Gennat. "Or **presume**? Or **once upon a time**?"

"At the same time, he starts to get it into his

head that he's performing a valuable public service in getting rid of these men. And that he can taunt us about it in the newspapers. That there's nothing we can do about it until we get lucky. Which is probably what it's going to take to crack a case like this."

"This is the part I don't understand," said Weiss. "The need to taunt us. Does he do it to have us chasing our tails, or just for the hell of it?"

"Simple," said Gennat. "He hates the police. I've heard it said that lots of people do, chief."

"And here was me thinking to run for election to the Reichstag," said Weiss. "Pity."

"Meanwhile, he helps build his notoriety by creating the public perception that we're just a bunch of village idiots," said Gennat.

I glanced at my watch. "I'd better get going."

Weiss smiled. "You're going to that ring bar, Bernie? The Sing Sing? Tonight?"

"I thought I might."

"With any luck they'll kill him," said Gennat. "Even the rats tiptoe past the front door of that place."

"Ernst is right, Bernie. Be careful. They don't like cops in there."

"I know. That's why I thought I'd take someone with me. Someone no one would ever suspect of being with a cop in a million years."

"Oh? Who's that?"

"A girl."

WHEN ROSA BRAUN finished playing her saxophone in the Haller-Revue orchestra, we left the club and walked north up Friedrichstrasse toward Oranienburger Tor. It was almost one a.m., but the streets were still full of sweaty Berliners gathered like damp moths outside the more brightly lit bars, loudly enjoying the high summer temperatures and the prospect of even further intoxication.

"I certainly didn't expect to see you tonight," she said. "And certainly not wearing that suit. Where on earth did you get it?"

"What's wrong with it?"

"You know perfectly well."

"Says the woman wearing male evening dress."

"These are my working clothes."

"So are mine, as a matter of fact. This bar we're going to, it's full of thieves and murderers. Which means it's best if I try to blend in."

"It's a little hard to imagine that suit blending in anywhere except a shooting party or a racecourse."

"Well, you're not so far from the mark. A couple of years ago, I had to spend a bit of time hanging around Hoppegarten, looking for some pimp we were after. And I bought this and the matching cap on expenses to make me look more like a sporting man."

"More Irish pimp, I'm afraid."

"Good."

"So you're working then?"

"In a manner of speaking. In truth I'm just keeping my eyes peeled for someone. But I thought it would be a good idea to invite you along and combine business with pleasure. Especially as the whole evening's on expenses. Which reminds me. The one subject we never mention in this place is that I'm a cop. Got that? You'll see why when we get there."

"So what's your name. Just in case anyone should ask."

"Zehr. Helmut Zehr."

"Nice to meet you, Helmut. But aren't you afraid someone will recognize you?"

"I'm a police sergeant, not the deputy commissioner. Besides, I figure by this time most of the patrons at Sing Sing will be too drunk to know me from a leprechaun."

"I've heard of this place, of course. People say Sing Sing is the most dangerous bar in Berlin."

"That's probably true."

"So what makes you think I'd like to go there?"

"Any girl who wears green lipstick and matching nail varnish strikes me as someone who likes to live dangerously. With a color combination like that, you should fit right in."

"I think we make a good combination ourselves, don't you? Your looks, Irish. My talent.

My green lipstick. Your green suit. People will think we're a couple. Albeit a couple without much in the way of taste. Mostly on your side."

"We **are** a couple. Seriously. While we're in Sing Sing we should watch out for each other like we're two convicts manacled at the wrist. Anything you hear that sounds remotely untoward, you should say so immediately."

"You're scaring me."

I put my arm around her. "You'll be quite safe as long as you mind what I say, Rosa."

"Ah, now I understand your technique, Irish. It's very sneaky. You aim to frighten me into your arms and, after that, who knows where?"

"I think we both know where, don't you?"

I stopped and moved to kiss her green lips.

"No, wait," she said. "Do you want to spoil my lipstick? You can kiss me all you want after we've been to this place. But for now, I need you to behave like Tannhäuser and treat me like a virgin princess. Does that sound about right?"

"It's a deal."

We walked on. She said: "Isn't Sing Sing a prison in China?"

"No, it's in New York. But don't ask me why it's called that. More famously they have an electric chair at Sing Sing called Old Sparky. Which is more of a nickname, is my guess. I'm told they have one at the club, too. But it's just for show."

"I'm glad to hear it."

We arrived at the rusticated club door. Like everything else in the place, it was designed to look as if it belonged in a prison, with a window grille and a door within a door. I rang the bell, and an eye and then a mouth like a vicious-looking mollusk appeared at the grille and demanded to know the password.

Without much confidence I said, "Hitler."

A few seconds later I heard the door being unlocked and bolts being drawn.

"Let's hope it's just as easy to get out of this place," I murmured, and then the inner door swung open, releasing a lot of boozy, smoky noise.

The spanner on the door was part man and part bull mastiff. His nose had a big scar running down the center so that it looked like it was two noses and one of his ears reminded me of an unborn fetus. He wasn't anyone's idea of a reasonable man unless your idea of one was Frankenstein. Wearing the uniform of a prison guard and carrying a truncheon, he smelled strongly of beer and when he smiled it was like looking at an ancient graveyard. He slammed the door shut behind us, locked it, and waved a waiter over. The shaven-headed waiters, all dressed like convicts, with numbers on their backs, were as tough-looking as the spanner. The one who fetched us to table 191819 looked like the rail tracks at Potsdam Station, he had so many scars on his face. I gave him five marks and told him to bring us a bottle of German champagne and two glasses; he was back quickly with a bottle of Henkell and two enamelware cups.

"No glasses here," he said. "Only prison mugs."

He wrote his number on the bill—191819/22—and placed it underneath the champagne bucket.

The champagne at least was cold. I poured some out and then toasted Rosa, who smiled at me nervously. She said something, but I couldn't hear what because the man seated next to us was shouting at a pretty girl dressed in stockings and suspenders, a tight basque, and not much else; they were both smoking marijuana. After a few seconds she spat the chewing gum out of her mouth and began kissing him. Her partner kept calling her Helga, so I assumed that was her name. Just looking at her you knew she was tough enough to survive another Krakatoa.

The champagne tasted a lot better than I'd expected, even in a tin mug. Rosa must have thought so, too, because she downed the mug in one and then came and sat on my knee.

"At least I can hear you now," she said, and let me pour her another.

Using Rosa's body as cover, I took the opportunity to look around. The place was set up like the mess hall at Plötzensee Prison, with heavy wooden tables, thick iron grilles on the windows, and, at the top of a tall stepladder, an observation guard who, our waiter informed us, was keeping an eye out for pickpockets. The place was full of Berlin lowlife, but I saw no one who fit the description of Prussian Emil I'd been given by the veteran outside the aquarium.

Up front, there was a small stage with a black curtain and I kept thinking a cabaret performer was going to show up and entertain us, but even as I thought this a man came to our table and did just that. In his hands were a set of manacles.

"Here," he said. "Look at these bracelets. Genuine coppers' clinkers, they are. Go on, folks. Check them out."

I took hold of the handcuffs and examined them carefully.

"They look like the real thing," I said.

"Look like? Of course they're the real thing. Go on, love, snap them on my wrists. Tight as you like. That's it. Go on, you're not putting on bandages, you know. There you are. Now what do you think? Am I your prisoner, or what?"

Rosa nodded. "I'd say your goose is cooked and no mistake."

I didn't see how he did it, but it took him less time to get out of the handcuffs than it took to take off his cap and solicit a coin, which I duly provided.

We drank some more champagne and settled

in. The man next to us was telling Helga about his time in Moabit Prison; in another place it was something you might have kept quiet about, but in Sing Sing it was like telling someone at the German Opera House that you were a trained tenor from Milan.

"How long were you in the cement, Hugo?" she asked.

"Five years."

"What for?"

"Writing poetry," he said, and laughed.

"There's a lot of poets who deserve to be in prison."

I couldn't disagree with that, but I kept my eyes and my opinion to myself. Keeping your opinions to yourself was essential in Sing Sing; some of the patrons seemed likely to take offense at the slightest remark. A fight was already breaking out on the other side of the club but the spanner quickly broke it up by the simple means of breaking the heads of both the combatants with his truncheon, to loud cheers and applause. They were carried insensible to the door and thrown unceremoniously into the gutter.

We'd been there almost an hour when desire for Rosa began to take precedence over my desire to find Prussian Emil; it seemed unlikely that he was going to show up now. I was about to pay the bill when a man dressed like a prison guard and wearing lots of makeup arrived onstage and blew a whistle. Some of the audience seemed to know what was going to happen and gave a loud cheer, and gradually the place fell silent.

"Good evening, ladies and gentlemen," he said, removing his peaked cap. "And welcome to Sing Sing!"

More cheers.

"Most Berlin clubs have bands or naked girls these days; or ventriloquists, or magicians. I've even heard it said that at certain clubs you can watch two people having sex. And sometimes three or four. So many cocks, so much mouse, so very **passé.** But Sing Sing has something unique in the annals of entertainment. I promise you that you will not forget what we have to show you. Because, ladies and gentlemen, and without further ado, once again I have the honor to introduce you to the greatest star in all Berlin cabaret. Please give a warm Sing Sing welcome to Old Sparky himself!"

More cheers and more stamping on the sawdust-covered wooden floor as the curtains drew back to reveal a large wooden chair equipped with leather straps. The master of ceremonies sat down in the chair and crossed his legs nonchalantly.

"As you can see, this is an exact working facsimile of the electric chair at Sing Sing prison in New York, which was most recently used to execute a Jewish housewife named Ruth Snyder who murdered her husband for his life insurance.

Poor woman. As if such a thing was in any way unusual. In Berlin, they'd probably have given her a medal and a pension."

Cheers again.

"Now, many of you will know that the use of the electric chair was introduced as a humane alternative to hanging. However, it has often been the case that the electrocution did not go as smoothly as the authorities or the condemned would have preferred. Sometimes they used too much electricity, in which case the victim caught fire; and sometimes they used not enough, in which case the victim lived and had to be electrocuted again. Of course it's all a question of money and a lot depends on whether the prison has paid its electricity bill. Or not. Fortunately the Sing Sing Club has no such problems with the Berlin Electrical Company. We always pay our bills. Not always with our own money, mind you. But we pay because without electricity there would be no Old Sparky for your entertainment.

"Yes, I'm pleased to announce that it's that very special, not to say galvanizing, time of the night when we invite a member of the Sing Sing audience to join us up here onstage and volunteer to be put to death by electrocution. What more could you reasonably ask in the way of entertainment? If only some of our politicians in the Reichstag were similarly inclined to volunteer for electrocution, eh? It's only what those bastards deserve. So do we have a volunteer? Come on, ladies and gentlemen, don't be shy. Old Sparky is keen to say hello and good evening in his own peculiar way.

"No? Well, I can't say I'm very surprised. Old Sparky makes everyone a little shy, doesn't he? After all, it's no small thing to be fried in the electric chair for the amusement of your fellow citizens. Which is why we usually choose someone by ballot. So ladies and gentlemen: If you check your bill you'll find that it contains a number. Please take a look at it while I select one of those numbers at random."

The master of ceremonies placed his hand into a large bag labeled SWAG, and came out with a piece of paper containing a number, which he read: "And the losing number tonight is 191819/22."

To my surprise and then horror I realized that the number was mine and I was about to crush the bill and head for the door but Hugo's friend Helga had already spotted the number and was helpfully pointing me out to the master of these grotesque ceremonies.

"He's here," she shouted excitedly, and suddenly everyone was looking at me. "The condemned man. He's sitting right beside me."

I smiled at her, though I'd like to have bitten

a piece out of Helga's neck. But I was cornered. I had little choice but to fake good humor and participate in Sing Sing's tasteless charade. With my ears full of applause I stood up as unseen hands started to pull and push me toward the stage. As I neared the MC, I looked around for Rosa, but all I could see were the sweating faces of my fellow citizens as they took a loud and sadistic pleasure at my obvious discomfort. A few people at the back were even standing on their chairs so as not to miss a minute of my last moments on earth and I was inevitably reminded of a public hanging on the old gallows at Neuer Markt, where Berlin's citizenry had once flocked in their thousands to see a man die.

"What's your name, son?" asked the MC as I stepped up beside him and he pushed me down into the chair.

"Helmut Zehr," I said.

The MC, who smelled strongly of illegal absinthe, took the bill from my hand and ostentatiously tore it up, as if my debt to the club had been canceled. Already two of the burliest convict waiters were strapping my arms and legs to the wooden chair; one of them rolled up my trouser legs and attached something cold and metallic to my calves as if they really did mean to electrocute me. It was about then that I saw the two huge H-switches on the bare brick wall, and another man standing beside these wearing heavy leather gauntlets. He seemed to be the only man present, apart from me, who wasn't smiling.

"Well, Helmut," said the MC, "in case you don't know how this works, there's an applause meter, so the more convincing the show you put on in this chair, the more money you will leave with tonight. By the way, you'll feel a small amount of current in your hands and legs, just to help with your performance." He grinned and then added, "Always supposing that you manage to survive the experience. Not everyone does. Just once in a while everything goes wrong and the man seated in that chair really does get toasted. But only if he deserves it."

The MC stood back and at a sign from the two waiters that the straps on my legs and arms were secure, raised his hands for silence before shouting, "Roll on one" to the man wearing the gauntlets. My executioner threw one of the H-switches and, as the lights in the club turned suddenly much brighter, the MC addressed me again in sonorously judicial tones. I wanted to punch his painted face and might have done, but for the straps that held me.

"Helmut Zehr: you have been sentenced to die by three judges of the German Supreme Court. Do you have anything to say before your sentence is carried out?"

The Sing Sing audience greeted my death sentence with great enthusiasm and I wouldn't have been at all surprised if they'd have viewed the real thing with just as much enthusiasm.

"Just get on with it," I muttered.

"Electricity shall now be passed through your body until you are dead, in accordance with Prussian state law. May God have mercy on your soul."

After a brief pause, the MC shouted, "Roll on two," and the gauntleted man threw the second H-switch. At the same time, the lights in the club flickered like lightning and I felt an electric current in my limbs that was strong enough to be uncomfortable. Anxious to end this loathsome spectacle as quickly as possible and get out of the club, I let out a yell, jerked around spasmodically for several seconds, and played dead. Then, from underneath the chair, a small smoke bomb went off, which made me jump one last time, and finally my ugly ordeal was over.

"Ladies and gentlemen," shouted the MC, "I give you Helmut Zehr."

With the straps on the chair undone, I struggled weakly to my feet and acknowledged the thunderous applause with a wave of my hand.

"Take a bow," said the MC. "You were a good sport, Helmut."

OUTSIDE THE SING Sing Club I leaned on the exterior wall to catch a breath of what passed for fresh air in that part of Berlin. My hands were trembling as they steered a cigarette uncertainly toward the biggest hole in my face, lit it, and then fumbled the rest of the matches onto the ground. Rosa regarded me with concern.

"That's an evening I'm not going to forget in a hurry," she said.

"Me neither."

"For a minute back there I thought you were dead."

"Believe me, I had the same feeling. There was real electricity in that damn chair."

"Are you all right now?"

"Just about. You might say what happened in there—touched a raw nerve. Once, when I was in the trenches, I found myself trapped up to my neck in a shell hole full of mud, unable to move my arms and legs and thinking I was going to drown. It's a recurring fear I have in all my nightmares. Not being able to escape. Thinking I'm about to die. After ten years you'd think I was over it. But I'm not. Most of the time I can handle it, but now and again it's every bit as vivid as if it had happened yesterday." I took a deep drag of my cigarette. "I'll be all right in a minute. In fact, I already am."

"What's in the envelope?"

I looked at the envelope in my hand; someone had put it there as we'd walked out Sing Sing's door. "I think it's the fee," I said. "For my performance. Look here, I should never have taken you there. I'm sorry. That was criminal."

"I'd say you already paid the ultimate price for that particular crime, Bernie."

I tried a smile. It felt a little tight on my face, as if someone had glued it there.

"Come on," she said. "I'll take you home. Let's find a cab."

BUT THE EVENING was not quite over. We hadn't walked very far when a brand-new Mercedes roadster pulled up and a man I half recognized leaned over the cream-colored door.

"Hey. Helmut Zehr. Need a ride?"

"Yes," I said.

"Get in," he said curtly.

It was Erich Angerstein, Eva's father.

I opened the door and nodded at a reluctant Rosa. "It's all right," I said. "We know each other. Sort of."

We climbed into the car, which still smelled strongly of the showroom.

"Where to?" he asked.

"Nollendorfplatz," I said.

"Good. That's on my way."

The big car took off smoothly. After a while Angerstein said, "You look like you need some schnapps. There's a hip flask in the glove box."

I helped myself to a couple of bites of

Angerstein's liquor and then nodded some thanks his way. He was wearing a smart single-breasted silk suit and a nice white shirt with a green silk tie. Only, the leather gloves on his hands seemed a little out of place. Maybe the car was stolen. Then again, he was probably a man who was always careful about where he left his fingerprints.

"You do know that was a ring bar you were in back there?" he said.

"Of course."

"What the hell possessed you?"

"You were there?"

"I saw the whole damn thing. You and Old Sparky. You're lucky it was only me who recognized you, otherwise they might have fried you for real."

"You're exaggerating."

"Am I?"

"When we met earlier I told you I was a cop. Otherwise I'd be just another Fritz to you. Rosa, this is Erich Angerstein. He's a gangster. But you can relax for now. He wouldn't hurt a fly. Not unless there was profit in it."

"Pleased to meet you, Herr Angerstein. I think."

"It's all right, sugar. I don't bite. Not when I'm driving a new car."

"Nice. What is this, anyway? The Mercedes Getaway?"

"Oh, I like her, Gunther. You should hang on to this one. She has courage."

"More than me, I think."

"Could be. Look here, Gunther, the people who run that club hate cops more than they hate losing money. Suppose I'd turned you in to them?"

"Why would you do that when you know I'm trying to find your daughter's killer?"

"Maybe so. But I still don't understand why you went there in the first place."

"I was looking for someone. A potential witness."

"To my daughter's murder?"

I didn't want to say too much on this score. The last thing I wanted was for Angerstein to find Prussian Emil and question him on his own. There was no telling where that might end up.

"I'm not really sure. It all depends on what he tells me when I catch up with him. He might know something useful. Then again he might not."

"Maybe I can help you find him."

"Maybe."

"This Fritz have a name?"

"Yes, but I'm not sure I'm going to tell you what it is."

"Why not?"

"In case you decide to go rogue and look for

him on your own account. Maybe even find him, too. A man with your education and background, I wouldn't be at all surprised if you did find him. But you might get impatient. And not knowing the right questions to ask, you might come up with the wrong answers."

"I see what you mean."

"Look, under the circumstances I could hardly blame you for taking the law into your own hands. But it really wouldn't help my investigation if you did."

"And if I gave you my word?"

"Come on, you're a Berlin gangster, not a Prussian Army officer."

"And that means my word isn't worth anything?"

"It could. Look, I don't know about you but me, I'm a cynical bastard. It's the secret of my charm."

"I told you before. I want to help you catch the man who killed my daughter."

"Sure, I get that. The difference is that I want to build a case against this Fritz and you want to murder him."

"In the long run, what's the difference?"

"Frankly, none. But my job is to see that the right man loses his head."

"So you're not going to tell me his name."

"I don't see how I can."

Angerstein sighed. "They've got a name for this in chess when, after several hours of playing, neither side can move and nobody can win or lose."

"A complete waste of time?"

"**Stalemate.** What, you never played chess?"

"Sure. I played Hamlet, too, but it certainly won't bother my conscience if I don't win or lose with you, Herr Angerstein. You're not the only informant in this town. There never was a detective who couldn't find himself another informer."

"No, but trust me, I am the best-informed informer you're likely to find. There's not much crime that happens in Berlin that I don't know about. The fact is, it's not just me who wants this bastard caught; it's all the bosses I represent in the syndicate. A killer like this is bad for business. There are too many cops out looking for him. With the result that they see more than they should."

"Now, that I can believe. But I already told you, I'm not the trusting kind, Herr Angerstein. They don't pay me enough to think too much. When it snows I know to stay indoors. These days that's considered enough to make detective."

"I think you're a lot smarter than you say you are. And you'd have to be smarter than that suit says you are. Look, Gunther, by the oath I took to the ring to which I belong, I'm supposed to finger cops for the benefit of our fellow members. But I didn't give you away back there. That has to be worth something."

"They have a name for that, too?"

"You could call it a sign of good faith. I see your dilemma. But I really do want you to get this bastard. Not just for me and Eva, but for all the others he's killed as well. And all the others he might yet kill. So please give me a chance. Let me help. The Berlin underworld is a sardine can without a key for a cop like you. But with my contacts I can probably find this fish in no time."

"That's the first reasonable thing you've said since you offered to drive us home."

"So you'll give me a name to work on?"

"I'm still thinking about it."

"Well, think up, copper, we're here."

"Don't rush me. My head still feels like a Chinese switchboard."

Nollendorfplatz looked a lot better from the inside of an expensive car; most things probably did. A new Mercedes roadster was like rose-tinted spectacles with wire wheels and hand-stitched leather upholstery. Even the exhaust fumes smelled good. Angerstein peeled off a glove, reached into the pocket of his silk suit, and took out a stiff little business card that he handed to me with nicely manicured fingers. On it was embossed a smart address in Lichterfelde on the Teltow Canal, a telephone number, and his name. They say crime doesn't pay, but the benefits looked just fine to me.

Rosa and I got out of the car. Then I leaned in the driver's window of the Mercedes and said, "Prussian Emil."

"That's it?"

"He's a yokel catcher and snow shoveler. Pretends to be a disabled veteran. But mostly he's a lookout for some of the city's burglars. Positions his **klutz** wagon outside a house and blows a bugle if any law turns up. On the night your daughter was murdered, one of the apartments in the vicinity got turned over."

"And you went to Sing Sing to do what? Ask the locals if anyone had done a job with him? It's amazing you've stayed alive this long, Gunther."

"I've got eyes as well as ears. As it happens, the man I went looking for is tall, cadaverous, vaguely military, with a port-wine stain on his neck like a careless waiter spilled something down his shirt collar. We detectives call that a description. You might have heard of it somewhere."

"It's not much, is it?"

"When you're a cop, sometimes not much is all there is to go on, Herr Angerstein. You should try it sometime."

MY HANDS WERE still shaking as I tried to undo my collar stud, prompting Rosa to come to my aid.

"Here, let me do that."

It felt strange allowing someone wearing men's clothes to help me undress but that problem soon disappeared when she herself was naked and lying beside me in my bed and looking more like a woman than I remembered—slender, her beautiful long hair, liberated from its tight bun, tumbling down her elegant back like a silk waterfall. There was a tenderness in her eyes. I'd had a severe shock, but not as severe as the one endured by poor Mrs. Snyder in the real Sing Sing, which made me feel a bit of a fraud and I almost apologized for the way my body was behaving. Still, I could hardly ignore the twitching of my own muscles, like a frog whose legs had been touched by Galvani's electrodes. But for her being with me, I'd probably have emptied the rum bottle that was in my desk drawer.

"It's all right," she said gently. "It's all over now. You're safe with me. Just lie still and close your eyes."

It had gone four a.m. but even though the window was wide open the room was stifling; we lay on top of the covers for a while, exhausted and sheened with sweat, listening to the symphonic adagio that was the city's smallest hours, too tired to smoke or to touch each other but knowing without having to say anything that there would be another time for all those mysteries. Somewhere a horse and cart were going about their early-morning deliveries; two cats had reached a stalemate in a game of feline chess; and, in the far distance, a barge was announcing its presence like a lost dinosaur as it made its lumbering way down the Spree.

Neither of us said anything and it seemed to me that for a fleeting instant we reached out into the void and touched a perfect innocence. After a while I stepped out of my body and stared down at these two intertwined lovers and marveled at the small differences between us that made Rosa so much more beautiful and desirable than me. I watched my lips move as if to form an elusive, loving phrase but since nothing really needed to be said in that department it stayed unspoken. Eventually Rosa yawned and then whispered something that sounded like, "What very peculiar lives we both lead, don't you think, Bernie?" and laid her head on my chest and went to sleep.

This seemed incontrovertible and not just because of what had happened that evening. Life itself was so fast-moving it was impossible not to feel that sometimes things were completely out of control, like being alone in one of Berlin's elongated open-topped tourist charabancs as it careered frantically around the metropolis, driverless, taking in the sights, heading toward some unknown peculiar disaster of our own making.

BERNHARD WEISS LISTENED to the tale of my night at Sing Sing and shook his head.

"It was a brave effort," he said. "And I commend you for trying. But you mustn't reproach yourself for having failed. The point is that the thinking behind what you were doing was sound. You couldn't possibly have anticipated what happened when you got to the club. That was just bad luck, coming up against the German sense of humor. I don't really understand it, myself. I suspect it is the kind of laughter that conceals a scream against modern life, man cut loose from all the certainties that once comforted him—God, tradition, love of country. Laughter that hides an existential crisis."

I tried to control my expression; I'd heard the man talking out of his arse before, but this was something new. I wanted to tell him that a lot of people were just cunts and that was all there was to it, but with a breakfast drink or two already inside me I thought it best to keep my face shut; the last thing I wanted was an argument with the boss about the true moral caliber of our fellow citizens.

"But you must be tired if you were out so late. Would you like some coffee, Bernie?"

"No, thanks, sir."

"I know. It's hardly the sort of weather for coffee. There is water if you'd prefer."

"I'm fine, thank you, sir."

He got up and crossed the floor to open a window. "You would think they could supply an electric fan that worked properly. But that one on my desk is more or less useless. Really, it's quite unforgivable when the temperature is as hot as this."

Weiss was slow coming to the point, which made me nervous. I half suspected he was going to deliver a dry-as-mummy-dust lecture about police discipline and then fire me from the Murder Commission before sending me back to the ranks of Vice, realizing that he'd made a mistake in giving me Lindner's seat and that Kurt Reichenbach should have had it after all.

Back at the desk he retrieved his cigar from the ashtray and relit it before sitting down. "Tell me, Bernie, do you remember the Klein and Nebbe case?"

"Everyone in Berlin remembers the Klein and Nebbe case."

"Well, I've been reading this essay about the case by a writer called Alfred Döblin. From Stettin. I recommend you read it. Anyone who's interested in criminalistics should read his essay.

It contains newspaper reports, trial records, medical testimony, everything. Only, it's not an attempt to sensationalize what happened but to understand it. To explain it."

"Two women poisoned one husband and attempted to poison the second," I said helplessly. "What's to understand or explain? That's a crime in any language."

Weiss took out a small notebook, opened it, and ignoring my objections, prepared to read aloud.

"One phrase that the writer uses in the essay struck me as particularly interesting. He says, **I had the impulse to travel the streets that they—the murderers—routinely traveled. So I also sat in the pubs in which the two women got to know each other. I visited the apartment of one of them, spoke with her personally, spoke with others involved, and observed them.**"

"There doesn't seem much point in going into it now," I said. "It was six years ago."

"Döblin wrote his essay in 1924. And I disagree with you. His is a brave attempt to examine where in society the noncriminal ends and the criminal begins. But it's not so much his conclusions that interested me as his whole investigative method."

I nodded. Anything to avoid giving my opinion of the case, which was that Ella Klein and

Margarete Nebbe were a lesbian couple who'd richly deserved much harsher sentences than those handed down by the court; there wasn't one cop in the Alex who didn't think they should both have faced the falling ax. Arsenic was every happily married man's abiding fear.

"You see, Bernie, I was thinking that this essay might provide the inspiration for a new kind of detective work. Something much more immersive than merely searching a crime scene for clues and collecting witness statements."

"Like what?"

"Like the same sort of thing you were doing last night, Bernie. You, investigating a crime undercover. At street level. No, really. This is the kind of detective work I'm talking about. No one is doing this at present. Not even Scotland Yard."

"I'm still not sure I understand, sir."

"It's just this. Detective work is based on the assumption that we are better than the criminals we investigate. Wouldn't you agree?"

"Of course."

"That we do not descend to the level of criminals ourselves. However, it occurs to me that in this respect we are missing an important trick. That there may be occasions when this is exactly what's required. That to solve the crime we need to be **pro**active rather than **re**active. That we need to inhabit the very milieu of the crime that has been committed. Do you see? We need to be in that world but not part of it."

I bit my lip and looked at my fingernails. It was like working for a school headmaster and I was the slow-witted pupil who wasn't quite following the line of his high-minded reasoning. I lit a cigarette and puffed it into life; if only Weiss's conversation could have combusted as easily; as it was, his words had yet to catch fire in my mind. By now I was more or less certain I wasn't being sacked. But was I listening to a lecture or merely a series of rhetorical questions?

"Are you still drinking, Bernie? Well, of course you are. I can smell it on your breath. I know, this isn't the Lutheran church. Men come off duty and they need a drink. But can you control it?"

"I am controlling it."

Weiss nodded sympathetically. "Because I think you'll need your wits about you for what I have in mind."

"I saved your life, didn't I?"

"Yes, you did. Which is why I think you're probably just the man for this. We have to do something. I'm under a lot of pressure from the minister to catch this Dr. Gnadenschuss. And what we're doing right now, well, it just doesn't seem to be enough." He paused for a moment and regarded me through a haze of cigar smoke. "What do you think?"

"Honestly? Until he kills again, I don't think we've a chance of catching him, no. The thumbprint on the letter they received at the **Berliner Tageblatt** didn't find a match with records, as you know. Right now we're just whistling while we wait for another corpse to turn up."

"And yet I think we have to do something more. In fact, I don't think we have any choice but to do something."

"What did you have in mind?"

"Before I tell you, I want you to feel free to turn me down. It won't in the least reflect badly on you, Bernie. You're young and I think you're still keen and you'll probably say yes without thinking. But you need to think about this carefully. Because what I'm proposing is a little out of the ordinary. What I'm proposing is to make you a kind of hunting decoy. In short, that you use the **klutz** wagon you recovered from Eva Angerstein's murder scene and pose as one of these unfortunate disabled war veterans yourself. Just as your friend Prussian Emil was doing. That's right. I want you to pose as a **klutz** in the hope that Dr. Gnadenschuss might try and kill you. And if he does try to kill you, then of course you would be perfectly placed to apprehend him. **In flagrante delicto.** But only if you're agreeable to the idea."

Weiss wasn't smiling. So I knew it wasn't a joke. But it certainly sounded like one.

"It will mean living on the street for a while, begging outside railway stations for pennies, maybe even sleeping in a hostel for the homeless, going without the odd meal, not washing regularly, accepting some abuse. And all the time keeping your eyes peeled for someone trying to kill you."

"If it's a question of catching Dr. Gnadenschuss, then I'm game."

"Are you sure?" He looked at me thoughtfully. "Yes, I think you are. Of course you'll have a bit of help in looking like a real **klutz.** With the army uniform and disability. As if you were an actor in a play. The **klutz** wagon you found helps because it was made for a man who isn't really disabled. For the rest of it, I was thinking of sending you to see a friend of mine at the Neues Theater on Schiffbauerdamm. A makeup artist and costumier called Brigitte Mölbling. She worked on that movie **Metropolis.** That is, if you're sure you actually want to do this, Bernie."

"I'd like to try. As you say, sir, we have to do something."

"Good, good."

"What does Ernst think about your plan, sir?"

"I haven't told him. In fact, I don't propose to tell anyone, and nor should you. The fewer people who know about this the better. What we certainly want to avoid is any other police officers coming to look at you, as if you were an exhibit in the zoo. Or tipping off the newspapers that one of our detectives is working in disguise. What I will tell Ernst is that I've given you some compassionate leave to get your drinking sorted out. Which, I might add, wouldn't be a bad idea anyway. And when you've decided where you're going to make your pitch, from time to time, I may come and check on you myself, if only to put a few coins in your hat."

BEFORE I LEFT to begin my mission I looked in on the new department at the Alex, the one handling commercial fraud. Created by Weiss, it was headed by Ulrich Possehl. He was a good officer, well respected, with an outstanding war record. But he was away on vacation and his deputy, Dr. Alfred Jachode, was an altogether different animal. By training he was a lawyer and an accountant and his office was lined with some very dry books. He was also an adherent of the Steel Helmet, and although this was supposed to be an organization above party politics, many of its members were quite open about their allegiance—in fact, many wore a miniature helmet on a stickpin in their lapels. In practice they were so radically anti-democratic and anti-republican they made the Nazis look reasonable. The minute I walked into his office, I knew I was probably wasting my time asking if he had any reason to suspect the owners of the Wolfmium factory of commercial fraud.

"You've got a nerve, do you know that? You're wasting your time if you think I would do anything to help a Jew's poodle like you, Gunther."

"If you're suggesting that my position in the Murder Commission owes anything to Bernhard Weiss, then you're wrong. It owes everything to him."

"What **do** you want?"

"I was hoping to waste your time, which looks like a better outcome. Besides, I wasn't thinking of you helping me so much as you helping the workers who were killed in the factory fire."

"Most of them were Russians, probably here illegally, so who gives a damn? I know I don't. They got what they deserved."

"You make me think that if Germany ever gets what it deserves, we'll have a very bad time of it."

"Communists."

"Actually, a lot of those workers were Germans."

"Volga Germans," he said. "There's a big difference."

"Is there?"

"I assume one or two of them are decent people. But most are probably thieves and rapists and murderers and therefore Russians in all but name. And every bit as illegal. It's only Jews and Jews' poodles who care about these people."

The Volga Germans were ethnic Germans,

largely descended from Bavarians and Rhinelanders and Hessians who were invited in 1762 by the Empress Catherine the Great—herself a Pomeranian native of Stettin—to come and farm Russian land. They'd helped to modernize backward Russian farming and, being German, had thrived, at least until the Bolshevik revolution, when their lands had been confiscated by the communists and they'd been forced to return to the Fatherland. It goes without saying that they were not welcomed back with joy.

"So the way I look at it is this: Fifty dead Volga Germans in Berlin is fifty damned Russians we won't have to send back to the eastern swamps when finally we elect a proper government that believes in protecting our borders." He smiled thinly. "Was there anything else?"

"No, I think we've covered it."

"It's not too late, you know," said Jachode. "For you, I mean. Personally. You could always join us. In the Stahlhelm. In making the new Germany."

"Yes, well, I'm afraid it's the **always** part I don't care for."

"Get out. Before I throw you out."

Most of the time I'm very proud to be a cop. I think there's nothing wrong with being a cop—unless there's something wrong with the cop, of course. But sometimes it took a great deal of courage to see the Berlin police force with all its faults and still love it.

—

THE NEUES THEATER was a tall neo-Baroque building with a high mansard roof and a bell tower. It was under the management and direction of Max Reinhardt and it frequently staged operettas and musicals. I never much liked musicals. It's the music I don't care for, but as well, it's the relentlessly jolly theater folk who cavort across the stage—I hate them. But mostly it's the idea that when the nearly always tenuous story reaches its greatest dramatic intensity, someone sings or dances, or sings **and** dances, and for no discernible reason. Speaking as someone who doesn't much care to be entertained, I always prefer dialogue to song because it takes half the time to get through and brings the sanctuary of the bar, or even home, just that little bit closer. I never yet saw a musical I didn't think could be improved by a deeper pit for the orchestra, and a bottomless chasm for the cast.

They were rehearsing a new opera when I showed up at the stage door and from the sound of it I knew I wasn't going to enjoy **The Threepenny Opera** any more than I'd enjoyed **The Cheerful Vineyard,** which was the last musical I'd seen at the Neues Theater some three years before. The band sounded desperately out of tune, like a waterlogged barrel organ, while the mezzo-soprano could hold a note no better than I could hang on to a hot poker. She was plain, too—I caught a glimpse of her onstage as I made my way up to one of the dressing rooms—one of those thin, pale-faced, red-haired Berlin girls who reminded me of a safety match.

By contrast, Brigitte Mölbling was an Amazonian blonde whose perfectly proportioned windswept head looked like the mascot on the hood of a fast car. She had a cool smile, a strong nose, and eyebrows that were so perfectly drawn they might have been put there by Raphael or Titian. She wore a plain black dress, more bracelets than Cleopatra's pawnbroker, a long gold necklace, a big ring on almost every finger, and an enormous single earring, on the end of which was a little frame containing a laughing Buddha. I figured the Buddha was laughing at me for playing along with Weiss's crazy idea. He was probably trying to work out what kind of animal I was going to be in the next life: a rat or a louse, or just another cop.

There was a black cigarette burning in the ashtray and a glass of something cold in her hand. She put the glass down and then rose from her armchair, before sitting again, this time on the edge of a big table that was covered with pots and bottles, a finished game of solitaire, and some ice in a bowl that matched the ice in her glass. "So you're the policeman who thinks he can play a **klutz,"** she said, sizing me up through narrowed eyes.

"I know what you're thinking: He's more leading man than character actor, but that's the part I've been assigned, yes."

She nodded, reclaimed the cigarette, and did some more sizing up.

"It's not going to be easy. For one thing, you're in good shape. Too healthy to have been living on the street. Your hair is wrong and so's your skin."

"That's what all the magazines are saying."

"We can fix that, I suppose."

"That's why I'm here, doc."

"And as for your teeth, they could use a bit more yellow. Right now they look like you chew tree bark. But we can fix that, too."

"I'm all ears."

"No, they're fine. A little clean maybe. It's the rest of you that needs some close attention."

"My mother would be pleased to hear it. She always said that in the final analysis it all comes down to clean ears and clean underwear."

"Your mother sounds very sensible."

"Unfortunately, I don't take after her. If I did I wouldn't be a cop and I wouldn't have volunteered to play the **klutz."**

"So what you're doing, is it dangerous?"

"Could be."

"Yes. I suppose there's always the possibility that Dr. Gnadenschuss might shoot you, too. That's what Bernhard Weiss said this was about, anyway. The crazy who's been shooting disabled veterans: I suppose he's more important than Winnetou. Isn't that just the thing? You murder a girl in this town and no one gives a damn. You murder a disabled war vet, they ask questions in the Reichstag. But you're taking a risk, surely."

"There's a risk, yes. But now that I'm here talking to you, it seems like a risk worth running."

"Smooth, aren't you? For a cop, that is. Most of the ones I've met were bullies in bad suits with ugly cigars and beer guts."

"You forgot the flat feet. But I seem to remember you didn't like my skin or my hair."

"No, your skin is good. That's why I don't like it. At least for what you've got in mind. But as I said, we can fix that. We can even fix your hair."

"I imagine there's not a lot you can't fix when you put your mind to it. Like some refreshment, perhaps. Is that a drink you're drinking?"

"I'm sorry. Would you like one?"

"Let's just say one will do for now."

She opened a bottle of Scotch and poured a generous measure on top of a piece of ice. Meanwhile, all her gold jewelry shifted in a vain attempt to distract my eyes from her breasts. She handed me the drink and I toasted her. Apart from the medicine I was holding, she was just what I'd have told the doctor to order.

"Here's to you and the opera. Whatever it is. From what I've seen on the poster outside, it looks as if I might actually be able to afford a ticket."

"You remind me of a comedian I used to know. He thought he was funny, too."

"Only you didn't."

"Not only me. Lots of other girls didn't think he was funny, either."

"I've had no complaints so far."

"You surprise me."

"I'm working on that."

"Save your breath. Didn't you know? There are no surprises in the theater. That's why we have rehearsals."

"Is that what's happening onstage?"

"It is. That's Lotte singing. She's married to the show's composer, Kurt."

"I guess that explains a lot."

"You don't like her voice?"

"I like it fine. The music, too. It's been a useful reminder that I need to call a piano tuner."

"It's supposed to sound like that."

"Is that why it's called the **threepenny** opera?"

"You **are** a detective, aren't you?"

"That's what they tell me at the Alex."

"You should really come and see the show. It's about cops and gangsters, beggars and pimps, a murderer called Macheath and a whore called Polly."

"I get plenty of the real thing at the office."

Brigitte smiled. "I bet you do."

"On the other hand, if you're **asking** me, then I'll check my schedule."

"We'll see, shall we?" She looked at the cripple-cart I'd brought with me. "This is a curious-looking contraption."

"That's a **klutz** wagon," I said. "But this one was made for a man who isn't crippled at all. He's a yokel catcher. A con man. He used to put his legs inside the thing, which made him look like he was a double amputee. Clever, eh?"

"I don't know. Seems a lot of trouble to go to for a few lousy coins."

"The main part of his work is selling coke and acting as a lookout for a burglar."

"So he wasn't sitting in this all day."

"No."

"And you're planning to be in this for how long?"

"I hadn't given that much thought."

"Then perhaps you should. I was at UFA studios before I came here and we made a movie featuring a character with one leg. A pirate. Only, he was played by an actor with two legs so he had to strap one up every day. He found it was very uncomfortable. After an hour or two his leg lost feeling and worse, he got cramps. So I recommend you get some liniment. And an alcohol rub. Better still, make friends with a good masseur. You'll need one."

"Thanks for the tip."

"How do they propel themselves?" she asked.

"Most of them wear leather gloves and use their hands. But I've seen one or two use short crutches. I'm going to see how I get on with leather gloves."

"And are you just going to beg, or actually sell something? Like some genuine Swedish matches?" She said the words **genuine Swedish matches** as if she'd been a beggar herself.

"I'm just going to beg. I'm not actually interested in making money. I'm watching people, not pennies."

"Good point." She finished her cigarette and stubbed it out. "I see you also brought your old army uniform. Well, put it on and let's see how you look, soldier. You can get changed behind that curtain."

I picked up my uniform and eyed it uncomfortably.

"Go ahead. I promise not to peek."

"That's not why I'm hesitating. I haven't worn this since 1919."

"Then let's hope it still fits, for my sake, otherwise I'll have to have it altered."

I went behind the curtain and put the uniform on. It felt strange wearing it again. It gave me a bad feeling of the kind that felt a lot better with some strong drink in my hand.

"What happened to this yokel catcher anyway?" she asked.

"He's disappeared."

I swept the curtain aside and stood to attention while Brigitte looked at me even more critically.

"Not bad," she said. "Now all you need is a rifle and a sweetheart."

"Are you volunteering?"

"I don't have a rifle. And I don't even have a sweet tooth. But I do recommend we shave your head. That way you'll also avoid catching head lice. We can do that now if you like. Your skin is going to be harder to fix. You could chew a small piece of cordite but it will make you feel sick and you don't want to deal with that every day. Better to use some white face paint. Like you were a Pierrot. I'll show you how to apply it. I also recommend you wear dark glasses, as if your eyes had been damaged; yours are much too healthy-looking. But the Iron Cross is a nice touch. Did you win it, or is it a prop?"

"No, they gave me that for cleaning out a trench."

"Seriously?"

"Sure. There were some Tommies in it at the time, but you know how it is when you want to clean up a bit."

"So you're a hero."

"No. Don't say that. I used to know some real heroes. And I certainly don't fit that description. Not like they did. Besides, I wouldn't like you to get any ideas about me being brave or honorable."

"Don't worry, I won't. Now let's see what you look like in the wagon."

I emptied my glass, knelt down in the contraption, winced, and then stood up again.

"Need a cushion?" she asked.

"Yes."

She picked one off the armchair and arranged it in the **klutz** wagon. I knelt in it once again and nodded to Brigitte.

"Better?" she asked.

"Much."

She nodded. "Not bad. Where are you going to beg? Any ideas about that?"

"I was thinking just across the river at the Friedrichstrasse railway station. There are plenty of pitches over there. Lots of people. Lots of trains. The killer likes it noisy, you see. A train rolls in, a shot rings out. Only, no one hears it because of the train. That's his cover."

"Maybe I'll come and see you. Check you're still alive. Toss a coin your way if you're breathing. Call an ambulance if you're not."

"I'd like that. But don't speak to me. That would spoil everything. Just treat me like vermin."

"Ask me to do something more difficult than that, please."

I thought for a moment. Of course I knew she'd made a joke because that was how we were talking, as if we didn't care for each other's company one little bit, but already I could see that this wasn't how it really was between us. I amused her and she amused me and we were like two fencers trying each other out with foils because that's how it is with men and women sometimes; it's fun not saying what you mean and not meaning what you say. Only now it suddenly occurred to me that if I leveled with Brigitte, then perhaps I could count on her to do something that really **was** difficult.

"Can I tell you something in confidence?"

"I'd like to hear you try."

"I'm serious. Look, what you were saying about Winnetou. I certainly haven't given up looking for that bastard. But before I say any more I'm going to need your promise that you won't tell anyone what I'm going to tell you now, Brigitte."

"All right, soldier. I promise."

"I think the yokel catcher who was using this **klutz** wagon witnessed the most recent Winnetou murder: Eva Angerstein. I found this cripple-cart near where her body was found. I think the owner ran away and I think that her murderer is killing other disabled war vets in the hope that he'll eventually eliminate someone who can identify him."

"You mean that Winnetou and Dr. Gnadenschuss are one and the same?"

"It's just a theory, but yes, I think so."

"Hell of a difference killing a whore and killing a **klutz,** I'd have thought."

"You might think so, but a lot of people believe that they're both bad for the moral climate of the city. That too many whores and too many beggars make Berlin look ugly and degenerate. That the city needs cleaning up."

"I've heard that opinion. And it's true, perhaps something does need to be done. Maybe things have gone a little too far and a bit of order and decorum need to be restored. You wouldn't believe the number of times I've been solicited on my way home from this theater. And once worse than just solicited. But some of these girls need help to get them off the streets—proper wages, for a start—maybe some of those poor men, too."

"That's what I've been saying—that and that the killer seems to want to embarrass the Berlin police. From the letters the newspapers have published, he seems to be playing with us. Trying to cause us maximum embarrassment. Maybe he's a Nazi, maybe he hates the fact that there's a Jew in charge of the criminal police. Then again, maybe it's just enough that he hates. There's a lot of it around these days."

"I can buy that. But what's the reason you're telling me all this?"

"What time do you start work?"

"I usually begin here around midday. Why?"

"Because it occurred to me that you might do a lot more than show me how to make myself look like a **klutz.**"

"Go on."

"What you said about the one-legged actor at UFA. That was smart. It's got me thinking that I haven't really thought this through, not nearly enough. I realize now that there's going to be a limit to how much time I can tolerate in this contraption. And perhaps, left to my own devices, to how convincing I am. Look, I know it's asking a great deal, Brigitte, but I was thinking I might come to this theater every day, at about eleven, before you start your proper work, when you could help fix me up, make me look like a proper **klutz** before I head across the bridge to beg. I could come back after a few hours and then go home. Maybe even leave my costume and the wagon here."

"Why would I do that?"

"Because I think you're a smart person, and helping me beats sitting around in here playing solitaire. Because I think that like any woman in Berlin, you want Winnetou caught. And because right now I'm the best chance of making that happen."

"You're very sure of yourself, aren't you?"

"Not in the least. When I said **chance** I meant one chance in a hundred. This is a long shot, bright eyes, a very long shot, with a long gun and a deep breath and only the slightest chance of succeeding or being accurate. But right now it's the only shot we've got."

THE NEXT DAY was almost worthy of a short poem by Goethe about a German summer, with the sparrows on the linden trees singing in the sun's warm clear rays. Above Berlin's grim gray buildings the sky was as blue as the stripes on a **Strandbad** chair and the air was already cooking nicely as if ready to steam all the human sausage that inhabited the metropolis. In front of the Neues Theater, the rippling river Spree glinted like a cut sapphire. Inside the theater, onstage, the band was already rehearsing one of the numbers from the opera, but it hardly seemed to be the weather to be playing anything that was deliberately out of tune. Call me old-fashioned but there's something about a perfect day that demands perfect music. Schubert, probably.

In Brigitte Mölbling's room I changed into my uniform and sat in the makeup chair. She tucked a sheet into the collar of my old army tunic and went to work on my shaven head with paints and sponges. I liked her attention to my face; it brought her own beautiful face nearer to mine, which felt like a good place for it to be. Up close I could smell the Nivea on her face and the perfume on her fingers; in other circumstances I might even have tried to kiss her. She hummed along with the band as she worked and before long I was humming, too; one of the tunes they were rehearsing was unfeasibly catchy.

"And now, because we don't want anyone to turn a deaf ear to your misfortune—" Brigitte burned a couple of small holes into the tunic with a cigarette and, in spite of my protests, made some stains with candle wax. "We need to ensure the pity of those who see you, Gunther. It certainly wouldn't do to walk into the rattrap looking like you've just come off the parade ground."

After thirty minutes she pronounced herself satisfied that I was ready to go out and meet my public. So I knelt on the **klutz** wagon and wheeled myself eagerly to her full-length mirror, where a seismic shock awaited me. I was staring at an abbreviated, nightmarish version of myself that made me gasp out loud.

"Holy Christ," I said.

The pitiful creature looking back at me was a badly damaged man who hadn't been as lucky as me; a Gunther who, blown to pieces by an enemy mortar bomb and then salvaged by the German Army medical corps against all odds, might easily have existed in Weimar Germany's half-Brueghel world of the blind leading the blind. The round dark glasses contrasted sharply with the creature's pale face and bald head, so that they resembled the empty eye sockets in a human skull. A living, breathing Golgotha, I felt like Faust being shown one of my alternative futures by a rather less than accommodating Mephistopheles who cared nothing for seductively indulging me with all the pleasure and knowledge of the world. It was enough to make any man count his blessings and swear off the drink—almost.

"Well?" she asked. "What do you think?"

"Holy Christ," I muttered again. "I look terrible."

"I'll take that as a professional compliment."

"Well, yes, you can. It's just that—I guess I never realized how very lucky I've been. I'm looking at the fellow in the mirror and asking myself what it must be like to wake up and be confronted with this horror every day."

"And what's the answer?"

I thought for a moment. Seeing myself like this had made me realize something important. Something profound that was probably going to affect me for the rest of my days. Thanks to Bernhard Weiss and Brigitte Mölbling, I'd achieved something useful, even if I never did manage to catch Dr. Gnadenschuss. I'd been given a genuine life lesson.

"It's this. That you can't put a price on good

fortune. It's the difference between two men: One, the man in the mirror with no legs and no future other than selling Swedish matches, and the other, a stupid, able-bodied idiot of a detective who's full of drunken self-pity instead of humble gratitude. I just got myself reminded of what a lucky break I had—to walk away from 1918 without a scratch."

"Well, you have to be smart to be lucky. But what you're saying sounds like an epiphany, if you ask me."

I took her heavily ringed hand and kissed it with fond gratitude.

"It's not Archimedes but yes, why not? An epiphany. They say that when you're drinking you have to reach rock bottom to turn your life around; I think I've just been shown a small preview of what rock bottom might actually look like. Thanks to you I may never drink again. Well, perhaps not as much." I kissed her hand again.

"If I didn't know better I'd snatch my hand away and fetch some disinfectant. I've seen stray dogs that had more to recommend themselves than you do."

"I get that a lot."

"So. Are you ready?"

"Yes."

"Hey, what will you do if Dr. Gnadenschuss

really does try to kill you? How will you protect yourself?"

"The usual way." I reached into my tunic and took out a Walther automatic.

"Good," she said, as if it mattered to her that I was able to look out for myself. And that was good, too: that it mattered.

She accompanied me to the front door of the theater, where she kissed the top of my shaven head.

"You're interesting to me now. So be careful, Gunther. There are plenty of other wicked bastards out there who can do you harm, not just Dr. Gnadenschuss."

I wheeled myself out the door and into the sunshine, onto the cobbled streets of Berlin, and headed across the Friedrichstrasse bridge in search of a killer.

part three
sexuality

Triptych: a set of three associated artistic, literary, or musical works intended to be appreciated together.

I WAS FOND OF seeing Berlin from a great height; the view from the cathedral roof is unparalleled. But the world looks different when you're no higher than a dog's arse and no more significant than that to the people around you. So close to the ground I felt like a small child, one of those street urchins in summer usually seen jumping naked into the river or shouting to a friend in some poor courtyard inside another courtyard, where the sun rarely if ever shone. I didn't know if **The Threepenny Opera** had any **klutzes** in the cast, but it probably should have done; my wagon played a squeaky little tune as it bowled lamely along that put me in mind of one of the numbers from the show. Perhaps it was because I was pretending to be a cripple, but it was only now that I noticed the theater was near the Charité hospital and on the edge of the city's medical district, where surgical bookshops and specialist clinics were in plentiful evidence, along with orthopedic stores featuring a variety of equipment, including shiny modern wheelchairs that looked far more attractive than the contraption I was in. But from the prices I saw advertised in the shop windows, anyone who could have afforded a decent wheelchair could never have passed for a beggar.

I launched myself across Schiffbauerdamm, dodging piles of horse shit—I'd forgotten how many delivery horses were still on the streets of Berlin—before being blasted by the horn of a tour company charabanc whose impatient driver leaned out his window and shouted at me:

"Watch where you're going, you dopey **klutz.** You're going the right way to lose your arms as well, do you know that?"

The travel group seated behind him stared at me and one of them even took a picture, as if I was a sight no less interesting than Old Fritz on Unter den Linden or the bronze bear in front of City Hall. I waved at them cheerily and made it onto the street corner, where I waited to cross with everyone else. I was surrounded by the shapely calves of young women who took me for a diminutive pervert spying on their stocking tops and by businessmen who assumed, not unreasonably, that I was a pickpocket and moved quickly away. They had good reason; many **klutzes** were thieves. No one took me for a person, least of all a person in need. But it was clear that people did take me for what I purported to be: a disabled beggar, and that was just fine. The stocking tops were fine, too. Can't see too many of those.

Across the Spree in Reichstagufer was a row of houses next to the railway station where I was now headed and behind these, the leafy charms of Dorotheenstrasse and the church where, at the age of nine, I'd once seen the tomb of the king's son, Count van der Mark, who'd died at the same age, something that had made an enormous impression on me because if a nine-year-old royal prince could die, then so, I reasoned, might I. It was perhaps my first intimation of mortality and I never went near that particular church again.

I crossed the bridge onto Friedrichstrasse, where a lethal sandwich-board man barged me aside. By the time I reached the station, I was feeling battered and my legs and feet were turning numb. I took up a position in an isolated pool of sunshine underneath the overhead rail track. I thought I'd chosen the spot well as none of the shoe shiners and news vendors were too near, the noise from the trains being as loud as it was—as loud as Fafnir the giant dragon breathing into an amplified microphone—and, Friedrichstrasse station being one of the busiest, the arrival of a train every five minutes made most types of commerce all but impossible. I was looking to get shot, not to make new friends.

I lit a roll-up, placed my army cap on the

ground in front of me, tossed a couple of coins into it for effect, and closed my eyes for a moment. Pushing myself around was harder than I'd imagined and I was already lathered with sweat. I laid my head back against the wall and the advertising mural that was painted there: **Telefunken radios: A touch of the hand and Europe plays for you.** Listening to the radio seemed a safer bet than sleeping.

Pay attention, I told myself; you've more to live for now you've decided to stop drinking. I knew it wasn't just the sight of myself in the mirror that had helped me make this decision. It was also the sight of Brigitte Mölbling. My imagination had been drinking her in for almost twenty-four hours and I was still thirsty. And could I have imagined what she'd said as I was leaving the theater? That she found me interesting? I was certainly interested in her. And what did interesting mean, anyway? Someone with whom she could discuss the ballet or what was in **Harper's Bazaar,** or someone she wanted to go to bed with?

After a while one of the news vendors came my way, squatted down at my side, and dropped a small coin in the cap. He was a sturdy, chaff-haired man of about forty with a chin like a boxing glove. His sleeves were rolled up and I could see a tattoo on his forearm that looked like the name of a regiment.

"My name's Gallwitz," he said. "Ernst Gallwitz."

"Helmut Zehr," I said.

"Listen, Helmut," he said, "it's none of my business where you ply your trade, friend. But where you're sitting is where another old comrade was shot just a couple of weeks ago. Fellow named Oskar Heyde. According to the newspapers it was that Dr. Gnadenschuss who did it. You know—the spinner who's been murdering injured veterans. Shot between the eyes he was and no one noticed. Least not for a while."

This was exactly why I'd picked the spot, of course; there seemed to be no reason Dr. Gnadenschuss wouldn't kill underneath the Friedrichstrasse station bridge again. But I wasn't about to tell this to the news vendor, whose concern would have touched me more if I hadn't also realized I was going to have to find another place to beg. I cursed silently; the last thing I needed or wanted was someone looking out for me. It was the sort of thing Dr. Gnadenschuss might easily notice.

"Thanks for the warning, comrade," I said. "I heard about that bastard. As if life wasn't already difficult enough. But I kind of figured that lightning doesn't strike in the same place twice. That this is as safe as anywhere else in Berlin. Perhaps safer because he's killed here before."

The news vendor nodded. "You may well be

right about that. Anyway, I'll keep an eye out for you."

"Did you know him? The man who got shot?"

"Oskar? Yes, I knew him. Believe it or not, he was my lieutenant in the war." The news vendor showed me his tattooed forearm. "That's us. The 107th Infantry. We were part of the Fiftieth Reserve. We were at Passchendaele, Cambrai, and then the Marne."

I wondered why I hadn't come across this man before. I was more or less certain that there had been no witness statement from a news vendor near the scene of Oskar Heyde's murder. And I couldn't help noticing the other tattoo on his hand: three dots, which usually meant "death to cops."

"What about you?" he asked. "You look like you've seen a bit of action yourself."

"Eighth Grenadiers. We were on the Somme. The best half of me is still there, probably, feeding some French worms."

"That's too bad."

"Cops got any clues as to who did it yet?" I asked, changing the subject.

"No. They're scratching their arses and sucking their thumbs. Just for a change. But I don't speak to coppers, no matter what, see?" His speaking voice, a dark, gravelly tenor, added to the impression of feral animality he conveyed. "In this town, the law doesn't care about the workingman. They're on the side of big government and can only see out of the eye that's on the right, if you know what I mean."

I sighed silently and wished I'd had a mark for every time I'd heard that horse-shit remark.

"No descriptions of what the bastard looks like?"

"I only know what's in the paper. That's my profession, after all. The killer waited for a train coming into the station, see? The noise covered the shot. Paper said it was a .25-caliber automatic that shot him, which doesn't make much more of a pop than an air rifle. So I reckon that's when you'll have to keep your wits about you, friend. When there's a train coming in."

I grinned. "That's every five minutes."

"So you want to live forever?"

"Not like this I don't."

"Look after yourself, will you?" he said, and went back to his stand, whistling "Ain't She Sweet"—which seemed to be on every damned radio—but not before giving me a copy of the early edition of the **Morgenpost,** now rendered superfluous by the recent arrival of the late edition.

As well as wondering why we hadn't come across Ernst Gallwitz before, I was also wondering how he knew it was a .25-caliber automatic that Dr. Gnadenschuss had used to kill Oskar Heyde. I'd persuaded the **Berliner Tageblatt** to leave out that particular detail from the letter they'd printed. A lucky guess, perhaps? Or something more? Apart from the three dots tattooed on his hand he didn't look like a murderer; then again, nobody does these days, especially not the murderers; it's one of the things that makes the job so difficult. All the same, his remarks about the Berlin police helped me decide to put him into my suspect file. After all, there was no one else in it.

I opened the newspaper and turned the pages almost mindlessly since it was mostly filled with advertisements. A full-page ad for a clearance sale of ladies' fur coats at Meine in East Berlin did little to persuade me I was wrong about this; buying a fur coat on one of the hottest days of the year looked every bit as crazy as staking yourself out like a goat for a man-eating tiger.

Still cursing the news vendor, I tried to figure out where I was going to move to; the next nearest station was at the Stock Exchange, which was at least half a kilometer to the east. A fifteen-minute stroll when you were on legs, but something else when you were confined to a **klutz** wagon. That was clearly out of the question. But perhaps I might find a spot on Georgenstrasse, close to the all-important overhead railway line, and after a while I had marked out a place in my mind's eye that was in front of the Trianon Theater, less than two hundred meters away. I waited a while, smoked another roll-up, and then set off.

ON MY THIRD day outside the Trianon I caught a glimpse of Käthe Haack, the actress, stepping out of a shiny Maybach limousine and going up to the stage door. She signed a few autographs, smiled her famous ingénue smile, and went inside, but not before putting a silver fifty-pfennig piece in my hat, which was the most I'd had since I'd started to beg and for which I blessed her, several times, and resolved not to think badly of her or her terrible movies ever again. A little later, Haack's much older husband, Heinrich Schroth, turned up—and gave me nothing except a look of withering contempt before going in through the same stage door. He was always playing Prussian aristocrats in movies and I think he almost believed he was one. He wore his broad-brimmed hat Bohemian-style and his coat hung on his shoulders like a cape; for a while I entertained myself with the idea that he might have been Winnetou because, at a stretch, he fit the description given by Fritz Pabst.

The Trianon had five entrances: the main one on Georgenstrasse, and the other four on

Prinz-Louis-Ferdinand-Strasse and on Prinz-Franz-Karl-Strasse. The back of the theater was a warren of alleys and small courtyards and gave onto the headquarters of the Green police, which was what the political police were called because it was their job to cover all outdoor political demonstrations, but it certainly didn't stop them from interfering with the normal day-to-day policing of the city that was handled by the regular cops, the Schupo. From time to time, a Greenie would harass one of the many prostitutes who, at all hours of the day, brought their clients to the back alleys of the Trianon from the various bars, theaters, casinos, and revues that were located in the famous Admiralspalast on Friedrichstrasse. But the sheer number of pricks that were sucked around the back of the Trianon was only exceeded by the number of pricks inside the theater, although Schroth was by no means the biggest of these; Mathias Wieman and Gerhard Dammann were usually in and out of the Trianon, and so was the biggest prick of them all, the stage actor Gustaf Gründgens, who couldn't have looked more pleased with himself if he'd been the devil incarnate. He wore a supercilious smile that persisted even after he'd flicked a half-smoked cigarette at my head. I wasn't sure if he meant to hit me or if he intended me to smoke it, but since beggars can't be choosers—and certainly shouldn't look as if they can be—I picked it up and saluted him as if he'd done me a favor.

"Thank you, sir. You're very kind. Very kind, indeed." I puffed the cigarette and found it was excellent Turkish tobacco. Nothing but the best for Gustaf Gründgens.

"What's this? Sarcasm? From a beggar?"

"No, sir. Never. Not me. Although it seems to me that even a great actor might learn something with a beggar for a teacher."

"True."

Gründgens fixed a monocle to his eye and regarded me as he might a strange species of beetle.

"You know who I am then."

"Oh yes, sir. I expect everyone knows who you are. You're the greatest actor in Germany, sir. At least that's what educated people say. You're the great Emil Jannings."

Gründgens's smile became a rictus and without another word he went on his way. It only takes a small triumph to make your day.

Actors were not the only artistes I saw at the Trianon. On my fourth day playing the tethered goat I realized that a man was sketching me. He was about forty, tall, handsome, with a good head, a rather boyish haircut, and a thoughtful knot between his gloomy, gray eyes. He wore a lightweight brown suit with plus four trousers, a rose-colored shirt with a collar pin, and a stiff pink bow tie. He didn't look like he wanted to shoot me, just to draw me. Irritated I turned my head away, hoping he might leave. Being closely observed was bad for my purpose; Dr. Gnadenschuss was hardly likely to strike while I was having my portrait done. My turning away prompted the artist to come over, first to apologize and then to offer me fifty pfennigs to resume my previous pose. He also told me his name was Otto.

"All right," I said without much grace.

"Where were you wounded?"

"In the legs," I said bitterly.

"No, I meant— Well, I was wounded myself, as a matter of fact. In the neck. Although not as you'd notice. August 1918. Actually the wound in my neck—it saved my neck. They sent me on a flying course after that and by the time I'd completed it, the war was over."

I grunted. "What's the idea, anyway?" I asked, playing the surly bastard, and playing it well, too. Brigitte would have been proud. "Drawing someone like me. It doesn't make any sense. After all, I'm no oil painting."

"I disagree. There's a certain beauty in the way you are. And I can assure you, you're not the first injured war veteran I've sketched in this city."

"You want to go around the back of the theater. You'll see many more interesting subjects than a **klutz** on a cart."

"Oh, you mean the whores."

"I do mean the whores. And their clients."

"No, I see enough of that when I go to a whorehouse. As a matter of fact, you and other unfortunate men like you are one of my favorite subjects. It's more or less unique to Berlin."

"Are you taking the piss?"

"No. Not at all. Look, everyone thinks they know what art should be—"

"A nice picture. Of something nice. That's what art **should** be. Something you can hang on your wall that doesn't make you feel like throwing up. That's what art should be. Everyone knows that."

"You might think so. But very few people have the wherewithal to experience painting as the sense of sight, to see colors and form as living reality."

I shrugged. "I'll tell you about living reality. You're looking at it. And it's shit. There's not a day that passes that I don't wish I was dead."

"That's exactly what I'm driving at. Germans are already beginning to forget what horrible suffering the war brought. I want to remind them of that. Drawing you, it's an expression of what's in my soul, that's all. Sketching you is just drawing my own most innermost thoughts."

I laughed. "Well, then, go ahead. But don't expect to sell any pictures. People don't want to be reminded of how crappy life is. They **want** to forget it. And there's nobody who wants to remember how terrible the war was. Me least of all."

He stopped spouting claptrap and went back to sketching me, which suited us both. After another half hour, he thanked me and then left on a bicycle, heading toward the university. I closed my eyes and told myself that if all artists were like Otto, if drawing a cripple on a **klutz** wagon really was what was in his soul, then Germany was in a lot more trouble than I could ever have imagined. And noting that an obsession with art depicting injured war veterans begging on the streets of Berlin was remarkable to say the least—almost as remarkable as George Grosz, who liked to draw the corpses of women—I mentally added him to the thin suspect file.

"YOU'RE ALIVE," SHE said. "Thank God. I was thinking of sending out a search party."

"I'm beginning to think this is all a waste of time."

"What? And miss my professional care and attention?"

"Coming here to see you has been the only real compensation. My last thought as Dr. Gnadenschuss presses a pistol to my forehead will be: 'I wonder if Brigitte can cover up this bullet hole and make me look like I'm still alive.' For the sake of my loved ones, of course."

"That's a cheerful thought."

"Oh, I've got others. But here's something that

will make you laugh. Someone drew my portrait today. A man wearing plus fours and a pink bow tie. The poor misguided fool mistook me for a work of art."

"Since I dressed and painted you myself I should be flattered."

"I never thought of it that way. But yes, maybe you're right. Like a student copying a picture in an art gallery."

"Not just any picture. Something by Velázquez, probably. A painting of one of those fashionable court dwarves owned by the King of Spain."

"Now, that's the kind of fashion you'd think a German must have invented."

Brigitte Mölbling helped me climb out of the **klutz** wagon and then knelt down and began rubbing my legs vigorously to get some feeling back into them while I washed my hands in the sink. She was wearing a very thin, clingy gray muslin dress with a matching scarf and a collection of South American silver jewelry that looked as if it was the understudy of the gold collection I'd met before. The dress was like a map since it showed every place I now wanted to explore.

"How does that feel?" she said.

"Beats my mother's coffee, I'll tell you that much."

"You look as though you need something a little stronger," she said, taking off my army trousers. "Shall I fix you a drink?"

"No, thanks. I'm leaving the hard stuff alone for a while."

"That sounds as if it's a new thing."

"As a matter of fact it is. I want to be sure I can take it without being unable to leave it, if you know what I mean. Frankly, I was in danger of not liking the stuff anymore; it was beginning to taste a lot like medicine. The next time I have a drink I want it to taste like it's something I'm doing only for pleasure."

"It sounds to me like you've had too much whiskey or too much sun."

"In Berlin? That seems hardly possible."

Brigitte slipped off my army tunic, and then steered me to the chair, where she began the business of removing my makeup. I was silent for a while, enjoying her breath and her scent and the brush of her breast against my shoulder and imagining the impression all of those might have on my pillow back home.

"I was thinking," I told her. "I still don't know much about you."

"I was born in Berlin. I've worked here for six months and I have an apartment on Luther Strasse, not so very far from you. I'm convent educated. Studied art history and theater in Paris. I was married for a while to a very minor Prussian aristocrat, but it didn't stick. One day I came home and found him wearing my clothes, including the underwear. Call me old-fashioned, but I don't like anyone wearing my clothes except me. Least of all my husband. He's happier now. Lives with a very poor boy in Hamburg and writes queer poetry that no one wants to read. Frankly he isn't much of a man. And I can't remember why I married him. Probably to please my father. It was all my fault, of course. My psychoanalyst says my problem is I like real men and, certainly since the war, they're in very short supply. That's probably the reason I like you. I get the feeling you've never worn a dress in your life."

"Only because I can never find one that fits. And then?"

"I told you. I used to work at UFA."

"That's it?"

"It is in Berlin. UFA opens all kinds of locked doors. I worked on Fritz Lang's **Metropolis.** Which almost broke the studio. That's why I'm working in the theater now. UFA couldn't afford to keep me."

"Then you must know Thea von Harbou."

"Sure. You know Thea?"

"I helped her out with a story she's writing for the cinema."

"It figures. She and Lang—they're a strange couple. In many ways they're not a couple at all. They have what you might call a free relationship and neither seems to mind what the other gets up to. She has an Indian lover who's not much more than a boy. And by the way, she's a Nazi, just in case you thought you liked her. As for him, he sees a lot of girls, mostly professionals, and not always with happy outcomes. I certainly wouldn't put anything past Fritz. Including murder, by the way. His first wife is supposed to have killed herself but like a lot of other people, I'm not so sure it was suicide. Thea and Fritz are fascinated with violent crime. The library in their house looks like it was assembled by Jack the Ripper, who's something of an obsession for them both. They even have objects related to the Ripper murders. They're just strange. Kurt—that's Kurt Weill, the composer of our little show—he hates Fritz. Don't ask me why, but pretty much everyone in theater and cinema hates Fritz Lang."

"What about Daisy Torrens? Do you know her?"

"You certainly know some very peculiar people, Gunther. Yes, I know Daisy. Good-time girl. Yank. Plenty of money. Lives with the present minister for the interior. Albert Grzesinski. Even though he's married. Still, he's an improvement on her last boyfriend. Rudi. Rudi Geise. He was a swine."

I'd heard this name before, but I couldn't remember where.

"Tell me about Rudi."

"He works for Reinhold Schünzel Films. Daisy said he was an assistant producer but the only thing I ever saw him produce was a knife. And a couple of grams of snow. Not sure why they were ever an item because Rudi hates women. Come to think of it, Rudi hates everyone. Something happened to him during the war. His boyfriend got killed, I think. Anyway, he told me that he got his revenge on the Tommies who killed him by mutilating their corpses whenever he got the chance. Cutting an ear off, he said. Slitting noses in half. I mean, he'd be a really horrible person even if none of that was true." She straightened up and looked at me critically. "There. I've finished. You look more or less normal. Or at least as normal as you're ever going to look for now."

After what Brigitte had said I could see no good reason not to add the names of Fritz Lang and Rudi Geise to my suspect file and, as soon as I was done playing the tethered goat, assuming I was still alive and hadn't caught Dr. Gnadenschuss, I resolved to go and interview both men. Especially Rudi. It was only a short step from slicing off ears to cutting off scalps. But right now I was more interested in Brigitte.

"I was thinking. The next time you're making me up, you should paint my toenails."

"Any particular color?"

"The same as yours. Whatever that is."

"Generally speaking, a woman chooses the same shade for fingers and toes." She kicked off one of her shoes and showed me her foot. There were five toes on the end of it and the nails were all painted lilac.

"Satisfied?"

"Not by a long way. It's a lovely foot. I like it a lot. I imagine you've another just like it. But please don't stop now you've started."

"You want to see the other one, too. Is that it?"

"Just to check that the colors match."

From the sound of things, rehearsals were going well; by now I knew the names of all the principal characters in the show and Polly and Macheath were presently singing a crappy love song. Maybe that's what started all the sexuality between Brigitte and me. **Sexuality:** I don't know what else to call this activity when it seems natural but also excessive. But it's amazing how sexy a woman's bare foot can look when the nails are painted lilac and there's toe cleavage and you've been sitting in the sun all day and she's locked the door, kicked off the second shoe, and is slowly gathering the gray dress at the hem and pulling it carefully over her head, and then draping it across the back of the chair I was still sitting on.

"I suppose you want me to take off my underwear."

"Generally that's recommended in these situations."

"Is that what you'd call this? A situation?"

"Of course."

"So what kind of a situation would you say this was?"

"An interesting one."

"Is that all?"

"Complicated, too."

She took off the underwear and tossed it silently onto the table, where it occupied not much more space than a handful of rose petals.

"One that I don't want to get out of in a hurry."

"Well, that's why I locked the door, Herr Commissioner. To keep you here for my selfish pleasure."

"That's just the way I was going to handle it. Your pleasure, I mean. Only, right now I'm a little distracted. It's not every day I get to look at the treasures of the world."

She came and sat on my lap and stroked my head and for some reason I couldn't put into words, I didn't throw her onto the floor; it wasn't that I couldn't think of any words, at least the ones with more than one syllable, just that my mouth was busy kissing her.

"So what happens now?"

"I should have thought it was fairly straightforward."

"You might think that. But then you're a man. Which means you really haven't thought this out at all. I'm happy to sit on your lap without my clothes on. As a matter of fact I'm rather enjoying the situation. If that's what this is. But for the next stage I want a large bed with nice sheets. Which means going to my place. I've never yet met a man whose bed linen was up to my standard. Just so you know, the way to my heart is through one-hundred-percent Egyptian cotton. Good bed linen is nonnegotiable as far as I'm concerned. And then maybe we'll have some dinner. Horcher's, I think. And before you say **policeman's salary,** I'm paying. Just because I'm working here doesn't mean I need the money. My dad is Curt Mölbling."

"The industrialist?"

"Yes."

"I'll check my diary. When were you thinking of?"

"Tonight. Now, if you can. Any sooner than that would be better."

AT AROUND ELEVEN o'clock the next morning, after having my makeup applied and in the hope of seeing something useful on the street, I sat outside Friedrichstrasse station under the bridge. If anything, the sun was even stronger than the day before and, always quick to complain, many Berliners were now grumbling about the heat and wishing for a rain shower. There was no sign of Ernst Gallwitz, the news vendor, and the shoe shiners had already packed up and gone home; they did a good trade first thing in the morning but not when it was getting near to lunch. I guess nobody wants a shoeshine in the middle of the day.

I'd been sitting listening to the monotonously atonal symphony of overhead trains for almost an hour when a yellow BMW Dixi pulled up at the edge of the sidewalk and, with the engine still running, the driver sat there looking to all the world as if he was waiting for someone to emerge from the station. But after a while he seemed to be eyeing me with real malice, so much so that I memorized his number, convinced I was looking at Dr. Gnadenschuss.

I put my hand inside my army tunic and took hold of the handle of my gun. In retrospect, I think he was probably trying to work out if the dark glasses meant I was also blind as well as crippled; but it was several minutes before I realized that he and his malice aforethought were waiting for someone else.

A Fritz came out of Aschinger, an old wheat-beer tavern with plain wooden tables and pictures of the Kaiser, and when he crossed Friedrichstrasse heading toward the station, the man in the car wound down the Dixi's window and shot him thirty-two times with a Bergmann submachine gun—the same kind of gun that an assassin had planned to use on Bernhard Weiss at the circus. I knew it was thirty-two times because that's how many the magazine on a Bergmann holds and the man in the car emptied the whole drum before throwing the gun onto the passenger seat and driving off.

Most people stayed back for fear of more shots being fired—a not-unreasonable precaution under the circumstances; this smelled like a ring killing, and it was safe to assume that there would be some kind of retaliation. Meanwhile, I wheeled myself onto the road to survey the bullet-ridden corpse at closer quarters; I didn't recognize the dead man but I'd certainly recognized the man in the car who'd shot him: it was the same thug who'd been sitting next to me at the Sing Sing Club. There was nothing about that evening I was ever likely to forget. The killer's name had been Hugo and his helpful girlfriend had been called Helga. Even as I recalled this detail, Helga herself came out of Aschinger, screaming like a prehistoric bird and in that same moment the true nature of the catastrophe was explained. It wasn't a ring killing at all, but a simple case of sexual jealousy. Hugo must have suspected Helga was seeing someone else and had resolved to eliminate his rival. And there could be no doubt he'd done that: I'd rarely seen a victim so comprehensively shot and killed as the torn and bloodied man lying on the street.

Helga ran toward her dead lover, dropped to her knees, and, still keening, cradled his leaky head on her lap, hardly caring about the blood spilling onto her blouse, at which point a piece of his skull detached itself in her hands and her screams grew even louder. I didn't say anything and having got halfway across Friedrichstrasse to check the man was dead, I didn't stop, or look back. I kept on going. The last thing I needed was to blow my cover by helping the local law. There would be plenty of time and opportunity to telephone the Alex later on, when I was Bernie Gunther again. Besides, there was no way that Dr. Gnadenschuss was going to show up now when the whole street was about to swarm with cops. I needed to be somewhere else, and quickly.

I wheeled myself east, thinking a cold wheat beer was just the thing on a hot day. My path took me past a shop selling foreign stamps and Diana air rifles and the local canine clinic, which was offering **docking, castrating, and painless destroying.** From the state of his corpse, I guessed that all three of those services must already have been provided for Hugo's unfortunate victim—except perhaps the painless part: being pumped full of bullets hurts.

OUTSIDE THE THEATER I resumed my position in front of the Trianon's poster. Recently transferred from the smaller Rose Theater, **The Spendthrift,** a play by Ferdinand Raimund, was now booking. Someone with a sense of humor had crossed out Raimund's name and substituted the name of Heinrich Köhler, the present finance minister. I could already hear the sound of police and ambulance sirens to the west. And so could the local control girls. One in particular was staring nervously into the distance, wondering if she dared risk taking her even more nervous-looking client around the back of the theater to conduct their business. She was wearing a pink cloche hat and a low-cut, thin pink dress that afforded me a fine view of her large unsupported pink breasts; evidently she'd been sunbathing. Then she saw me.

"Hey," she said. "Hindenburg. Can you see?"

"Yes."

"Then why the glasses?"

"It's sunny."

She shrugged. "Fair enough. Well, now you've had your free look at today's special, do you want to make yourself some money?"

"Sure. Why not? How, and how much?"

She tossed a coin into my cap and then handed me a police whistle. "That was twenty-five pfennigs. There's another twenty-five if you keep a lookout while I take care of this Fridolin's signal box. If a bull shows up before I come back, just give a toot on that whistle, right?"

"I wouldn't worry about it, love," I said, keen to avoid any kind of role in their transaction. "There's been a shooting outside the station on Friedrichstrasse that should keep the bastards busy for hours. That's what all the commotion is about."

"I'm not worried. It's my friend here who's worried. Just blow that whistle if a bull turns up, right? One blast, that's all. Got that?"

"How long will you be?"

The whore looked at her client, whose blushing face told us both he was young and inexperienced, and grinned.

"We'd better ask him, hadn't we?" She looked at the boy and smiled. "How about it, Fritz. How long will it take to get you off?"

The boy blushed a deeper shade of red, at which point the whore looked at me and said: "Ten minutes, tops."

But as things turned out they were gone for a lot less than ten minutes. I didn't see where the two Greenies came from who arrested them, but as they marched the pair out from behind the theater and around the corner to the police station, the whore shot me a look every bit as homicidal as the one I'd seen on the face of the man in the yellow Dixi.

"What, are you blind as well as stupid, you legless prick?" she yelled. "Christ, I hope you're a better beggar than you're a lookout. Did you actually lose those legs, or just forget where you left them?"

"Sorry." I shrugged an apology but thought no more about it until half an hour later, when I was awoken from a light sleep and a dream of summer rain by something wet and the sound of a woman's laughter. I opened my eyes and the first thing I saw was a woman's genitals close to my face; it was another few seconds before I realized that the whore who'd been arrested by the Greenies had come back to the Trianon to hoist her dress up, plant one foot on the wall above my head, and then piss on me like a dog. By the time I realized what she'd done, she'd dropped her skirt and run off, shrieking with laughter, leaving me soaked in her stinking urine.

"That'll teach you, dumbhead," she yelled back at me. "Next time someone asks you to keep a lookout, try opening your fucking eyes."

IT'S HARD TO describe the shame I felt at this latest turn of events. I told myself it was no less than what Anita Berber used to do at the White Mouse on Jägerstrasse, until the place had closed. But the fact was, I felt curiously emasculated by what had happened. So much so that when I returned to the Schiffbauerdamm Theater and saw

Brigitte again, I couldn't bring myself to tell her exactly what had happened and instead chose to make a joke out of it; at least, that's how I explained it to myself.

"A dog pissed on me," I said, removing my reeking army tunic. "I must have dozed off in the sunshine and when I woke up a damn dog was pissing on me. I guess it mistook my field-gray uniform for a street corner. If I wasn't so disgusted with myself I'd be laughing, so go right ahead, be my guest. Because it is kind of funny. Some detective, huh? If the boys at the Alex find out about this I'll never hear the end of it."

"You worry about me. Not them. My sense of humor is every bit as cruel as any man I ever met."

"I can believe that."

"What kind of a dog was it, anyway?" she asked, restraining a smile.

"A big one. With lots of teeth."

"That's not much of a description."

"I don't know about breeds. Next time I'll pat it on the head, ask if it has a name, and get it to go and fetch me a stick to beat it with."

"The poor thing was just marking out its territory." Brigitte fetched a bottle of cologne from her bag and sprayed the air with it. "Really, you should feel flattered."

"That's just what I've been telling myself on

the way back here. But that's a little hard; now that the sun's dried it off and I smell you, I realize I stink like a **schnapper.**"

I draped the tunic on a hanger, hung it out the window, slipped off the army pants, and washed my hands and face. Brigitte lit a black cigarette, which helped with the smell, and then threaded it in my mouth. I sucked the smoke down like it had come from an altar boy's thurible.

"I can get that uniform cleaned if you like. Overnight. The cleaners we use here are very reliable."

"If they're anything like the overnight service I got from you then they must be the best in Berlin."

Brigitte smiled. "I'm very glad to hear it. But that wasn't a service. That was an errand of mercy."

"So you're an angel as well."

"There are a lot of angels in the theater. Someone has to pay for these shows. My dad, mostly." She shook her head. "You know, talking of angels, I thought of you today. As a matter of fact, for a while back there I got quite worried. There was a murder on Friedrichstrasse and I thought it might be you who was playing a harp."

"What persuaded you it wasn't, angel?"

"As soon as I heard about it I walked down to Friedrichstrasse and asked a cop."

"What did he say?"

"Said it was a gang thing. But by then I knew it wasn't you. The dead guy's hand was sticking out from under the sheet. You didn't have a girl's name tattooed on the base of your thumb when you left here. Or pants with a cuff. And I wasn't sure you had that amount of blood in you. No one does."

"You were worried about me? I'm touched."

"Don't make a big thing about it. Besides, I needed the exercise and the fresh air."

"And when you knew it wasn't me who was dead?"

"I came back here."

"Is that all?"

"No, I lit a candle in St. John's, went down on my knees, and gave thanks to the Almighty."

"You on your knees. I'd like to see that."

"Your memory stinks worse than your army uniform, copper."

"As a matter of fact, I was a witness to that murder. I saw the whole thing. I even recognized the killer."

"What does that make you? An innocent bystander?"

"Kind of. Except that I wasn't standing. And unless it's a blue moon or a Sunday, I'm not so innocent."

"After last night's errand of mercy I can testify to that. But it is handy that it should be you who happened to see the whole thing. You being a cop 'n' all. You think the defense lawyers will believe you? When it goes to court? **I just happened to be sitting in a** klutz **wagon on another case when your client shot the dead man.** Meanwhile, maybe the police commissioner will give you a promotion. Or a medal. Or a new magnifying glass. Whatever he does when you hand him the murderer's head on a plate."

"As soon as I get my own clothes on I'm going to telephone the Alex to make a report."

"What's your hurry? I like you just fine with your pants off." She kicked off her shoes and showed me her toes. "Besides, the victim looked as though he would keep for a while."

"You're forgetting the killer. He might get away."

"I very much doubt that. You look like the kind of cop who always gets his man. Not to mention his woman. And if not his woman then someone else's. Maybe anyone else's."

"Now, what makes you say a thing like that?"

"You've got a way with women, Gunther. A nice way, but a way nonetheless. The same way a professional gambler knows the way to count cards. Or a good jockey knows how to handle racehorses."

"You make me sound very cynical."

"No. That's not it. I'll work out a name for it the next time I have a thesaurus in front of me. Anyway, now that I know you're all right I was thinking of celebrating by locking the door again."

"Just as long as I'm on the inside."

"I can't think of a better place for you to be."

THE NEXT DAY, after my army uniform had been cleaned and Brigitte had swept the floor with it for good effect, I decided to cut my losses at Trianon and beg somewhere else: I chose Lehrter Bahnhof, which was west of the theater. It was a little farther away, but I was gaining confidence on the **klutz** wagon. I could go faster now. My arms and shoulders were stronger and I could bowl along without raising a sweat. On the journey down Friedrich-Krause-Ufer, I'd gone so fast I'd dropped my cigarette case and had to stop to look for it. The station was right at the junction of the canal and the river and, with its central nave and aisles, resembled the basilica of a site of modern pilgrimage, receiving millions of visitors per year, which wasn't so far from the truth. There's nothing Germans worship more than getting to work on time.

It was only when I got there and saw the newsstands that I found out a fifth disabled veteran had been murdered. I bought the lunchtime edition of an evening newspaper and discovered that Dr. Gnadenschuss had struck again, only this time he'd killed someone I'd actually met: Johann Tetzel, the one-legged sergeant with the bushy white mustache. I'd talked to him in front of the Berlin Zoo aquarium, and that's where he was killed. It had been Tetzel who'd given me the tip about looking for Prussian Emil at the Sing Sing. Like the others, he'd been shot through the forehead at point-blank range by a small-caliber pistol.

My first thought was that Tetzel was the only one-legged man that Dr. Gnadenschuss had shot; and this only seemed remarkable when I remembered that Tetzel had partnered with another veteran, a man called Joachim who, like all the previous victims, was a double amputee. Why had Dr. Gnadenschuss killed the one-legged man and not the other? Unless Joachim had moved his pitch. My second thought was that I was probably wasting my time; it seemed highly unlikely that Dr. Gnadenschuss would kill again so soon. He was probably already composing another boasting letter for the newspapers alleging police incompetence. Possibly he was right about that. We seemed to be no nearer to catching him.

In my mind's eye I pictured Weiss and Gennat in front of the Berlin Zoo aquarium with the murder wagon and I could already hear Gennat grumbling about my not being there. He had a point, too; and for a while I considered abandoning my disguise and reporting back to the Alex, sober and ready to do my proper job. Try as I might I couldn't help but think there was something demeaning about what I was doing, especially after the events of the previous day. And I still had to make my report about the shooting in Friedrichstrasse. I'd already telephoned Bernhard Weiss a couple of times but, on both occasions, he'd been with Grzesinski at the Ministry of the Interior. Given that only he knew I was working undercover I had been reluctant to speak to anyone else for fear that I'd have to explain how it was that I'd come to be on Friedrichstrasse in the first place.

I was still processing this new information when I saw a gang of wild boys swaggering down Wilhelm-Ufer. In their distinctive attire—leather shorts, top or bowler hats, striped vests, and large pirate earrings—they were easy to spot. Unfortunately they had also spotted me and I found myself quickly surrounded.

"Well, well, well," said the leader, a tall, muscular youth of about seventeen, with a cowboy-style bandanna around his neck. He carried a heavy blackthorn walking stick and was covered with tattoos proclaiming his allegiance to the "Forest Pirates"—which meant nothing to me. "And what do we have here? The legless wonder, is it? The human centipede, perhaps? The Red Baron? Half man, half shopping cart."

His four delinquent friends thought all this was very funny. But the leader hadn't finished with me; indeed, it seemed he'd hardly started.

"That's a nice medal you're wearing," he said. "The Iron Cross. First class. Did they give you that for courage? For raping Belgian women? Nice work if you can get it. Or just for killing Franzis? You know, you should paint your cripple-cart red, like Manfred von Richthofen. And you could fly around Berlin as the red **klutz.** Then you really would look like that medal was deserved. I think I'd like a medal like that. In fact I think I'd like **your** medal. It will match my vest. What do you say, boys? Don't you think a nice medal would suit me?"

More laughter from the pack of hungry young wolves. Other Berliners coming out of the station were wisely giving them a wide berth and I could see no one was going to come to my aid. I was in trouble and was already reaching inside my tunic for the automatic.

Except that it wasn't there. And realizing it must have fallen out of my tunic when I'd dropped my cigarette case on Friedrich-Krause-Ufer, I felt a look of alarm on my face which, to my interrogator's hard blue eyes, must have looked very like fear.

"Don't worry, Baron. We won't hurt you, not unless we have to. Just hand the medal over and we'll leave you alone."

He patted the thick handle of the blackthorn walking stick meaningfully. I didn't doubt that if he hit me with it, I'd be in serious trouble. Already I was flexing the muscles in my hidden legs in the expectation that I was going to have to stand up and defend myself. Which, of course, was misinterpreted as another sign of fear on my part.

"Look, Erich." One of the bull's acolytes laughed. "The bastard's shitting himself."

"Is that right, Manfred? Are you shitting yourself?"

I was beginning to think that perhaps Gennat had been right about the Gnadenschuss killings—that it was vicious kids who were responsible after all.

"You're not getting this medal, sonny," I said. "Since I was almost killed winning it, I'm not about to hand it over because I'm scared of getting killed again, least of all by a nasty little queer like you. If you want a medal, why don't you go and buy one from a joke shop? Better still, why don't you join the army yourself and then win one? Posthumously. Yes, that might be best, I think. Best for you and best for society in general. Because what the country certainly doesn't need are cowardly pipsqueaks in greasy shorts whose idea of courage is to try and rob a man with no legs."

The rest of the wild-boy gang uttered a long

and girlish groan of camp horror and one of them whistled as if this insult from me would have to be answered. The bull of the gang was going to do something now, I could see that.

"I'm sorry. What was that you said, Manfred?"

"I think you heard him clearly enough," said someone out of my sight line. "But in case you're deaf as well as stupid, the man said that if you want a medal of your own you should join the army and win one, posthumously. And I must say I agree with every word."

The gang leader turned around and was immediately felled by a big-fisted right hook, which looked to have broken his nose. One of the others took a savage blow on the shoulder from a thick rattan cane. And then the rest ran off. All of which left me looking up at my impeccably dressed rescuer. And moreover at a rescuer I recognized.

It was Police Inspector Kurt Reichenbach.

I TOOK OFF my sunglasses to make sure it was him, at which point he frowned and then looked down at me, rubbing his eyes incredulously. When he stood immediately in front of the sun it was like he was a black hole in space. Someone who wasn't there at all, but it was my good fortune that he was.

"Jesus Christ. Gunther? Bernhard Gunther? Is that you down there?"

My disguise was good, but it wasn't so good it could deceive a man I'd known for several years, moreover one who was a good detective. But as usual Kurt Reichenbach was more flaneur than cop. He was wearing a smart lightweight beige suit with a blue-and-white-striped shirt, a white waistcoat and a white tie, a blue silk handkerchief in his top pocket and a carnation in his buttonhole; a light brown bowler worn at a jaunty angle topped off the whole ensemble. He might have been off to the racecourse in Grünewald, or to a nice lunch in Wannsee. His gray beard was longer and more luxuriant than usual and there was a ruby twinkle in his eye; he almost made being a cop look like it might be fun.

"What the hell do you think you're doing? I could—you could have been killed. Those young bastards—I mean, they're vicious. Heartless." He kicked one of the wild boys still lying on the sidewalk, which stirred the youth enough to drag himself away. "I was at the local apothecary getting some drops for my eyes. It's just as well I hadn't yet used them, otherwise I might not have seen you at all and you'd be on your way to the Charité. One more bleeding body for my poor wife to patch up. You know she's a nurse, right? Why, just the other night she had to fix up a hotel doorman who got himself beat up by some of these feral queers because they wanted to steal his top hat. Maybe these were the very ones who did it. But I still don't understand—why the hell are you sitting here dressed up like a half-eaten war bagel?"

I waited until the remaining wild boy had run off before answering.

"Working undercover," I said. "You might say I'm a tethered goat playing the **klutz** in the hope of ambushing Dr. Gnadenschuss."

"Ambush, how? By rolling your wagon wheels over his toes before he can shoot you?"

"No, I've got a gun. At least I had one until this morning. I must have lost it when I was rolling myself over the bridge. I was looking for it when you showed up and saved my hide. Thanks, by the way. You were just in time to save me a beating. Or worse."

"Who thought up this crazy scheme? No, don't tell me. It was that idiot Bernhard Weiss, wasn't it? Gennat would never have gone along with something as dumb as this. The Big Buddha's got common sense. But Weiss—like any ex-lawyer, he reads far too many books. Typical Jew, of course. Always got his nose in a book. He should have been a rabbi, not a cop."

"You're a Jew yourself, Kurt."

"Yes, but he's a clever Jew and people don't like that. I'm not a clever Jew like him. Weiss is the kind of Jew who has a surfeit of new ideas. People don't like new ideas. Especially in Germany. They like the old ones. The old lies best of all. That's what Hitler is all about. Says he's got new ideas but they're just the old ideas, reheated, like yesterday's dinner. New ideas, nobody likes that. People are afraid of the new. Look here, we work for the Berlin police force, not a laboratory of human behavior. Jesus, you should never have been asked to do this without some backup. Some other cops to watch over you. One at the very least."

"I think we both thought that Dr. Gnadenschuss is too smart not to spot something like that."

"I don't think he's smart. I think he's been lucky, that's all. Probably because there are some people who just don't want this monster to be caught. Who think he's doing God's good work. Cleaning up the streets. You know, respectable window-box folk who like things neat and tidy. And there's nothing tidy about the way you look and what you're doing. Believe me, I know what I'm talking about. I know this city like I know my own prick. Do you ever ask yourself why I'm on the street so much instead of being in the office, Bernie? Walking around like I'm just a citizen? I talk to the meat, that's why. I'm a social animal. I like to talk. I chat to whores, pimps, thieves, and rapists. Shit, I'll even speak to cops in uniform. I collect their stories like I'm a writer and, sometimes, I even see a connection. Hell, that's true detection. When you talk to the meat on the street you hear things. And we both know that there are ways of keeping a man under surveillance without drawing attention to yourself. I wish you'd asked me. I could have helped."

"In that outfit?"

"Listen to Lon Chaney."

"Look, we thought we had to do something. Especially with those letters he keeps writing to the damn newspapers. They're beginning to hit home. We're no nearer to catching him now after five victims than we were before he killed anyone."

"Sure, sure. But still, it's a risk you're running here, Bernie. When you play in the street, you risk getting yourself run over. It's not just **klutzes** and whores who get killed in this city. It's cops, too. Maybe you've forgotten Johannes Buchholz."

"That was other cops who shot him."

"If you say so. But those two cops they booked for it were acquitted. All I'm saying is that you need to be more careful. The first law of police work in Berlin is to go home at night without a new hole in your head; everything else is of secondary importance, my friend. So what are you going to do now?"

"Stick it out here for a while. See if I get a bite."

"Really? Surely you've scared the fish away with

all this commotion. You won't get a bite now. I can guarantee it."

"It's not even lunchtime. Besides, if you knew how long it takes me to get this makeup on—I have to make that seem like it was worthwhile."

"Yes, I can see you put a lot of energy into that disguise. It's a good look for you. I suppose your legs are folded away inside your cripple-cart. Ingenious. Never seen that before."

"I found it abandoned at the site of Eva Angerstein's murder."

"You did?"

"A yokel catcher had been using it. A burglar's **achtung.** That's what helped to give Weiss the idea."

"I see. You know, it strikes me that Weiss looks more like a genuine **klutz** than you do. He's small enough. Makes me wonder why he didn't take on the role himself. But suppose he does turn up—Dr. Gnadenschuss. Without a gun, what can you do? Talk him into surrendering?"

"I'll think of something."

"And while you're thinking he'll blow your brains out. No, I don't think that will work." Reichenbach smiled and put his hand in his side pocket and produced a little pistol, which he handed to me. "Here. Take this. Just in case. Let me have it back when you're through with this foolishness. Don't worry. I've got another." He unbuttoned the top button of his jacket to reveal a Walther in a shoulder holster. "Catch me, a Jew, walking around this town without a Bismarck. I should say not. I've got a lot of enemies. And not all of them work at the Alex. By the way, have you noticed the number of Nazis there are around the Praesidium these days? There's something about the warmer weather that brings them out of their holes, like cockroaches. That bastard Arthur Nebe, for one. Not to mention that bastard who took a swing at you on the stairs at the Alex; Gottfried Nass, wasn't it? Yes, Nass is another cop I'd like to shoot." He nodded firmly. "Let me know if you need my help. Anytime."

"Thanks, Kurt. Listen, one good turn deserves another. The fellow who got himself shot on Friedrichstrasse yesterday."

"Pimp called Willi Beckmann. What about him?"

"I know the name of the Fritz who did it. At least, half his name. Hugo something. Hangs around the Sing Sing Club. Built like a wrestler. The girl who was weeping and wailing over Willi's body was Hugo's girlfriend, Helga. At least that's what he thought. Which is why Hugo put all those coins in Willi's slot. So it wasn't ring related. It was a love triangle. You can have the collar. Like I say, one good turn."

"Thanks. But how do you know all this?"

"Long story. But I was there when it happened.

Playing **klutz.** And I saw the whole thing, from the quiet prologue to the fiery finale. Unlike the girl. Whatever she says now, she saw nothing except Willi's dead body."

"And you don't want the credit, because?"

"Because I'm the witness. And because I don't want to come into the Alex and do the paperwork. Not yet. And not dressed like this. I figured that maybe you could pick him up and see if he still has the Bergmann MP-18 that he used to kill Willi. And the car he was driving when he did it. A yellow BMW Dixi, registration IA 17938. If he does, you may not need a witness at all."

"You're wasted as a cop, you know."

"How's that?"

Reichenbach tossed a coin into my hat. "All that detail? You should have been a scientist. Or a philosopher." Grinning broadly, he lit two cigarettes and put one in my mouth. "That's made my day, Bernie. There's nothing like arresting someone who's guilty as sin itself to put you in a good mood, is there?"

"It certainly beats arresting someone who's innocent."

I WATCHED KURT Reichenbach as he walked away, whistling and twirling his cane like Richard Tauber as if he didn't have a care in the world. He was wearing spats, which I hadn't noticed before. **A cop wearing spats.** I almost laughed; I wouldn't have been at all surprised if he'd started to sing and dance. On the other side of Wilhelm-Ufer, he paused by a new open-top Brennabor—the car with the outside trunk and the tool kit on the running board—and opened the gray door. Before he climbed into the front seat, he turned and waved back at me, which did little for my cover, but made me grateful that Reichenbach was a friend. And he'd been right, of course. I should have had some backup. In too many ways I hadn't thought through what I was doing at all. And I resolved to call Bernhard Weiss and discuss my undercover adventure with him as soon as I was home again.

But on my way back to the theater and Brigitte, my mission seemed to end when one of the axles on the **klutz** wagon snapped. For a moment I just sat there; then a taxi driver asked me if I needed some assistance and I was obliged to tell him against all evidence to the contrary that I could manage perfectly well, which left the poor fellow looking both puzzled and irritated.

It was already clear to me that Prussian Emil hadn't been using the contraption to get around the cobbled streets of the city but just to sit in, for the sake of appearances. It wasn't nearly as sturdy as it needed to be and I imagined the burglar he worked with must have transported him to the scene of a crime in a nice comfortable car. For a second I debated taking the **klutz** wagon to a bicycle shop for repair, but that would have meant carrying it through the streets and risking the contempt and wrath of my fellow Berliners, who would very reasonably have concluded that I was a yokel catcher just like Prussian Emil. The possibility that they might assume the worst about all veteran beggars—even the genuine ones—and stop giving them money was enough to make me throw the thing into the canal, which I did when I was sure no one was looking.

I took off my army tunic and cap and dark glasses and walked back to the theater on Schiffbauerdamm, relieved that the whole masquerade was very likely over. Rehearsals were finished for the day; the orchestra was already heading out the front door to the beer hall across the road. I went up to Brigitte's room, and she removed my makeup. She didn't say much because we had company: one of the stars of the show, the redheaded Lotte Lenya. She was smoking a cigarette, drinking whiskey, humming, and reading a copy of **The Red Flag.** I didn't mind that she might have been a communist as much as that she seemed to mind me. It wasn't that I was a cop: I'm sure Brigitte hadn't told her. But as Brigitte worked on me and I began to relax, I started to whistle, which drew a look of such fierce hostility from Miss Lenya that I felt obliged to stop.

"My Viennese mother once told me that she couldn't ever trust a man who whistles," said Lotte, looking critically at me over the top of her spectacles. "Not ever. It's the most damnable noise there is. When I asked her why she thought such a thing, she told me that thieves and murderers use whistling as a way to send each other coded signals. Did you know that even today whistling is banned in the Linden Arcade for this very reason? Oh yes. They'll think you're a rent boy and you'll be asked to leave. But even worse than that, when some evil people wish to summon horrible devils and wicked demons that should not ever be named, they also whistle. This is why Muslims and Jews forbid it. It's not just the fear of being ungodly; it's the more ancient fear of calling something evil to your side. A dog that may not be a dog. A woman that may not be a woman. Or a man that may not be a man. A goat that may be the devil himself. The Vikings believed that whistling on board a ship would cause evil spirits to generate storm-force winds and they were quite likely to throw the offending man over the side to placate the gods."

Lotte's wide, heavily lipsticked mouth split open like a large fig in a mischievous smile. "All ignorant superstitions, of course. And much more important than any of these, the fact remains that you should never ever **ever** whistle in a theater. The stage crews use whistling to communicate scene changes. People who whistle in theaters can confuse the stagehands into changing the set or the scenery and this can result in serious accidents. I know because I've seen it happen. Generally speaking, we just call this bad luck. And you know what theater folk are like about that. Just remember that, my handsome friend; the next time you're tempted to whistle in this place. Please, even when the lovely Brigitte is around, try to restrain your lips."

With that, Lenya left. "Don't mind her," Brigitte said. "Lotte's famously cantankerous."

"No kidding."

"She's something though, isn't she?"

"Not a female I'm likely to forget in a hurry. You'd best fetch some vinegar. I can still feel her sting." I made a face. "Is she a ladies' club scorpion, do you think? One of those irregular lilac-hued females who can do very well without men? You know, like Sappho and my old schoolmistress?"

"I told you. She's married."

"So were you. And look how well that turned out."

"I can assure you, Lotte likes men as much as the next woman."

"Well, if the next woman's you, then that's all right. But if the next woman is a sharper or a **garçonne** from the Hohenzollern lounge, then I'm not so sure. Besides, Weiss has got a friend called Magnus Hirschfeld who estimates that there are more than two hundred and fifty thousand lesbians in Berlin."

Brigitte laughed. "Nonsense."

"No, really. He counted them all as they came out of the city's eighty-five lesbian nightclubs and sports associations. Not to mention all the theaters."

"Why would anyone do such a thing?"

"Hirschfeld is pretty interested in sex. All kinds of sex. But don't ask me why."

"By the way, where's your **klutz** cart?"

"It broke."

"You broke it?"

"I guess I'm a bigger **klutz** than I realized."

"What are you going to do now?"

"I don't know. Call the boss, I guess. See what he wants me to do. But I'll tell him I'm thinking of throwing in the towel before someone strangles me with it. I had a run-in with a gang of wild boys today and I almost ended up being crippled for real."

"That doesn't sound good. And just as I was getting used to you coming here."

"There are other places we can meet. Restaurants. Bedrooms. We might even do something really crazy and go for a walk in the park one day."

"Sure. But in here you're under my control, and I like that. You're very different from most of the men I meet in the theater."

"I guess I must be. Now if I can only learn to control my whistling."

"Can you?"

"Not when a first-division, bubble-bath blonde like you is around, angel. You're going to make every Fritz you meet inclined to whistle like a castle in winter."

LATER THAT DAY, when I was looking comparatively normal again, I returned to the house on Nollendorfplatz, where I found that Frau Weitendorf was again worried about Robert Rankin.

"You know I clean his room," she said.

"I wish you'd clean mine."

"You don't pay me what he pays me. Anyway, look, I'm not worried about him so much as the rest of us. I was cleaning his room yesterday and I found this on the floor."

She held up a bullet and then dropped it into the palm of my hand. It was a bullet for a .25-caliber automatic.

"No law against carrying a gun," I said. "Even a Tommy's entitled to look to his own self-defense."

"I understand that. But he drinks. He drinks too much. My old man used to say guns and alcohol don't mix."

I smiled and restrained myself from telling her that I'd probably drunk alcohol on every day of the four years I'd spent in the trenches. Sometimes being drunk is the only good reason to pull a trigger.

"A man loading a gun while he's drinking heavily," she insisted, "is a recipe for disaster. If it's done at all, it's best done well. And best done sober. Besides, I don't like guns in the house. They make me nervous."

"I have a gun." I remembered that while I might have lost the Walther somewhere, I still had Reichenbach's little pistol. It felt snug against my abdomen as we spoke.

"That's different. You're a policeman."

"You'd be surprised at the number of complaints the police receive about us shooting innocent people."

"It's not a joke, Herr Gunther. Besides, he's English. They hate us, don't they? Not him, maybe. But the rest of them hate us almost as much as the French."

"Very well. I'll ask him about it when I next see him."

"Thank you. You might also mention that I don't approve of his having women in his room at night any more than I approve of his having a gun. Specifically Fraulein Braun. I wouldn't mind so much but they make a noise, which keeps me awake."

"Was there anything else, Frau Weitendorf?"

"Yes, someone called Erich Angerstein telephoned. Twice. He asked you to call him back. But I didn't like him. He sounded very common. I asked him for his number and he said you already had his business card, but that if you'd lost it you could find him at the Cabaret of the Nameless every night this week after midnight. Not that it's any of my business, Herr Gunther, but I've heard that the Nameless is a place all respectable people should avoid."

"I'm not respectable people, Frau Weitendorf. I'm a policeman and that means I go to evil places so you don't have to. When I've been to the Nameless I'll tell you all about it and you can thank me then."

I telephoned Angerstein's number but there was no answer. Then I telephoned the Alex. This time I got through to Weiss and told him that nothing much had happened except that I'd broken the **klutz** wagon. There was a long silence. He seemed to be thinking.

"That's a pity."

"I was wondering if you wanted me to stay out on the street," I added, hoping that he would say no. "But without the contraption, I would have to adapt my look. Get myself a crutch and go begging with one leg instead of none at all."

"And what's your feeling about doing that?"

"I suppose I could do it."

"Really, it's up to you, Gunther."

"But honestly? I'm beginning to think I'm wasting my time. Especially now that there's been another murder. I do believe a change of tactics is called for."

"Well, it was a brave attempt. A noble failure, if you like. I still am convinced we have to try everything to catch this killer, even when what we are doing seems unusual or disagreeable. But perhaps you're right. Maybe now is the time to change our tactics. To try something new. Whatever that might amount to. Grzesinski is tearing his hair out. We're really short of ideas. The public has been less than helpful. I don't have to tell you how many time-wasters we had in response to my own newspaper article appealing for help. You'd think Berliners don't want this man caught."

"That's certainly a possibility."

He paused. "But you're all right, in yourself. Feeling well?"

"If you're asking me if I've stopped drinking then yes, I have."

"That's something, I suppose. What I mean is, you're not getting tired of police work."

"Not in the least, sir. And I want to get this murderer as much as you do."

"Good, good."

"But I haven't changed my theory that Winnetou and Dr. Gnadenschuss are one and the same. For this reason, and with your permission, I'm going to have to speak to the minister's girlfriend, Daisy Torrens. It seems that her previous boyfriend, a fellow named Geise, Rudi Geise, used to have a penchant for mutilating enemy corpses during the war. Cutting off ears and that kind of thing. Apparently he still carries a knife. So if you add that to the fact that by all accounts he hated women, then he might make a useful suspect. As I've said, it's only a few centimeters from cutting off an ear to cutting off a scalp. Worth a look, I'd have thought."

"Very well. But please tread very carefully. Right now I'm not so popular with the minister. I do believe he would fire me if he could. It would certainly make him look good in front of his enemies if he could dismiss a Jew from the police. Especially as he's a Jew himself. He can even produce a good reason to get rid of me. It seems that President Kleiber of the Stuttgart police has complained about my book. Accused me of settling old scores. Which simply isn't true."

If I'd ever got around to finishing his dry book I might have agreed with him, loyally. Meanwhile, I decided not to tell Weiss that I was half inclined to interview Fritz Lang about his first wife and his interest in Jack the Ripper. It might have sounded like one fishing trip too many. Instead I gave him something else.

"This latest victim, sir: Johann Tetzel. I met him in the course of my investigations. Questioned him outside the Berlin Zoo aquarium not so long ago. It was Tetzel who gave me the tip about Prussian Emil."

"Prussian Emil is the one whose **klutz** wagon you were using, right?"

"Yes, sir. As a matter of fact I'm going to follow up a lead on him tonight."

"Excellent. It might interest you to know that Gennat is currently working on a theory that the murderer is a member of the Steel Helmet. We found a membership stickpin in Tetzel's dead hand. As if he'd grabbed it from the murderer's lapel. Do you remember Tetzel wearing such a pin himself?"

"No. I don't, sir. And he didn't strike me as a right-winger either."

"Well, we can talk more about this when you come in to the Alex. You **are** coming in tomorrow, aren't you? I mean, if you're not out playing **klutz** any longer."

"I'll be in tomorrow, sir." If nothing else, I needed to report the missing Walther and put in for a replacement.

"Good. We can catch up. Share some ideas. Then I wondered if you'd care to come for dinner with me one night soon."

"Thanks. I'd like to."

"My wife is keen to meet you, Gunther. I didn't give her any details but I'm afraid I told her that you saved my life. She and I don't have secrets from each other. Besides, I'm a terrible liar. Comes of being an honest cop, I suppose."

"Take my word for it, sir; we honest cops have to lie like all the rest. Sometimes that's what keeps us alive."

IT WAS WELL past eleven but the Thomas Cook charabanc was collecting excited English guests from some of the more exclusive hotels to take them on a late-night tour of Berlin's famous sex clubs: lesbian clubs like the Toppkeller in Schwerinstrasse, where there was a famous Black Mass featuring several naked girls; or the Zauberflote with its separate floors for queer men and queer women. These sex tours were especially popular with the English, since it was certain that there was no sex to see nor any to be had back home.

Since the English sex tourists were only interested in visual stimulation it seemed unlikely that the Thomas Cook charabanc would be stopping outside the Cabaret of the Nameless; while being a byword for Berlin malevolence and bad taste, it was not a sex show. The cabaret involved a series of ten-minute amateur acts. All the players were poor deluded souls especially selected for their astonishing credulity and lack of talent by the sadistic conférencier, Erwin Lowinsky, who, in the face of all evidence to the contrary, managed to convince the performers that they had real talent and that there were some influential people in the audience who could give the poor wretches a head start in show business. Meanwhile, the audience—which thought itself quite sophisticated—enjoyed the cruel contemplation of one entertainment catastrophe after another. The Cabaret of the Nameless was very popular; for many a Berliner it was nothing less than a perfect evening. A cultural anthropologist seeking to understand the German character could not have done better than to go to the Cabaret of the Nameless.

I found Erich Angerstein seated near the back of a busy room behind a bottle of good champagne and accompanied by a couple of table ladies who seemed to be enjoying the show although their smiles might just as easily have been owed to the fact that he had a hand inside each of their brassieres. Seeing me, he made no attempt to remove his hands to somewhere more respectable—nothing was out of bounds among guests in the Cabaret of the Nameless—nor to introduce me to his two companions, who appeared to be twins.

"Gunther," he said. "I've been wondering when you'd show up. Margit, pour Bernie a drink, there's a good girl. You like champagne, Bernie?"

"Not particularly."

"Horrible stuff. Smells of goat and tastes of cheese. Like a woman's mouse. Women drink it because it's expensive, which they think implies quality. But it's a lot of gas, really." He jerked his head, summoning a waiter, and I asked for a glass of Mosel. "Where have you been anyway? Getting a haircut, I suppose."

"Something like that."

"If I were you I'd ask for my money back."

Up onstage, a woman in a wheelchair with one arm and one leg was singing "Nobody Knows the Trouble I've Seen." Hers was an untrained voice—a bit like Lotte Lenya's, only there the similarity ended; the woman in the wheelchair couldn't have hit the right note if she'd swallowed a whole canteen of tuning forks. Every so often the laughter from the audience became too bovine and she stopped, at which point Erwin Lowinsky—"Elow"—would cajole her into believing she had a sweet, natural voice and that she might best ignore the audience. "Ah, Lucy," he told her, "these fools have had too much to drink and wouldn't know real talent when they saw it."

And then she would start all over again, to gusts of laughter.

"The trouble you've seen," shouted a wag in the audience. "I'm just guessing, but might it involve an arm and a leg?"

The waiter came back with my Mosel. I sipped it slowly, even carefully, and then lit a cigarette.

"Is there a reason we're meeting in this torture chamber?"

"In the front row. Table by the piano. Do you see the flax-haired Fritz with the cellar-mistress girlfriend? You can't see them from here, but the girl is wearing spurs on her button-up boots."

I looked over that way and saw a tall woman showing a good deal of snow-white thigh and quite a bit of purple garter. Beside her was a taller man wearing a coarse yellow wig. They were both in helpless fits of laughter, red-faced, tearful, slipping off the edge of their seats. The man looked like he was having an asthma attack.

"I see him."

"That's Prussian Emil. His real name is Emil Müller. Comes here regularly just before twelve after finishing work, so to speak. Last night he was in with a burglar by the name of Karl Szatmari, a Hungarian, I think. Both of them belong to a criminal ring called the Hand in Hand. I hope you're impressed with my patience, Gunther. Sitting here and watching him for the last three or four nights has been a real test of character for me. I've just about chewed off my fingernails wanting to drag that bastard into an alley and beat some information out of him."

"In that respect at least you strike me as the kind of man who needs a regular manicure."

"I hope it's been worth it. Which is why I'm going to have to insist on being there when you question Emil. I'd hate to think I've been coming here for no reason."

"We'll speak to him tonight. After he leaves we'll follow him outside. How long does he normally stay here?"

"Couple of hours. I had him tailed one night. He went to the Heaven and Hell and then home to an apartment in Wedding."

"Please try to remember what we agreed to. We do things my way. And you'll be helping me with a witness. Not a suspect."

"Sure, sure. But you try to remember this: These bastards don't like giving out information at the best of times. Sometimes they need a little friendly persuasion."

"Then let's keep it as friendly as possible. I want him talking, not bleeding. He can't talk if he's spitting out teeth."

"Whatever you say, commissioner. Always glad to help the Berlin police."

I laughed. "If you mean the same way that Elow is helping poor Lucy's singing career, then I can almost believe that."

"He's a genius, isn't he?" said Angerstein. "How he can manage to persuade this one-legged no-hoper that she has a scintilla of talent is beyond me. He makes Svengali look like the Good Samaritan."

But after my time on the street pretending to be a **schnorrer,** I had developed a certain sympathy for people with one leg, even the tone-deaf songbird who was at last leaving the stage in tears, followed by gales of laughter and derision. I stood up and started to applaud, as if I'd enjoyed her act.

Erich Angerstein looked at me with amusement and then pity. "You're a decent man," he said. "I can see that. Says a lot about you. But the people in this audience will only think you're being sarcastic. You know that, don't you? There's no room for anything genuine in this place. You probably thought that show you and Old Sparky put on in Sing Sing was the cruelest spectacle in Berlin, but you were wrong, my friend. It's not just dreams that are broken in here; it's souls, too."

Finally he removed his hand from Margit's brassiere, but only to light a cigarette. For a moment I caught the girl's narrowed eye and knew that she wasn't much enamored of her host's attentions. Or of the Cabaret of the Nameless. It wasn't everyone in Berlin who enjoyed cruelty for cruelty's sake or being constantly pawed.

Still looking at Margit, I said: "I wonder how the poor girl ended up in a wheelchair, anyway. With one leg and one arm, treated like she was shit on the cabaret carpet, pinning all her hopes on these heartless bastards."

"You missed the beginning of her act," said Margit. "She explained how she lost the arm in a factory accident, and the leg in hospital, as a result of losing the arm."

Margit's twin added: "She wanted to be the first one-legged actress and singer since Sarah Bernhardt."

"Some people have all the luck," said Angerstein. "While it seems that others have none at all. When it comes to good fortune, everyone believes they're entitled to a fair share. And they're not. They never were. And that's where people like me come in."

I sat down again. "Can you see all of human creation from on top of that high mountain, Siegfried?"

"My point is this: Can **you** imagine how much of existence would be impossible if people didn't believe in a certain amount of luck in the face of all evidence to the contrary? The true essence of human life is delusion. That's what we've got in here. And it's been that way ever since the first Roman soldier blew on a handful of dice. It's simple human nature to believe your luck is going to turn."

"I'd hate to comb your hair, Erich. I'd probably cut myself."

"Could be your own luck will turn tonight."

"I hope it does. This case needs a break."

"I've got a good feeling about that, Gunther. You're going to crack this case wide open and turn yourself into a local hero. I'm sure of it. You're going to catch Eva's murderer. That man is going to have his head cut off. And I'm going to be there to see it, even if I have to bribe every guard in Plötzensee."

He meant it, too. And just for a second I gained a small insight that perhaps Erich Angerstein was the wickedest thing in the club. I glanced around at the cabaret audience, just to make sure: Lucy was gone now, her hopes as dead as the Archduke Franz Ferdinand and his poor wife. I had not thought vicious, conscience-free killing was so very common in Berlin. But in the Cabaret of the Nameless, it was the name of the game; and worse was to come. A one-eyed juggler with a bad speech impediment who couldn't juggle; a grossly overweight impersonator who pretended to be Hitler and then Charlie Chaplin but looked and behaved more like Oliver Hardy; and a tap dancer who had no more sense of rhythm than a dying rhinoceros. Worst of all perhaps was the woman with the large breasts who fancied herself a mezzo-soprano and inexplicably had chosen to sing an aria from Richard Strauss's **Salomé** and Elow had persuaded the poor creature that she might find more favor with the audience if, like Salomé, she removed her clothes while she was singing—this provided the most depressing sight of the evening when Salomé turned out to have a very large cesarian scar. Even Prussian Emil seemed to find this revelation too much, and soon after Salomé had left the stage, he and his hook-heeled girlfriend suddenly stood up and headed for the exit. Angerstein tossed some banknotes onto the table for the waiter and the twins. Then he and I followed our bewigged quarry outside.

"Where shall we pick him up?" I asked.

"This is your picnic basket, copper."

"You said you had someone tail him to his place in Wedding?"

"Yes, it's on Ackerstrasse. You see it and you'll understand why he's on the flypaper with the rest of them in that club we just came out of."

"Well, let's pick him up there. Are you in your Mercedes?"

"Not tonight. It's having a little tune-up. Get it back first thing tomorrow." He pointed at a little two-seat Hanomag. With its single headlight mounted in the middle of the hood, it looked more like a car in a children's storybook than something a man such as Erich Angerstein might drive. "Which is why I'm driving that piece of shit toy. It's my wife's car. She's away on vacation right now, so she doesn't need it."

PRUSSIAN EMIL DROVE a black Dixi north up Mauerstrasse, which traced the path of the old city wall. The curve of the street used to irritate Frederick the Great: Like any good Prussian, he much preferred straight lines. I was hoping to get a few myself when we caught up with Prussian Emil. With Angerstein driving, we headed across the river, into Red Wedding. It was red for a reason; like Schöneberg or Neukölln, the poverty in Wedding was the dispiriting kind they'd had back in Gaza, where sightless Samson had been forced to work grinding grain in a mill. Crushing poverty was the reason none of the thousands of Berliners who occupied Wedding's sorry-looking tenement buildings would ever have dreamed of voting for anyone other than the communists or, at a pinch, the socialist SPD. Judging by the peeling signs painted on the gray walls of the Russian-doll courtyards, all human life was here: coalmen, dressmakers, butchers, pumpernickel bakers, car mechanics, kosher bakers, pigeon shops, cleaning ladies, briquette suppliers, fishmongers, housepainters; and quite a bit that was inhuman, too. The place was rat-infested, patrolled by mangy stray dogs and spavined horses and probably a Golem or two. Anything went in Red Wedding, and nobody paid much attention to what was deemed respectable by middle-class Berlin standards. Although it was the middle of the night, there were still small, undernourished children loitering in the lightless arched entryways under the watchful eyes of men and women wearing shabby **Trachts** and military surplus. It was the kind of place that made you feel lucky if you had a clean collar and a shine on your shoes.

"I hate this bloody neighborhood," confessed Angerstein.

"Any particular reason, or are you just a student of fine art and architecture?"

"I grew up here. That's the best reason of all."

"Yours must have been quite an education."

"That's right. It was. I've had a lucky escape, right enough. Whenever I come back to Wedding it reminds me of what life might have been like if I'd had to—well, you know."

"Make an honest living? Yes, I do see that."

"No, you don't. Nobody who hasn't lived here can know what it's like to grow up in a shit hole like this."

Angerstein slowed the car to a halt for a moment; since he knew exactly where Prussian Emil's car was going he wasn't afraid of losing him. He looked at me with eyes that were brown and unflinching and almost lifeless, like cold rock pools in granite. They were the most intimidating eyes I'd ever seen. Gradually he smiled, but it took a while and there was little mirth in it.

"You see that stone bench? That's the Wedding gamblers' bench. My father sat on that bench for twenty years, playing skat and betting away what money he made from whatever temporary crap job he'd managed to get while my mother slaved her guts out taking in laundry and making children's clothing. I swore I wasn't ever going to end up like those poor bastards. The number of times since then I've wished I could go back in time and give them just a few hundred reichsmarks. Which would have transformed their lives. And mine." He shook his head. "Sometimes it seems like it must have happened to someone else. Like a schizophrenic, you know? You ever want to know why people become criminals, just come and spend some time here and you'll learn a thing or two."

"Not everyone who lives here becomes a criminal, Erich. Some people manage to stay honest. A few even manage to better themselves. The hard way."

"You're right, of course. But mostly they get stuck here, see? Living their hopeless lives. And I'm not. If I had to live in Wedding again I think I'd kill myself. Or someone else, more likely. But murder's not such a big crime when you live in a dump like Wedding. That's called binding arbitration around these parts. A quick way to resolve disputes, one that doesn't involve cops or courts. Leastways, not unless someone opens his flap."

His laugh reminded me of just how dangerous a man he was. The Middle German Ring was one of the most feared in the whole of Germany.

"Which violates the first law of Wedding: Always keep your mouth shut, especially when there's a cop around." He shook his head. "I got out of this place for the sake of my family. I wanted something better for my children, you know? And when Eva got her Abitur, I couldn't have been more proud. Kids round here wouldn't even know how to spell Abitur. I was even proud when she got herself a job working as a stenographer for Siemens-Halske. I could have found her something better, but she was independent and wanted it that way. So I let it be. I didn't interfere. Then something went wrong. I'm not sure what, exactly. Maybe a bad boyfriend, I don't know. I'm still trying to find out. She started taking cocaine and going on the sledge now and then to help pay for it. You might even say she started to revert to type. And now that Eva's dead I'm wondering why I bothered. Would she be alive now if we'd still been living here? I don't know."

"You did what you thought was right," I said. "Even if what you did was wrong. That's what matters. You give people chances. What they do with those chances is their own affair. It's not down to you if she made mistakes, Angerstein. It's not down to anyone except the person who makes those mistakes. At least, that's the way I look at it."

"Thanks for that, anyway. Even if you don't mean it."

Erich Angerstein's life story over, we drove on a bit and then he pulled over, parking the car immediately behind the empty Dixi; Emil and his girlfriend had already gone inside the tenement. We followed through one gloomy courtyard and another, then up a narrow stone stairway that smelled of coal fumes and tobacco and fried food and carbolic and something worse. The whole place was like a black-and-white engraving of a deep pit and dry bones scene from **The Divine Comedy.**

"Top floor," said Angerstein.

I looked up at the side of a building that was all wall cracks and dead concrete window boxes.

"Suppose he doesn't answer the door," I said. "I'm not sure I would answer it in this place and at this time of night."

"Then it's just as well we're not going to knock," said Angerstein.

At the top of the stairs were two apartment doors and, down a small flight of steps, a third, ill-fitting door that led outside again; this door was secured from the other side until Angerstein prised it open with a folding knife. "I know all these old tenement buildings like the back of my hand," he explained. "From when I first started stealing. And other things."

He led the way out onto an iron fire escape that overlooked a small, dark, rat-infested courtyard. Above us the sky was full of smoke and the sound of a couple having a furious argument—the kind that promised violence. I followed him quietly through a web of washing lines until we came to a grimy window. Inside, the lights were on, affording us a ringside view as Prussian Emil's girlfriend finished tying his wrists and ankles to all four legs of a kitchen table with a selection of her client's neckties. She herself was naked but for her boots and stockings and as soon as she was quite satisfied with her knots, she pulled down Emil's trousers and underpants, picked up a cane and swished it in the air.

"Looks like we're just in time for the late show," said Angerstein.

"Somehow I can't see the Thomas Cook sex tour making it up here."

"No, but it saves us time."

"How's that?"

"You've read Kant, haven't you? A man's more likely to see reason when his trousers are around his ankles. And there's no chance of his losing any teeth. Just like you said. It seems to me that he's just waiting for us to question him."

He walked along to the next window and while the cellar mistress went about her work, Angerstein silently jimmied it open with his knife and we climbed inside. It wasn't much of an apartment. A green linoleum floor. A bed that looked and smelled like a nest of mice. A large wardrobe full of fur coats, probably stolen; and on the door, a military uniform and a bugle. We went into the living room where the cellar mistress was caning her client. He took it well enough, I thought, crying out only a little, but seeing us in the room he began to yell loudly—with outrage, not pain.

"Who the hell are you? Get out of here before I call the police." And other words, most of them obscene, to that effect.

"What's the twenty-mark word for this particular perversion?" Angerstein asked the mistress. "Algolagnia?"

The mistress nodded. Angerstein handed her a banknote.

"Get your clothes on, darling. Go home. Forget you ever saw us. We'll finish up here with the algolagnia."

The woman grabbed her clothes and ran. She could tell we meant business. For one thing, Angerstein had a gun in his hand.

"Put the Bismarck away," I told him. "We won't need it. Not now he's trussed up and ready for some Socratic dialogue."

He shrugged and slipped the pistol into a little holster on his belt.

"I don't pretend to understand why anyone would want to be punished like this," he said, picking up the cane. "But it takes all sorts. Especially in Berlin. Personally, I put it down to the armistice. We're still beating ourselves up for the way the war ended. Or paying someone else to do it."

"What the hell do you want?" demanded Emil.

"Answers to some questions," I said, pulling a chair up beside his head, which was the much preferred alternative to the other end of the table. His wig had disappeared and the birthmark on his neck was just as Johann Tetzel had described; it looked as if a careless waiter had spilled something down his shirt collar. "As soon as we have those answers we'll leave you alone. If you're good, we may even untie you before we leave. Simple as that."

"And who wants to know the answers?"

"Let's get something straight," Angerstein said, and hit him hard on his bare backside with the cane, which had me wincing with vicarious discomfort. "We ask the questions."

"Yes, yes, yes. Whatever it is you want to know, I'll tell you."

"A few weeks ago," I continued, "you went on a job one night with your friend Karl Szatmari. South of Wittenbergplatz, at the back of a building on Wormser Strasse. I found your **klutz** wagon. You were his **achtung.** That horn in the bedroom: You were meant to blow it if the cops turned up."

"Who says?"

Angerstein beat him again. "Answers only, please. Not questions."

"I'm not interested in any of that. What I want to know is why you ran away. What you saw that made you abandon the **klutz** wagon and leg it."

"I haven't a clue what you're talking about," insisted Emil. "You're right. I used to play **schnorrer** and spot cops for Szatmari when he was on a job. Yokel catching. I plead guilty to that. No question. But I lost that wagon on Wittenbergplatz. Had to make a run for it when a nosy cop started asking me awkward questions. I've no idea how it turned up where you said it did. But Wormser Strasse isn't so far away from Wittenbergplatz."

"A woman was murdered that night," I said. "Murdered and mutilated. And I think you caught a glimpse of the man who was responsible. I believe that's the reason you ran away. Because you were afraid he might kill you, too."

"Whatever gave you that idea?"

Angerstein beat him a third time and Emil's face turned an interesting shade of purple. "Didn't they teach you anything at school?" he said. "The difference between a question and an answer?"

"All right, all right. And not so hard, eh? I've told you. I'll tell you whatever you want to know."

"So far you've told us nothing," said Angerstein.

"Look, Emil, there was a burglary in Wormser Strasse on the same night as the murder. That's a fact. And I'm guessing it was Szatmari who was responsible. If we ask him and he says it was you who was cop-spotting for him, and we have to talk again, then my friend here is going to do more than just beat you. But you shouldn't worry about that. You should worry about what's going to happen right now." I lit a cigarette. "This is your last chance, Emil. If I have to ask you the same questions once more I'm going to tell my colleague to beat you like an old carpet. And when he's tired of doing that, then I'm going to beat you myself. Which will be worse because I won't enjoy doing it. Not for a moment. I'll be very embarrassed and because I'm embarrassed I'll be angry. Maybe angry enough to beat you harder than anyone has ever beaten you before. You understand? So I urge you to start telling me some things I don't already know. Before you really do get hurt."

"All right. I did see something. Only it wasn't much. Hardly anything in fact. But look, if you're cops I really can't imagine anything I could tell you would be of any help."

"Why don't you tell us from the very beginning?

And we'll be the judge of that." I leaned back on the chair, flicked my ash onto the floor, and waited expectantly.

But Erich Angerstein was shaking his head and giving me his best stoneface.

"You read books?" he asked.

"Of course I read books. What's that got to do with anything?"

"Well, I read people the way you read books. I'm an avid reader, you might say. But the fact is that in my business you have to be. It's my observation that you've got a lot to learn about interrogation, my young friend. When a man minimizes the importance of what he's about to tell you, you can be damn sure he's not going to tell you anything worth hearing. What you want is a whore who hasn't eaten dinner for several days, someone who's very keen to please her Fritz. And we don't have that here. Not yet. Do you agree?"

I nodded. Emil was already repeating his willingness to answer all of our questions, but I was forced to agree with Angerstein. I didn't want him to be right about this, but he was and we both knew it. And we both knew what was going to happen next. I didn't like it, but all I cared about now was that we got whatever information we could get from Emil so that I could be out of that room and away from that loathsome scene as soon as possible. I nodded again.

Angerstein produced a folded white handkerchief, shook it out, and then stuffed it into Emil's mouth. Then he turned to me. "So here's what's going to happen," he said calmly, taking off his jacket and rolling up his shirt sleeves. "You're going to go back in the bedroom, close the door, smoke a cigarette, and wait there patiently for five minutes. That's because I don't want you and your capacity for decency and fair play of the kind you exhibited back in the Cabaret of the Nameless interfering while I beat this bastard. **Like an old carpet.** Your words. That is what you said, right? I'm going to beat this bastard until he wants to tell me everything that's happened to him since he let go of his mother's teat."

SITTING ON THE edge of the malodorous bed I smoked a cigarette to keep my mind off the smell and stared around at the blank room that stared back at me. As I waited uncomfortably—but not as uncomfortably as Prussian Emil—for Erich Angerstein to come and fetch me from the bedroom, I felt like a ghost and probably looked like one, too. But it was easier to keep my nose off the smell of the bed than it was to keep my ears detached from the sound of what was happening in the room next door. It was cowardly of me to let the gangster do the dirty work but that part of it seemed unimportant now beside the absolute imperative necessity of getting a name and a man I could arrest. I suppose I convinced myself that the end justified the means, which, in a case that refuses to crack, is always the honest policeman's dilemma. Five minutes, he'd said, five minutes for me to smoke a cigarette and for him to force Emil to tell us everything he knew. Next to the lives of some other men and women who might yet be killed that didn't seem so bad, but still, it was a long five minutes. I heard a little of what was going on, of course. I heard the slicing cuts of the cane and Emil's muffled screams; and if I heard it, the neighbors very likely heard it, too, only no one would have tried to fetch the police in a building like the one we were in. It wasn't as if cops or public telephones were plentiful in that part of Berlin. After a couple of minutes, I put the cigarette between my teeth and plugged my ears with my fingers, which only seemed to make my every guilty thought throb inside my skull as if I was suffering from a low fever.

When at last he came to fetch me, Angerstein was breathless, his forehead beaded with sweat and his cheeks flushed, as if he'd really put his shoulder into the beating, and the minute I laid eyes on Emil I knew that he'd done that and more. The man had passed out; his backside was the color of a crushed insect; blood was running down his thighs; and his face was as pale as goat's cheese. The crimsoned cane lay on the floor like a murder weapon and in my guilty haste to erase the scene from my mind I kicked it angrily aside and bent down beside the unconscious man to retrieve the handkerchief from his mouth before he suffocated.

"I think he'll tell us what we want to know now," said Angerstein calmly. It was obvious that he didn't despise himself in the least, as I would have done; he had probably intended to inflict the maximum violence necessary, and experience had told him the limit of what his victim could take. He rolled down his shirt sleeves and collected his jacket from the floor as I slapped Emil's cheeks as firmly as I dared; and gradually the man started to come around. Angerstein was much less circumspect; he grabbed the man's ear and lifted his head up.

"Now then," he said. "Let's hear it. Tell us the whole story. From the beginning. Exactly the way I told you a few minutes ago, Emil."

It was a curious remark but at the time I thought no more about it.

"Tell my friend what you saw outside the building in Wormser Strasse. Or we'll start again."

"I was watching the street while my friend turned over an apartment," said Emil. "I was supposed to . . . to blow my horn if any bulls turned up. Or anyone that looked like the apartment's owner. I hadn't been there for long when I saw this Fritz go into the courtyard with the girl.

And I saw him when he came out again . . . just a few minutes later. Alone. Got a good look at him, too. Saw the blood on his—on his hands. I guessed what must have happened. That he had murdered her. But not only that. I recognized him. He was a cop."

"A cop?"

"Yes. From Kripo."

"A detective?" I said. "Are you sure?"

"Sure I'm sure. That's why I didn't want to tell you before. I was afraid you would kill me."

"What's this man's name, Emil? I assume he has a name."

"Don't know his name. Right? I don't know that. Please believe me. But I knew his face. From way back when I was being booked in the main hall at the Alex by another detective for a job I did. And this one saw I'd recognized him. Which was why I ran away. Before he could kill me. Laid low after that. As soon as that first **schnorrer** got shot, I guessed what it was about. That he was looking for me. Had to be."

Shaking away my disbelief, I remembered what the homeless man, Stefan Rühle, had told me and Otto Trettin back at the Palme: that he'd seen the murderer, too, and that the murderer was a cop. Then I'd assumed the man was a lunatic, but now I wasn't so sure. And already I was trying to match the policemen I knew with what sounded like Rühle's description of Satan.

"Can you describe him?"

"Not very tall. Ordinary. I don't know. I'm not very good at descriptions."

"You're not trying to put one over on us, are you? About the murderer being a copper."

"No! I swear it was a cop that did it. A detective. I just don't have a name."

"A cop. I don't believe it."

"Please. You've got to believe me. I couldn't take another beating."

"It's all right, Emil," said Angerstein soothingly. "My friend is just a little surprised to hear this, that's all. Unlike me. I'm much more inclined to believe the worst of Berlin policemen. All the same, I wouldn't like it if you were taking the piss."

"I told you everything I know, right? But please don't hit me anymore."

But Angerstein was already untying Emil's ankles and hands, as if he was satisfied with what we had heard. Which surprised me; he wasn't the type to be satisfied with anyone's explanation of anything, let alone with a cursory description of the man who had probably murdered his daughter. Emil's revelation that the suspect was a cop seemed to beg as many questions as it answered. Angerstein looked at me and shook his head.

"Well, that's a bit of a turnup, eh?" he said. "A copper from the Alex. Narrows it down a bit, I suppose. Who was that other copper who was fond of murdering whores? The fellow who thought he was doing God's work cleaning up the city."

"Bruno Gerth."

"And where is he now, exactly?"

"Still in the asylum at Wuhlgarten. Last I heard."

"I don't suppose a kind judge could have been persuaded to let him out?"

"No. As a matter of fact I went to see him just a couple of months ago."

"Might I ask why?"

"I was seeking some information on another case." This hardly stated it. I'd gone there specifically at the behest of Ernst Gennat, who knew I was well acquainted with Gerth, to see if he couldn't help us with a few unsolved murders. More important, however, I'd been asked to check on a story circulating about Bruno Gerth at the time of his conviction; it was never confirmed but it was widely rumored that he'd had a partner. He'd denied everything, of course. It was obvious to me that he hoped at some stage to "prove" that he was sane again and effect his own early release: A late confession would have spoiled that.

"So he's quite sane then. In spite of the fact he's in Wuhlgarten. Otherwise you'd hardly have gone there asking for his help."

"In my opinion, quite sane. He knew how to

work the legal system, that's all. To avoid a death sentence."

"Any other homicidal cops you know that spring to mind?"

"Plenty," I said. "But not like this. On the other hand."

"Yes?"

"If he really is a cop, then it might explain the way he salted those crime scenes with clues. Like he knew the best way of making us waste our time. And maybe some other things, too. The way he taunted the police in the newspapers. As if he wanted to get back at Kripo—to show all of us up as incompetent."

"It's a pity Emil didn't give us a name."

"That's the only reason I get paid to be a detective. To try and work it out for myself."

Angerstein tapped Emil on the head with his knuckle. "We know where you live. And you know who I am. You know that I can find people and hurt them very badly. You think of anything else to do with this copper you saw, then you get in touch, Emil."

"Yes, sir."

Angerstein took out his wallet and laid some cash on the kitchen table. "Here. Go and see a doctor and get your stripes attended to."

"Thanks."

"We need to leave. Now." Angerstein took my arm and moved me toward the door. "In case anyone heard something and decided to report it. Even in Berlin that's just about possible."

ANGERSTEIN DROVE ME back to Nollendorfplatz.

"You're very quiet," he said.

"I'm thinking."

"Would you care to share some of that thinking with me, Gunther?"

"I'd be wasting your time. I'm still drilling for oil here. But I'll let you know if I hit a gusher. Until then I'm just going to whistle a tune and keep my hands in my pockets."

"If there's one thing more ridiculous than the idea of a policeman who's thinking, it's a policeman saying he expects something important to come of it."

"I'm glad we fill you with such confidence."

"The police?" Angerstein laughed. "Maybe you weren't there when I was beating that carpet. I just learned it was a cop who murdered my daughter. I'm doing my best not to blame you for that. You being a cop yourself and part of the general conspiracy of silence that afflicts this town."

"It's the part of me that's a cop that's doing the thinking."

"Don't take too long. The sooner you arrest someone, the sooner I can stop pecking your head."

"Sorry, but a man has to do his thinking in private."

"Maybe back in the day when you were a theology student in Heidelberg. But these days you've got to write reports so your superiors can help guide your thoughts with wisdom. If they can. That's why they put cops in teams, isn't it? It's not the bar bills they expect you to share, it's the brain work." He lit a cigarette. "All I'm saying is that maybe I can help."

"And all I'm saying is that if you're expecting ninety-five theses nailed to your front door tomorrow morning, you're going to be disappointed. Look, Herr Angerstein, I'll tell you something just as soon as I have it. Until then, have a good night."

I went inside the house and crept upstairs. There was a light under Rankin's door, but I didn't knock. And I didn't go to bed; my mind was too active for sleep. Instead I went to my desk and drew a paper pad toward me and sat thinking and making idle marks with my pen, hoping that the business of writing and reconsideration might fix a number of things that remained jumbled in my thoughts. I was trying to remember a few forgotten facts, some blurred details, and any lurking inconsistencies. In short, I hoped to set something down on paper that had appeared altogether trivial but now nagged at me as being piercingly significant. I looked at the bottle of rum in my drawer and turned it down, like a man of real character, and kept on scribbling things on the pad as they occurred to me, in no particular order. And after a while I found myself yawning and thought it best to leave such compelling considerations to the subterranean part of my mind, about which nothing seemed clear except perhaps the antithesis between sleep and wakefulness, and a good policeman and a bad one. But was there ever any such antithesis in fact? A lot of good cops were capable of some very bad behavior, myself included. Some more than others. Which was why my thoughts returned to the meeting of the Schrader-Verband at the Schlossbrauerei in Schöneberg, and the anti-republican cops I'd seen there. Many held opinions that I found objectionable—and one, Gottfried Nass, had even attempted to kill me—but were any of them capable of psychopathic murder? The only truly psychopathic cop I'd ever met had been someone I actually liked: Bruno Gerth. At the time I visited him, I'd thought bad policemen didn't come much worse than Bruno Gerth, and yet he'd been warm and courteous and, to my layman's eyes, more or less sane. We'd known each other since before the time I'd joined Kripo, when I was still in uniform like him; and he'd greeted me in his room at the asylum in Wuhlgarten like a long-lost friend.

—

"BERNIE GUNTHER," SAID Gerth, shaking my hand. "How long has it been?"

"Four years." I lit us each a cigarette and transferred one to him.

"Four years. Incredible, isn't it? I heard you were out of uniform. In plainclothes."

"Who told you that?"

"Oh, I couldn't say. But I get visitors. Tell me, are you enjoying being a detective? You're in Vice now, aren't you?"

"Vice. That's correct. It's all right, I guess. But I'm never off duty. That's the thing about wearing a uniform. Once you hang it in your locker, you're finished for the day."

"So what brings you to east Berlin? I take it this isn't a social call."

Bruno wasn't much older than me. With his blue eyes, blond hair, and regular features, he was also a war hero and a policeman with a commendation for bravery. He fit no one's profile of a violent murderer; certainly not that of the judge of the court that had tried him. His lawyers had argued that he would never have killed anyone if he hadn't also been an epileptic. I wasn't so sure about that. Not only had the detectives investigating Elsie Hoffmann's and Emma Trautmann's murders described a scene of horrifying brutality, they'd also revealed Gerth's obsession with a book by a popular criminologist by the name of Erich Wulffen. Gerth's copy of **The Sexual Criminal** was heavily underlined and annotated, and both his victims were eviscerated in a way that seemed to be a copycat version of what was in Wulffen's near-pornographic book.

"I could tell you I'm here because I wanted to see how you are, Bruno. Because we're **Bolle** boys. To see if there was anything I could do for you. But that would be a lie. The truth is, Ernst Gennat found out we'd been colleagues and prevailed upon me to come and talk to you. Not as a friend but as a cop."

"Hoping I might help with his clear-up rate, I suppose."

"Something like that."

"I already put out my wrists for those two whores, Elsie Hoffmann and Emma Trautmann. I don't see how I can help any more than I have already."

"That would be true if they were your only victims."

"What makes you think they weren't?"

"Not me. Gennat. He likes you for another girl called Frieda Ahrendt."

"Never heard of her."

"As well as some others we don't even know about."

"He's fishing in a cold spot, Bernie. Let me tell

you as an old friend. Those two women were the only ones I killed. But I suppose if I hadn't been caught I would have killed again. Depending on my physiological state at the time."

"Then as a friend, let me ask you this: Why the hell did you do it? And don't say it was because of a preexisting medical condition. I'm not buying it. That book they found in your apartment was also covered in your own handwriting; lurid accounts of fantasy sexual murders."

"Which were themselves the result of my condition. But I will say this, Bernie. And you being a detective in Vice will appreciate it. At the time I killed those women, the absolute logic of what I did seemed unassailable. You can hardly deny that Berlin has been suffering from an almost biblical plague of prostitutes. Killing one or two to put the fear of God in the majority and perhaps deter them from their profession seems an effective means of control. Much better than registration and medical examinations."

"So it wasn't that you just wanted to kill them for the pleasure of it, like the prosecutor said?"

"Really, what kind of man do you take me for?"

"It's also been suggested by some that you may have had a partner. Another copper who agreed with what you were doing and who looked the other way. Who shielded you from arrest. At least for a while."

"Lots of police agreed with what I did. Surely you must know that by now. Following my arrest, no less a figure than the chairman of the Schrader-Verband, Police Colonel Otto Dillenburger, told me he fully supported my actions. Now, that's what I call a union."

"I'm more interested in what police support you might have received **before** you were arrested, Bruno."

"Now, that would be telling. Let's just say that I had my fans. I get lots of letters in here, you know. From people who applaud what I did. Those who think that something has to be done to help turn the tide of filth and immorality that threatens to engulf this town. From morally minded women, too, who strongly disapprove of prostitution. I've even had offers of marriage."

"After the war there's a severe shortage of single men, right enough. I guess you just about pass in that respect."

"Don't knock it. Some of them have money. I could marry well if I play my cards right."

"Is that how you were able to afford to retain Erich Frey to defend you? Because someone else paid for it?"

Gerth didn't answer.

"And not just him. No less a figure than Magnus Hirschfeld was the physician for the defense."

Again Gerth didn't answer.

"But for those two, your head would be leaking in a cold bucket."

"Yes. That's true. Isn't liberal German justice wonderful?"

AFTER MY VISIT I had gone to see the director of the asylum, a doctor by the name of Karl-Theodor Wagenknecht, who had the most unruly joined-up eyebrows I'd ever seen; they looked like the nest of a very large and untidy species of eagle.

"Do you keep a record of a patient's visitors? I'm particularly interested in those people who've visited Bruno Gerth."

"Yes."

"I'd like to see it if I may."

He disappeared for several minutes, leaving me in his curious office, half of which was given over to what looked like a sort of electric chair; I decided not to inquire about it in case the doctor offered me a free demonstration. When he returned, he handed me a sheet of paper.

"You can keep that," he said.

I glanced down the list. One name drew my attention immediately. It was the name of Police Commissioner Arthur Nebe.

Ever since that visit to Wuhlgarten Asylum, I'd been possessed of the idea that there was a lot more to Nebe than met the eye, and his speech to the Schrader-Verband at the Schlossbrauerei in Schöneberg had left me convinced that if there was anyone in the Berlin police who approved of ending useless or criminal lives it was Commissioner Nebe.

I CLOSED MY eyes and laid my head on my forearm, drifting somewhere in the middle of nowhere near a tall house on Nollendorfplatz. For a moment I thought I was back at the Palme, in Dr. Manfred Ostwald's office, with Stefan Rühle and Lotte Lenya and Arthur Nebe and Frizt Pabst, among several others. There were solid clues all over the place but I didn't pick them up because I didn't trust them. If only Ernst Gennat could learn to take his own advice. Lotte was whistling a snatch of a tune from **The Threepenny Opera** only it wasn't, it was from **The Sorcerer's Apprentice,** by the French composer Paul Dukas—the very tune Fritz Pabst remembered his or her attacker whistling when she was being Louise Pabst. Meanwhile, Rühle was babbling at her about a devil in white shoes whose face was covered in hair and whose eyes were red; and Nebe was making a tidy speech about cleaning up Berlin's streets and how the Nazis were going to fix everything because nobody else could, especially not Bernhard Weiss.

After a while Gottfried Nass came into the office and succeeded in throwing Weiss out the window. Then it was my turn. Two other officers arrived to help him: Albert Becker, who'd assaulted a senior officer because he was a communist; and Kurt Gildisch, who was a violent drunk given to singing Nazi party songs when he'd had a few. But Nass was the most determined of the three; like Bruno Gerth, he'd also been tried for the murder of a prostitute, albeit acquitted. None of them succeeded in my defenestration because I had the door with the wet green paint and the handprint from the Patent Office on Alte Jakobstrasse and I was able to keep it pressed shut against all three until Kurt Reichenbach came to my aid in his usual timely fashion and hit them on the head with his stick and then walked away whistling and dancing. Which pleased Brigitte Mölbling enough for her to shed some clothes and try to sit on my lap while I was still standing up, much to the amusement of Robert Rankin, who was pointing a small gun at the center of my forehead. Meanwhile, someone was screaming in pain, and Prussian Emil was being beaten with a cane for the pleasure of the crowd from the Cabaret of the Nameless, a prospect that I, too, enjoyed, albeit from the comfort of an electric chair. Then I was briefly out of the chair and flat on the bed in Nollendorfplatz with my clothes on.

That was the last thing of which I took any notice. After this there was just the dark and silence and a general sense of impending doom.

ON AWAKENING, I felt strongly that much of this nagging vivid dream made sense. Scowling at the clock, which told me I was late, I found pen and paper and, even before I could shave and throw some cold water in my face, I hurriedly began to write, intent on preserving some memory of the dream.

I had the strong sense I was on the edge of understanding everything about the case, as if, like van Leeuwenhoek with his primitive compound microscope, I was about to see the great significance in all that was small, but at this moment I was summoned to the window by a loud commotion in the street below: a running battle between Nazis and communists that detained me for almost ten minutes. On returning to my desk, I found, to no small surprise, that though I still retained a dim recollection of what I had so clearly understood in my dream, with the exception of a few scattered words and phrases, all the rest lay hidden away in the clouds, and no amount of staring at the sky could restore it.

Cursing, I shaved and washed, put on a clean

shirt, and went to the Alex—my first day back in the Praesidium since my adventures with the **klutz** wagon—and immediately joined a meeting that had just begun in Weiss's office, where Ernst Gennat was explaining his latest theory: that Dr. Gnadenschuss was a member of the Stahlhelm because a Steel Helmet stickpin had been found in the latest victim's hand.

I listened patiently until Gennat finished and then made my objections.

"I'm afraid that Tetzel's stickpin sounds suspiciously like a soft clue to me."

"A soft clue?" said Weiss. "What the hell's that?"

"It was Ernst himself who thought Winnetou was deliberately planting soft clues like that to put us off the scent. Or onto the wrong one. Don't you remember the Freemason cuff link that was found at the scene of Helen Strauch's murder? And the British pound note we found next to Louise/Fritz Pabst? And the cigar holder next to Eva Angerstein's corpse?"

"Yes."

"A Steel Helmet stickpin fits the same pattern. An object for us to waste time on."

"Yes, but the stickpin would fit in with the Nazi profile of the killer that we've seen in his letters to the newspapers."

"Would it? I'm not so sure. Members of the Stahlhelm regard themselves as conservative nationalists, yes, but above politics and very separate from the Nazis. At least that's my understanding."

Gennat wasn't about to give up on his theory without a struggle.

"There must be plenty of those bastards who admire Adolf Hitler as much as they hate the Jews," he said. "Wouldn't you agree? And unless you've had some luck finding Prussian Emil, it's about all we've got to go on right now." He paused and lit a cigar. "Well, have you?"

I shook my head. I wasn't ready to share what I'd learned from Emil nor the circumstances in which this information had been acquired. Not without some very hard evidence. I didn't think any of my superiors—and certainly not the newspapers—were going to welcome the news that eight Berliners had all been murdered by a single cop in the city's police department.

"No, I thought not. Gunther, I want you to spend the rest of your day in the records department, looking for anyone with a conviction for violent assault who happens also to be a member of the Stahlhelm."

"I don't know that something like that would be recorded," I said.

"When arrested, a suspect is obliged to empty his pockets, isn't he? A Stahlhelm membership card would be part of a man's personal effects. You'll find it listed there."

"It would probably be quicker," added Weiss helpfully, "to see what Commissar Dr. Stumm has in that respect. And then to cross-check with Records. Wouldn't you agree, Ernst?"

Commissar Dr. Stumm was with the political police, created to forestall attacks by political agitators against the republic.

As it happened, some time in the records department suited me very well; the last place I wanted to be was at my desk manning the telephone. I needed somewhere quiet to think about what Prussian Emil had told me, and Records was as good as the public library in this respect.

"Yes, probably," said Gennat. "Although as you know I've never been a fan of having a political police force in Germany. It smacks of spying on your own citizens. But however he does it, I think it will make a nice change for Gunther to carry out some good old-fashioned police work."

I STAYED LATE in Records before returning to my desk, having found nothing in the files of any consequence. Not that I'd expected to, and not that I'd tried all that hard.

I hadn't been at my own desk for very long before the telephone rang. It was Erich Angerstein.

"So what have you found out?" he asked.

"About a murderous cop? Nothing yet."

"I thought we narrowed it down quite nicely last night. From a population of four million Berliners to one crazy cop."

"You know, you ought to take a look at the number of cops there are in Berlin sometime. Oddly enough, even the sane ones are in plentiful supply. As a matter of fact, there are fourteen thousand uniformed police, three thousand detectives, three hundred cops in the political police, and four thousand police administration officials. It'll take me a while to sift them out and figure which one of them is a murderer, Erich. You're going to have to be patient for a little longer."

"Not something I'm good at, Gunther. You should know that by now."

"And I told you that we were going to have to do this my way. I've spent the whole day going through criminal records looking for what's called evidence."

"Find anything interesting?"

"Look, I'm a detective at the Alex."

"You make that sound like it's something respectable."

"At the Alex we take a bit of time making up our minds. We're known for it. Justice requires that we do a little bit more than just pick a name out of a hat."

"I'm not in the Alex. I'm in a hurry. I want this bastard caught and punished. And I don't much care about justice. At least not the way you understand it. Punishment—proper punishment—is what I care about. Retribution. You know, I checked out your friend in Wuhlgarten, the one who escaped the ax: Bruno Gerth. And it seems a lot of people thought he had police protection. Maybe I should speak to him. Maybe he has a disciple. These bastards often do."

"I'd be careful about trying to get in there. They might not let you out."

"They say you shouldn't yell at a sleepwalker in case he falls and breaks his neck. But this is me yelling at you now, Gunther. Find this man. Find him soon. Otherwise, it's your neck."

He rang off, which was just as well, as I was on the verge of telling him to go to hell. But I was only **thinking** about it. With a man like Erich Angerstein it was as well to speak softly. I'd seen what he could do with a cane when he wasn't even angry.

HEADING HOME, I caught the double-decker bus west. I went upstairs and smoked a cigarette. I like riding on the upper deck; you see the city from a whole different angle up on top so that it almost seems unfamiliar. It was the very opposite of being on the **klutz** wagon. As we headed down Unter den Linden I glanced in at the Adlon and was thinking of Thea von Harbou when I saw some of the white-shoe types going in for dinner. Except that they weren't white shoes but **spats.** And I suddenly remembered a cop who wore spats. One of the very few cops—apart from Weiss himself—who ever wore spats. Spats that might easily have looked like white shoes to a man like Stefan Rühle. It was about then I remembered the tune this same cop was fond of whistling: **The Sorcerer's Apprentice.** The same cop who had a thick beard, fine clothes, and a heavy walking stick that could have looked like a scepter, I suppose, and who'd been on his way to an apothecary to get something for his red eye. Just as Rühle had described. The same cop who bitterly resented Bernhard Weiss. The same cop I'd always thought of as a good friend. **Kurt Reichenbach.**

Was it possible that he'd been about to shoot another disabled veteran, but had stopped when he realized that the vet was me? The more I thought about it, the more it seemed quite possible that instead of Reichenbach saving me from the wild boys outside Lehrter Bahnhof, it might have been they who'd saved me from him. The gun he'd lent me afterward was still in my pocket. I took it out and looked at it now: a Browning .25-caliber automatic—the same kind of vest pocket gun that had killed all those men; lots of cops carried one as a spare, only this one might actually have been a murder weapon. Reichenbach was certainly arrogant enough to lend it to me all the same. And why not? Who would ever have suspected him of being Dr. Gnadenschuss? He probably had another. He might have several. Reichenbach had never looked like a man who was short of anything, let alone a gun.

About the only thing I was still short of was a motive. Why would a man like him viciously attack nine people? To embarrass the Murder Commission and Weiss in particular? To clean up the streets just like he'd said in the letters to the **Berliner Tageblatt**? To put the blame on the Nazis? Somehow none of it seemed to be quite enough. And yet, lots of people had been murdered for less.

Of course this was all nonsense. Had to be. Reichenbach was a good cop. All the same, a cop who could afford a new Brennabor motorcar. And an expensive leather coat. Where did he get the money? Not from his wife; how much did a nurse at the Charité hospital make? No, the money had to be his. Could Reichenbach have been the source of the new ten-reichsmarks note I'd found in Eva Angerstein's handbag?

It was all mostly circumstantial. I had no firm proof. But it seemed possible even if I couldn't bring myself to believe any of it. Suddenly I had to get off the bus. I had to get back to the Alex.

SOMEONE WAS STILL working at the firearms laboratory in the cavernous basement of the Alex. I knew who it was before I walked in. I could smell the cigarette. Paul Mendel was quiet but ambitious; the open copy of Commissar Ernst van den Bergh's book, **Police and Nation—Their Spiritual Bonds,** told me that much. I knew he hadn't ever read it and kept it there next to Weiss's book and **History of the Police** by Dr. Kurt Melcher to impress the commissars in case any of them came calling. He was gently spoken and bespectacled with lots of thick curly hair. He smoked foul-smelling Russian cigarettes that he always pinched twice to control the flow of the acrid-tasting smoke. He wore a lot of lime water—which is not my favorite cologne unless there's plenty of good gin it—and I suspected he was queer, but not enough to make it noticeable, which was probably wise around Berlin policemen; even the queer ones were difficult about that kind of thing. He might have been working late, but he still looked like he was about to go home. All three buttons of his jacket were done up and he was wearing a natty silk scarf against the evening heat.

"I hate myself for bringing you some work this late."

"I know exactly how you feel. So don't worry. I'm not staying."

"Come on, Mendel. It won't take long. Besides,

what else were you going to do this evening? It's not like you had tickets for the opera. Besides, you love your work. Almost as much as I love mine."

"All right. I'm listening. What have you got for me?"

"A chance to help me crack the Dr. Gnadenschuss case."

"Hmm. That's a big sell you're making there. You're not just saying this to persuade me to work late."

"No. I'm absolutely certain of it."

"So then. A .25-caliber automatic. Probably a Browning. No spent brass. Just the bullet. Last-known victim, Johann Tetzel: shot in the head at point-blank range. The case file with the bullet is still on my workbench. Has there been another killing?"

"No. But I've got something better: a possible murder weapon."

I laid the little automatic Reichenbach had given me on Mendel's desk.

"Safety's on," I said. "And it's loaded."

"Interesting," he said, picking it up and sniffing the barrel. "The Browning Vest Pocket pistol. Nice little gun. I have one myself. No real stopping power, but not bulky in the pocket. A Jew can't be too careful these days. Did you hear that someone attacked Bernhard Weiss? You did. Of course you did. Yes, a lot of people think these guns are Belgian but in fact they're American. John Browning was a Mormon, did you know? Born in Utah, of course. Several wives. Don't know if he shot any. But he himself died in Belgium."

"I almost died there myself. Lots of Germans did."

Mendel took off his jacket and removed his scarf, donned a brown cotton coat, and rattled his pockets, which were usually full of ammunition. What Mendel didn't know about guns could have been written on the back of a postage stamp. He ejected the Browning's magazine, inspected the barrel, checked the number of rounds it contained, and laid the gun down again.

"This pistol has been cleaned, and recently, too. You can still smell the gun oil. If this is a murder weapon then the killer knows how to look after a weapon."

"So you'll do it. A test."

Mendel smiled. "As it happens, you're in luck, Gunther. We just took delivery of a new piece of equipment and I've been dying to try it out."

"Oh, what? A human target? After the last meeting of the Schrader-Verband, I can think of a few people in this place I'd like to test a gun on. Even that one."

"Me too. But nothing so messy. No, we have an expensive new toy in the lab. Just arrived today. A comparison microscope."

"How does it work?"

"Well, as you know, when a gun is fired, all imperfections in the gun barrel leave a unique pattern of marks on the bullet. Two bullets fired from the same gun bear identical characteristics. With the comparison microscope we can now view a test bullet side by side against a bullet from a cadaver without touching either one. One eyepiece, two microscopes. Very convenient for a man like me. We bought this one from America. It was a microscope like this that helped put Sacco and Vanzetti in the electric chair."

"That's a cheerful thought."

"Do you think they were innocent?"

"I don't know. But a lot of other people do. Of course a trial like that could never happen here. German courts are rather more careful about proper legal procedure. Especially when it's a capital crime."

"I'm glad you think so. Me, I'm not so sure."

Mendel switched on a light that illuminated a shooting range and then produced something square and wobbly and wrapped in brown paper, which he laid on a table. He unpeeled the paper to reveal a slab of what looked like aspic jelly.

"I get my local pork butcher to make these blocks of gelatin for me. They're great for observing how bullets behave, and for retrieving them without too much trouble. Now then. If you'll do the honors, Gunther. Someone's stolen my spare ear mufflers so you'll have to make the best of it, I'm afraid. Just shoot the pistol into the block."

Using Reichenbach's Browning, I fired off three test bullets. The shots were noisier than I'd expected and they left my ears ringing for several minutes. When I'd finished, Mendel cut the block open with a knife and retrieved a couple of spent rounds that could be examined underneath the comparison microscope, side by side with the bullet that had killed Johann Tetzel.

"By the way, you're the first person in here in a while who hasn't made a joke about how it is that a Jew can handle pork gelatin. You wouldn't believe how many anti-Semites there are in this building."

"**Is** there a joke?"

"Not a funny one. Besides, we're only forbidden to eat pork, not to shoot it."

"You know what they say about anti-Semitism. It isn't a big problem for Jews. It's a bigger problem for Germans."

"Let's hope you're right. But if you are, who's going to tell them?"

Mendel positioned one of the new rounds under the microscope and turned the focus bezel; but it wasn't very long before he was frowning. **The test was negative.** The bullet retrieved from Johann Tetzel's skull was not the one Mendel had cut from the gelatin block.

"I'm sorry. But this is not the gun that killed him."

"That blows my theory out of the water," I said. "Pity. I was quite sure this was it."

"Not necessarily. You're forgetting. This fellow shot more than one man. So let's try a comparison with one of the earlier bullets that we have. Victim number two: Oskar Heyde."

I held my breath and waited patiently while Mendel peered through his comparison microscope again. After a while he started to smile.

"Yes, In my opinion these two bullets match perfectly. Obviously the killer has used more than one weapon. But this is one of them. Without a shadow of a doubt. Take a look for yourself."

I peered through the eyepiece. To my untrained, inexpert, and tired eye, the mangled bullets looked, at best, not dissimilar.

"You're sure these were fired from the same gun?"

"I'm certain of it."

The Browning .25 Reichenbach had so coolly lent me was a murder weapon.

"Well, I must say, you don't look very pleased, Gunther. Surely this is a major step to solving the case."

I was thinking of the scandal that was about to engulf the Alex, a scandal that might very well end up costing Bernhard Weiss his job. The right-wing newspapers were just looking for an excuse to go after him again, and this time even he wouldn't be able to sue. What could have looked more incriminating for the Jewish deputy police commissioner than a multiple murderer who was a Jewish detective in Kripo? They would hang him out to dry. But who was going to believe me anyway? Not Ernst Gennat. He probably still thought I was a drunk. And it was Kurt Reichenbach's word against mine that he had ever owned the Browning. What I needed was more evidence. But what kind of evidence? And how to get it?

"I'm grateful, Mendel. Don't think I'm not. But while I may have the gun I don't yet have the man who owns it in custody. So I'd be very grateful if you didn't mention this to anyone for now."

"Sure. No problem."

"That Browning you said you own. Have you got it on you?"

"Of course."

"Would you lend it to me?"

"Sure. But why?"

"Let me see it."

Mendel fetched the little jet-black automatic from his jacket pocket and handed it to me. I examined it carefully. It looked identical to the pistol I'd brought with me.

"The murder weapon. I can't take it with me.

Not now you've proved that's what it is. But I need to return a Browning pistol to the man I borrowed it from. Even if it's a different one."

"Sounds dangerous."

"So wish me luck."

"Mazel tov."

I went upstairs to look for Reichenbach. He wasn't there. But one of his colleagues in Kripo was and told me he hadn't been seen all day.

"But that's not unusual."

"Anything to do with a lead I gave him? About the mob killing outside Aschinger. He said he was going to check it out."

The detective, a sergeant named Artner, shook his head.

"He hasn't mentioned it."

KURT REICHENBACH LIVED in an apartment on the top floor of a smart building in Halensee, at the west end of Kurfürstendamm, where Berlin turns very green. There were some lights on in the windows, and his car—the new Brennabor—was parked on the street outside. I rang the doorbell, ready to give him a story about how I was just passing and saw the car, and then the lights on in the apartment and had thought to quickly return his gun. I also had ready a follow-up story to the effect that I appreciated his offer of watching my back and how I wondered if he was prepared to keep an eye on me when I posed as a **klutz** again the following day. I'm not sure what I was expecting to find out, maybe I just wanted to look him in the eye. I certainly didn't think a full confession was in the cards, but I did nurse a vain hope that somehow I might come away from his apartment with some of my suspicions allayed. After a minute or so I heard a window open upstairs and a woman, presumably Reichenbach's wife, Traudl, called down to me.

"Yes. Who's there?"

"Police. Bernhard Gunther, from the Alex."

"Has something happened to Kurt?"

"No. Not that I know of. I was hoping to find him at home."

"He's not here. Wait. I'll throw some keys down. Top floor. Number ten."

I found the keys and let myself in the front door. I took the stairs instead of the elevator, only because it gave me time to adjust my story. If I was going to speak to his wife, then there might be a way to get some information out of her without raising the woman's suspicions; at the same time I was thinking that if his car was there and he wasn't at home or at the Alex, then where the hell was he?

Traudl Reichenbach opened the door to the apartment wearing a nurse's uniform and a look of deep concern. I showed her my warrant disc just to reassure her that I was on the level.

"Are you sure there's nothing the matter?" she asked, ushering me inside. "It's just that Kurt still hasn't come home from work. That's not so very out of the ordinary, him being a detective, but he usually manages to let me know. So this is not like him. Plus his car is still where he left it yesterday."

"Are you sure?"

"It's not like there are many other cars in the street."

"I see. Well, I'm sorry to have missed him. I was in the area and thought I'd drop in and ask him if he wanted to come out for a drink."

"Would you like to wait for him? Perhaps you'd like some coffee, Herr Gunther?"

She smelled, lightly, of sweat, as if she'd just come from work, but was no less attractive for that: a tall, fair-haired woman with brown eyes, wide hips, and strong, defensively folded arms.

From what I could see of it, the apartment's interior was modern with the kind of expensive furniture you only see in magazines. We stayed in the entrance hall, which was patrolled by a black cat and smelt lightly of cinnamon, as if she'd been baking. The cat wrapped its tail around my leg, prompting her to shoo it away impatiently.

"No, thanks," I said. A minute later I spotted a typewriter on the dining table and regretted turning down the coffee. It was an Orga Privat Bingwerke. I wondered if it was going to be possible for me to check to see if the machine displayed a horizontal alignment defect in which the capital letter **G** printed to the right, which would have certainly proved that it was Reichenbach who'd sent the letters to the newspapers. But it was clear that an examination of the machine would probably have to wait until later. The same way I was going to have to wait to try to match Reichenbach's handprint to the one we'd found in the wet paint of the door to the Patent Office on Alte Jakobstrasse.

"I'm worried," she confessed. "This isn't like Kurt at all. He knows I worry enough about him as it is."

"All copper's wives worry. It's natural."

"Maybe. But he suffers from extreme melancholy, you see. Has done ever since the war. Sometimes he's suicidal."

I shrugged. "I'm that way myself sometimes, Frau Reichenbach. There's hardly a man who came out of the trenches who isn't scarred in some way. Often those scars aren't obvious."

"I suppose so."

I glanced through another door at an impressively equipped kitchen, where a second black cat stared back at me with unblinking green eyes as if, like a cynical lawyer, it knew what I was up to.

"But look, maybe I can help. Maybe he left something in the car that will help tell us where he is. Would you like me to go and have a look,

Frau Reichenbach? It's the gray Brennabor, right?"

She fetched the key from a hook on the kitchen wall and handed it over and I told her I wouldn't be long.

I went back downstairs and unlocked the car. There was nothing in the front or rear seat, so I went around the back and opened the enormous trunk. There was a flashlight and I picked it up, turned it on, and lifted an old army-style woolen blanket. Underneath a surprise awaited me, and not a pleasant one: There, on the floor of the trunk, I found a heavy hammer, a razor-sharp knife, and a fedora hat to which a bit of yellow wig was attached on one side; there was also a loden coat with a smudge of green paint on the sleeve. And looking at these four objects it was immediately plain that Reichenbach was Winnetou. The only thing missing was a motive explaining why he had murdered all those people. Because it made no sense to me. Frau Reichenbach seemed like a nice woman; it was hard to imagine how a man married to her could have brutally murdered three prostitutes. The anticlimax of my discovery was only exceeded by the terrible disappointment of being proved right; I thought of some of the other policemen I'd have preferred the killer to have been and realized I had little or no appetite for arresting a brother officer I liked and admired.

I covered the evidence with the blanket, closed the Brennabor's big trunk, locked it carefully, and trudged back upstairs, wondering what to do next. I badly wanted to speak to Reichenbach himself before doing anything, but after what I'd found in the trunk, the sensible thing would have been to telephone the Alex and summon the murder wagon. I may not have had a suspect in custody but I already had more than enough evidence to justify a search of Reichenbach's apartment and to get a warrant for his arrest.

"How long has it been since you last saw him?" I asked when I reached the top floor.

"This morning, before we both went to work. I'm a nurse at the Charité, and sometimes, because we both keep such irregular hours, we don't see each other for days. But we managed to have breakfast together. Which hadn't happened for a while."

"How did he seem?"

"In good spirits. He said he was about to make an arrest. Which always put him in a good mood."

"Did he say who?"

I thought of Hugo, the man who'd murdered Willi Beckmann in front of Aschinger, and concluded that it might have been him that Reichenbach had planned to arrest following my own tip. But it was impossible to imagine that

Reichenbach would have tried to arrest a man like that by himself; he was much too experienced a policeman, especially given Hugo's willingness to use a Bergmann machine gun. It was clear that I was going to have to speak to someone else on Reichenbach's team back at the Alex. But I was almost hoping that something might happen to Reichenbach while I was making this arrest if only because it looked like a less ignominious end for him.

"No. He didn't."

"Oh well, I expect there's a perfectly innocent explanation," I said, trying to think of one. Perfect innocence was already something far beyond my own understanding. I was beginning to wonder if such a thing could even exist in Berlin. "There was a meeting tonight of a new police union: the Betnarek-Verband. It's always possible he went to that. I was going to go myself and then thought better of it. Don't worry. I expect he'll come through the door at any moment. And when he does, tell him Bernie Gunther was here."

"Bernie Gunther. All right. I'll do that."

She opened the apartment door so that I could leave.

"There is one thing," she added. "And I don't know if it's worth mentioning. It's probably nothing, but when I went to work I noticed there was a brand-new Mercedes parked near Kurt's car. I had half an idea that the two men inside were keeping an eye on it. As if they were waiting there for Kurt."

"Oh? Did you get a good look at them?"

"Smartly dressed. I might have thought they were policemen but for the car. I was paying more attention to it, really. An expensive item. A cream-colored roadster."

I felt my heart miss a beat. The Mercedes roadster was not a common car. I knew of only two people who owned a cream Mercedes roadster: one was Thea von Harbou; the other was Erich Angerstein, and the thought of him knowing half of what I did about Kurt Reichenbach filled me with alarm.

"You're sure it was a Mercedes?"

"Oh, yes. I'm sure about it because that was Kurt's favorite type of car. They've got one in the Mercedes showroom on the Kurfürstendamm. We would stop and admire it when we were out for a walk. I used to say that one day I was going to win the Prussian State Lottery and buy the car for him."

"I see. Well, thanks. Like I say, I expect he'll turn up safe and well before long."

But hearing this latest information I had a strong sense of foreboding that this was never going to happen, that Kurt Reichenbach was probably dead, or worse.

—

I OUGHT TO have despised myself. At the very least I'd been very stupid. I'd trusted Erich Angerstein to keep his word when all my better instincts had told me he wouldn't. It was now obvious what must have happened in that awful apartment in Wedding. No wonder the bastard had asked me to leave the room before he'd started to beat the man, and like a fool I'd done it. A few minutes before Prussian Emil told me that the man he'd seen near the scene of Eva Angerstein's murder had been an anonymous policeman from Kripo, he had informed her father that this same cop was called Kurt Reichenbach. With me sitting safely out of the way in the bedroom, all Angerstein had to do was order Emil to withhold Reichenbach's name from me. That would give him ample time to find Reichenbach and then take him to a ring hideout to exact his own personal revenge. The earlier telephone call I'd taken at my office desk from Angerstein had doubtless been designed to help bolster some sort of deniability when, eventually, I discovered Reichenbach was missing.

I'd made it so easy for him. But all that was over now. Angerstein wasn't the only one who could turn up armed and unannounced. I had a gun. I had the gangster's business card. I had an address in Lichterfelde.

THE ANGERSTEIN HOUSE was a white stucco building near the former cadet school at the southwest end of the Teltow Canal. A three-story Wilhelmine, with a short Corinthian portico, topped with a balcony about the size of a laundry basket; it looked like the most expensive house in the road. I'd have been disappointed if Erich Angerstein had been staying anywhere else. The carriage light that hung in the portico was lit, and the cream-colored Mercedes roadster was parked out front. I laid my hand on the bonnet and felt the still-warm engine underneath. Angerstein hadn't been home long.

There was a small garden with a cherry tree in front of the house, and a larger one at the back, which was where I began my search, having climbed over a low picket fence. The ground-floor windows were dark and fitted with louvered shutters that prevented my peering in, but all the lights were on in the upper floors and, having tried, unsuccessfully, to gain entry through a kitchen door and then a set of French windows, I returned to the front door and prepared to ring the bell, which is to say I took Mendel's Browning out of my pocket, worked the slide, put one in the barrel, and kept it close to my armpit, ready to point at whoever answered.

I was angry enough now to go all the way. I'd been suckered by Angerstein, but that was over now. I felt sure of it. All the same, I wouldn't have minded a drink to put a little iron in my soul. I told myself I wasn't prepared to kill him, but I was ready to shoot him; with a little .25 there were all sorts of places I could shoot Erich Angerstein without killing him.

Behind me the Teltow district steamer let out a mocking toot as it headed down the canal to Potsdam. The purpling night was clear and warm, with just a hint of honeysuckle in the air, or perhaps it was jasmine; something sweeter than the way I was feeling, anyway. I pulled on the butcher's-weight brass doorbell and waited while the big bell in the entrance hall did its job, sounding as if it were summoning the local people to mass. I heard a couple of bolts slide away and then the door opened to reveal Erich Angerstein.

"Where is he?"

"Who?"

I pushed him back into the double-height entrance hall and kicked the door shut behind me.

"Don't waste my time. You know perfectly well who I'm talking about."

In his silk dressing gown he looked as if he'd been about to go to bed, but I frisked him for a gun anyway and while I did, he smiled like a schoolteacher who has been obliged to humor an unruly pupil, which did very little for my own humor.

"I haven't the least idea what you're talking about, Gunther. I thought you were here to tell **me** something interesting. In which case, come in, take a load off, sit down, and have a drink."

"Yesterday I was an idiot, Angerstein, but not today. Today I'm smarter than the paint on a new car. Today I know you're a lying bastard and that it was you who snatched Kurt Reichenbach from outside his apartment in Halensee."

"Who's he? The man who killed my daughter, I suppose. I told you on the telephone, Gunther. I'm impatient. But I'm not a mind reader. It's me who's following your lead, remember?"

"That's how it was supposed to be. Only, you persuaded Prussian Emil to give the cop's name to you but not to me. That gave you a head start—enough time to deal with him yourself."

"That's crap."

"I don't think so."

"For Christ's sake put the gun down and let's have a drink."

I shook my head. "Not tonight."

"You don't mind if I do? Look, whoever it is you're searching for, he's not here. Take a look around, if you don't believe me. I'm quite alone. My wife's away. And just as well for you, my friend. She wouldn't like this at all."

Instinctively I glanced at my surroundings. The entrance hall was largely given over to a bar under the curving staircase; on the other side of the room was a white grand piano; and on one of the taller walls was a full-length painting of an old bald man with rotten feet copulating with a generously endowed naked lady that owed more to the artist's sense of humor than it did to accurate draughtsmanship or skill with a paintbrush. Angerstein moved slowly toward the bar, where he picked up a bottle of schnapps and filled a small schooner.

"You wouldn't have brought him here, to your lovely home," I said. "I expect your friends in the ring are holding him somewhere quiet where nobody will complain about his screams. And you're going to tell me where that is. Or he's already dead. In which case I'm going to need some evidence. Like a body."

"Listen to me, Gunther. And listen to yourself. You're like some crazy scientist with a dumb theory. Flat earth. Phlogiston. Or maybe the planet Vulcan. But whatever you think you know for sure, you don't."

"I was crazy ever to think a scumbag like you would keep his word. My own mother could have told me that."

"Mothers can be wrong. They often are. Otherwise they wouldn't have sons. At least that's what mine always told me."

"So you're not going to tell me where he is."

"I'll admit, I've made some inquiries of my own. Asked around. Sure I did. You can't blame me for that. I figured I could help."

"You're an interesting man, Herr Angerstein. I've learned quite a bit from my brief association with you. Not all of it good, I'm afraid. Principally, I've learned that I'm quite like you in a lot of ways."

"Really? You surprise me, Herr Gunther."

"Yes. You're not the only person who can thrash another man until he tells you exactly what you want to know. Metaphorically speaking. Thanks to you, I've realized that at the right time and in the right place, I'm capable of almost anything. The same way you are."

"Like what, for instance."

"Like this, for instance." I smiled thinly and then shot him in the shoulder. He dropped the schooner and suddenly the air was strong with the smell of liquor and gunpowder.

"Jesus." Angerstein winced with pain and grabbed at his shoulder. "What the hell did you do that for?"

"I tell you what I'm going to do, Herr Angerstein. If you don't tell me where Kurt Reichenbach is, I'm going to shoot you again. I might not kill you. But I will inflict the maximum amount of pain this little gun can provide.

I haven't got the time or the inclination to ask you more politely."

Angerstein sat down on the piano stool and glanced uncomfortably at his shoulder; the silk dressing-gown was now shiny with blood. He shook his head. "You're making a big mistake."

So I shot him again, this time in the pajama leg.

Angerstein yelled out with pain. I figured the second one hurt more than the first.

"I can't believe you shot me."

"Shouldn't be too hard to believe, what with two bullets in you. And I will shoot you a third time if I have to. Just count yourself lucky it's this little peashooter and not my usual cannon."

"That little peashooter, as you call it, hurts like hell, damn you."

"All the more reason for you to tell me where you've cached Kurt Reichenbach." I pointed the gun at his other leg.

"All right, all right. I'll tell you. Reichenbach is dead."

"How do I know you're telling the truth? How do I know he's not being tortured somewhere even as we speak?"

"He's dead, I tell you."

"Tell me exactly what happened. Convince me he's dead and maybe I won't shoot you again."

"What do you care, anyway? He was a multiple murderer. The city's well rid of a man like that.

But I'd like to know how a public trial would have helped anyone. Least of all this city's cops."

"That's not for you to say."

"Why not? He killed my daughter."

"I'm asking the questions, remember?"

I pulled the trigger on the Browning a third time, only this time I let the bullet graze his earlobe.

"Isn't that what you said to Prussian Emil?"

"What do you want? A confession? You might think you've got my neck under the blade, but I certainly didn't kill him. And I didn't order him to be killed. Not that it matters. None of this will stand up in court."

"Eva was your daughter. Fine. I get that. And you have my sympathy. But she was my case. The law's still a set menu in this city, Angerstein. You don't get to pick and choose what you'll have and what you won't." I lit a cigarette. "So what's it to be? An explanation of what exactly happened, or another bullet in the leg?"

"That's the trouble with cops. You people think you own every meter of the moral high ground between here and the Vatican. So he goes to court. And then what happens? A smart Jew lawyer invokes paragraph fifty-one and before you know it another sharp-witted murderer like your pal Bruno Gerth is serving out his sentence weaving baskets in a home for the bewildered instead of getting the sentence he deserves. I couldn't risk that happening."

"You better let me have it, Angerstein. And don't give me that crap about you being a father. After seeing you in action with a cane I figure you haven't got a kindly bone in your crooked body, let alone one that resembles anything paternal. I want the whole story beginning with when you picked him up in your car. Otherwise you'll be picking these little slugs out of your teeth for the rest of the week."

"ALL RIGHT. YOU guessed what happened between me and Prussian Emil. I'll give you that. While you were out of the room I gave him a few extra hard ones with the cane and then told him he was a dead man unless he told me exactly what he knew about the man who killed Eva. Which is when he dropped the bombshell and said it was a cop called Reichenbach. But here's the real reason I didn't let you in on that. With you being a cop, I asked myself if Reichenbach being a cop might persuade you to go easy on him, the same way it went for Bruno Gerth, and concluded it might and I couldn't take that risk. So I stuffed the handkerchief back in Emil's mouth and told him that I didn't want you to know the name, just that it had been a cop who'd killed her. I figured that by the time you could put a name to the description, I'd have Reichenbach safely in the bag. I couldn't have told you any more than I did about what I was planning. You wouldn't have stood for it."

"You were right about that much anyway."

"I didn't have time to figure all the angles, but it seemed like a good idea. I still think you should let things lie the way they are."

"I can't. It's just not in me. I've got standards and I try to live up to them. Whereas you've got no standards at all, and you certainly live up to those. I should have realized that. So. Let's have the rest of it. The whole story. Exactly what happened to Kurt Reichenbach."

"If you insist. Just don't shoot me again."

"LIKE MOST COPS in Berlin you actually know very little about it. The city, I mean. For people like you, German society is very simple. It's the one familiar social order that has existed since time immemorial, a hierarchy in which everyone knows his or her place. The reality is very different. For more than a century there has existed another world that lies beyond the bounds of this hierarchy—a world of outcasts and people who belong to no recognized social class—which, for better or worse, people like you call the underworld. At the center of this underworld are professional criminals, bandits, robbers, thieves, and murderers. Oh, some of you—Ernst Engelbrecht, perhaps—they think they know this netherworld, but believe me, they don't. No one does who is not a part of it.

"This underworld exists deep beneath this city, like an intricate labyrinth of old mine shafts and tunnels. A criminal society, yes, but one with its own rules and institutions: a professional brother-and sisterhood that is restricted to those who've done time in the cement and that severely punishes not just those who inform on one another to the police, but also those who scorn our influence, or whose crimes are considered so heinous that they are beyond the merely criminal; crimes that fly in the face of what it is to be human, such as compulsive murder. In short, it's the Middle German Ring that brings a bit of order and stability to the criminal world."

I laughed. "If you're telling me that there's honor among thieves, I don't believe it."

"Oh, it's much more than honor, I can assure you. It's about organization where otherwise there would be chaos. The Middle German Ring imposes statutes on the local gangs and clubs, controls their activities, exacts money tributes, and punishes those who break our laws, which are as binding as anything a German jurist would recognize. We even have our own court to judge what sanctions and punishments are to be inflicted on those who have broken our laws."

"Next thing you'll be telling about Esmerelda and Quasimodo and the court of the gypsies."

"You asked me to tell you what happened to Reichenbach and I'm telling you now. It's your business what you believe."

"Go on." I tossed him my handkerchief to mop some of the blood off his thigh and shoulder. "I'm listening."

"This people's court meets once a month or by special session in the cellar of an old disused brewery in Pankow."

"Which one?"

"The Deutsches Bauernbrauerei near the water tower on Ibsenstrasse."

"I know it. There's a hole in the west wall as tall as the Brandenburg Gate from when they took the copper fermentation tanks out."

"That's right. It's the kind of place where we can meet without disturbance. The court's judges are the ring's most senior bosses, but the jury is made up of some of the city's thieves, pimps, prostitutes, drug dealers, yokel catchers, illegal gamblers—all of whom are paying members of the local clubs—in short, all those men and women who can't go to the police for protection."

"Hell of a country club you have there."

"Just give your mouth a rest and listen. You might learn something. So, as you surmised, this morning I kidnapped Kurt Reichenbach outside his own apartment and took him before a specially convened people's court. In your world this has no official standing, of course, but in mine, it is a legitimate judicial authority, as important as the Imperial Court of Justice in Leipzig. As many as a hundred people were present to see that true justice was done. I myself acted as his prosecutor, and Prussian Emil was my chief witness. Reichenbach was given a defense attorney appointed by the court and allowed to argue his case. But the evidence—more evidence than you were aware of, perhaps—was compelling, not to say overwhelming.

"The chief witness told the court he saw the accused enter the courtyard with my daughter, and not soon after, he saw him again, **with blood on his hands.** And if that wasn't enough to convince the court he was Winnetou, a second witness, a prostitute, came forward to say that months before any of the Winnetou murders, she'd met with the accused and they'd agreed to have sex, but he'd changed his mind and started calling her the vilest names and said it was wrong that decent men like him could be tempted in this way, and how it was high time someone cleaned up the streets.

"A few days later, she said she was attacked from behind by someone who hit her on the back of the head with a stone in a sock and that she was only alive because her attacker had been interrupted, as she was quite certain he'd meant to kill her. The man ran away leaving the sock and the stone. She is convinced it had been Reichenbach because she recognized the sweet smell of his cigars. Not only that, but one of the women who saved her life found a cigar stub at the scene and she'd kept it in her handbag intending to give it to the police when she reported the attack, but she changed her mind and never did. Decided she didn't need police attention. Well, who does? Anyway, she told the court she had thrown away the cigar but remembered the brand on the wrapper clearly enough because it was such a beautiful name: Dominican Aurora. It was this information that truly sealed his fate, since a summary search of the accused's personal effects had revealed some unsmoked Dominican Aurora cigars in his breast pocket, which, one of the judges informed the court, could only be obtained in Germany as an import from Amsterdam.

"In the face of this damning evidence, Reichenbach's defense attorney then argued a simple case of diminished responsibility: only a lunatic could have killed so many people. The court was not persuaded. At that point, the accused, asked if he had anything to say for himself before sentence was pronounced, demanded to know by what right the scum of Berlin were putting **him** on trial—his words, not mine—and it was then that he confessed to his crimes, which he justified by saying he'd intended first to drive Berlin's whores out of business, and then to make the city's streets fit for decent law-abiding citizens to walk in. It seems he had a closer acquaintance with Bruno Gerth than even you did. It was when Gerth got arrested that Reichenbach decided to carry on the good work."

"Did he say why he scalped them?"

"No, but I should have thought it was obvious; he wanted to cause the maximum amount of terror among the city's whores. And he succeeded, too. After all, it was this part—the scalping—that made the killings newsworthy. Let's face it: Whores being murdered in this town is almost commonplace."

"This is what I was afraid might happen. I now have a hundred questions that will very likely never be answered."

"Such as?"

"Such as why did he wait until he'd killed Werner Jugo before he wrote a taunting letter to the newspapers? And why didn't he admit to killing any of the girls in either of those two letters? He suggested he might get around to killing some prostitutes, but that's not the same as admitting he'd already killed three. It's almost as if he wanted to make sure we didn't establish a connection between Winnetou and Gnadenschuss. Which, of course, would have doubled our chances of catching him."

"Is that all you've got?"

"Not by a long chalk. In the first letter he suggests that the veterans were not only a disgrace to the uniform, they also reminded everyone of the shame of Germany's defeat. But in the second letter it seems the mission has changed and he's intent merely on cleaning up Berlin's streets. These are important questions to which I should like to have had some answers. Only, I don't suppose he left a written confession."

"You know he didn't. A verdict of guilty was delivered by the people, a sentence of death—to be carried out immediately—was then pronounced and Kurt Reichenbach was hanged in the brewery yard. He made a poor end. Fear got the better of him: He tried to resist and then begged for his life, which reduced him even more in the eyes of those who were present. No one likes a coward. The body was cut down and taken away for disposal. I say disposal; I'm more or less certain the body was not buried. So I very much doubt that you could be taken to see it. The last time the people's court carried out a capital sentence, the body was burned in secret. But if you'd been there you would have been convinced of his guilt, I can assure you."

"Oh, I am. As a matter of fact I was convinced of his guilt before I came here tonight. Earlier this evening I found enough evidence in his car to send Reichenbach straight to the guillotine: principally the murder weapon—a hammer—and a scalping knife. I even have the pistol with which he shot those disabled war veterans. Short of seeing the word **murderer** chalked on his back, it couldn't be more obvious."

"Then I really don't understand. What are you doing here? If you knew all that, why the hell did you shoot me?"

"Because I don't believe in lynchings."

"He got what he deserved. And how often can you say that these days? Do you honestly think the end result would have been different in the courts you serve?"

"You can dress it up any way you like, Angerstein, but that's what it was. A lynching. And what he deserved most was a fair trial."

"Because he was a cop?"

"Because he was a citizen. Even a rat like you deserves a fair trial."

"And you say that even though you say you had ample evidence of his guilt."

"**Because** I had evidence of his guilt. Sometimes being a cop is difficult because the law says the guilty get treated the same way as the innocent. It sticks in the throat a bit to respect the rights of a man who's a piece of shit. But this republic will fall apart if we don't stick to the legal process."

"On the contrary. In this case I think there's every chance the republic would fall apart if the legal process was observed. Can you imagine the scandal that would have resulted from the news that it was a serving police officer who carried out these murders? Moreover, a serving police officer who was a Jew? The nationalists would assume Christmas had come early this year. I can almost see the headlines in **Der Angriff** and the **Völkischer Beobachter.** Bernhard Weiss would be out. Maybe even Gennat. Albert Grzesinski, too, probably. And I doubt the SPD could hope to keep a government together for more than a few hours. Very probably there would have to be another federal election. With all the economic uncertainty that such a thing entails.

"Of course, it's up to you what you tell the commissars. But if you'll take my advice, Gunther, you'll keep your mouth shut. This way everything can be swept neatly away and forgotten. In three months nobody will remember him or any of the people he killed. Not that you could use any of this against me in court, anyway. My lawyer would get any charges thrown out in a matter of minutes."

"I don't doubt that, either."

"Then there's the dead man's wife. She's a nurse,

isn't she? What do you think she'd prefer? To be known as the spouse of a multiple murderer? Or as the poor wife of a cop who disappeared, heroically, in the line of duty? Maybe you should ask her opinion before you go blundering down the road of absolute truth, Gunther. Can you imagine what her life would be like with every one of her friends knowing what her husband has done? Many would assume that she must have known something. Perhaps she did, at that. How could a wife not know that kind of thing? Take it from me, very soon she wouldn't have any friends at all.

"And lastly, there's the great German people. Do you think any of them give a damn if someone like Kurt Reichenbach gets a fair trial? Nobody thinks in terms of justice and the rule of law, so why should we? Ask a bus driver or a boot boy if he thinks it's a good idea to spend thousands of taxpayers' reichsmarks putting a man like that on trial, or if it's better just to put him to death quietly. I think I know what they'd say.

"You're guarding an empty safe, my friend. No one cares. The only people who profit from a trial are the lawyers and the newspapers. Not you. Not me. Not the ordinary man in the street.

"Well, that's what happened. There isn't anything else. You can take it or leave it."

Erich Angerstein stood up and walked painfully to the telephone. "And now if you don't mind, I'm going to call a doctor." He gave me a quizzical look. "Unless you're going to shoot me again. Are you going to shoot me again?" He gave me a cynical smile; it was the only type he seemed to have. "No, I thought not."

That's the trouble with listening to the devil; it turns out that his most impressive trick is to tell us exactly what we want to hear.

Angerstein picked up the candlestick and started to dial a number, which is when I started to walk out of there.

"Hey, stick around, Gunther. I'll make it up to you. You'll need another collar to help deflect the criticism that will come Kripo's way when you don't solve the Gnadenschuss case. I said if you helped me find Eva's killer I'd give you the true facts about the Wolfmium factory fire. And I will. This will help you make commissar."

But I was shaking my head.

"What's the matter, Gunther? Don't you want to be a commissar? Don't you want to know the truth about what really happened back there?"

"I don't want anything from you, Angerstein. Especially when it's something as precious as the truth. Even truth sounds like a damned lie when it's in your mouth. So I'd hate to have to rely on it or use it in any way to advance myself. If ever I make commissar, which I doubt, it will be as the result of my own doing."

"Have it your own way. You're a stubborn

bastard if ever I met one. I almost admire you for it. It seems it's true what they say: There's no fool quite as foolish as an honest fool. But ask yourself this: One day, one day soon if I'm not mistaken, when you're the only honest man left in Germany, who'll know?"

I WAS BACK at the Alex the next day, going through the slippery motions of investigating a series of murders I had already solved, just for the sake of appearances. I didn't doubt for a minute the truth of what Erich Angerstein had told me, not with two bullets in him; nor the cold pragmatic wisdom of my not telling Weiss or Gennat anything of what I'd discovered about Kurt Reichenbach. Angerstein was just as right about that in daylight as he'd been the previous night; identifying Reichenbach as Winnetou **and** Dr. Gnadenschuss looked like a quick way of bringing down not just Kripo, but also the fragile government coalition; another federal election so soon after the last one would have been a great opportunity for the German National People's Party, the communists, the Workers' Party, or even the Nazis. So I spent a dull, quiet afternoon in Records, as ordered, compiling a list of five potential suspects from the Stahlhelm for Ernst Gennat. It was a total waste of time, of course, but then again, so much of my job in the Murder Commission looked like it was going to be a waste of time, at least for the next few weeks. And the longer I spent going through the motions, the more I came to realize that my deception could only end when there occurred another unrelated murder for us to investigate. But when, after forty-eight hours none came, I told myself that the quickest way to divert attention from Dr. Gnadenschuss was by solving an existing murder case, if I could. It was fortunate that I had half an idea which case this might be.

IT WAS SOON obvious that Reichenbach had done nothing about arresting Hugo "Mustermann"—the man I'd recognized from Sing Sing, the same man who'd shot Willi Beckmann. Arresting him was now my secret priority. I telephoned the Office for Public Conveyances in Charlottenburg and asked them to check the owner of the yellow BMW Dixi, registration IA 17938. They told me that the car was owned by a man called Hugo Gediehn. On the face of it, this now looked like a straightforward bit of detective work. I'd seen the murder myself, and it doesn't get much more straightforward than that. But there was something about it—a minor detail—I wanted to check out first with Brigitte Mölbling before I called on Hugo Gediehn.

I arranged to see her for lunch at Aschinger. It wasn't just because I liked the beer at Aschinger that she and I met there, although I did. I wanted to ask her about the shooting and assumed that being on-site would help her to remember everything she'd seen on the street outside.

"But you already told me you saw the whole thing," she said.

"I did. And I just found out the killer's name and address from the Office of Public Conveyances. He has an apartment in Kreuzberg."

"Are you going to arrest him?"

"Yes. As soon as you've helped me sort something out in my own head."

"Me? I don't see how I can help. You've got his name and address, what do you need from me?"

"The fact is, I didn't pay too much attention to the dead man's corpse. You told me that you came down here to check it wasn't me lying on the street. Correct?"

"Yes. I did. Can you imagine that? Me being concerned about you?"

"I try to, when I'm alone and naked, but somehow it's difficult to picture."

"Shouldn't be too difficult if you think of all the other pictures of me that ought to be in your head by now. The ones I wouldn't like anyone else to see."

I picked up her hand and kissed it.

"You mentioned seeing a tattoo on the dead man's hand. A woman's name. On the base of his thumb. You see, I didn't see that."

"That's right. I did."

"Can you remember what the name was?"

"No. I don't remember very much, actually."

"Was it Helga?"

"I don't think so. Besides, there was too much blood for me to remember very much. It's been preying on my mind ever since."

"I guess that means I have to go to the city morgue and take a look for myself."

"You mean that place by the zoo? On Hannoversche Strasse?"

"I do. Perhaps you could drive me there."

"Now?"

"Sooner the better. Before someone claims Beckmann's body."

"All right."

We found her car, another BMW Dixi, and drove west to the morgue. She parked out front, and I kissed her hand again.

"Will you wait here for me? I won't be long."

"If you like. But it's open to the public, isn't it?"

"It is. Only, I don't recommend you go in. You wouldn't like the show any more than you'd enjoy a hard-boiled egg rolled in sand."

"Lots of people do go in there, don't they? There are people going in there now."

"Almost a million people just voted Nazi, but that doesn't mean you should do what they do."

"It can't be that bad. Otherwise they wouldn't let the public in, surely."

"The Prussian state authorities let the public in because they want to scare them into submission. The sight of violent death is usually enough to cow the most rebellious spirits. Even in Berlin."

"In case you hadn't noticed, Gunther, I'm kind of rebellious myself. At least that's what my father says. Maybe I'm not the little snowdrop you think I am."

"If you'd just finished telling me that crime pays, I might recommend that you go in and see the sights, sure. But not otherwise. Look, angel, it simply hadn't occurred to me you might want to go inside. If it had crossed my mind, I'd have caught the bus. Or taken the U-Bahn."

"You're beginning to sound suspiciously like a hero."

"Maybe. And what kind of a knight in shining armor would I be if I didn't try to talk the princess out of walking into the ogre's castle?"

"I get that. And I'm grateful. But I like to think I can look after myself. Since my ex-husband started wearing my underwear instead of shining armor I've learned to be a lot tougher than people take me for. You included, it would seem."

"That's the trouble with real men, sugar. They expect women to behave like real women."

She was already getting out of the Dixi. "That doesn't mean you should treat them like they're made of Venetian glass. Or is it just me you want to wrap in some tissue paper?"

"No, I'm against the existence of this place in general. It's bad enough that there are so many men who remember how abominable things were in the trenches. I see no use for a public morgue in which we afford women and children an approximate sight of that same horror."

"Maybe women should know something about this side of life."

"All right. But bear this in mind. When it comes to seeing lots of dead people, your brain is like a camera with the shutter open. Everything gets recorded on the film. I was a schoolboy the first time I went in this place. I sneaked in, without permission. What I saw then has stayed with me forever. Somehow it always seems worse than anything I've seen since. So please don't complain to me when you don't sleep because you can't destroy the negatives."

She followed me inside and while I went to ask to see the body of Willi Beckmann, I left Brigitte to stroll around the morgue on her own. Maybe she was right. Thanks to people like George Grosz and his friends, you could probably see things that were just as unpleasant in the city's modern art galleries.

Beckmann's body contained more lead than

Berlin's water pipes. Fortunately for me, his right hand was one of the few parts of his body that had not been hit with a machine-gun bullet. So it took only a few minutes to satisfy my own curiosity; but rather longer than that for Brigitte to satisfy hers. I went outside, leaned against her car, and smoked a cigarette. When eventually she came out of the morgue she looked a little pale and was very quiet. Which was only to be expected, I thought.

"Well, that was horrible."

"To say the least."

"Is that all you've got to say?"

"See anyone you recognized?"

"Funny."

"That's why it exists. To help the cops identify the unidentifiable."

"Did you find what you were looking for?" she asked, starting the engine.

"Yes."

"Did he have a girl's name tattooed on his hand?"

"He did."

"Good. And was it Helga, after all?"

"Better than that. It was Frieda."

"Where to?"

"I have to go back to the Alex."

She turned the car around and drove east, on Lützowstrasse.

"Are you going to tell me about Frieda?"

After what she'd just seen I decided she could probably handle the whole story. I was wrong about that, too.

"About a year ago a man walking his dog in the Grünewald found some female body parts wrapped in butcher's paper and buried in a shallow grave. There was no head. Just a torso, a foot, and a pair of hands. Which was thoughtful of the killer in that the girl's fingerprints enabled us to identify her as Frieda Ahrendt, and they revealed that she had a record for petty theft. She also had the name **Willi** tattooed at the base of her thumb. In spite of all that, we never managed to find a family, a job, not even a last known address. And certainly not the murderer, who is probably still at large."

"And you think Willi Beckmann—the man in the morgue—might be the same man."

"I don't think Willi Beckmann was dumb enough to chop her up and bury a severed hand that had his name on it. But it's possible he could have told us something more about her. If he hadn't been shot. Maybe enough to find her killer—the man the newspapers had dubbed the Grünewald Pork Butcher." I'd already decided to visit Willi's apartment in Tegel, to see what evidence I could find before I went looking for Hugo. "Who knows? Maybe he still can."

Brigitte listened in silence and then said: "My God, the things that must be inside your head.

You go looking at things that no one should ever have to see, with no idea of the effect it's going to have on your mind, and all for not much money. I don't think you even know why you do it. Do you?"

"Sure I know. Because I have nothing to say as a painter. Because I couldn't finish my unfinished symphony. Because being a cop is a job for honest men, and since there are not many of those around these days, they'll take anyone they can get."

"Well, I think you're crazy. And if you're not, then you soon will be. Still, I suppose that's what being a detective is all about."

WILLI BECKMANN HAD lived in Tegel, part of the northwestern borough of Reinickendorf and not far from the giant Borsig locomotive works. The whole area was dominated by a modern red brick ziggurat that was the model for the New Tower of Babel in Fritz Lang's **Metropolis.** That had been a silent movie—with talking pictures now arriving on the scene, it already looked like a remnant from the past. As for the Borsig works, there was nothing futuristic about it; noisy and dirty, it seemed a throwback to an industrial Berlin that was fast disappearing. Willi's apartment was on the top floor of a more traditional Berlin building with its mustard-yellow walls, red-tiled mansard roof, and a curving balcony that was home to a spectacular window box full of pink carnations, which possibly explained the buttonhole poor Willi had been wearing at the time of his death. The concierge admitted me to the apartment. He was a man of few words and those he had expressed a kind of awed pride in the size and layout of the accommodation.

"I'd forgotten what a nice big apartment this is," he said. "All these rooms. And the ceilings so high. You could play tennis in here."

He had very little curiosity about what I was doing there or indeed about Beckmann's death. To my relief, he quickly left me alone.

There wasn't a lot of furniture but what there was was good stuff—Biedermeier copies, mostly, and on the walls were prints of hunting scenes in the gardens of Schloss Tegel. Of course, the police had already been there searching for leads to the identity of the dead man's murderer and, according to an official notice taped to the apartment door, they had taken away some photographs and papers.

Not knowing what they were looking for, they'd removed very little.

I had better luck. In a cylinder cabinet, I found a couple of photograph albums, and in these were pictures of a quartet of good friends. Several had been taken at a nearby restaurant on the edge of Lake Tegel. The quartet was made up of Willi Beckmann, Hugo Gediehn, Helga "Mustermann"—I still didn't know her surname—and Frieda Ahrendt. What was clear from the photographs was that Hugo and Frieda had once been lovers. Some time after the photos were taken Frieda and Willi became lovers, which was when they each had the tattoos made. None of the pictures provided a neat explanation for Frieda's murder, but they were all the excuse I needed to detain both Hugo **and** Helga. These four wouldn't have been the first good companions to fall out violently. There's nothing like an old friendship to provide a solid basis for a lasting enmity.

Since I had the free run of the apartment, I spent another hour raking through drawers and closets, which is how I found several letters addressed to Frieda from her **loving sister, Leni** in Hamburg. I wondered if Leni even knew her sister was dead. I was still short of an ironclad motive as to why two of the people in the pictures had been murdered, but everything else seemed to be falling into place.

Leni's letter had included a telephone number and since there was still a working telephone in Willi's apartment, I called her.

"Forgive me for telephoning you out of the blue like this," I said, "but my name is Bernhard

Gunther and I'm a detective with Berlin Kripo." Choosing my words carefully, I added, "I've been investigating your sister's disappearance."

Leni sighed. "It's all right, Herr Gunther. I know she's dead. If she were alive she'd have contacted me. But it's been almost a year. And I gave up all hope of ever seeing her again several months ago. We were very close, you see, always in touch. Also, the man she was living with in Berlin at the time of her disappearance, Willi Beckmann, he came to see me here in Hamburg and told me he thought she was dead, too."

"But why didn't you contact the police?"

"Willi said that for his sake and for mine we'd best not say anything about it to the police because the man who told him she was dead was a member of a criminal ring and very dangerous."

"Did he say what that man's name was?"

"He did. But I'm not going to repeat it now, even after all this time."

"Willi Beckmann's dead. Did you know that?"

"No."

"The man who murdered him is called Hugo Gediehn. And I'm going to arrest him today or tomorrow. Is that the name Willi told you?"

"Yes, it is."

"I have him cold for Willi's murder."

"May I ask how you know that?"

"Because I have a witness."

"A witness who'll stand up in court?"

"Yes."

"Sure about that?"

"Yes. I'm the witness. I saw him pull the trigger on Willi. But he's also my only suspect in your sister's murder. Frankly, I was hoping you might be able to help me out there." I paused, and hearing nothing, added, "You'll be quite safe, I can assure you. No one need ever know I spoke to you."

"How can I help?"

"I have a suspicion as to why Hugo killed your sister, but I have no real proof. Getting proof would be help enough, I think."

"The why is quite simple. Hugo and Frieda were lovers. Then Willi enticed her away from Hugo—Willi was a very attractive man—and Hugo decided to get his revenge. Killed her. Buried her in a shallow grave somewhere. That much he told Willi. To torture him. Of course, Hugo knew that Willi was also in a ring, and that the last thing he could ever do was talk to the police. But I don't understand, Herr Gunther. Why did Hugo kill Willi now, after all this time?"

"I can't be sure, but I think it was because Willi went and stole Hugo's new girl, Helga."

"Makes sense, I suppose. If you're looking for him, Hugo has an apartment in Kreuzberg. But I expect you know that."

"Yes. I do."

"Will you let me know what happens?"

"Of course."

"Thanks. And good luck. Hugo being Hugo, you might need it."

BACK AT THE Alex I made out a good case for Hugo Gediehn's arrest to Weiss and Gennat and, accompanied by several heavily armed uniformed officers, we proceeded to his apartment in Kreuzberg and took him into custody. To my surprise, he came with us quietly, saying very little except to insist we had the wrong man, a detail to which we might have paid more attention if it hadn't been for the Bergmann MP-18 that was still in his car and my discovery in his desk drawer of a single souvenir photograph of Frieda's severed hand, the one featuring the tattoo of Willi's name. It was what the lawyers called **prima facie** evidence, which is just a fancy way of saying that as soon as Gediehn saw that we had the photograph, his expression changed and all the color drained from his face as if we'd introduced him to a pack of hungry wolves.

The rest of the day and half of the night was spent interrogating him and eventually he confessed to both murders, with no sign of remorse. If I'd known that the court would later sentence him to just fifteen years in prison I almost might not have bothered, but of course clearing up a couple of murders was only part of the reason I'd gone after him. There's nothing like solving a cold case to deflect attention from several hot ones.

For days no one mentioned Dr. Gnadenschuss. Bernhard Weiss was able to call a press conference and make a big song and dance about the fact that Frieda Ahrendt's case was almost a year old and to call for a little more patience when it came to reporting crime in the city. He even singled me out for praise, but this did little to allay my feelings of guilt at having covered up a greater crime.

Even Gennat offered me his congratulations although I could tell he was convinced that there was rather more to my tenacious detective work than met his eye. It was the elapse of time between my witnessing the murder of Willi Beckmann and the arrest of Hugo Gediehn that seemed to cause him the biggest problem.

"You had the car registration number, a description of the killer, and his Christian name—you almost had his shoe size—and yet you didn't call it in," he said. "I don't get that. Suppose Hugo Gediehn had taken off? He could have slipped across the Polish border and we'd have been none the wiser."

"It was a risk I was prepared to take."

"That wasn't your decision to make. And that's not how this Commission operates. You should know that by now. You could have telephoned me or someone else in this department and dictated the car's registration number without breaking your cover."

"Look, when I saw Frieda's name tattooed on Beckmann's dead hand I wanted to see if I could make him a suspect for her murder. I couldn't do any of that until I was through playing the **klutz.**"

"But Willi Beckmann wasn't going anywhere," objected Gennat. "He was dead. No, it looks very much as though you wanted to make yourself a hero. On the face of it, that would make you a glory seeker."

"Maybe you're right. Maybe I am. Maybe I decided that we need a bit of glory around here."

"But only on the face of it. You're not out for glory. Why say it when we both know it's not true? That's not who you are. I think I know you well enough to say that."

"I don't know where you're going with this, sir. The Murder Commission just put two unsolved murders to bed. What's wrong with that?"

"Nothing. Nothing at all."

"I was doing my job."

"Come on, Gunther. You're playing an angle here. Only, I can't see it. And that irritates me, because I'm supposed to be smart. They don't call me the Big Buddha for nothing."

"I don't know what you're talking about, Ernst."

"Then I'll spell it out for you. It's the way this digs the Murder Commission out of a hole that I don't like. It's too convenient. All the bad press we were getting for not doing our jobs properly and now you come along and fix that overnight by solving two cases for the price of one. They'll make you an inspector for this. Maybe give you a medal. Bernhard Weiss is ecstatic. So's the minister."

"But you're not."

"I'm a man with an ulcer. And when that's not grumbling, I am. You're a good detective, Gunther. One day you'll be an excellent commissar. But you're a man with secrets. That's what I think. That there's a lot more to you than meets the eye. I can't help thinking that there's a reason you solved these two murders when you did. And so very neatly it's like they had pink bows on them."

"A reason?"

"**A reason.** I haven't figured out what that might be. But I will. And when I do I can promise you we'll have this conversation again. Until then, try to remember this: You can't cut corners in our business. And you can't make deals with the truth. That's good advice, from one who knows. Otherwise, one day you'll try to do the right thing and discover you're so out of practice you can't."

IT DID NOT, of course, go unremarked that Kurt Reichenbach, a serving detective, was missing. But Police Praesidiums are busy places and it wasn't long before the buzz about his absence subsided to little more than a murmur. There were some at the Alex who ascribed his sudden disappearance to a nefarious Prussian land deal gone wrong, that he'd been obliged to disappear before he could be arrested by his own department. One or two mentioned a rich mistress in Charlottenburg and were adamant that he'd run away with her; someone even claimed to have seen him taking the waters in Marienbad. Others suggested that he'd been murdered by the Polish intelligence services as a result of his supposed acquaintance with the Weimar foreign minister, Gustav Stresemann, who hoped to annex the so-called Polish Corridor and much of Upper Silesia. (It transpired that Reichenbach had occasionally acted as Stresemann's bodyguard and, at the foreign minister's request, had once met with agents of the Soviet OGPU, who were collaborating with Stresemann in opposing Polish statehood.)

But the majority of the men in Kripo, including

Bernhard Weiss, were convinced he'd been murdered by right-wing nationalists simply because he was a Jew. It wasn't just German politicians who were attacked because they were Jews, as Weiss himself knew only too well; several German bankers and businessmen had also been attacked, one of them fatally. What was more certain was that if Kurt Reichenbach hadn't been a Jew, then perhaps some of his Kripo colleagues would have tried a bit harder to find him. Without a body or a witness, however, it was soon a case of out of sight, out of mind.

Even Traudl Reichenbach seemed reluctant to demand answers to her husband's sudden disappearance, and eventually I wondered if she'd actually known more about the Winnetou murders than any of us could have suspected. I kept thinking of the Brennabor and the contents of the car's trunk: the hammer, the razor-sharp knife, the coat, and the hat with the piece of wig attached. How innocent were those? Would anyone other than a homicide detective like me ever have connected those objects with a series of vicious murders? Surely there must have been one night when she had suspected her husband was guilty of something unusual: some blood on his shirt cuff perhaps; a trace of another woman's perfume on his collar; a single stray hair. A wife just knows these things, doesn't she? And what about those human scalps? What had Kurt done with the scalps? I don't suppose I'll ever know. But did she know? If anyone could handle that, it was Traudl. Being a nurse, she was likely made of strong stuff, stronger stuff than most women, stronger stuff even than Brigitte Mölbling.

"ROBERT HAS INVITED me to his home in England," Rosa told me. "To meet his mother and father."

"That sounds serious," I said.

"Oh, it's nothing like that."

"I wouldn't be too sure. The minute you start speaking to parents you've got some innocent bystanders."

"No. It's just that he wants me to meet them because they're very old."

"So's the Sabre of Charlemagne, but it's not every girl I want to take to Vienna to see it."

"It isn't how you think it is."

But of course it was; it always is. Four weeks later I received a gold-embossed invitation to their wedding in Oxford and I never saw either of them again. Later on, Frau Weitendorf told me they were going to live in Cairo, that Rankin had been offered a job teaching English at the university. I was glad for them both, of course, especially Rosa, not least because I still had Brigitte in my life; at least I thought I did.

Then one day, like Orpheus, I looked around

expecting to see Eurydice and found she'd vanished. Brigitte had written me a letter that tried to explain why she was ending our relationship; she even offered to meet me to talk about it but I couldn't see the point; it's hard not to take that kind of letter personally.

My darling Bernie,

This is not an easy letter to write, my dear, but I have to stop seeing you, for the sake of my own sanity. This will sound like an exaggeration but I can assure you it is not. At first it was exciting to be around you because you're an extraordinary man—you know that, don't you?—and not just by virtue of your vocation. Ever since I went to the morgue and encountered the reality of what you do, day in, day out, I've been thinking about who and what you are, and how you make a living. You did warn me not to go into that terrible place, of course, and I wish now I'd had the good sense to listen to you. One should always listen to a policeman. But I'm afraid my spiritual independence got the better of me.

In effect the city pays you to go all the way to hell and back again, doesn't it? But hell's only a small word. For most people, that police morgue on Hannoversche Strasse is a gateway to a place most people couldn't ever, shouldn't ever possibly imagine. To another infernal world. But for you hell is so much more than just a word. And what that does to you—what it must do to your mind—it makes me shudder.

The fact is, I don't believe you can be around all that horror without something of the grave attaching itself to you like a ghost or perhaps the angel of death. And what scares me most is that you're not even aware of it, my love. When you started drinking heavily I'm sure you believed that it was just a legacy of the war but to me it now looks more like a simple corollary of what you do: of your being a homicide detective.

If I was telling you this in person, you'd smile a cute smile and probably make a joke about it, and then tell me I was overreacting—you'd be much too polite to tell me I was being hysterical. Well, you can fake a smile; but you can't fake what's in those blue eyes, Bernie; the eyes tell you things that a person's body might not reveal. Your eyes are like the windows of a car: the transition between two worlds; there's you looking out at one world; and there's me from another looking in and increasingly scared of what I will see lying on your backseat. When I look at you, Bernie, I see eyes that half an hour before might have seen a woman with her throat cut, or a man with his skull bashed in like a grapefruit; either way, something terrible. What's more, I feel this as if I had been there to see it myself. Eyes so familiar with violent death now looking at me, it makes me uncomfortable.

And the jokes—I understand now where they're coming from; if you didn't make a joke I think you'd scream. Maybe you don't even realize that yourself. I would tell you to get out of the police, now, while you still have a chance of leading a normal human life, but we both know I'd be wasting ink; you're good at what you do, I can see that. And people remain what they are even if their faces fall apart. That's what Brecht says. Why would you give up something you're good at because some hypersensitive woman you'd met and who was fond of you thought it could only get worse? Which it will. I am very sorry.

If you want, we can meet and talk about this but you should know that I've thought a great deal about this before putting pen to paper and my decision is final.

Your own very loving Brigitte

"You know you should write a book on how to be a detective, angel," I said out loud to no one except the ghost of Eurydice. "You almost make it sound interesting. From a metaphysical point of view."

I burned her letter. It wasn't as if I hadn't had one before, and I suppose that before my time is up, I'll have others. Never forget, always replace. That's the first rule of human relationships. Moving on: This is the important part. Which is why later on I telephoned Fritz Lang's wife.

"Thea, it's Bernie Gunther. I was wondering if we might meet for dinner again. I've got some great ideas for your script."

author's note

Bernhard Weiss fled Berlin with his family just a few days before Hitler was made chancellor of Germany in 1933. He moved to London, where he opened a printing and stationery business and died in 1951. The forecourts at Friedrichstrasse railway station and the Alexanderplatzstrasse are named in his honor.*

All the members of the Schrader-Verband described in the early part of this book achieved

* There is some confusion about his formal titles: According to his daughter Hilde Horton, nee Weiss, he was both chief of the Berlin Criminal Police and vice president of the Berlin police during the Weimar Republic (Weiner Library for the Study of the Holocaust and Genocide, https://portal.ehri-project.eu/units/gb-003348-wl1768). Moreover, Philip translated the title **Polizeivizepräsident** as both "deputy police president" and "deputy police commissioner." Although our team at Putnam made a valiant attempt to identify the preferred titles, in this—though nowhere else—their search was unsuccessful, and we decided to acknowledge the inconsistency, which may well be what Philip intended all along.

positions of importance under the Nazis, not least **Arthur Nebe**, who commanded an SS-Einsatzgruppen in Ukraine that massacred some 40,000 Jews. His postwar fate remains something of a mystery.

Ernst Gennat remained in Kripo until his death in August 1939.

Frieda Ahrendt's death was never officially solved by the Berlin police and remains open to this day.

Albert Grzesinski fled to Switzerland in 1933. It is not known to the author if **Daisy Torrens** went with him; he died in New York, in 1948. Her fate is also unknown.

The double-murderer **Bruno Gerth** remained in a Berlin mental institution for the remainder of his life.

The **Berlin morgue** was built on the site of the Charité hospital's old cholera cemetery. The main viewing hall was twenty-five meters long. Bodies were displayed for three weeks and then buried by the city in a coffin that Berliners called a **Nasequetscher** (a nose crusher). The morgue was closed to the public; since the Nazis were now responsible for most of the murders in Berlin, it may be that they wanted to keep their crimes as quiet as possible.

George Grosz was one of the Weimar Dada movement's leading artists. To say the least, his work, not to mention his appearance—he really did walk around the city dressed as a cowboy—was challenging for conservative-minded Berliners. Here he is in his words—and this goes a long way to explaining just why the Nazis thought his work was degenerate and banned it: "My drawings expressed my hate and my despair. I sketched drunks, puking men, men shaking their fists at the moon. I drew a man, his face filled with horror, washing blood from his hands. . . . I drew a cross section of a tenement house: through one window could be seen a man beating up his wife; through another two people making love; from a third hung a man, his body covered with flies. I drew soldiers without noses, war cripples with crab-like steel arms; I drew a skeleton dressed as a recruit having a medical for military duty. I also wrote poetry." He emigrated to the USA in 1933, returning to Berlin in 1956, where he died, in 1959.

Thea von Harbou was a German screenwriter married to Fritz Lang, the film director. Her screenplays include the **Dr. Mabuse** films, **Metropolis,** and **M.** She and Lang divorced in April 1933, soon after Hitler came to power. She was loyal to the new regime, which may have had something to do with it. Imprisoned by the British after the war and subject to denazification, she died in 1954. **M** was released in May 1931; the leading detective in the story, Inspector Karl Lohmann, is based on Ernst Gennat.

Theo Wolff was editor of the **Berliner Tageblatt** until 1933, when the Nazis took control of the paper. It was finally shut down by the Nazis in 1939.

Walter Gempp was head of the Berlin firefighting department at the time of the Reichstag fire, in February 1933; in March 1933 he was dismissed from the fire department for suggesting that the Nazis had had a hand in the fire. In 1937 Gempp was arrested and accused of malfeasance. He was sent to prison, where he was strangled in his cell.

The biggest criminal rings in Germany were the Grosser Ring, the Freier Bund, and the Frei Vereinigung; these were all part of a larger syndicate called the **Middle German Ring**.

The **Sing Sing Club** really did have an electric chair; it was closed down by the Nazis in 1933.

The Threepenny Opera opened at the Theater am Schiffbauerdamm on August 31, 1928. Despite an initially poor reception, it became a great success and played almost four hundred times over the next two years. But both Brecht and Weill were forced to leave Germany in 1933. **Lotte Lenya** also left Germany in 1933; she and Weill remained together until 1933, when they divorced. But they remarried in New York in 1935, and the marriage lasted until Weill's death in 1950. Lotte Lenya died in Manhattan in 1981.

Otto Dix was a friend and contemporary of George Grosz; his works are perhaps even more visceral: some remind one of Goya at his darkest. He was also regarded as a degenerate artist and was obliged to leave Germany in 1933; he did not return until after the war and died in Baden-Württemberg, in July 1969.

The Cabaret of the Nameless, which reminds me of **Pop Idol** and anything with Simon Cowell, was closed in 1932.

LIKE WHAT YOU'VE READ?

Try these titles by Philip Kerr,
also available in large print:

Greeks Bearing Gifts
ISBN 978-0-525-58924-2

Prussian Blue
ISBN 978-1-5247-5615-4